# BIG THUNDER

BY PETER ATKINS

Novels
*Morningstar*
*Big Thunder*

Screenplays
*Hellbound*
*Hell on Earth*
*Fist of the North Star* (with Tony Randel)
*Hellraiser: Bloodline*
*Wishmaster*

# BIG
# THUNDER

## PETER ATKINS

HarperCollins*Publishers*

This novel is entirely a work of fiction.
The names, characters and incidents portrayed in it are
the work of the author's imagination. Any resemblance to
actual persons, living or dead, events or localities is
entirely coincidental.

HarperCollins*Publishers*
77–85 Fulham Palace Road
Hammersmith, London W6 8JB

Published by HarperCollins*Publishers* 1997
1 2 3 4 5 6 7 8 9

A catalogue record for this book
is available from the British Library

ISBN 0 00 224596 5

Set in Meridien by Rowland Phototypesetting Ltd
Bury St Edmunds, Suffolk

Printed and bound in Great Britain by
Caledonian International Book Manufacturing Ltd, Glasgow

To my family, living and dead

We seek the Fire but fail. We only bring some
Cinders from the Furnace of the Sages.
We weep behind the bars of this world's cages
Like Adam in the ruins of the Kingdom.

*Desiccation*, JOHN WILLIAM ADAMS

Man is so made that all his true delight arises from
the contemplation of mystery and, save by his own
frantic and invincible folly, mystery is never taken
from him; it rises within his soul, a well of joy
unending.

*Introduction to Middleton's
'The Ghost Ship'*, ARTHUR MACHEN

# CONTENTS

# PROLOGUE

## *The Fields of Heaven*

The way the sky looked wasn't new to him.

He'd seen this before. Only five or six times in his life, and most of them in childhood, but he'd seen skies like this, seen this perfect summer moment: the sun low in the sky, heavy and full, looking so ready to fall suddenly and rapidly below the horizon that when instead it slid slowly and gently down it seemed like an elegant miracle.

He'd seen before the shadows such suns made, long and deep. Seen the grass that such suns shone on, green and rich. Seen too the light of such suns disseminate across the sky so that blue married gold and half of heaven glowed like a glimpse of vast and distant fires . . .

But those moments had always been moments. Here it was forever. This perfect day would never end, the sun never fall, the shadows never dwindle, the green unending hills never disappear into darkness.

On those rare occasions when his new friends weren't keeping him busy with their wine, their laughter, their conversation, he would wonder idly about how long he had rested against this tree, how long this lazy contentment had gone on. But he had no answer. And he never wondered long.

Once, many years ago, he had walked the boulevards of Paris with a friend from student days. He had asked Greg, whose French was better than his, how Champs Élysées would translate. When he was told that *champs* meant fields and *Élysée* related to Elysium or Paradise he himself had completed the puzzle. *The Fields of Heaven*, he'd said, and instantly an image had flashed in his mind. This image. This sky, these gentle hills, this eternal afternoon. So

1

he knew precisely where he was now. He was in the Fields of Heaven and, though his companions were wingless, in the company of angels.

# PART ONE

## The Blue Valentine

# 1

Listen, and I'll tell you.

There was once a man who came home from the war.

This was in Liverpool. That's in England. You knew my mother was English, right? No? Doesn't matter. It was Liverpool and it was 1946. The Japanese had had this man but now he was coming home. His house was at the top of the small terraced street in which my mother lived with her parents. She was still a little girl then.

It was a bright summer afternoon. She and the other children were playing in the back alley behind the street, sent there by the grown-ups. They weren't to see the man come home. He'll be very tired, the grown-ups had said, you can all see him tomorrow.

In the street itself, the grown-ups all stood at their front doors. There were no banners. There were no balloons. But it was meant to be a kind of collective welcome anyway. Other men had come back, of course, but he was the last resident of the street to return. Now the war would really be over.

But the man stopped the taxi short of the street. He wanted to walk anonymously up the alley and slip into his house through the back door.

The children were throwing a ball around. My mother had the ball and pitched it at her friend. My mother didn't understand at first why her friend simply let the ball hit her on the chest and fall unheeded to the uneven grey stone of the alley floor. Then she saw her staring down at what was coming toward them.

All of the children flattened themselves against the walls of the alley. Some turned their face to the cold bricks. One small boy began sobbing in fear. My mother just watched wide-eyed as it walked directly up the centre of the alley looking neither right nor left.

The skeleton was dressed in a brown pin-striped suit and walked with the aid of a stick. The suit flapped distressingly around the absence beneath it and the nub of the stick was grasped by five unfleshed fingers. The exposed bones of its hands weren't white and nor was the naked skull. They were more the kind of translucent brown that you see on walls that have accrued twenty years of cigarette smoke. My mother could hear the bones creak against each other as it moved slowly up the alley toward its back door.

Its head swung only once, pivoting loosely to stare into the eyes of my mother and hold her there pinned in one long frozen second. I always asked her how a skeleton could stare if it didn't have any eyes. It remembered where its eyes were, she always said.

'Yeah, but it wasn't actually a *skeleton*,' her visitor said, reaching up for a cigarette from the bedside table.

Avis turned sharply to stare at him.

'You calling my mother a liar?' she said.

He laughed and shook his head as he lit the cigarette. Taking a deep drag, he lay back on the pillow and looked up at her. Sitting up, she had the sheets pinned primly beneath her arms to cover her breasts but the whole curve of her naked back was visible to him. He ran a caressing finger down her spine as he spoke.

'Of course not,' he said, 'but she was a kid. She *thought* it was a skeleton. He must have been starved in those Japanese camps. The thinnest man she'd ever seen.'

'That's not how she told it.'

'Stories grow in the telling.'

Avis looked at him for a moment, gesturing with her head for him to get her a smoke too. As he reached for it and lit it for her, she repeated in her head the phrase he had just used.

*Stories grow in the telling*. A truism. A platitude. She'd heard it a hundred times without thought or reaction. Probably used it herself almost as many. So she had no idea why a thrill of wonder

6

and fear had run through her on hearing it said just then. It had suddenly felt unaccountably important to her – not for any retroactive light it shed on her mother's anecdote but in a strange precursive way, like an initial signifier of something as yet unknown that was heading toward an inevitable intersection with her life. She thought about being on the freeway at night. Sometimes you can't see the traffic on the merging lane until quite late because the roads are at different heights or the shrubbery along the buffer has grown taller than its planters intended and therefore your first indication that another car is about to join the road you're on is a pool of light in the distance ahead thrown from the other car's headlights. That's what this felt like. A light from something unseen but heading her way. She remembered Stacy Brown, a girlfriend from college, telling her that the first time she had heard the name Dale Chandler in a conversation she'd had a strange reaction as if it was a name she knew but couldn't remember. When they were introduced by mutual friends a week later she'd realized she was wrong and that they'd never met. But now they had two kids and a house on Staten Island.

Avis doubted there were any bridegrooms in her future with the name of Stories Grow In The Telling, but *something* was out there. She'd just seen the glint of its headlights and soon their roads would merge.

She took a deep drag of the cigarette to clear her mind and smiled at (*Oh Christ. Jim? Jack? John? Jeff!*) Jeff.

'Yeah. Whatever,' she said and settled back down beside him against the propped-up pillows.

# 2

The sounds of his hammering heart and pounding feet were louder in Richard Sharnock's ears than that of the driving rain bulleting against the pockmarked concrete of the alley. Neither, though, were as loud nor as insistent as the steady unhurried tapping of the black leather shoes of his pursuers as they walked inexorably toward him through the rain, through the city, through the night.

That's what frightened him the most, the fact that they *walked*. Sharnock himself was running – running like he hadn't run since high school, running now for twenty desperate minutes, running so that every new breath slid down his protesting lungs like a swallowed razor blade – and these three bastards *walked*. And never lost ground. No matter how fast he ran, he couldn't shake them. Despite their never breaking stride and never breaking a sweat, the distance between him and them remained impossibly and terrifyingly constant. Like a pursuit out of a nightmare, it was as if they were linked to him by some invisible and inflexible chain and the most that he could do was to keep it taut. And Sharnock knew that very soon his body would betray him and the chain would slacken and they would reach him.

They looked *ridiculous*. The tiny part of him that wasn't terrified knew that but the vast part of him that *was* didn't give a fuck. Clowns looked ridiculous too but if some white-faced red-nosed idiot in slap-shoes had you tied to a table and was practising golf swings with an open razor using your face as the putting green you wouldn't actually be thinking about how silly he looked. And these guys weren't even clowns. They were accountants, for Christ's sake! Or at least that's what he'd first thought twenty-five minutes ago when he'd noticed them turn onto 18th

Street at the same time as him but several blocks further down.

Any late-twentieth-century urban dweller has certain in-built triggers of fear but, despite it being after midnight, none of Sharnock's triggers had been pulled when he first saw them. Three men in overcoats, that was all. Triggers change with time and geography, of course, and had this been Prohibition Chicago Sharnock may well have been alarmed but it was 1990s New York and terror was younger and wore different clothes, brighter and less formal. So he'd simply been mildly amused at the anachronistic sight they made in their matching black overcoats, matching black homburg hats and matching black umbrellas held up against the rain. He hadn't been far from the garment district so his initial and fleeting assumption that they were accountants had given way to a thought that three Jewish tailors had had a late night – the black coats were similar to what Hassidim might wear – and that was fine. Tailors were no more harmful than accountants. A great deal less harmful in fact – as far as he knew, nobody'd ever gone to jail for following the advice of their tailor. Besides, he was heading in the same direction as they were and they were at least fifty yards behind him so what did it matter?

They must have had good old-fashioned shoes on for the rhythmic and steady tapping of their feet on the sidewalk had carried through to him despite their distance. It was the sound of the tapping – or, more specifically, the curious synchronicity of it as if each of them was putting his foot down at precisely the same moment as his companions, all three of them keeping time with the eager precision of West Point cadets – that had made him glance back for the first time.

His heart had jumped then. There had still been nothing overtly menacing about them but little oddities about their appearance had suddenly registered. They were almost certainly not Hassidic, he'd realized, because all three were clean-shaven. All three were also wearing sunglasses, a strange affectation after midnight even for rock'n'rollers and positively bizarre for men such as they. Something else, too. Their faces. Perhaps it was heightened by their all-black outfits and the solid black of their shades, but the pallor of their faces seemed extraordinary. The streetlights could be misleading, he'd acknowledged, but even so he'd felt a sudden

9

twitch of irrational terror at the distinct possibility that their faces were white. Not pink. Not pale. *White*. But the major source of his anxiety had been none of these details. It was the fact that he could make these details out; in the few seconds since he'd first noticed them, the men had more than halved the distance that kept them from him and were now no more than twenty yards away.

Perhaps if he'd started running right that second, Sharnock thought, he might have got away from them. But no. That would have been infantile, wouldn't it? He might have looked stupid. Might have felt a fool. How he yearned to feel a fool now. To look stupid. To be infantile. How he hoped that in the very few moments from now when his stamina and his breath finally failed him and he turned, panting and slobbering, to face his pursuers like a harried and helpless fox finding the baleful and glittering eyes of the hounds, how he hoped that the nearest of the men in black would walk toward him with an apologetic grin and proffer the wallet or the keys that Sharnock had dropped twenty minutes earlier. But that wasn't going to happen. There were many things that weren't going to happen. In fact, the list of possibilities left in Sharnock's life was very short and the items on that list were far from pleasant.

He hadn't started running when they'd first got closer. He hadn't even started walking faster until the next glance back and the realization that the men were now ten yards from him. He'd picked up his pace then but had only started to run when, after several more increasingly frequent looks back, he'd finally grasped the idea that these people had no intention of being left behind. They had business with Richard Sharnock, it seemed, and were single-mindedly eager to begin it.

And suddenly they were about to get their chance. With a gasp of a despair more profound than Sharnock had ever had reason to believe possible through his twenty-eight years of life, he realized that the alley into which his most recent panic-fuelled turn had led him was a cul-de-sac. A dead end. Emphasis on the dead.

Pointlessly, automatically, Sharnock continued to run until he reached the wall at the end of the alley. Twenty feet high, its bricks plastered to a cruel and unclimbable smoothness, it stood there before him, slick with the pouring rain, as solid and real as any metaphor for the end could ever hope to be.

Had Richard Sharnock been a man more inclined to the dramatic, he might have beaten his fists against the unyielding brick in a final acknowledging flourish of defeat and defiance. Instead, he simply turned to look back along the alley and wait for the three figures to reach him. An absurd thought surfaced, as absurd thoughts will at inappropriate moments: Sharnock found, hiding behind his terror and exhaustion, a ridiculous hope that he could avoid humiliation, a tiny wish that the sheeting rain soaking his face would blind his pursuers to the tears of fright that were pouring from his eyes and running saltily into his nostrils and his mouth.

The pace of the three figures neither slowed nor increased. The expressions on their cold ivory faces, unalteringly impassive every time he'd looked at them, remained impassive now. It was as if his stopping and turning and waiting had as little effect on them as his flight had. They were moving toward a moment. That moment would happen. His actions made no difference one way or the other, they were as relevant or as important to the inevitable moment as the actions of the fly in the web – it could struggle or it could be still; the moment would happen, the spider would feed.

As they reached Sharnock they finally broke rank, the figures on the right and left moving forward to stand on either side of him and take hold of an arm each. The sensation as their hands gripped tightly was intense but Sharnock, if asked, would have been genuinely unable to say whether the touch was numbingly cold or blisteringly hot. It was at that point of extremity where each sensation imitates its opposite. He made no resistance, he made no comment. He felt the rain pelting down on his face and shoulders and heard it drumming against the curved black surfaces of their umbrellas. He heard the ragged sound of his own exhausted breath and the silence of their own. He raised his eyes to stare at the third figure, who stood only a foot or so in front of him beneath his own umbrella.

A moment of silent study passed, though the opaque lenses of the figure's sunglasses made any judgement or decision on his part invisible. The man in black lowered his umbrella, furled it, clipped it, and let it fall to the ground beside him. From the inside pocket of his overcoat he drew a clipboard. Easing the pen from the attached holder, he made a few ticks against various places on the piece of paper on the clipboard and then returned both pen and clipboard to their proper places. He gave a tiny inscrutable nod like that of a bureaucrat satisfied that certain proper conditions had been met, certain proper authorizations signed. Things could go ahead now.

'When you get to where you are going, Mr Sharnock,' he said, his voice quiet with understated authority, its only tonal coloration an all but oblique reptilian hiss on the sibilants, 'report at once to my chambers. Chastisement will continue there.'

Sharnock had no time to profess either innocence or ignorance. The other two figures dropped their still-open umbrellas onto the rain-soaked alley floor and, while keeping hold of his arms with their near hands, took firm hold of the back of his head with their other hands, keeping it rigidly in place.

The figure in front took half a step forward and leaned in slightly so that his face was only inches from Sharnock's own. Then he opened his mouth wide. The tongue that jetted out, twitching and writhing in the rain, was startlingly pink against the terrible cold whiteness of the face. It was unnaturally long, inhumanly thin, and forked for the last two inches of its length.

Sharnock finally screamed, though not for long. With an accompanying tilt of the head to aid direction, the tongue flew forward with incredible speed, burrowing through the yielding jelly of Sharnock's left eye and burying itself deep within his brain.

The figure who had had the clipboard leaned in a little closer, his hands crossed lightly behind his back, the calm stillness of his body in contrast to the dervish excavations of his tongue.

Sharnock was dead within seconds but the other two men in black continued to hold his body professionally in place until its reactive spastic twitching had finally stopped.

There had been no witnesses to what had happened and nor were there any witnesses to what happened next. The three figures –

who had seemed so implacable in their purpose when there was a pursuit to be performed and a punishment to be administered – seemed now, when their immediate purpose was done, almost at a loss. The two who were supporting Sharnock's body simply let it drop and wandered aimlessly to either side of it, as if it had no meaning at all to them. The leader, the one who had spoken, the one who had killed, looked around himself curiously, almost as if he had woken from a dream to find himself somewhere else entirely than the place in which he had imagined himself to be.

Their movements, which had been so precise and so co-ordinated, were now indecisive and random, their arms swinging wantonly like those of bored and confused children, their heads turning as if awaiting instruction or elucidation. Like a pack of highly trained attack dogs who, having ripped to shreds the appointed quarry, look around in confused disorder until the voice of their master should give them new orders, the three men in black stood waiting. A goal had been set, a climax had been reached, and now they had nothing to do. Creatures of a single function, they were – when not performing that function – essentially pointless. They had no meaning. And now, as if demonstrating the literal truth of some philosophic concept that held that meaning is the basis of being and the glue that holds the material world together, they began to lose their hold on their existence.

Guided by a final lingering notion of appropriateness, they shambled over to the edge of the sidewalk, the tips of their black leather shoes protruding a couple of inches over the gutter beneath them, and stood still. The rain was still falling steadily and heavily. It splattered against their black overcoats and bounced from their black homburgs until, with a communal shuddering motion, a brief spasm of something being released, they surrendered to the rain and, instead of splashing *off* them, it began to drive *through* them, as if their matter had devolved to an amoeboid jelly-like consistency, apparently solid but actually permeable.

Slowly, with no apparent pain, indeed with no acknowledgement at all of what was happening, the three figures dissolved, slipping into shapelessness as the rain pelted through them. The white of what had been their flesh and the black of what had

13

been their clothing ran together, streaming down from their central masses like wax rivulets down candles.

Though their expressions were no longer readable – for there were no longer any faces on which to read them – their bodies stood there impassively as their transmutation into liquid continued like the slow dissolution of snow figures carved by a disturbed child.

The blackness of the liquefying figures overwhelmed the white as the process continued so that, by the time the fully liquid remains of all three poured into the gutter, running together, pooling and circling, it looked like nothing so much as old ink, washed away down the storm drain like abandoned stories from the mind of a madman. A bottle of ink is full of stories or drawings the way a pubescent male is full of babies. It looked now as if a reluctant or exhausted storyteller was throwing a bottle of nightmares away down the drain, diluting it with cleansing and disseminating rainwater.

# 3

*Fall, 1935*

THE MONSTER DEMANDS A MATE! proclaimed the huge six-sheet outside the 42nd Street theatre.

Norbert Read, arrested by the size and four-colour glory of the poster for *The Bride of Frankenstein*, stopped walking and stared at it. Though he had heard of the film and was eager to see it, it had yet to reach his home-town theatres in Cedar Rapids, Iowa. He glanced at his wristwatch. 12.45. His one o'clock meeting would surely be over within an hour. If it went well, perhaps he could come back here and reward himself with a matinée before making his way to Penn Station and the train back home. Hell, if it went *very* well, maybe he could spring for another night at the inexpensive uptown hotel he had left half an hour earlier. He could buy himself dinner on Broadway. Maybe even pick up a date. This was New York. Anything could happen.

Set back from the sidewalk, between converging poster-hung walls that ran back to two sets of window-studded double doors, was the theatre's freestanding ticket booth. Read looked at it, at its strange elaborate design, its silver shell and streamlined wing-shaped mouldings. The glass that gave on to its counter was curved like a cockpit windscreen. The whole thing looked to him like a stranded scientific wonder, a time machine that had escaped from the pages of the fantastic and touched down just that second in this unlikeliest of locations.

Behind the glass, a uniformed girl; alas, no chrono-pilot motif here – just the usual braids, buttons, and scarlet cloth that made her look like the daughter of a Toytown general caught in Daddy's Sunday best. She was pretty but her expression of boredom looked profoundly genuine and not simply a pre-emptive female defence

15

against predatory male ticket buyers. She caught Read's eye and her glance was neither challenging nor welcoming but a simple act of registering a presence.

Read smiled his automatic small-town smile. The girl had no response, not even a blink. She simply kept looking. He was either going to buy a ticket or he was not. That was the only issue in her mind, the only point of connection between them. Read's smile faltered in the face of her Manhattan indifference and he turned away to continue along the sidewalk.

The corner with 8th Avenue was several yards ahead. He was going to make a right there. The street map was folded and hidden in his hip-pocket. He had no wish to consult it. People more well-travelled than he had told him about that. *Don't look like a rube. Walk like you know where you're going.* So he'd planned his route before leaving the hotel and – though the grid-like layout of the city had already made it clear to him that it was actually pretty difficult to get lost here – he was sticking to it. Five blocks along 8th and then left on 47th. And then destiny, whose name was Aylward R. Jacobs.

'Who?'

The secretary, a spiritual sister of the ticket booth girl, lent the question no urgency, either of suspicion or apology.

'Read. Norbert Read,' he repeated, 'I do have an appointment.'

'And he said to come *here*?'

Read thought about it. Actually, Jacobs *hadn't* said to come here but this was 219 West 47th, the address on the masthead, so what else was he to assume?

'Well, I figured this is where he'd be.'

The secretary shook her head. Read liked the way her old-fashioned bob-cut swayed around her powdered face.

'Not at one o'clock, he wouldn't,' she said.

Read nodded his head in a reasonable imitation of understanding and awaited further elucidation. When none was forthcoming his head slowed to stillness and his hands, palm out, made a silent request of the girl for further information.

She was smiling now and her chin was cupped in the hand of one arm, the elbow of which rested on her desk. She waited

16

another second or so, eyes sparkling in inoffensive pleasure at his confusion.

'Did you ever see *The Murder Man?*' she asked.

Now Read was really at a loss.

'Uhh . . .' was all he managed to get out before she continued.

'Spencer Tracy? Dipso newshound? No? There was a kid in it. His first movie. James Stewart. He's making a musical now. *Rose Marie*. It was in *Photoplay*.'

Read was nodding again, though only God knew why.

'You remind me of him,' the secretary said, 'all tall and helpless and cute.'

Read felt the blush begin to burn its way up from beneath his collar. She spoke again.

'Emmett's Grill,' she said.

Finally, he found his voice.

'What?' he said. Not much, but a start.

'Emmett's Grill. Broadway. Between 50th and 51st. That's where you'll find Mr Jacobs.'

She'd swung back on her chair almost before she'd finished speaking and her fingers were flying over her typewriter keyboard before Read could stammer out his thanks and stumble out of the office.

Emmett's Grill was a no-nonsense coffee shop whose Broadway address gave it no pretension but plenty of business. The place was packed, noisy with the buzzing of New York conversation and cloudy with the burning of Virginia tobacco.

Fortunately, the white-capped guy at the counter – Emmett himself, perhaps – knew Jacobs by name. He pointed towards a back booth and Read weaved his way between the closely packed tables. Unaware of his approach, Jacobs, a heavy-set middle-aged man, was busy getting outside of a chopped-steak sandwich. He ate with no indication of pleasure but rather a steady purposeful efficiency as if he feared his meal's escape. After every fifth bite he'd take a quick swallow of coffee, more, it seemed to Read, in the spirit of necessary lubrication than of anything like enjoyment.

Read reached the booth, which was set for four. Given how busy the place was, he took this as a tribute to Jacobs's standing

17

as a regular customer. Swallowing his last mouthful of meat and bread, Jacobs finally broke his concentration and turned to Read, giving him a quick look up and down before speaking.

'You Read?' he asked.

'Yes. A pleasure to meet you, Mr Jacobs.' Read extended his hand, which Jacobs shook perfunctorily without rising.

'Name's Aylward. Sit.' He nodded in indication at the place opposite him on the curved leather booth.

As Read slipped himself between the seat and the table, Jacobs passed him a coffee mug from the place setting next to his own. Read glanced momentarily at the mug in his own place but decided it was better to say nothing. Jacobs wanted to feel like the gift-giver, the man of benison. And Read wanted a gift. If a redundant mug was a metaphorical overture to a contract, then so be it.

Jacobs wasted no time on preamble.

'I like your stuff, Read,' he said, 'like your stories. Can't buy 'em, but I like 'em.'

He must have caught the falling of Read's face because he rushed on before Read could say anything. 'Chin up,' he said, 'the news isn't all bad. I said I like the stories and I do. I mean, your *style* ain't gonna give Scott Fitzgerald any sleepless nights. But at least you write in sentences. And the ideas are good, which is what counts in our game. The ideas are real good. Creepy. Get under your skin, know what I'm saying?'

Read nodded, taking the compliment, though he was still at a loss as to what Jacobs actually *was* saying.

'You got things in there made my skin crawl,' Jacobs continued. 'Nasty. Real nasty. And that's good. But you don't *explain* things. Not rationally. See, my magazine, everything has to be explained. The readers like that. You can have all the weird crap you want but in the end you gotta pull the curtain back and show them the bad guy who's been faking it, who's been engineering all the stuff.'

'What kind of stuff?' Read asked.

'Bad stuff. Whippings. Burnings. Broads in bras tied up by dwarfs and ready for the mad doctor's scalpel. That sort of stuff. Here . . .' he fumbled in the briefcase beside him on the red leather of the booth and drew out three magazines, 'take a look at these. Take 'em home.'

Read took the proffered pulps and looked at them. *Strange Thrills*, they were called. The cover illustrations certainly lived up to the title. While the specifics differed – a lab table here, a dungeon floor there – they were all essentially the same picture, the same fever-dream of male confusion: a semi-naked woman at the mercy of grotesques, all of whom were armed with weapons ready to open, to expose, to mark, to control. Read laid the magazines on the table and flicked to the contents page of the issue nearest to hand. The titles of the stories were astonishing: 'Lust of the Leper King', 'Dead God's Flesh', 'White Brides for Satan'.

'See, once we establish you with the readers you can do what you want,' Jacobs said, 'but right now this is the kind of thing I'd need to get you in. Think you could come up with something?' Before Read could reply, Jacobs turned and signalled to the passing waitress to fill Read's mug and to refill his own.

Read turned the magazines face-down as the waitress poured the coffee. He caught Jacobs's amused glance but still waited till the waitress moved on to the next table before speaking.

'How about "White Skin, Red Weals"?' he asked. Jacobs moved his mouth as if tasting the idea and made a non-committal noise.

'Too on the nose?' said Read. 'Okay . . . "Love in a Mummy's Tomb".'

Jacobs brightened immediately. 'Yeah! You got the idea. That's perfect. Love in a mummy's tomb. Good. So what happens?'

Read had no idea what happened but he took a long sip of coffee and thought about it.

'A husband and wife are visiting a –'

'Newlyweds,' Jacobs interrupted.

'Okay. A pair of newlyweds are visiting . . . no. No, they're on their way to a honeymoon hotel. But they nearly run over a body in the road. It's night, of course. Lonely road. No traffic. Body just lying there. They pick up the man . . . no, woman. And unconscious, not dead . . . and take her to a nearby house. In fact, the only house for miles. And a man answers the door who –'

'A scientist.'

'An Egyptologist.'

19

'Right! An Egyptologist.'

'Who tells them it's his wife. She's troubled. Disturbed. Mad. She'd run away from home. He thanks them, offers them a meal. Can't do that, they say. A drink, then, at least a drink. Okay. They have a drink. They have a drink even though the wife is beginning . . . I mean, *our* wife, the newlywed . . . to be suspicious of this guy. But it's too late.'

'Drinks are drugged.'

'Exactly. Blackout. End of a chapter. Whatever. So she wakes up and she's in a dungeon. Well, we'll know it's a dungeon eventually but as far as she can tell it's an Egyptian tomb. We play it that way. She doesn't know how long she's been out, what he's been up to. For all she knows, she might have been shipped to Egypt. Christ, for all she knows, she might've been shipped back in *time*. Her wrists are chained to the wall above her head. There's all kinds of stuff in there – treasures and things . . .'

'But it's creepy?'

'Creepy as hell. There's a big gold sarcophagus across the room from her. She's screaming for help, for her husband, but nobody seems to hear. Except that the lid of the sarcophagus starts to come off. Now she's really screaming. And then it flies off completely and a mummy crawls out of it and starts staggering towards her. Bandages. Dust. The works. Centuries old. You know. She's twitching and hollering now, for sure. He comes closer and closer . . .'

'Wait a minute. Is she dressed?'

'Not for long. Because the mummy's hand reaches out and snatches her dress away. She's all exposed. And she realizes the mummy isn't going to kill her – well, maybe he's going to kill her but not before . . .'

'Giving her some old-time Egyptian loving.'

'Precisely. So he's just about to . . .' Read paused, threw in a question. 'Can we actually . . . ?'

'No. No, of course not,' Jacobs said, looking almost offended. 'Cops'd have it off the newsstands quicker than a Tijuana bible.'

'Right. Right. Okay, where was I? Okay, his withered hands are roaming her body and his dry ancient face is leaning in toward hers, eyes shining with unholy lust, when suddenly the door

20

opens and a shot rings out. He falls dead and her husband and the supposedly mad wife run into the room. Hubby starts snapping her out of the chains while the other wife rushes over to the mummy and . . .'

'Takes the mask off and it's the scientist!'

'Of course. And his wife explains that it was *he* who was mad. His studies had driven him crazy, made him think he actually *was* some old Egyptian mummy. That's why she was running away. Because he made her play this little game all the time. Once she woke up upstairs and found the drugged husband, she realized what was going on and gave him *her* husband's gun.'

Jacobs lit a cigarette, nodding vigorously. 'Okay. Okay. I like it. What do you think – five thousand words?'

'Easily. Maybe more.'

'No. I got a five thousand word hole in the next issue. If you can make it fit I can buy it tomorrow.'

'Great. And when would you want the story?'

'Tomorrow. That's what I said.'

Read stared at him. 'Tomorrow!'

Jacobs stared back. 'What's the matter with you?' he said, lip curling in some semi-polite relative of derision. 'You ever hear of Walter Gibson? Or Arthur Burks? Those guys'd write it for me while I went to take a piss. It'd be on this table waiting for me while I was still buttoning my fly! Can you do it or what?'

Read nodded. 'I can do it. Sure I can.'

'Okay. Get it to me before five. I'll see you then.'

Jacobs stood up, shook the hand of the still-rising Read, and was half in his overcoat and half out of the coffee shop door before Read realized that he had been left at the table in the company of his own half-drunk cup of coffee and Jacobs's drained cup, empty plate, and unpaid bill. They hadn't discussed payment for the story at all but Read tried to think of the thirty-five cents the editor's chopped-steak sandwich was going to cost him as a kind of commission. Or an initiation fee. He was *in*. He was a professional. It was all going to happen. New York was full of wonders, a place where dreams came true.

# 4

The effect of the drinks had started to wear off by the time the subway deposited Avis at the corner of Spring Street and Lafayette but she came out just north of Little Italy and the proximity of the many people still sitting out at sidewalk tables working on their pasta, their chianti, and their pick-up lines kept her feeling safe for the first hundred yards of her walk home. It was only after she'd left those people and the massed sound of their conversations behind and covered four blocks or so on Spring Street to start heading east on Bowery that Avis had begun to be fully aware of the fact that it was one-thirty in the morning, that she was a woman on her own, and that she had been out of her fucking mind to give up so easily on finding a cab.

That thing she'd christened The New York Change had happened. Manhattan was a city of suddenness in all aspects, some good, some bad. The New York Change was the one she liked least. In all the European cities she'd known, the transition from a good area to a bad, from a safe to a dangerous, was a slow dissolution, a process that you could observe happening at a speed with which you could cope: buildings became shabbier, stores less ostentatious, people less civil. It was like a four minute warning and allowed the choice of continuing to head for the explosion site or turning back towards the viewing point. Not in New York, pal. It could change from block to block. No warning. Ground Zero. A blink of the eye and a single sidewalk crossing could take you straight to Hell.

The drunken bravado that had propelled her onto the F Train somewhere between Park Avenue and 3rd, the happy jokes she had shared with her midtown friends as they waved her through the turnstile seemed not only irretrievable now but also hollow and impossible. Nobody was that stupid, she thought, nobody actually believed that urban dread was something that could be dealt with simply by denial dressed as humour. It was the way she felt every time she fastened a seat belt on a plane and a wave of anxiety would suddenly clear her head and allow her to realize where she irrevocably was. As if blinkers were suddenly lifted and reality came back and you realized that, through some combination of divine malice and your own idiocy, you had brought yourself back to the thing that would kill you.

There was no immediate threat. The street was deserted. But that wasn't the point. These three blocks that led to her building simply felt bad. Always did. Even during daylight she didn't like to walk alone along them. And now, with the paltry street lighting and the glimpses of the ugly shattered buildings swelling into the light and shrivelling back into darkness, she would be hard pressed to name anywhere on earth that she wouldn't rather be than here on the street where she lived.

Imaginary assassins lurked in every shadowed doorway. No. Wait a minute. Who was she kidding? Assassin was far too elegant a word for the creatures her imagination conjured. To be pursued by an *assassin* would almost lend an air of importance, of dignity, to her fear. That wasn't its nature at all. Vacant-eyed soulless thugs, poor, stupid and brutal and as priapic as they were murderous, *that* was what she peopled her nightmare with.

'Why do you *create* this?' she could hear Fern ask in her voice of New Age inquiry, the voice that could, with apparent seriousness, search for karmic reasons for cancer, infidelity, or the loss of a limb or two as if the victim of any or all of these things not only sought them out but, on some etheric level, actually put them into action.

'Fuck you, Fern,' Avis said aloud. She liked her flatmate, liked her a lot. So, just on the off chance that even half of the rubbish Fern believed in was true and just on the off chance that the ears of Fern's astral self were tuned to Radio Avis at that precise moment, she added a silent rider that the cursing of her wasn't serious and that she hoped Fern would understand. It just gave Avis an excuse to use her voice and somehow, irrational or not, the use of her voice gave her a sense of control which, even

23

if specious, was at least comforting and made her feel safer.

The thought of Fern, coupled with her brief glimpse of Little Italy, led her to remember John's comments when he'd persuaded them all to buy the building. Avis, Fern and Michael had all had reservations despite the relatively low price and the staggering realization that, by pooling their resources, they could actually *own* property in Manhattan. For four people of their age (John the eldest at thirty-one, Fern the youngest at twenty-three) it was an astonishing possibility. But it was in the Bowery – which meant not only that the majority of their neighbours were unlikely candidates for invitations to any parties the four newcomers might throw but that a lot of them were neighbours simply because it was in that area that they chose the doorways and alleys and decimated buildings in which they slept.

John, though, had been both confident and convincing.

'There's nowhere else left for croissantization,' he'd said, 'this place *has* to be next. We'll be there *first*. And the galleries and the coffee houses and the bandwagon-jumpers will follow and we'll be sitting pretty on a prime piece of real estate.'

'And what then?' Michael had asked. 'We sell up and do the same pioneer act in the South Bronx?'

'Maybe,' John had replied over Avis and Fern's laughter, 'maybe. See, your problem is you're only seeing the *now*. What is, *is*. But – just like what was, *isn't* – so what is, *won't be*. Get it?'

Actually, Avis hadn't got it at all. Hadn't had a clue what the hell he was talking about. Seemed to work for Fern, though.

'Listen,' John had said, 'you know where the safest area in New York is? Little Italy, that's where. Owned by criminals. Established criminals. Time-served professionals. And they do a much better job of keeping the violent element out than any city-paid official.'

'So?' Avis had asked.

'So we're *four blocks* from there!'

Avis came back to the present. She was retroactively pissed with John. First, he'd exaggerated the proximity. And second, even four blocks was four fucking blocks too far when they were dark and creepy and frightening and ugly.

She was out of her mind. How long could she possibly have had to stand waiting for a cab? Ten minutes? Twenty? Call it half an hour if you like, those thirty minutes would still have seemed much shorter than the three minutes she'd been walking home. A bored and frustrated minute feels pretty long until you compare it to a so-scared-you-could-scream one.

From an alleyway entrance a few yards ahead of her a mass of garbage protruded onto the sidewalk, the scores of black plastic bags and the vast amount of unbagged trash spilling over in a downward slope that was as tall as her where it emerged from the alley and still tall enough to require stepping over or around where it settled on the sidewalk. It looked like the alley had taken all of the crap it could and was literally disgorging it onto the street. It was the same all around the neighbourhood. Alleys were refusing to recognize the difference between the streets and themselves. Barriers were coming down, divisions dissolving, and the neighbourhood could no longer keep up the pretence that it was anything other than what it was – the lower intestine of New York, the place where shit happened.

Avis reached the trash and, holding her breath at the appalling stench as she sought its narrowest point, stepped over a low and lumpy pile of dark cloth.

It barked at her and grabbed at her calf.

Avis screamed and threw herself forward, simultaneously turning round to stare back at the thing. A grime-blackened hand – still clutching spastically at the air where her leg had been – was sticking out of the ragged shape she had stepped over. Avis's adrenal system was pumping its overload through her in a nauseating rush that she could actually hear hissing like white noise inside her head. There was a hammering in there too, that she'd last heard as a child when succumbing to gas pumped into her mouth by a dentist. Oh God, don't let me faint, she thought, don't let me faint.

A movement rippled along the dark shape as if something loose and disconnected was trying to find a way out. A face as filthy as the hand emerged from the raggedness, its dryness-cracked lips curled back from yellow teeth in an aggressive snarl.

Avis was frozen, her mouth open and pulling in air in rapid and short gasps, the closest approximation she could make to breathing. Her eyes were wide and unblinking as she stared at the face of the woman whose sleep she had disturbed.

The woman stared back. She was about fifty as far as Avis could tell – though the margin of error demanded by dirt and circumstance was at least ten years – and her eyes, startling in the grime that surrounded them, were a piercing blue. Neither of them said anything as they held each other's gaze.

Avis was freaked. Her initial and specific fears (*rape, robbery, murder*) were disappearing, though her system was still in shock, and now she was feeling something different – the kind of helpless mix of ignorance and anxiety that city dwellers feel when coming face to face with a harmless but strange wild animal. That sense of confrontation with the alien was what she felt as she and the woman regarded each other. She recognized now that the woman's mannerisms were defensive rather than aggressive – Avis had invaded her territory and had had to be warned off – but it distressed her profoundly that that was the sum total of the possible connection between them. This wasn't like meeting the eyes of a stranger on a train or a bus or a crowded street, this was more like members of two different *species* surprised by each other at a common watering hole. This woman wasn't even going to ask her for money or try to bum a cigarette. She was long past that. She was a woman who had fallen off the edge of the world and Avis's sighting of her now was like a cosmic accident – as if some dimensional interface had been temporarily breached and a glimpse afforded from one plane to the next.

Avis dropped her eyes and turned, hurrying on down the street without looking back, hearing behind her the sounds of the woman resettling herself.

Okay. Two more blocks and she was home. Once inside, she could allow pity and guilt to replace shock and repugnance but right now she just wanted to keep moving and be grateful that that was the only surprise the street had had to show her tonight.

Avis could see her front door now. It wasn't lit from outside – John had argued against that, saying that in this neighbourhood it would be more magnet than deterrent – but there was a street-lamp only a doorway down which lent some visibility and Avis began to feel safe. There were no more alleys or cross-streets between her and the door and there was nobody else in sight.

Her hand moved to her purse to bring out the keys (having your keys ready and aimed before reaching the door was a piece of street-smartness that was now instinctive with her) but she felt them catch against something in there and looked down for a second to free them. No problem – a pack of mints had pyramided with a tampon and a fold-down hairbrush, that was all. She didn't even break stride as she manoeuvred the keys out from beneath them. Holding the keys tight, she raised her eyes back up to look straight ahead.

There was a man outside her front door.

Avis jerked to a halt, gasping in shock. A whole new wave of tingling fear capered through her body, as if maliciously gleeful at its resurrection and laughing at the frailty of her recent sense of safety.

Frozen, she stared at the man at the door. How could he be there? From where had he come? The street had been empty when she'd glanced down into her purse but now here he was, not fifteen yards from her. She thanked God that at least he wasn't looking in her direction – which meant she had the grace of a second or two should she need to start running.

The man, in fact, was simply staring at the front door with a slightly puzzled look on his face that was half recognition and half confusion. It was like the expression of somebody who had wandered home paralytically drunk and, surfacing out of a black-out, suddenly found themselves right in front of their home.

Avis, though still rooted to the spot, was calmed a little by this look on his face. The man's appearance helped, too. He bore no weapons and was impeccably dressed – so impeccably dressed indeed that Avis wondered if he'd been to a costume party in some other outpost of civilization in the Wasteland. He was in evening clothes, but evening clothes of an elegance and formality that bespoke an earlier time. Nobody dressed like that now, not even for fancy dinners or theatrical first nights. His black dinner jacket had tails, his gleaming black leather shoes were half-covered by equally gleaming white spats, and, at an appropriately jaunty angle, he sported a silken and shining top hat.

Tucked with elegant precision into a buttonhole on the lapel of his jacket was a midnight-blue flower of a type that Avis didn't recognize. The man glanced down at it and gave its position a minor adjustment. Looking up, he glanced away from the door to look around the street and take in his surroundings. A small frown of surprised distaste creased his features for a second at the nature of the neighbourhood and then his gaze found Avis.

She was still standing where she had stopped at her first sight of him and, as their eyes locked, her face remained as frozen as her body. Though calmed a little by his clothes and his manner, she was still very much aware of the time, the locale, and their proximity on an otherwise deserted street. There was no way she was going to initiate any greetings, no way she was going to send out any signal for him to interpret in some psychopathic language as invitation or consent. Let him make the play, if play there was going to be.

A small but charming smile blossomed on his face at the sight of her. He straightened himself up, placed one arm across his waist and bowed, raising his other hand to his top hat to lift it slightly from his head in courteous and respectful greeting.

Avis couldn't help but relax somewhat and nor could she help the smile of mixed parentage (as much amusement as greeting) that, answering his, grew on her face. She was calmed. And intrigued. She began to move toward him. But she didn't move too quickly – she was as susceptible to charm and good manners as the next girl but she wasn't an idiot and she knew of no law that said Death couldn't come robed in fine silks and cottons and bowing like a gentleman.

'I live here,' she said, proud of her tremor-free voice, 'can I help you?'

The man, having risen from his bow, opened his mouth to reply. Avis watched his lips form the shapes of words (A name? A greeting? A request? What was she, a lip-reader?) as nothing but silence emerged from his throat. He seemed not only embarrassed by this but as surprised as she was and promptly closed his mouth. He looked away from Avis back to the door, then out again at the street. The puzzled look Avis had seen on his face earlier was back now, the look of a man who, while perfectly sure of where he *was*, was far from sure as to *why* he was where he was.

Avis hadn't liked the dumb show. It had been creepy and unusual. But it had obviously bothered him too and so she hadn't slowed down – well, hadn't slowed down *much* – and now, reassured further by his little-boy-lost confusion, she spoke again.

'Are you okay? I mean, are you . . .' she hesitated – what was she going to say? *Dumb*? Was there a PC way to put this? Verbally challenged? Fuck it. 'Can you talk? Can't you talk? Is anything the matter?'

The man became transparent.

Avis's stomach lurched in shock. She felt a sudden warm wet rush between her legs and realized she had lost control of her bladder. She was sure she should hate that but she had no con-scious space to spare for something as trivial as shame. Her brain was busy being metaphysically challenged. (*There* was one for the PC-ers: Help. I need a government grant. I have a coping disability when it comes to supernatural manifestations.) It was bizarre. It wasn't *fear* she felt – though it was a bloody close relative – but something for which she didn't have a name. She was in the presence of the unknown and she and her body knew it instantly. She had no doubt about what she was seeing, entertained no possibility that this was some trick of the light. No. She was look-ing *through* him, looking straight through him at the street scene beyond. He was transparent. Increasingly transparent. He was slowly vanishing from her sight like a cross-fade dissolve in a movie.

Avis moaned in distress and – though he was now as insubstan-tial as gossamer – the man seemed to hear her. He looked at Avis one more time, gave an apologetic shrug as if to say that, while he was painfully aware of how rude such behaviour was, matters (*his* matter, at least) seemed to be beyond his control, and then disappeared.

Avis swallowed, a difficult job given how dry her throat had suddenly become. She felt a kind of post-traumatic numbness, not just emotional but physical, as though some over-eager dentist had given her an elephantine dose of Novocaine; she could hardly feel her body at all. It was as if her inhabitation of her flesh had suddenly become tenuous and her soul had already started its preparations to leave, as if somewhere her spiritual bags were packed and the celestial engine of some supernatural taxi was throbbing and waiting. Unfeelingly, automatically, she walked forward and, just as automatically, walked wide of the spot on the street where the man had stood as if it still held some kind of dangerous paranormal power. She reached her door and realized she was still holding her keys out and ready. As she fitted the first key in the lock, she watched, as if watching detachedly the curious behaviour of some foreign object, the unceasing trembling of her hand.

# 5

The soup had been cleared and the egg rolls served when the dragon blinked its dark stone eye.

None of the four people at the table noticed. Why would they? The place was full of dragons. They were in a private dining room at the rear of a second-rate Chinese restaurant in the theatre district, a restaurant that was patronized more for the camp pleasures of its over-the-top decor than for its merely adequate dishes. The price of your food actually bought you admission to a stage set China, a dream Orient of beaded curtains, paper screens, vast glazed pottery, silk-robed attendants, and carved stone monsters. Some of these monsters sat on pottery plinths, fat and gilded, while others glowered from the ceiling, long, sleek, and winged. The one immediately above their heads – four feet long, as elegant as it was ferocious, and painted in primary reds and greens – had excited some comment from the four men from the small software company as they'd taken their places at the table but, like all decorations do, it had become invisible to them as the meal progressed and thus, when its eyelid lowered – slow, silent, and impossible – over the highly polished piece of jet that was its eye, it did so without response from those below.

Chip Peters, the owner of Byte-Syze and the host for the day's dinner, held his half-eaten egg roll out in front of him like a teacher's educational aid, angling it in several directions towards the objects in the room to help illustrate the lesson he was imparting to his staff.

'See, you don't get this stuff in Chinatown,' he said, gesturing with his battered pointer at the chinoiserie scattered about, 'they get enough tourists down there. Don't need to work hard for their custom. This place is the real thing.'

Graham Edwards had his doubts. While Artie and Ray nodded enthusiastically in support of their boss's contention, Graham (the youngest at the table, the newest at the business) remembered the faces of the patrons in the main dining room. The demographic had been about eighty per cent Caucasian and the rest African-American or Hispanic. He didn't recall seeing a single Asian face. Graham's grandpa – who was not, Graham would be the first to admit, a great source of wisdom on most subjects – had had one rule of thumb when it came to eating out: If you're going to eat ethnic, make damn sure you eat where the ethnics eat. Don't eat Irish stew in a place full of Polacks. Don't order your tortillas amidst a swarm of WASPs or your cannelloni where the customers are blonde or black. Or, if you do, don't expect them to be any good. Graham, like most of his generation, had probably eaten out more in his twenty-four years than his grandpa had in his entire life but he had yet to see his grandpa proved wrong. And so, though the won ton soup had been passable and the egg roll was okay, Graham had considerably lower expectations about the courses yet to come than Chip was implying he should have.

Unfortunately, though he was yet to realize it, Graham had tested his grandpa's culinary theory for the last time in his life.

Chip took another mouthful of egg roll. He leaned forward after his bite and he was almost in time to ensure that the bean sprouts and pork juice that his bite pulled from the portion that remained in his hand fell on his side plate rather than the red cotton tablecloth.

'Mmm. Good. Very good,' he said, chewing and looking once more to his staff for signals of assent. Perhaps Artie and Ray provided some. Graham couldn't be sure that they had because it was at that moment that the creaking of the stone wing of the dragon as it sought to free itself from anchor drew his eyes upward and away from the table.

He wasn't sure what he was expecting to see. He was merely responding to an unidentified noise that appeared to come from overhead. Now he was puzzled. Something looked different, and he wasn't sure what it was. Then it hit him. The wings of the heavy stone statue above their heads – hadn't they been sym-metrical when he and the others had arrived? Now the left wing

32

was lower and apparently unfurled. Fuck, was the thing coming loose? Was it going to fall on them? Graham looked at the dragon. And then the dragon looked back at Graham.

For a second, he said nothing. For a second, he *felt* nothing – other than mild surprise. Then, just as his mind grasped the irrationality of what he was seeing and just as his body shuddered at the first wave of a primal fear that he hadn't felt since the day his father had finally convinced him that there really *weren't* monsters under his bed, the dragon beat both its wings against the air, opened its terrible mouth wide in a reptilian grimace of aggression, and dropped to the surface of the table.

'What the fuck . . . !' Artie screamed, while Chip jumped in surprise, his egg roll dropping from his jerking fingers, and Ray's jaw sagged open in shock.

'It's alive!' Graham finally managed to shout – realizing that the other three were under the misapprehension that what had just happened was merely a dangerous accident.

'Don't be a prick,' Chip snapped at him contemptuously. He was about to say more but the words shrivelled in his mouth, devolving into a moan of terror as he – as all of them – saw what happened next.

The dragon raised its head, its long curved neck coiling back with all the deadly elegance of a cobra, and looked rapidly at each of them in turn, taking the measure of the situation like a beast that had just woken in the camp of its enemies. It hissed at them in warning and three viciously sharp curved claws blossomed from each of its four feet, clicking on the table like the tapping of fingernails from Hell.

Perhaps if all of them had remained motionless, things might have gone differently. But when they had decided an hour ago to go out and eat not a single one of them had felt the need to discuss a group strategy in the event of a confrontation with a legendary monster. Chip was the first to move. While fear froze Graham, Artie and Ray in their places, he pushed himself back from the table, rising to his feet and sending his chair flying to the floor behind him.

The movement of the dragon, had any of the men had the leisure or the calmness to observe it dispassionately, would have

33

been seen by them as a magnificent display of grace, speed, and economy. Its feet not moving at all, it propelled its body forward, its neck outward and its jaw toward the, by contrast, slow-motion Chip. But they neither saw nor appreciated this display of beautiful efficiency for what it was. All they saw was that the beast lunged forward. All they saw was that its awful mouth was wide and fierce. All they saw was that with one snap of its jaws it sliced Chip's face completely from his head.

Chip had had no time to scream and now had no mouth with which to do so. The sound that emerged from the lipless hole in that flat plane of blood and raw tissue that used to be his face was more a primal roar of the acknowledgement of death than a cry of pain or terror.

The dragon's rippling body flowed back into itself long before Chip's body began its fall to the floor. For a brief second the creature was once again motionless. It wasn't even chewing. Like some Juggernaut of the deep, it had simply swallowed Chip's face and was letting its stomach acids do the hard work. It had other things to concentrate on – like the flailing arms and screaming voice of Artie and the blur of movement that was Graham rising to his feet and turning his back to the table, ready to run. The dragon did two things at once. It swung its head in Artie's direction and flicked its great and heavy tail toward Graham. It opened its mouth and issued a searing jet of flame at Artie as, at precisely the same moment, its tail smashed into Graham's back at the base of his shoulders.

Graham fell back awkwardly into his seat. He knew he was falling because his eyes told him so – but *only* because his eyes told him so: he had no feeling whatsoever in his body. He felt as if his strings had been cut, as if some puppeteer God had decided that Graham Edwards's part in the marionette show was irrevocably over. He knew he had reached his seat only because his eyes told him he had stopped falling. He tried to turn his head. He couldn't even do that. He had felt the massive blow to the bottom of his neck and had felt nothing since. Not even his mouth would open to emit the cry of anguish he desperately wanted to unleash. All he could do was watch in mute and helpless horror as Artie's head became a fiercely burning torch atop his shoulders.

It was maybe five seconds since the beast had landed on the table. A second ago, the door from the kitchen to the private dining room had been flung open and two members of staff, alerted by the noises, had begun to rush into the room. Now they were frozen in the doorway, unable to believe what they were seeing.

Graham heard the door bang open against the wall but found he could not turn his eyes far enough to the side to see if there was any help coming from that direction. He had no problem looking straight ahead, however, and thus had a very clear view of what happened to Ray. He saw Ray hesitate, as if he understood dimly that it was the movement of the other three men that had brought their doom to them. Graham again wanted to cry out, to shout his agreement to Ray, to tell him to stay absolutely still. But he couldn't speak. And Ray couldn't stay still. Whatever tiny impulse was telling him not to move, it was as nothing in the face of the instinct to flee, to be as far from this horror as fast as he could. He broke to the left, screaming. The dragon was faster. One of its front paws flew out as quickly and as smoothly as its head had lunged earlier. Even as it was moving, the paw had turned upside down so that by the time its inch-long claws had buried themselves in the pit of Ray's stomach they were pointing upwards.

For a second Ray was simply stopped – held in place by the strong hooked claws that were anchored deep inside his flesh. Then the dragon ripped its paw upwards, its claws passing as effortlessly through the splintering ribs and shattering breastbone as through the bursting flesh of muscles and organs. It laid Ray's torso completely open in one sweep. Graham watched Ray look down to see his own viscera spilling onto the floor like offal escaping a rotted butcher's sack.

Ray looked up and found Graham's horrified eyes. There was a bemused expression on Ray's face, as if the shock of what he had just seen and the realization of what it meant had moved him beyond fear or pain into a childlike confusion.

'Graham,' he said, 'look at all the colours. Look at all the colours in me.'

He was right. Graham was as surprised as Ray at the bright-

35

nesses of purple and yellow and green that had spilled from the torn torso of his associate but even if Graham had been capable of replying Ray would not have heard him for as soon as he finished speaking his eyes turned glassy and his body followed his guts to the floor as if in some vain attempt at corporeal reconciliation.

Graham found his eyes drawn away from Ray by another movement on the table. The dragon was coming toward him. Unlike its lightning-fast killing strikes, the beast's motion now was very slow as if it knew precisely the nature of the damage it had done to Graham and that he was incapable of avoiding its advance.

And yet, despite the terrible and unforgiving face of the monster that was, second by second, coming closer to him, something else was bothering Graham more.

His body had forgotten how to breathe.

His lungs useless, his entire respiratory system paralysed, he was dying already as the beast approached. His brain, starved of oxygen, was making a final attempt at conserving what was left and, rather than squander it on the luxury of sight, was allowing his eyes to cloud.

In what was possibly his last insight in this life, Graham realized that something similar was happening to the dragon. He saw now that its slowness was not just the cruel play of the predator closing on the crippled prey. The flesh of the dragon was remembering that it was stone.

Mounted on the table, its head now only inches from Graham's face, its will still urging it forward in a struggle against its increasingly unyielding limbs, the dragon was re-ossifying. Whatever unnatural ichor had pumped magically through its veins for the brief moments of its killing spree was once more thickening and becoming solid. For the dragon, as for Graham, life had already slipped the skin. For man and for monster, breath and the spirit were already memories. Graham knew that his soul had left for home and knew too that the consciousness that let him know this, the consciousness that appeared to remain in him now, was only a shadow, an accidental imprint left in his body like the ghosts of words burned onto a switched-off computer screen.

36

Fearless, he stared at the dragon, a brother to it at the last in their diminishment and their nostalgia for the flesh.

As if it too sensed this bizarre and last-minute kinship with Graham, the beast locked its cold black eyes on his. The rhythms of their closure came together, Graham's fading heart keeping slowing time with the winding-down of the great flicking tail of the fireworm. Frozen in place by his severed spine, Graham gazed deep into the hardening eyes of the dragon, watching, helpless and dying, as the beast retreated back into the impossible.

A sound came into Graham's head as all other sound deserted him. He wondered if, in some strange terminal empathy, he was hearing what the dragon heard: the dreadful sounds of the dreaming place to which it was returning. It was a low hellish rumbling on the very edge of perception like a distant echo of unimaginable machines, indescribably vast and inexpressibly malicious.

# 6

Avis wasn't sure what she did for a living.

That scared her for a moment until she realized she wasn't really awake yet so it was okay. She relaxed and let memory come in. Well, it wasn't so much letting it in as *accessing* it, making the gear change from a dreaming state to a waking one. She didn't actively remember who she was and what she did, it was just that that information simply clicked into place along with everything else that came with the territory of living in her body. As her eyes remembered how to let the world in and her mind remembered how to dress the information which her eyes received, so did she know that her name was Avis Llewellen, that she was twenty-five years old, and that she earned her keep by processing small-claims forms on the forty-first floor of the midtown offices of a large insurance company. And that last night she had seen a ghost.

In the comfort of her bed and the safety of daylight that last piece of knowledge didn't frighten her so much as thrill her. She'd seen a ghost. A *ghost*. What a trip. Out the other side of the experience, away from any danger it might entail, she could retro-actively revel in it.

As a quality, fear is aggressive and territorial, rendering invisible any other aspects of the thing that is feared. The gaping jaws and terrible teeth of a timber wolf are all that will be seen by a traveller who stumbles upon one by surprise in the wild. To the calm patron of an urban zoo, however, or the casual reader of *National Geographic*, it is the animal's natural grace and magnificent beauty that dominate. Behind the glass, behind the bars, behind the painted image, things can be seen for what they are. Putting the beast in the cage allows the contemplation of the thing itself, rather than the dread which it induces, and Avis's ghost was now safely in the cage called Time and Avis was enjoying her view of it.

She felt the way she felt the morning after a plane flight. Flying was something she loathed and feared while she was doing it but it was also something that, once survived, was actually exciting. The exhilaration that she supposed most airline passengers felt while flying was something she could only feel in retrospect. Safely on the ground, she could appreciate the wonders of speed and elevation that, when they were in operation, were sources only of terror and a nerve-tingling knowledge of mortality.

Frightening – and only frightening – at the time, last night's apparition was now something she could appreciate for the marvel it was. Far from something that made her tremble and sweat, it was something that made her feel special. Made her feel like the recipient of a rare gift. It was many years since she'd set foot in the Roman churches of her father's religion. She wasn't Catholic any more. Hell, she'd never been Catholic as far as she was concerned. As a child, she had figured it was just a label that had been stuck on her as a convenient method for drawing name-calling and abuse from classmates in the non-Catholic schools she'd attended. It was probably marginally preferable to having *Give me shit* tattooed on her forehead, but it served the same purpose. Nevertheless, despite her distance, both chronological and philosophical, from the Church, she found herself remembering a word. Sacrament. There were seven of them, as best she recalled. She couldn't name one if you paid her but she knew what the word meant. A thing of mysterious and sacred significance. That's what had happened to her last night. She'd experienced a sacrament – an unveiling, a glimpse of something from beyond. She'd gazed briefly through a temporary sundering of the veil that separated her from . . . from *that other stuff*. That other stuff was the name she gave to the hodgepodge in her head where elements of various categories of the indefinable collided and hid from reason and reality. A catch-all category composed of the divine, the paranormal, and the science-fictional, it was where she filed UFOs and angels, telepaths and poltergeists, anything from newspapers, TV, or gossip that didn't fit with the way the everyday world was supposed to work. So her friend in the suit, her well-tailored phantom, was ready to be filed there too. She wasn't quite sure *where* exactly because she wasn't sure of the provenance of her vision. Was he traditional – a tortured spirit not yet free of the claims of this earthly realm – or was he modern? Modern in this context would mean that he would have something to do with some vague science-fictional idea about ruptures in the space-time continuum. Her ghost, after all, had not merely seen her too but had seemed, in a different way, as confused as she had been – which gave her the idea that, to him, *she* might've been the ghost. She knew she wasn't making this shit up. She'd read as many stories in which the future faced the past and they frightened each other as she'd read those in which somebody hung around after dying because somebody else (or they themselves) had been a right bastard and needed a lesson. She and the guy in the Cary Grant hand-me-downs had been ghosts to each other, staring at themselves across a temporary dimensional flux that had allowed a brief two-way glance between past and present. Yeah, she liked that reading a lot more. Somewhere in 1933 or whatever the fuck year he was from, he too was waking up and thinking about the strangely (and probably scandalously) dressed girl he'd seen materialize and disappear the previous night. The only difference, she decided, was that back there in his Avis-free world of breadlines and black-and-white movies he'd already be pining for the girl he'd glimpsed, waking to the first day of a life which the poor sweet fool would spend in a romantically hopeless yearning for the beautiful vision with which time and chance had tortured him. Cool.

A part of her mind found it interesting that, despite all this recasting, retelling, and redefining she was doing, it was not occurring to her at all to question what she'd seen. And she wasn't going to. Whatever doubts she might have as to the explanation of what it *was* she saw, she had no doubt at all that she *saw* it. Though it brought analysis and definition, the daylight brought no qualification, no rationalization or dismissal. Whether its home was the realm of the supernatural or the realm of quantum physics, she had been in the presence of something other than the everyday. And she liked it.

Once was enough, though. She didn't want to see him, or anything like him, ever again. She'd had the experience – different from all the other stuff in *that other stuff* only inasmuch as it wasn't reportage or the tales of friends of friends, it was hers – but it was filed away now and it could stay filed away. That was the way she wanted it. Stored and safe. Something she could pull out occasionally and smile at. A souvenir. A dried flower pressed between the pages of memory's book but redolent still, when sniffed, of the aromas of an alien orchard, the perfumes of a stranger's garden.

She stopped briefly in the kitchen on her way to the bathroom for her morning shower. She'd lain thinking a little too long to allow her to grab breakfast before leaving for the office but she figured a few fluid ounces of juice would hold her till she could meet the muffin-man in the lobby of her building and take coffee and banana-nut up to her desk on the forty-first floor.

She was standing in front of the open fridge door, mid-swig from the carton, when Fern entered the kitchen. Wrapped identically to Avis in a towelling robe half-dragged over a baggy T-shirt (Fern's reading CUDDLE UP TO SOMEONE FROM GEORGIA, Avis's I'M WITH IDIOT), she stopped halfway to the cabinets, her face crumpling in exaggerated disgust as she stared at Avis.

'Gross,' she said.

Guiltily, Avis lowered the carton, swallowing hard.

'Couldn't see a glass,' she got out the second her mouth had room for words.

'Couldn't see a *clean* one, maybe,' said Fern, grabbing up a semi-encrusted plastic glass from the sink. Turning the faucet on full, she held the glass up to be pounded in the flow.

Avis cocked her head, watching with interest.

'So let me get this straight,' she said, 'you're expecting water pressure alone to do the job that all those companies spend thousands of millions a year persuading me that only the grease-cutting ingredient in their product can do?'

'Uh-huh,' Fern nodded. She took the glass out and held it up for Avis's inspection, killing the faucet with her other hand. 'See? It's easy. Long as the water's hot enough.' She picked up the carton from the shelf in the still-open fridge and filled the glass.

'You better be drinking that,' Avis said.

'As opposed to . . . ?'

'As opposed to playing Mom. Teaching me by example.'

Fern laughed. 'Relax,' she said, taking a sip, 'and you know what? I'm not even going to insist that you label this carton and buy us another. Me and the guys'll risk your germs. And they won't even know.'

'John would freak,' Avis acknowledged.

Fern nodded in agreement, then looked thoughtful. 'I might tell Michael, though.'

'Why?'

'Make his day.'

'What?'

'Come on. He'd love it. I'd tell him that, scientifically speaking, it's practically the same as you putting your tongue in his mouth.'

'Oh, stop it.'

'He *likes* you, Avis.'

'Does not.'

'Does too.'

'Does not.'

'Right. That's why every time you bring a guy home he disappears to his room . . .'

'Stop.'

'. . . to sulk . . .'

'Stop.'

'. . . and masturbate.'

'*Stop!*'

Fern laughed. 'Hey,' she said, 'just giving you something to think about at work.'

Work was the magic word that broke the mood for Avis. 'Fuck,' she said, 'I'm going to be late.' She swung round and headed out of the kitchen calling an over-the-shoulder goodbye to Fern as she went.

She was on the second turn-the-water-down-to-nearly-freezing part of her shower before she even began to wonder if she should tell Fern about her experience the previous night. Actually, she

42

didn't wonder about it at all. She knew that she wasn't going to. It was more that she acknowledged that she wasn't going to and wondered *why*. Because it's *mine*, part of her said. Because Fern would think it was outlandish and insane, another part offered. Because Fern would think it was entirely normal, give me some shit about empathetic vibration and channelling, and take away its specialness, said yet another. Avis was inclined to the arguments of this third voice as she slapped the lever on the tiled wall to knock it back round and turn the thousand tiny freezing needles that had been pricking at her skin into a thousand tiny lasers seeking stinging entry into her flesh. She gasped at the thrill of contrast and, after the initial millisecond of tension, surrendered herself to the sensation.

The soaping and shampooing stages were long over. Avis liked to get that shit out of the way almost immediately she got in there. Her morning shower was only incidentally about hygiene. Its real function was as her day's first moments of sensuality. She thanked God that one of the few major improvements they'd been able to bargain out of the previous owner of their property was the installation of a private bathroom each, one per bedroom. She remembered the jokes and abuse she'd suffered in house-share situations in her student days regarding the time she'd spend in the shower. The jokes usually revolved around the amount of soap it must take to get her clean though there had also been the occasional imaginative barb, based on her nominal Catholicism, that involved guilt, expiation, and the impossibility of cleanliness in the eyes of the Lord. She'd never bothered explaining that the cleaning part of her time in there was over within ninety seconds at the most because she'd never known whether an acknowledgement that she was in there for ten or fifteen minutes at a time *enjoying* herself would have made things better or worse. Anyway, fuck 'em; she had her own bathroom now and was free to indulge herself every morning. And indulge herself she did. The gamut of temperatures (scalding, hot, warm, tepid, cool, cold, freezing), the gamut of pressures (stinging needle-nose pin-pricks, pounding three-fisted massage-jets, stroking soft-rain streams), she ran them all, back and forth, one to the other, her body surrendering itself to each in turn to be scalded or frozen, stroked or spanked.

43

It was her time of secret and private pleasure. One boyfriend, in a particularly Neanderthal mood, had asked her, when she tried to explain it to him, whether she ever brought herself off in there because he'd once read a letter in *Penthouse Forum* or some other highbrow rag that extolled the joys of shower-driven orgasm. She'd stared at his glittering eyes and adolescent expectation and kept him guessing (*Prick. Let him wonder. Let him wish.*) but in fact she never did. It was a more generalized pleasure she sought in there, an ecstasy that had little to do with sex.

But even ecstasy had to work to a schedule when there were mortgage payments and food-money to be earned and so, as reluctantly as ever, Avis turned the lever back to zero and, sliding the glass door back, stepped from the shower cubicle onto her bath-mat. Her bathroom was foggy with warm moist mist, droplets forming and sparkling on the tiled walls and faux-marble sink. The mirror on her cabinet door was completely fogged over. More often than not, Avis would finish up her shower with invigorating coldness and so this steam-room effect wouldn't happen but every now and then she felt like stepping out warmed up and today was one of those days. From the rack beside the shower-stall she grabbed a large towel and wrapped it around her body and a smaller towel and wrapped it around her head, turbaning her wet hair. She stared into the fogged-up mirror at her unfocused self, an amorphous shape without detail or clarity, and was just figuring she'd move back into the bedroom and give the surfaces in the bathroom time to adjust and dry out when something moved beside her in the mirror.

Avis gasped and swung to her side, simultaneously taking a step backward, her heart pounding. There was nothing there, nobody next to her. She glanced back at the mirror. At first, all she saw was the surface of mist and the same unclear Avis somewhere behind it. Her pulse slowed and her breathing resumed and she leaned forward, moving her head to see if what she thought she'd seen had been a trick of the light. No, nothing shifted as she moved. It was still just as if she was looking at some alien planet, a world of fog, a world the atmosphere of which precluded its inhabitants from seeing each other's real faces. Avis moved forward, pulling a Kleenex from the box beside the sink.

Bunching it into a ball as she raised her hand toward the mirror, she brought it swiftly down the surface of the glass in a long and decisive wiping motion, removing the mist, removing the obscurity, revealing clearly the reflections of the shower cabinet door, the towel rack, Avis herself, and the silk-hatted man immediately behind her.

This time Avis screamed as she turned around. Even as she completed her turn and saw that, apart from herself, the room was completely empty, she could hear Fern running down the hallway to her room calling her name. By the time she'd swung back to look at the mirror again – and saw that it too registered her as the only animate presence in the room, Fern was just outside her bathroom door, calling out again.

'Avis? Honey? You okay?' followed by a tap on the bathroom door.

Avis took a breath. 'Yeah. Yeah, I'm fine,' she said through the closed door. 'Thought I saw something. It's nothing. Sorry if I scared you.' Avis was surprised that her voice sounded as steady and normal as it did. She heard Fern's mumbled answer and the sound of her housemate moving away and was suddenly hungry for a glimpse of humanity. She flung open the bathroom door and leaned out, still wrapped in towels, in time to catch Fern just before she let herself out of Avis's bedroom door.

'Hey,' Avis called and continued, as Fern turned to look at her inquisitively. 'Thanks for coming running. I mean it. Thanks a lot.'

Fern made no answer other than a warm smile as she let herself out. The smile lit up her whole face and, as the door closed behind her, Avis once again found herself wondering just how beautiful her friend would be if she'd indulge just a little in some old-fashioned bad-for-the-environment-and-probably-bad-for-you cosmetics. Her mind let her hide in that thought for all of a second before it directed her eyes back to the mirror – still clear, still tuned to the real world – and set her chewing pensively at her lower lip.

It wasn't the first time she'd had to face terror in the bathroom, Avis thought as she stood pressed between other handle-grippers in the packed subway train to midtown, but the last time reason

45

and reality had helped her. The last time there'd been direct cause and the only person haunting her had been her brother. Little bastard. He –

She was plunged into blackness as the train suddenly stopped short of the next station and its lights went out, accompanied by the dying groan of its electrical system. It was a common occurrence and nothing to be frightened about but Avis held her breath for the two seconds before the lights came back up, irrationally convinced that she'd suddenly find herself surrounded by flappers and playboys in a jazz-age F Train hurtling into a lost decade and a monochrome Manhattan, a nightworld of Art Deco clubs and long-dead sophisticates where an implacable maître d' would take her powerless arm and steer her to her appointed table and its patient guest, a man with a blue flower in his lapel and a knowing smile of terrible welcome.

The power surged back on with a rising atonal screech of which Stockhausen would have been proud and the train jerked forward as the lights flickered back into neon life. Nothing had changed. It was still the nineties not the thirties and everybody stuffed into the overcrowded coach when the lights came up had been stuffed there when the lights went down. Avis would have called herself an overimaginative idiot if she wasn't so busy thanking Christ that nothing had happened. She heard groans from some of the passengers and wasn't sure what was going on until a teenager with an out-of-date Kurt Cobain T-shirt and a really bad haircut shouted out to some invisible engineer in the sky, 'A-C, man! Where's the fucking A-C?!'

The kid must have had a direct line to God or the Transit Authority because he'd hardly finished bitching before the air conditioning hissed its acknowledgement of his complaint and resumed its duties. Avis hadn't even noticed it was off but she lent silent endorsement to the sighs of relief issued by several other passengers. She only had three stops to go but she'd ridden this route one too many times on trains with fucked cooling systems and she knew that even a one-stop ride could be hell without the fans blowing. She wondered for a second which she'd prefer – her nightmare trip to the tuxedoed quarter of the Dream Country *with* air conditioning or her everyday ride to reality

46

*without.* Tough choice, she told herself. Yeah, right. Tough choice when the *lights* were on. No fucking contest in the dark.

She turned her thoughts back to her brother and his long-ago idea of fun. It was when Danny had been about eight and Avis herself either six or seven – there was an eighteen-month age gap between them and so sometimes it sounded like he was two years older than her and sometimes only one – and they'd been living in the Elmwood Park house. It was the first of her parents' houses that Avis could remember properly – she had photos of her two-year-old self outside the Hoboken apartment but she had no memory of it – and she could picture very clearly the front yard in which Danny had asked her the question.

He'd been sitting cross-legged on the grass pretending to re-read the comic book that he'd snatched from her a minute or so before with the brotherly logic that it was his and he needed it. Avis had decided not to cry and was sitting watching him. After a moment more, he'd looked up and asked her who the scariest character in comic books was. She'd said the Hulk and he'd laughed at her. She hadn't understood why – his only offered explanation (that the Hulk had his own *book*) not making much sense to her at the time. Four or five years later she'd realized that his eight-year-old logic had been saying that, if the Hulk had his own book, he must, by definition, be a *hero* and therefore, no matter how monstrous he looked, he couldn't be scary. She'd also realized at that time that, despite his age advantage, her brother wasn't as smart as she was, that his thinking was already trapped and trammelled by convention and labelling. Danny at eight had used a formalistic tradition to reach his conclusion. Avis at six had used the tool of the true philosopher – her *eyes*. The Hulk was a massive green monster with a nasty temper. She found that scary. Fuck her brother. He'd carried on laughing for an hour.

It was about three days later and Avis had been out in the yard again when Danny, strolling out of the house and parking himself beside her, had asked her if she'd ever considered something unusual about their bathroom.

'What?' she'd asked in reply.

'It's on the second floor and it's only got one window and one door.'

She'd giggled at him. She knew there was nothing unusual about that even if she was only six.

'Don't laugh,' Danny'd said. 'What about the corridor?'

She'd stared at him. She hadn't known what he meant but she'd known she didn't like the tone of his voice.

'What *about* the corridor?' she'd asked.

'It's long and thin and dark and I *hate* walking down it. Don't you?'

Avis had nodded guardedly. She did hate walking down it but she was getting worried about giving Danny any information that might prove useful to the nasty part of his mind. Which was quite a large part.

'Not only that,' he'd said, 'there's no doors. It only leads to the bathroom.'

'Yeah. So?'

He'd looked at her and grinned in a mean, knowing way.

'*So* – what if you were in the bathroom and you heard a noise from the top of the corridor and you looked through the keyhole . . .' he'd paused for dramatic effect, knowing that he had Avis's complete and undivided attention, and then finished in a grinning rush, 'and it was the Hulk walking down? Or a giant spider with a human head and huge teeth?'

Avis had screamed at that point and her brother, after quickly quietening her in case a parent should run out and stop him before he'd done the real damage, had carried on.

'See, it's not just that the scary thing is coming for you – it's that there's nowhere you can go. You'd just have to wait and watch as it walked down to you. And, Avis, that corridor is *long*.'

He'd waited then, satisfied with her silent sobbing and wide staring eyes, before concluding cheerily, 'Neat, huh?'

Avis had tried to fight back with terror-fuelled denial disguised as reason.

'It *wouldn't* be the Hulk. It *wouldn't* be the spider,' she'd cried, 'it would be Mom or Dad!'

'Yeah? So, if you heard the noise – would you look through the keyhole to see? Or would you just wait? Would you take the chance that the noise isn't what you think it is and just wait? Wait to open the door? Wait for *it* to open the door?'

'It isn't it! It isn't it!'

'But what if it *is*, Avis? Would you look through the keyhole or not?'

'Hey, lady! I'd like to get off the train. That okay with you?'

Avis blinked herself back into the present and realized that the stocky balding guy pressing against her had already asked her twice to let him pass. She moved aside with a mumbled apology, trying not to respond to the contemptuous shaking of his head as he squeezed his way to the open doors of the compartment. Her eyes followed him out and it was only when the doors, with a low percussive gasp, began to close after him that she realized that this was her stop too. She slid between the remaining passengers with a hard-learned ease that would be the envy of many an electric eel and managed to jam her hand between the doors just before they met. The doors' electrical system growled in protest and a woman standing just inside them whose face was as old as New York but whose bright orange hair was as young as her last colour-rinse caught Avis's eye.

'Forget it, sweetheart,' the woman said in a voice so low and so rich in gravel that Joe Cocker would have sold his mother's soul to possess it, 'take the next stop. Walk'll do you good.'

Avis pulled a face at the woman, the convoluted and multi-purpose semiotics of which were meant to convey gratitude for her concern, acknowledgement of the wisdom of her advice, warmest wishes for a long and happy life, and complete fucking determination that this was her stop and she was getting out at it no matter what. She forced more of her arm through behind her hand and applied a sideways leverage with her forearm.

For a moment she thought that it wasn't going to work and that she was going to have to ride to the next stop with her stupid and defeated hand waving embarrassedly through the doors' windows at her and the antediluvian redhead but finally the doors yielded and slid back to their hiding places along the outside walls of the train. Avis jumped smartly onto the platform and turned back to see the doors close, the train start to move, and the woman mouth unheard words of congratulation before she and the train were lost to the darkness of the tunnel. Avis turned and headed for the turnstile exits, wondering if it was actually likely that a woman of that age had said *Fucking-A!* Hell, it was New York. Anything was possible.

Her feet on autopilot as they led her out of the station, onto the streets, and towards work, Avis found her thoughts drifting back to her brother. The scene in the yard had only been the set-up. It was the next day when Avis was in the bathroom that he'd staged the main event.

She'd just finished peeing and had been pulling her pants up when she'd heard a heavy footfall echoing down the length of the corridor to the bathroom, followed rapidly by another. She'd screamed, shouted, 'Daniel, is that you?!', and received no response other than the increasingly frequent sounds of heavy footsteps coming down the corridor, getting louder, getting closer.

Though scared, Avis had finally realized the flaw in Danny's plan. The reason he'd gone on about the keyhole so much was in order to frighten her away from using it and thus seeing that it was only *him* heading toward her. She'd rushed over to the door. Below the modern fitted-by-daddy sliding bolt was a large old-fashioned keyhole, the brass plate of which had been paint-stripped, wire-brushed, and polished up by her house-proud parents despite the key having been lost who knew how many owners ago. Avis had knelt down to look through . . . and had been unable to see anything. Wadded thickly into the keyhole was an unidentifiable mass – Avis had later learned that it consisted of newspaper strips and aeroplane modelling glue – that completely blocked any view she might have had. She'd realized instantly that it had been wedged there by her brother probably days before. Now, of course, had Avis been in a less frightening situation at the time or had maybe been just a little older, she would have been able to have seen this wedging as irrevocable proof that it was her brother fucking around in the corridor. But she'd been scared and she'd been six and all the blockage had meant to her was that she couldn't see if the monster was real and was coming. But she'd been able to *hear* and what she'd heard were the foot-steps getting louder, getting nearer, and getting faster. Was it Danny? Was it a monster? She hadn't known and she'd had no way of finding out – other than sliding back the bolt and flinging open the door. But part of her had known – *known* – that it was

50

the Hulk out there, or the spider with the human head or the six-foot boy-doll with the tiny pointed teeth or the nightmare-mommy, the mommy with a different face and a sharp knife, and she hadn't been able to do it, hadn't known if she would have been able to stand seeing the monster. And having it see her. Seeing it growl or grin or whatever it wanted to do at the sight of her small, terrified self.

She'd stood up and backed away from the door, staring at it. What was she going to do, she'd asked herself, wait till the monster smashed the door in or stood outside scratching at it with impossible nails and whispering her name? She'd wanted to cry, wanted to call out, wanted to shout accusingly at the Daniel that another part of her knew it to be. But she hadn't. Couldn't. What if it's the monster and somehow it didn't know she was in the bathroom, she'd reasoned – any shouting, any noise, would just alert it to her presence. She'd been paralysed with fear and indecision. And the footsteps had drawn closer and closer, ringing out loudly as each foot was smashed down.

That had been it. Somehow, even through her fear, even at six, Avis had suddenly been able to find a clue in that. *Smashed.* The footsteps had *smashed* onto the echoing wooden floor of the corridor, slammed down so hard that she had been able to hear the effort in it – hear the raising of a small leg and its strenuous stamp down in an attempt to imitate the kind of noise that would be made effortlessly by the raising and lowering of the feet of a full-grown monster. Avis had held her breath, clenched her teeth, drawn back the bolt, and flung open the door.

It had been Danny, of course. But he'd done something unintentionally clever. He hadn't turned the corridor light on and, windowless and doorless as the corridor was, he'd therefore been, despite his size, simply a black hulking shape halfway down the corridor and for one terrible frozen second Avis had been convinced that she'd been wrong and that she had just opened the door to the monster and delivered herself into its hands. Fortunately for her, having done something unintentional and clever, Danny had then done something intentional and stupid. He'd raised his hands above his head and growled at her. He was eight. The Hulk he wasn't. The scream which he'd hoped to pull from Avis's throat (and which, God knows, had been there to be pulled) mutated instead into what was, for a six-year-old, a very good imitation of seen-it-all-and-bored-by-most-of-it sophistication: Avis had looked at him impassively for a second, yawned, and said, 'Daniel, what on earth are you doing?'

His howl of frustrated fury had been scarier than his far from convincing growl of a moment before. Screaming, 'Shut up!', he'd turned and ran back up the corridor toward the embarrassment-free zone of his bedroom. Avis had stood there, six years old and warm with triumph, a baby sister astonished by victory. She'd waited till she heard the door of his room close and then had started to laugh and had kept on laughing, had laughed so hard and so long that suddenly she'd had to pee again and had run back into the bathroom. This time, she'd kept the door open and a wise but cautious eye on the corridor. One game was enough, one victory sufficient.

Avis's mental replay of the sweet but long-ago defeat of her brother (and, by psychological association, the defeat of the monster) had kept her company all the way to the corner of 6th and 54th. Glancing anxiously at her watch as she approached her office building, she saw that skipping breakfast and fighting her way out of the subway train had between them managed to bring her here more or less on time. She felt a great sense of relief, a sense to which she suddenly objected, recognizing it as disproportionate at best and, at worst, practically neurotic. What was with the panicking need to be punctual? Why had it felt like such an issue? Not that she'd known it was even a fucking issue till she'd experienced that wave of relief. She'd been late before. Many times. No big deal. In fact, not only had she always felt guiltless about it but she'd usually found a secret enjoyment in it, a feeling that, though she might be as much on the leash as every other poor bitch that had to work for a living, she could at least take the occasional nip at the hand that fed her. Now she felt like all of a sudden she'd turned into a *good* dog, had become Lady instead of the Tramp, had woken from a dream of chain-rattling and attitude into a life of walking at heel. And worse, *liking* it. What the hell deal was that?

She stepped into a quadrant of the revolving door of her

building and stepped out inside. She didn't break stride as she headed for the elevator doors but she still, as she did every day, found time to enjoy the lobby. Her building wasn't famous in Manhattan. It wasn't the Empire State. It wasn't the Chrysler building. It wasn't even the Brill building but it was still fantastic. Designed and constructed at the confident height of the American Empire, its lobby glowed still with streamlined pride. All marble, gilt, and swagger, it had a single message for everyone who walked into it: *You work in the capital of the world. Walk tall.*

Crammed with fourteen other people into an elevator that was supposed to hold ten, Avis looked back out at the lobby as the elevator door wiped it from her eyes and suddenly felt a stab of anxiety at the sight of it.

'Forty-one,' she called automatically to whichever unseen hand was nearest the floor buttons while at the same time trying to analyse what had just bothered her. Anxiety? Her lobby? She *loved* her lobby. Loved thinking of its history, loved thinking of the various people who had walked its length on who-knew-what business down its proud decades. She could see them stretched out into the past, period by period. The seventies – polyester kings and queens walking in bleary-eyed after Donna Summer nights in disco infernos; the sixties – Zapata-moustached guys and panda-eyed girls, lip-service revolutionaries and reluctant nine-to-fivers; the fifties – the men with their narrow ties and buzz-cuts and a four-foot stick up their ass, the women with tiny waists and impossible breasts; the forties – former GI's with too-much-world in their warrior eyes and dreams of suburbia in their little-boy hearts and their women, Rosie the Riveters ready to devolve into Lucy Ricardos; and, finally, the people who'd been there the decade the place was built, the . . .

Oh. Right. That decade. *His* decade.

Her whole morning suddenly made unpleasant sense. The lobby made her anxious because it came from his time. Boy, *there* was a tough connection. Idiot. And she'd turned into little-miss-loyalty scurrying to be on time because . . . because it was *safe* there. Not the building, but the world-view. She was shrinking back into the world of order and rules because it offered a deal. If everybody behaved exactly as they should, it promised, then

53

reality would behave exactly as *it* should. Rocks wouldn't flower, cigars wouldn't speak, cows wouldn't jump over the moon. And ghosts wouldn't hide in your mirror.

Avis exited the elevator with four other people. Walking down the corridor she realized, belatedly, that she knew two of them – Lance was from marketing and Sherry from claims investigation – and that she'd completely blanked them in the elevator. Tough. Sherry was an idiot and Lance had once put his hand on her ass and pretended it was an accident. Fuck 'em. She walked faster, keeping her eyes straight ahead, and felt rather than saw them exchange a what's-with-*her* glance behind her back.

Avis thought back to how she'd felt first thing this morning. It had been an adventure then. What had she called it, a sacrament? Sacrament, her ass. That was before the return engagement, the little looking-glass encore. That wasn't how it was meant to work. Once is fine. Once is something useful – social currency, a topper for somebody else's campfire stories. Once is once. Unique. Past. Over. *Twice* is something different. Twice is deliberate – the start of a pattern, a habit-in-embryo.

She pushed open the swing door to her department, tense and worried, and headed for her desk halfway down the third aisle in the open-plan office. She tried to remember her joy at her defeat of Danny. Little bastard. She'd shown him. He'd deliberately pushed open the door to her fear and she'd slammed it right on his mean little fingers. She'd . . .

Avis suddenly realized that she was walking about twice as fast as normal and that her face was pulled into a rictus of anger. She stopped in her tracks, about four desks shy of her own, and took a deliberate and deep calming breath, using her memory of the routing of her brother not as a source of anger but as a source of peace and self-confidence. She let the breath out slowly and felt her body easing down from overdrive. Okay. Okay. Good. That was better. Every muscle loosened. Boy, she must have been wired. She felt as weak and over-relaxed as after the come-down from an adrenaline high. In fact, maybe she'd geared down too much. She was all out of tension, all out of anger, but she suddenly found she had surplus stock in the depression department. So she'd beaten Danny. So what? Danny was easy. Danny was a little boy. As she started walking to her desk again, she felt the quiet re-emergence of fear. Nothing like the panic-attack – which she now realized was what it was – that had hit her in the elevator and propelled her down the corridor and into the office like somebody in training for an attempt on the land-speed record using only her feet, this was smaller, subtler, and seemed to have every intention of taking up permanent residence. A little nugget of worry, a gnawing anxiety that her life had been changed, that something had been opened which she had no idea how to close.

She reached her desk. Looked at it. Looked at it again. Perched on the nearside corner, out of place amongst the paper-clip dispensers and correspondence trays, was a black silk top hat.

# 7

The tiny part of Avis that wasn't busy screaming was quietly impressed with how relatively quiet the scream itself was. Not that that lessened the sudden and unpleasant shock of it for everyone else.

It was still a couple of minutes shy of nine o'clock and, though the office was nearly fully manned, people hadn't settled in to work yet. They were all still part-way through the easing-in rituals – hanging at each other's desks, fetching coffee or water, shooting the breeze, playing smuggled-in games on their computer terminals, whatever.

The desk next to Avis's belonged to Nancy Lieberman. Nancy was sitting there, tipped back in her chair which was half-turned toward the aisle between the desks, her long legs stretched out in front of her and crossed at the ankles. Standing at the side of Nancy's desk was Anthony Bellisario. Three seconds ago he'd been talking to Nancy and trying to be subtle about his enjoyment of the sight of her dark-stockinged legs. Now he was pondering the mystery of how it was that coffee which tasted just the right side of lukewarm in your mouth could burn like fuck when you spilled it on your damn fingers.

Anthony swung round to face Avis, transferring his Styrofoam cup to his left hand and shaking his right hand wildly to free its fingers of the coffee.

'Jesus, Avis! What the hell's wrong with you?' he said.

'God, you gave me a heart attack!' said Nancy, pulling herself upright and pressing the splayed fingers of one hand against her breasts.

Avis's eyes did a sweep of the entire room. Practically everyone had turned to look at the source of the scream but already, once convinced that it hadn't signalled the arrival of a disgruntled fellow worker with a handgun, were turning back to their own business. So she only had Nancy and Anthony to deal with. And the hat.

She pointed at it, her eyes on Anthony's still-angry face.

'What?' he said. 'I only put it down to get some coffee. What's the big deal?'

Avis's first question was to have been a whispered *Can you see it?*, but already embarrassed understanding was taking the place of terror.

'Is it yours?' she said instead.

Anthony looked confused – not by the question so much as by the curious urgency with which Avis had asked it. He shot a glance at Nancy, who made a small grimace with her mouth. *Don't ask me*, it said, *I'm not the one asking the dumb questions.*

'Yeah,' he said to Avis, 'Broadway Novelty. By 49th. Picked it up on the way in.'

Avis let out a breath. She glanced at the hat, nerves still jangling, and said nothing.

'It's his cousin's birthday,' Nancy threw in, as much to fill the awkward silence as to elucidate matters.

'Fancy dress,' said Anthony, 'I'm going as Slash.'

Avis's eyes were still on the hat but gradually Anthony's words seeped in. What the fuck was he talking about?

'Who?!' she snapped back. Didn't want to snap. Didn't mean to snap. Snapped anyway. She looked back to Anthony and spoke more softly.

'Sorry. Who?'

Anthony looked at her the way he might look at someone coming back to consciousness after a blow to the head, as if concussion's confusion was a real possibility.

'Slash,' he said. 'Jesus, Avis. Get with it. Slash. Guns'n'Roses? Guitar-player? Curly hair, cigarette? Top hat?'

He reached over to her desk, picked up the hat, and perched it at a canted angle on his head. Fishing in his pants pocket, he brought out a pack of Marlboro, shoved one in his mouth in a lazy Robert Mitchum dangle, and then played some air guitar, looking back and forth at Avis and Nancy for approval.

'You should've got a wig too,' said Nancy.

'I'm on it, babe,' he said, for a moment still in character, 'my sister's friend, Geneva.'

'Geneva?' Nancy said, incredulous. 'What the hell name is that?'

Anthony shrugged, like names are names. 'Got stacks of wigs,' he said.

'What, she got alopecia?' Nancy asked, grinning.

'No, man. Cancer.'

Nancy's hand flew to her mouth. 'Oh God,' she said, 'I'm sorry.'

'No. Treatment's going good. Doctors are pleased.'

Avis looked at them, lost back in their conversation, her own screaming faux pas apparently forgotten along with their puzzlement as to its apparently innocuous source. She moved quietly past Anthony and sat at her desk, staring at her blank computer screen. After a few moments, she realized Anthony had moved back down the aisle towards his own desk, taking the hat with him. Nancy was looking at her.

'Avis,' she said, 'you okay?'

Somehow Avis managed to summon a smile that was at once apologetic and reassuring. 'Yeah. I'm fine,' she lied, 'I'm sorry.'

'I mean, it was like . . . a *hat*. You know? Just a hat. What was . . .' Nancy let her voice trail off, completing her question by holding her hands, palms out, in the air.

Avis gave a little laugh. 'Don't even ask,' she said – and managed to make the implication of the phrase merely one of *So I'm an idiot. Give me a break.* She smiled at her co-worker again. Nancy looked concerned and then tacitly agreed to let it drop.

'You want a coffee?' she asked. 'Let me get you a coffee.'

Without waiting for a reply, Nancy was up and out of her chair and heading down the room toward the coffee-maker. Avis watched her walk, watched her pour, watched her come back, realising that she hadn't after all stopped in the lobby to buy a breakfast. She also realized that she wasn't at all hungry. She didn't even know for sure that she wanted a coffee.

'Black. No sugar. Right?' Nancy checked, handing over the Styrofoam cup.

'Right,' said Avis and took it with a grateful smile. Wanted or not, she wasn't going to refuse it because she knew – and appreciated – that Nancy's gesture was more an expression of concern and friendship than anything else.

She switched on her computer, took a sip of the coffee – which actually tasted pretty good for something she wasn't sure she wanted – and grabbed at the contents of her in-tray. She didn't look up again for two hours.

Avis was not someone who defined herself by what she did to pay the mortgage and was secretly (and sometimes not so secretly) contemptuous of those in her office who seemed to find either meaning or enjoyment in their job or, worse, simply suffered through it till the weekend, turning their real selves off for five days of every week. She'd once evolved a theory that the perceived life-span (as opposed to the actual) of those people was horrifyingly short. They played a mental trick on themselves, turning Monday-through-Friday into a single block of time, living for the weekend, living for the summer vacation, living for Christmas or other public holidays. Thus, a month began to feel like a week, a year like a month. Forty years would pass in the blink of a comatose eye and one day Death would come for them and – despite their shouts of astonished protest at its premature arrival – they would be led away from this world, casting a horrified glance back over their shoulder down all the unlived years, weeping at last for the moments that had passed while they were sleeping.

But Avis felt different today. Today she took comfort from dullness and found peace in the familiar, respite in the routine. She was re-confirming her deal with reality. She was going to be a good girl and the universe would return the favour. *Was* returning the favour. The hat hadn't been his hat. It was just a nasty coincidence. But it might have been otherwise. She felt hideously and irrationally aware of the possibility that, had she arrived at the office still stupidly enamoured of her brush with the unknown last night, things might have gone somewhat differently. It was like flirting with the wrong guy. Don't send signals that you don't want received and acted upon. She read *Time*. She read *Newsweek*. She'd heard of Probability. She'd heard of Chaos. She knew that scientists' latest model of reality was one of an astonishingly fragile system in which every moment could blossom into a thousand different scenarios and she had no wish to be the beating butterfly wing that could induce some metaphysical hurricane. There were worlds on either side of her. In one, there'd been no hat on her desk at all and Anthony Bellisario had decided to attend his cousin's birthday dressed as Groucho Marx. In another, Anthony didn't have a cousin. In another, the world didn't have Anthony – his great-grandfather had never immigrated or his great-grandmother, a knockout in 1917, had told the ardent but impoverished tailor's assistant that no he couldn't have a date. And, in yet another, a foolhardy Avis had wandered into work to find a hat on her desk and, turning, find its ectoplasmic owner and an office full of phantoms.

No more rocking the boat. Last night she'd sailed too close to uncharted waters and something from its depths had found her scent and liked it. She needed to retreat to the shallows. She needed to stay in this world of files and familiarity and not break surface lest something break surface beside her.

Files were good. Files – whether hanging in card folders somewhere in a cabinet or hanging in invisible storage somewhere in cyberspace – were where you expected them to be and, once opened or accessed, were *what* you expected them to be. People too. People – whether boring or brilliant, bestial or beautiful – were people. Real. Solid. Audible. They wouldn't fade into transparency if you looked at them too long and their mouths, once opened, would – with the exception of that mouth-breather from the twenty-second floor whose jaw opened and closed with the terrible and vacant regularity of a particularly dull goldfish – emit words, not word-shaped silences.

Avis embraced it all. Her yesterday self would never have believed how delighted she could be to listen attentively to all the details of the visit to the paediatric chiropractor of Tommy, the youngest boy of Phyllis-from-accounting nor how warmly she would greet the clumsy but inoffensive overtures of Ben Chepstow. Ben, who worked just across the hall, had been after a date for nearly a year now and despite regularly getting shot down would wander back to stand within firing range with all the stoicism of the old plains buffalo. Avis was in no danger of accepting

dinner and a movie with Ben as the price of renewing her sub-
scription to normality, no matter how much she longed to confirm
her membership, but she made a special effort to be nice today.
Indeed, her warm friendliness through a shared coffee and cigarette break gave Ben such hope and excitement that, charged
with a new sense of his own attractiveness, he moved on through
the course of the afternoon to the office of another woman to
whom he'd been laying court and, reeking of confidence as he
was, was suddenly seen by her in another light. She said a tenta-
tive yes, enjoyed the first date, enjoyed the second, slept with
him on the third and, two years from that afternoon, was married
to Ben Chepstow by an Elvis impersonator in a Las Vegas chapel.
They were happy the rest of their lives, were looked after by their
children when they grew old, and would often entertain family
and friends through their long years with the funny story of how
they might never have got together if it hadn't been for that pretty
little blonde from the forty-first floor putting some lead in Ben's
pencil one day by holding his coffee for him and putting her
lipsticked cigarette in his mouth so that he could try a drag. Sally
could never remember her name and Ben would always pretend
that he couldn't either but both of them would wish her well and
wonder whatever happened to her.

What happened to her after her transparently flirtatious move
with the cigarette and Ben's trembling lip was that she spent the
rest of the working day trying to kid herself that she was enjoying
her stay in a shrunken life. She caressed the details of banality
like a contented lover or, at least, a practised courtesan. By the
time she got back to the Bowery that night she almost felt all
right, felt almost reconnected, felt as if whatever had loosened in
her in the street the night before had tightened its grip again. The
good ship Avis, though it had slipped its moorings last night and
briefly glimpsed a vast and unknown sea, was tethered once more
to the dock and dry land.

When she let herself into the house that evening, Fern and
Mike were watching a re-run of Dick Van Dyke. Avis took a quick
glance but, as soon as Morey Amsterdam mentioned walnuts, she
moved on. It was the scary episode. The dream episode. Soon
Rob would have no thumbs and Laura would have an eye in the

61

back of her head. Not tonight, thanks. Not for Avis.

She moved on into the kitchen and started to put the blender together. She leaned back to let her voice carry through to Fern and Mike.

'I'm making frozen Margaritas,' she called, 'anybody want one?'

She got a yes from Mike and a no from Fern and measured out the ice accordingly. The tequila was an easy grab from the lower cabinet to the side of the dishwasher but the tall glasses were up on the second shelf of the other cabinet, the high wall-mounted one. She and Fern had already complained about the male-oriented kitchen designer this place must have had but John, of course, had managed to turn it round and claim it as a probable point of feminist triumph that kitchens were no longer being designed with the assumption that they would be staffed exclusively by women. John had minored in Philosophy – quite a cool-quotient enhancer for a Business major – and its Logic 101 course had bequeathed him an annoying ability to apparently defeat you in an argument even when you *knew* that he was talking out of his ass. Avis had stopped bothering. John's reading of this was that Avis had acknowledged his intellectual superiority. Avis's reading of it was that she had better things to do than waste her breath on a smug prick.

Anyway, the point was that the glasses – indeed, anything above the first shelf in that high cabinet – were difficult for her to reach. She thought for a moment about calling Mike in but Fern's amused insistence this morning that Mike was attracted to her made her decide against it. Standing on tip-toe, she was able to reach her hand in and send her fingers spidering along the surface of the shelf. Provided the glasses – which were actually *plastic*, she pointed out to herself, so could you actually call them glasses? Better that, she supposed, than tumblers or some equally ugly new word – provided they hadn't been pushed too far to the back the last time they'd been loaded up, she should have been able to reach them and edge two of them forward to tip them into her other hand. Her fingers moved, tapping and clawing, until they reached something. Avis recoiled instantly with that special shock that comes when, reaching blind with a preconceived tactile

62

expectation, we in fact touch something completely different. It needn't be frightening, dangerous or offensive. Its very difference is enough to startle us and make us recoil.

Avis cursed herself as her hand shot back. So what that her fingers hadn't felt the smooth coolness of plastic? Big deal. It had hardly felt sharp or poisonous, either. It had felt like soft fabric. Somebody must have folded up one of the dish-cloths or one of the towels and shoved it up there by mistake. She reached up again and grabbed at the item, flicking it forward to send it dropping into the upraised and outstretched palm of her other hand.

As she brought it down into her sight, she realized that she'd been wrong. It was not a towel. It was not a cloth. Resting on her hand was a white cotton glove. She also realized why she had initially recoiled. Her fingers had been smarter than she. There had been an oddness about the feel of the thing. The glove, unlike something that had been stuck up in the dark cool of a cabinet, out of sight and forgotten, was curiously warm – as if it had only recently been peeled from the hand of its owner.

Avis stared at it for a moment, unblinking. It wasn't as if she needed time for recognition to set in. She knew instantly what it was and to whom it belonged. She'd seen it and its matching partner on his phantom hands last night. It wasn't as if she was waiting for a reaction, either. It wasn't as if she was going to start screaming or anything. Her reaction was already there. It was fear, but not the sharp kind. It was the nauseating slow dull throb of a terror that promises never to go away until the matter is resolved, the sure and steady ache that gnaws at the belly of the condemned as they wait through the peeling away of each day that clouds their view of the inevitable rope.

Avis didn't tremble. Avis didn't scream. In fact, she didn't even scream when the glove began to dissolve in her hand, suddenly softening and collapsing into a runny white mucus that oozed over her palm and trickled between her fingers to hang down in vile jellied strings. If it wasn't for the brilliant white of the colour, Avis would have been horribly reminded of a handful of ejaculate. She suddenly couldn't escape that metaphor and felt as if the tuxedoed stranger had somehow violated her. Haunting wasn't

63

enough – he had to find some loathsome supernatural way of *coming* on her. She felt a dizzying wave of helpless disgust which at least galvanized her and sent her rushing over to the sink where she turned on the faucet hard and thrust her hand beneath it. She let the water blast away at the sticky white mess in her palm till it was driven completely off her and sloshed around in the sink itself – viscous strings and globules of it suspended in the rushing, circling water like oil or mercury or some other indissoluble thing. It didn't stay indissoluble, however. The process that had begun in Avis's palm continued as the ectoplasm that had masqueraded as a glove continued to lose its cohesion, continued to lose its ability to be manifest in this world. Its mucoid nature now gave way to something of a thinner and runnier consistency so that as the rushing water circled the drainhole it was streaked and peppered with what looked like swirls of white paint or ink. Soon even they were gone, whirlpooled away down the drain into the New York sewage system, and the sink was full only of water. Avis watched it for a full minute before she turned off the faucet. Just as she did so, a hand touched her shoulder from behind.

She whirled at once to her left, her right hand already bunched into a fist. She still wasn't screaming. But she was growling with anger, her face contorted into a nostril-flaring, teeth-baring rictus of animal rage.

'All right. Okay. Jesus!' said Mike, taking a dancing step backward, the hand that had tapped Avis's shoulder still held upright but pulled back sharply to his body. He looked shocked. More, he looked *scared*.

Avis stared at him. She dropped the fist. She relaxed the face. But she held on – albeit guiltily – to the strange and new satisfaction she'd felt blossom in her stomach at the sight of his fear.

'I asked how it was going,' Mike said, 'but you had that faucet on so fucking loud I guess you didn't hear me. Sorry if I scared you.'

Sorry if I scared *you*, Avis said in her head while merely nodding dumbly at him. And she *was* sorry that she'd scared him. But she wasn't sorry that she'd seen evidence of her ability to scare. No. That made her feel better, smothering as it did the flames of her own anxiety in the blanket of a fury that she was astonished to find was equally her own.

Her heart-rate began to slow back to normal as Mike moved past her to reach up and grab a couple of the tall glasses and her hidden joy at her anger began to give way to distress at its misdirection. She watched dully as he brought the glasses down and set them on the counter beside the sink. Jesus Christ. What if she'd had a knife in her hand? She'd have swung and . . . who the fuck knows? Taken his eye out? Slit his throat?

'Mike, I'm sorry,' she said. 'You know what? Why don't you make them? The ice is in the blender. Give mine to Fern.'

'She doesn't want one,' he said.

'She'll drink it. Trust me. I gotta go to bed.'

Mike turned and looked at her. 'You okay?' he asked.

Avis shrugged. 'I had a hell of a day,' she said, trying to keep her voice clear of anything beyond standard big-city blues, trying to keep her eyes clear of a dread he wouldn't understand.

'Anything I can do?' he asked.

'I don't know,' she replied. It was the simple truth. Was there anything he could do? Was there anything anybody could do?

Avis astonished herself by managing to fall asleep. It wasn't immediate, of course, but twenty minutes' worth of anxiety, confusion, and disbelief seemed to be enough to send her mind into an overload that hit some mental circuit-breaker and produced a void that was a reasonable imitation of relaxed peacefulness.

A lethargy crept over her, as sweet as any she'd felt, and Avis surrendered to it, grateful for the ticket it offered to whatever destination in the Dream Country it might take her. She felt like one of those guys in the old gangster movies, getting out of town in a hurry. First train available. Fuck the cost. Fuck the destination.

It was dark in her room, the moon not as yet over in her side of the sky. She wasn't sure if her eyes were open or closed. She blinked a few times and decided that, of the alternating black and red washes which were all she could see, the red ones were probably the times she had her eyes closed. She couldn't be sure though because there was a window of black inside the red against

65

which, every now and then, there would be flashes of light that seemed very distant and flashed past the window at great speed. She laughed silently to herself as she realized her mistake. It wasn't the lights that were moving. It was her. She was speeding past outlying towns, their tiny lights occasionally breaking up the darkness outside the window beside her seat. She looked back to her other side. The compartment was relatively empty but she figured that was probably normal for a night train. She looked around again at the fixtures and fittings in the carriage. Very old-looking. Kind of elegant, though. Nice. Maybe they hauled these due-for-retirement cars out of the sheds to make the night runs while the newer ones got serviced. She wasn't sure she liked the quality of light in the carriage – an oppressive muted yellow that, while it showed everything very clearly, seemed somehow the opposite of brightness. It seemed strangely familiar to her though she couldn't remember ever seeing such light before. She also couldn't recall ever riding a train where the seats were essentially benches, wooden and pew-like. They weren't particularly uncomfortable, though. And movement, she remembered, was the issue. Couldn't remember why, though. Still, she was moving. That was good.

The door at the back of the compartment opened and Avis turned her head to see a heavy-set man enter. He was somewhere in his mid-fifties, she guessed, and well-dressed. Old-fashioned, though: heavy brown pinstripe suit and a green-felt fedora. He took the hat off as soon as he noticed Avis, which she found quaintly charming. She smiled at him and he nodded in response. It was only then that she noticed how nervous he was. There was a film of perspiration across his brow and his eyes flicked from side to side like those of a skittish animal expecting attack.

'You made the train,' Avis found herself saying, which rather surprised her as she'd had no intention of starting a conversation. Also, how did she know he hadn't been on the train for hours? The man took it as an invitation and settled himself in the pew opposite Avis, facing her.

'The far side of crimson,' he said in greeting. Avis knew exactly what he meant. His upper body was leaning forward in the pew, his elbows resting on his knees and the fingers of his hands interlaced, the green hat hanging from them. He looked at the fedora for a second as if puzzled by it and then laid it down on the bench beside him. Throwing a quick glance at Avis to check she wasn't going to object, he slipped a hand into his inside jacket pocket and pulled out a small draw-stringed suede purse. Loosening the brown leather draw-string, he tipped several small objects into the palm of his other hand and placed the purse down beside his hat. He held his hand out in front of him, staring intently at the seven human teeth resting on his palm. His brow furrowed and Avis couldn't tell if it was simply concentration or if he was displeased with what he saw. She didn't think it was polite to ask.

After a moment, he brought his other hand up and, like a crap-shooter agitating his dice, shook the teeth furiously within his cupped hands. He took his other hand away and stared once more at the new alignment of the teeth. He looked up to meet Avis's inquisitive glance and let out a strange and sharp burst of hysterical laughter which ended as quickly as it had begun, after which he put the teeth back in their purse and the purse back in his inside pocket.

Avis, disturbed by the laughter, turned to look out of the window again. The train was travelling over water now, the waves occasionally splashing silently against the glass. Far in the distance there was a glowing mass. Avis found it uncomfortable to look at and turned her face away. Sitting opposite her was a small man of about forty. What was left of his dark-brown hair was combed forward into what would have been a widow's peak if it was not set so far back on his scalp. There was a fat moustache between his expansive nose and his thin lips. He wore a white shirt beneath a heavy burgundy jacket and there was a silk scarf around his neck that tucked into the shirt.

'I am a Prince of Aquitaine,' he said, 'whose tower has fallen.'

'The light hurt my eyes,' Avis replied.

The man glanced out of the window, winced in pain, and looked up at Avis as if shocked that she would have directed his eyes to such a sight.

'We're very close to their territory,' he explained.

'Is that bad?'

The man shrugged. 'It can be,' he said, 'but my understanding was that your specific appointment was with the man in the mask.'

Avis knew precisely of whom he was speaking but felt obliged to set him straight on the mask issue. 'No,' she said, 'he wasn't wearing a mask.'

'Next time he will be,' the man replied confidently and then let a second or two's silence pass before asking Avis in a hopeful-but-ready-to-be-disappointed voice whether she had seen his lobster.

'I may have left him in Paris,' he added, as if that might aid her in answering. 'My star-studded lute bears the black sun of melancholy.'

Avis looked down at her hands. One of them was stained with black ink. Embarrassed, she covered it with the other and then looked up quickly to see if he had noticed.

He raised a hand sharply in the air as if calling for quiet or attention. His eyes flicked rhythmically from side to side and then, with a sudden cry of understanding, he fished out of his jacket pocket a large pocket-watch, the silver casing of which was tarnished with age. Popping it open, he stared closely at its face for a moment and then looked up to meet Avis's eyes.

'Somebody's coming to see you,' he said, his voice as impartial and as implacable as that of a black-capped judge.

Avis didn't like it. She glanced over to the far side of the carriage. She noticed that the light had grown dimmer, its yellow tinge becoming even more oppressive. The other man was there, the fat gambler in the pinstripe. He was standing up in front of the far window with his back to Avis, doing something. Finishing up, he stood aside and turned round to face her, smiling. She looked to his side. He'd misted up the window with his breath and then written with his fingers in the fog. *Somebody's coming to see you*, the message read.

Avis turned back to the little man opposite her.

'What do I do?' she asked.

'Wake up!' he said, and clicked his fingers.

# 8

Avis woke up in darkness, confused. She had no idea what it was that had awakened her, she only knew that she was awake. She had a lingering sense that she was going to be late for an appointment but that didn't make any fucking sense at all because, according to the glowing red numbers on her bedside clock, it was three in the morning. What the hell was she doing wide awake at three in the morning? But awake she undeniably was. Not a trace of drowsiness nor a vestige of dream insulated her from the cold dark reality of her room and her awareness that she was awake and alone in the middle of the night.

She couldn't see anything right away and she ordered her heart to stop pounding quite so much – at least until her eyes adjusted to the darkness and she could see if there was anything of which to be afraid. They did. There wasn't. At least, nothing visible. But she knew something was wrong. She'd woken with that certainty and nothing was happening to change it. She raised herself up a little on her pillow, bringing her arms out from under the sheets as her ears strained to hear. Was it a sound that had disturbed her? As soon as she tuned in, of course, what had seemed like silence was revealed as cacophony – somewhere a faucet dripped rhythmically, outside the wires and power cables hummed and the engines and horns of distant cars growled and honked, from the kitchen the fridge added a low bass murmur, and the walls and doors creaked with the night-time sounds of settling. Many noises, many sounds. And then one more joined them – the sound of footsteps creaking their way toward her bedroom door. Something was moving in the house and heading her way. Avis felt her body jerk as the shock of fear ran through her. She fought an instinct to cry out and then wondered why she had fought it.

She answered that last thought pretty damn quickly – she had no desire to alert the house to the terrifying fact that Mike had got up to take a piss or John to raid the fridge. For a moment she was astonished at herself – or, rather, astonished at her ability to hold two completely contradictory thoughts in her head and believe both of them. She wasn't calling out, she realized, because, rationally, she knew that the footsteps she was hearing belonged to a member of the household. She was sitting up in bed, throat tight, heart beating fast, she realized, because, emotionally, she knew that the footsteps she was hearing belonged to a stranger who was coming to keep their appointment. One of these things was going to be revealed to be true. And so Avis waited.

She could see her own room fairly clearly now because of the fullness of the moon, the light of which, for about an hour every night, managed to find its way through a gap between two buildings on the other side of the street and send a narrow band of itself through Avis's window. So what. Nothing to see here. All the action was outside. Avis's attention was focused completely on the sound of the footsteps. She was waiting to be proved right or to be proved right. Once she knew, then she could think.

The sound of the footsteps changed character. Avis knew. And thought she'd never think again. It was impossible for her mind ever to be clear enough for her to think again because it was a screaming, jangling, klaxon mix of alarm signals via which all her nerves were bellowing at her to do something, crying out to her that danger was coming.

All that had happened was that the footsteps had suddenly sounded different, sounded as if they were walking on bare wooden floor instead of carpet. But Avis knew what that meant. It meant that options had disappeared and the world had narrowed to a single reality. It meant that she'd been right, that something was coming, and it was coming for her. It meant that the feet were now walking down the narrow uncarpeted walkway that led exclusively to her bedroom, that she was now hearing the undeniable creaking that signalled their single destination. Kitchen, sitting room, other people's bedrooms – these possibilities had passed. There were no more doors save hers, no more visitees save Avis herself.

For the luxury of a long single second, Avis indulged in a self-flagellating I-told-you-so moment. She'd liked this room since the first time they'd all looked over the property and Fern had encouraged her to take it for her own. Avis had glanced at the long narrow corridor that ran to the room's door, however, and had not been so sure. Fern had misinterpreted her glance and congratulated her on grabbing what was essentially the most private room available but that hadn't been what had occurred to Avis. It had reminded her even then of Danny's corridor, of the monsters' walkway to the bathroom in her parents' house. And now she was really really pissed off with herself. She'd known. She'd known all along. She should have listened to herself, should have told Fern that *she* could have the room, that Avis herself would be much happier in a room that was sandwiched between those of the two men in the house. But no. She had to pretend to be a grown-up. She had to kid herself that childhood fears belonged only in the past and that there was no lesson to learn from them. And now look.

Self-abuse gave her that one second of relief and then fled, like everything else, before the fear that demanded total occupation of her psyche. Stupid or not, her own fault or not, the fact was that there was now no exit between her and whatever it was that was coming and Avis was as paralysed as her six-year-old self had been. The monster was on its way and she had no idea what to do. Should she get up and meet it coming? Should she lie very still like a good little girl and pretend to be asleep? Pretend to be *asleep*? What the fuck was she thinking? That it wouldn't do anything to her if she wasn't awake to let it enjoy her fear? Yeah. Good plan, Avis. That'll do it. Unless of course it decided to wake her up. Stupid bitch. That's not an option. She had to get up. Had to. If only for the sake of doing something. If only to be ready to do something else.

But it was too late. The footsteps suddenly stopped. Avis's eyes fixed on the far end of her room as the door was pushed open from the other side and a piece of darkness detached itself from the black corridor and slipped into her room.

Avis didn't even hear herself moan in fear as an overwhelming nausea swept through her, part the result of terror itself, part the

71

result of seeing a long-held and loathsome prophecy finally fulfil itself. She'd always known this moment was coming and this time it was true. She was back on the runway, back on the Bowery at midnight, back in her parents' bathroom, back on all those occasions when God had played games with her. And this time the punch line was coming. This time the plane was going to crash, this time the vagrant was going to hurt her, this time it wasn't her brother outside, this time it wasn't a game. This time something was coming and all games were over. And others just beginning.

Avis still hadn't moved (still *couldn't* move) as the dark figure shuffled nightmarishly into the room. It walked like a marionette in the hands of a retarded puppeteer, lurching forward one step at a time and wobbling in place before lurching forward in another, its arms dangling loosely at its sides and twitching reactively at each spastic jerk of movement. Finally it staggered into the thin band of blue light where the moon crept into the room and, as the light folded around its indistinct black mass like a cloth thrown over an invisible man, its features swam into clarity. There was no top hat, no white gloves, no unidentifiable blue flower in a tuxedo buttonhole. There were none of these things because the figure was not a ghost. The figure was not a man. It was Fern.

For a brief and beautiful second Avis was delighted to see her housemate. She didn't quite have time to call out a neighbourly greeting, however, because, before she got around to doing so, she got around to having a closer look at Fern. And suddenly felt as if maybe her signals to her body to relax had been a little premature.

Fern had stopped four or five feet from the end of Avis's bed as if the blue band of moonglow was a spotlight, as if the invisible idiot pulling her strings had finally dragged his unwieldy doll to the appropriate part of the stage and was about to send her into her act. Her being there allowed Avis to see certain things clearly. Fern's mouth was widely and loosely open and her tongue, flaccid and unnaturally long, was hanging over her lower lip halfway to her chin. Like her mouth, her eyelids too were wide open but both of her eyes were rolled up into their orbits, leaving visible

72

only a shining whiteness glistening wetly under the moon.

A warm rush of adrenaline billowed up from the pit of Avis's stomach, leaving her charged and breathless. The rational part of her mind was trying to tell her that everything was all right, that Fern was sleepwalking. Avis had never seen evidence of this nocturnal habit in Fern before and nor had she ever heard anything to suggest that a sleepwalker's gait was so unnatural and disturbing but she'd read all the books – well, seen the talk-show synopses – about this stuff and knew that it was harmless and normal and that she must be considerate of her friend and not wake her up too sharply. Meanwhile, the irrational part of her mind was telling her that something was very wrong.

A drop of transparent saliva gathered on the tip of Fern's tongue and dripped from it. Avis watched it fall while registering that Fern herself was as unaware of it as a panting dog would be. Fern seemed in fact completely unaware of any aspect of what was happening – including her presence in Avis's room and Avis's own presence in her bed, for which Avis was very grateful. Grateful too that Fern had at least stopped moving, she stared in dumb horror at her friend. This wasn't just sleepwalking. And this wasn't just Fern. There was something else in her room, something else in her friend's body. Avis didn't know whether to speak or not, whether that would make things better or worse. It was no longer just for herself that she was worried. If she spoke, would she summon Fern safely back from whatever neighbouring region of oblivion in which she was currently exiled? Or would she instead simply draw the unwanted attentions of whatever it was that was currently in control of her body?

Fern's head swivelled loosely on her neck as if seeking something by means of a sense beyond sight or smell. It lolled to a stop at an angle facing the bed and the sightless eyes fixed on Avis as unerringly as if they were blessed with pupils. There was a subtle twitching at either side of Fern's slackly open mouth as if whatever was possessing her body was doing its level best to smile in glee at having located Avis but lacked the muscle control to move the lips properly – which made it all the more unsettling when a tiny high-pitched giggle sounded impossibly from within that still unmoving mouth. Avis's body jerked in shock. And then

Fern spoke. Or, rather, an approximation of Fern's voice issued from somewhere inside the dark slackness of that mouth, disturbing neither the lips nor the dangling tongue, as if somebody or something was broadcasting from somewhere else entirely and using Fern's head as a receiver and her larynx as an amplifier.

'Using his favourite is good,' the voice said. 'A strong signal, with echoes left behind. And no irrevocable decay. He can be sent again and the presence established firmly.'

A pause, and then a second voice – still Fern's but lower-pitched – responded to the first.

'I liked the Chinese Dragon.'

The higher voice came back. 'A flourish, no more,' it said, 'it wasn't his. As ever, the focus was impossible to hold.'

Avis was frozen in place. But her stillness was now voluntary, a conscious choice rather than the paralysis of terror. She was frightened of the voices of course, frightened of the bizarre circumstance in which she was hearing them, but it was a less personal fear. She, it seemed, was no longer the specific target of whatever unnatural event was taking place. When Fern had come into her room Avis had felt as if she herself was being particularly sought, singled out for torment like a new kid at school triggering the radar of the local bullies. But this was something different. Fern was tuned in somehow to a conversation to which Avis seemed irrelevant, to which she – and Fern too if Fern was somehow hearing this – was only an eavesdropper.

'The Corridor Walkers, too,' the lower voice said, 'they were his but still could act only from memory, performing by rote their basic function. No opportunity to move them beyond.'

'But were you there? Did you see?' asked the first voice, a tone creeping into it of prurient excitement like that of someone discussing forbidden pleasures and finding their mouth awash with arousal.

'I had no sight but, for moments at least, I felt the flesh.'

'Ah. Long forgotten. But sweet, yes?'

A laugh sounded from inside Fern's mouth before the second voice replied. 'Sweet indeed,' it said, 'and ripe for the work we would have it do.'

'Soon we will walk within it –'

74

'In the ruins of the kingdom –'

'And the wound will be healed –'

'And the veil rended . . .'

The voices were now alternating rapidly, speaking as one, giving the unpleasant impression that this was not after all a conversation between two distinct entities but the fractured monologue of a schizophrenic. Avis didn't like it. Didn't like what they were saying. Didn't like the way they were saying it. Didn't understand it either, but that was the least of her worries. She just wanted it to stop. And so, she suddenly understood, did Fern. Fern's body was trembling wildly, spasming from head to foot, and tears were pouring from her rolled-up eyes as they tried to compensate for the unnatural length of time her eyelids had been held wide open.

Fuck this, Avis thought, her fear giving way to an angry concern for her friend. She threw her covers aside and, scrambling out of her bed, rushed instantly over to Fern, grabbing her by the shoulders and shaking her.

'Fern!' she shouted, 'Fern, wake up! Come back!'

The voices stopped immediately but Fern remained in the same puppet-like state. She was completely loose in Avis's hands, showing no signs of strength or will, her head lolling on her shoulders as Avis shook her. Avis grabbed her chin, moving the unresisting head to face her. She pressed up on the chin and found Fern's mouth surprisingly easy to close. Drool trickled from between her lips as Avis reached up to lower her equally unresisting eyelids. Her body was still twitching and quivering, still in the grip of whatever spell she was under. Biting her lip in apologetic regret, Avis let go of her, stepped back, and, drawing one arm back behind her, slapped her friend hard across the cheek.

Fern's body stopped shaking at once. Her eyelids flew open and for one dreadful second Avis found herself staring into a pair of eyes that couldn't possibly be those of her friend. All pupil, all black, they glared at her with a hostility of a depth so measureless that Avis gasped. It was like looking down twin black tunnels that led impossibly but directly to the very heart of Hell, like gazing into the crystallized points of a hatred so huge, an anger so ancient, that to gaze any longer would be to despair.

And then Fern blinked and, when her eyelids raised themselves again, it was only Fern's eyes that were there, green, moist, and terribly confused. She looked at Avis in bewilderment and suddenly fell forward, her body finally surrendering to the unconscious strain it had been under.

Avis made a half-step forward, caught Fern before she could fall to the floor, and manoeuvred her friend's body into a sitting position on the edge of the bed, crouching in front of her and holding her steady.

'Fern,' she said. 'Fern, can you hear me? Are you okay?'

Fern sighed, blinked, looked around the room, and raised a weary arm to her brow, combing the fingers back through her hair. Eventually, she fixed her confused gaze on her friend.

'Avis?' she said. 'What the hell happened? What am I doing in your room?'

'Sending me a message. I think.'

'Huh?'

'Never mind that now. How are you feeling?'

Fern shrugged and shook her head. 'I don't know,' she said, 'I had the weirdest dream . . .' She broke off, looked around herself again to confirm which room she was in, and resumed with an incredulous tone, 'Was I *sleepwalking*?'

Avis nodded.

'No shit?' said Fern. 'That's amazing. I never do that.'

'What were you dreaming?' Avis asked.

'Fuck knows,' Fern said. 'It was bizarre. I can't remember it all. There was an old guy who . . . I was sleepwalking? Really?'

'Really,' said Avis. 'What happened? Who was the old guy?'

Fern thought for a minute, screwing her face up in an effort to recollect.

'No. He wasn't anything to do with it,' she said after a moment. 'He came earlier. You know the way that happens – different bits all flow together. It was the soldier. The soldier and the conch shell. Oh yeah. Yeah! Wow, this is wild!'

Her tiredness and confusion apparently forgotten, Fern was suddenly animated and enthusiastic. She grinned as memory came back fully. Avis, still crouching in front of her, pressed her knee to prompt her.

'What is? Tell me,' she said.

76

Fern, still grinning, looked down at Avis and pointed her finger at her. 'That's why I'm in your room,' she said. 'Far fucking out!'

'What?!'

'I was little again. I think. Maybe not. Anyway, I was playing. On a beach. Right by the water's edge. And this soldier came up. I didn't know him but in the dream I did – you know what I mean? – and he pointed to a shell that was by me. He was young but he must have been old . . .'

'What do you mean?' Avis interrupted.

'Because his uniform was old. I mean, it was new on him but it was old. Old-fashioned, I mean. You know, like . . . I don't know . . . World War One or something. Anyway, he pointed to this shell and said *Can you hear the voices?* and I lifted it up and listened and I could and he said *Let Avis hear them* and I said something about should I like take the shell to her and he said *No, she's on a train* and . . .'

'Oh shit,' said Avis, falling out of her crouch to sit heavily on the floor. Her own dream had suddenly flooded back into her.

'What's the matter?' asked Fern.

'I *was* on a train.'

'In a dream? No shit? Wow.'

Avis stared up at Fern, shocked at her apparent pleasure in all this. 'You think this is *fun*?' she said.

Fern pulled an I-dunno-whadda-*you*-think face, shrugged, and said, 'Sure. What's the big deal?'

Avis shook her head. She had to remember that Fern didn't have the background information, didn't see this apparent confluence of their dream-lives as only the latest piece in a bigger puzzle, didn't know that this was anything other than a single interesting and pleasurable incident.

'It's okay,' she said, 'forget it. What else did he say?'

'He said I should just close my eyes and get to you and let you hear the voices. So I did. At least, I guess I did.'

'You didn't hear any of it? You didn't know you were in my room?'

'No. It was weird. I closed my eyes like he said and then I was . . . somewhere else.'

'What do you mean, somewhere else?'

'The Colourfield,' said Fern and then paused as if surprised by the name. 'Man,' she said. 'How do I *know* that? This is so cool!'

'What was it? Where was it?'

'I'm not sure. It wasn't anywhere. And I wasn't anything. I mean, it wasn't like a dream. A normal dream. It wasn't a place. There was nothing there. But it felt like everything. It was . . . a series of colours. All the colours. And some I'd never seen. They were just going on for ever. And I was just seeing them. Or maybe I was one. I don't know. It's hard to describe. But it was . . . all right. Everything was *all right* there. I don't know how else to say it.'

'How long were you there?'

Fern shrugged again. 'I don't know,' she said, 'two seconds? Ten thousand years? I don't have a clue. Next thing I knew, I was here and you were sitting me on the bed. What's your story?'

Avis wondered how much to tell her, decided to keep it simple for now. 'You came in,' she said, 'freaked me out, by the way. Stood at the bottom of the bed and voices came out your mouth.'

'Other people's voices?' said Fern, increasingly delighted with how this was going. 'Like I was *channelling*?! Far fucking out! What they say? Was the soldier one of them?'

'I don't know what they said. Didn't make any sense. And how would I know it was the soldier?'

'Did he say anything about a Frenchman's head?' Fern said with a laugh in her voice.

Avis went cold. 'What?' she said, in a very small voice. Fern was too busy delighting in this latest snatch of dream-memory to notice her reaction.

'That's right! I'd forgotten. Before he pointed to the shell, I asked him what he was doing and he said he was looking for a Frenchman's head. He was laughing, like it was a private joke or something.'

Avis's whole body was tensed as she asked her next question. 'What was his voice like?' she said.

'I don't know. Foreign. Kind of British. But weird. More sing-songy. You know what I mean?'

'Welsh?' said Avis, looking down at her awkwardly crossed legs, not meeting Fern's gaze.

Fern shrugged again. 'Maybe,' she said. 'Why?'

There was a pause. And when Avis finally spoke it was as much to herself as to her friend.

'Private William Llewellen,' she said, 'King's Own Fusiliers.'

Fern stared down at Avis, shocked and excited. 'What?' she said. 'Who?'

Avis lifted her eyes to look straight at Fern.

'My grandfather,' she said.

# 9

It was two in the morning but Irma didn't like to use the night-light. Sometimes she'd put it on if the book she was reading at home had come to a part that was interesting enough to make her want to take it to work with her but that didn't happen often. Most nights she left it off. She liked to sit at her post and watch the old man and have the room illuminated only by the green and red lights of the machines that kept him alive.

It was a good gig, she figured. The old man was no trouble, bless him. Coma cases rarely were. Unless they woke up, of course – but even then it only meant hitting some alarms and checking vital signs till a doctor came. That didn't worry her – she was a trained nurse, for God's sake, even if she hadn't had to do any practical nursing for the last couple of years – but she didn't particularly want it to happen. She was forty-two years old and twenty years' service had been enough. She'd done it all and seen it all. She'd helped people be born, she'd helped people die. She'd done the filthy work and the fulfilling – emptying bed-pans one day, encouraging people to walk again the next. She'd given injections, administered enemas, pressed her staunching finger against gouting arterial wounds, and stroked fevered brows. When she'd hit forty she'd looked at her pension plan and kissed it all goodbye. After all, she'd owned the house ever since her step-mother died five years before and, being unmarried, she'd had no kids to send through college. So she'd retired. But she kept her name – Vanborough, Irma S. – on the Rolodexes at the agencies, calculating that two or three of these freelance baby-sitting jobs a year would keep her solvent and sane. They'd called her two weeks ago when the old man was first admitted and she'd been here every night since. They knew she didn't mind working nights.

Made no difference to her. Fact, she preferred it. Peaceful and dark. Just her and the old man.

She looked over at him, at the tiny rising and slow falling of the sheets above his thin and ancient chest, and strained her ears to hear the shallow rattle of his respiration. The monitors were a surer sign that he was alive, their pulsing and pinging and constantly self-renewing lines of light a clearer indication than his all-but-invisible breath that he hadn't slipped effortlessly from near-death to the thing itself.

'Poor thing,' said Irma in a whisper barely louder than his breathing. 'Poor old thing.'

She stood up from the recliner and walked quietly and slowly over to the bed. Poor old thing. Eighty-four years old, bless him. Irma thought about the car crash that had put him into this coma and wondered again at how he'd survived it at all at his age. The chauffeur'd been killed outright, she knew. Probably deserved it. Probably his fault. No other cars involved. Just the Van Wyck Expressway on a rainy night. The chauffeur hadn't cared about the old man. Nobody cared about him. Irma knew that it was only money that was keeping him alive, only money that paid for this private room in this far-from-inexpensive private hospital, that paid for these machines and paid for her. There was no love, no concerned family offering prayers or sitting with him and letting him hear the sound of their voices calling him back from wherever the car-crash had sent him. There was a lawyer somewhere or a business manager, somebody simply processing the bills that kept him in here, but there was no family to care if he lived or died. All alone. Poor old thing.

She looked out of the window on the wall beside the bed and saw the lights of Long Island stretching back towards Brooklyn. The hospital was halfway up a hill and the rooms on this side afforded a good panoramic view.

'You have a nice room,' she whispered to him. 'A nice view.'

She'd started talking to him her third night in when she'd been looking at his charts. His year of birth had registered with her. 'Hey,' she'd said, 'you were the age I am now when I was born. How about that?'

There'd been no response of course but she'd walked over to take a closer look at this person who was exactly twice her age and decided she liked his face. She looked at it again now and saw the same thing she had seen then. He was kind, she thought. Irma wasn't an idiot. Kindness was not a quality commonly found in rich old bachelors, she knew, but in her time she'd had the opportunity to look at many an elderly face and, if she knew anything, she knew how to read wrinkles. The old man's face was as lined and cross-hatched as any she'd ever seen but all of his wrinkles looked earned by years and not engraved by cruelty. The only thing that had been at work on his face was time. He was a nice old man. Somebody worth her attention. Somebody worth talking to.

In the two weeks they'd been together, Irma felt they'd established a rapport, developed a friendship. She knew he was lonely. Friendless and without family. In need of conversation.

'You know what the doctor says about you?' she said. 'He says you're a very smart guy.'

That wasn't actually what the doctor had said. Irma'd found him – a baby, maybe twenty-seven years old – just as he was leaving for what was undoubtedly a swank house in the Hamptons and had asked him a couple of questions. After failing to mask completely his astonishment that Irma would even be inquiring about such esoteric medical details – like it was none of her business, like who was she to give a shit – the surly little bastard had reluctantly let slip what he referred to as the most interesting aspect of the old man's case. Some machine or other had revealed that, despite the coma, despite medical science's inability to reach him, there was an astonishing amount of brain activity going on inside the old man's head.

Irma thought the old man had no need to know that some young prick found his plight *interesting* but surely it would comfort him to hear that people knew his mind was still buzzing, that he was a smart old guy.

'I knew you were smart anyway,' she whispered, 'didn't need him to tell me.'

Of course he was smart. He'd made all that money, after all. He was an oil executive – retired maybe but a retiree who could obviously afford to run a chauffeur-driven Lincoln and pay for an indefinite stay in this place.

Irma reached down her hand and stroked his forehead.

'You doing okay?' she asked. 'Want me to stay awhile?'

He didn't say no. Irma smiled. She patted his head one more time, glanced again at the window and the lives beyond it, and walked back over to the recliner to settle in for the rest of her watch. They had four more hours together. And she'd be back tomorrow night. And the night after. For as long as he needed her.

She looked from his still and silent body to the busy and beeping machines that told her of his life. She watched his heart beat. She watched him breathe.

'Sweet dreams,' she whispered.

# 10

It was nine-thirty at night and Avis's feet were on the Bowery. Her head though was in Liverpool, England, on a summer's day in 1975 and she was barely aware of her neighbourhood, hardly conscious of the bad lighting, the street trash, and the run-down buildings as her autopilot legs led her home.

Much clearer in her mind's eye was the small English house in an anonymous north end suburb of the birthplace of the Beatles. Clear too was the sweet and incredibly ancient face of William Llewellen, the face of her grandfather.

He'd wept when Mom had made her hug him hello and that had made Avis uncomfortable but within an hour, her five-year-old arm possessively round his eighty-year-old neck, she was sitting on his lap basking in the pungent smell of pipe tobacco that came off him like some exotic cologne. By the end of the afternoon, grandparent and grandchild were bonded completely.

At that time – the only time they met – they didn't even share a second name. Not until after her mother had divorced her father in 1980 did Avis and Danny become Llewellens. But this was before all that, before Dad's cheating and drinking had driven his wife and children away from him, and he was with them on what was Avis and Danny's first visit to the country in which their mother had been born, the country to which their grandparents had moved from Wales shortly after getting married in 1930. In fact, it was Dad who prompted the story. Avis might otherwise never have heard it.

It was after tea and cake and William was on his umpteenth pipe of the afternoon. Everybody else was sitting but Dad was on his feet walking round the small sitting room, checking out the numerous framed photographs. He stopped at one, a formal studio portrait in which a pretty four-year-old girl clutching the hand of what was presumably an older sister stared with suspicious nervousness at the unseen cameraman.

'Is that . . . ?' he asked, completing his question by a smiling gesture at Avis's mom.

'Aye. That's your wife,' said William, chuckling at the memory. 'Thought the camera was going to bite her, I reckon. Had it done at Jerome's. Nice studio he had there. London Road. Mmm. 1944, I think. How old were you, love?'

Avis's mom shrugged and smiled. 'Four?' she ventured. 'Five?'

'Aye. Something like that,' said William. He glanced down at the little bundle on his knee. 'She looks like you, doesn't she, pet?' he asked.

Avis nodded solemnly, ready to agree with anything her new friend said. William looked at her face.

'Got your grandad's eyes, though,' he said. 'Haven't you? Eh?'

'If she has,' said Dad, having moved on to another photo, 'then this fine young fellow must be you because the eyes look awfully familiar.'

The picture, from a much earlier period than that of the girls next to it, was of a uniformed soldier standing stiffly to attention as if the camera was a commanding officer. William glanced at it and confirmed its identity.

'That's me all right,' he said. 'Nineteen years old. Just signed up. Hadn't even got my uniform dirty.'

'Not seen action?' asked Dad, sitting down beside Mom on the short sofa that seemed to be almost as old as the photograph.

'Not then,' confirmed William. 'Saw plenty of it soon enough, though.'

'He was four years in France,' said Mom to Dad.

'Four years? Jesus.'

'Aye. Four years. Shouldn't really be here, you know. Odds were I should've been feeding the rats like all the other poor buggers.'

'You must have seen some sights,' said Dad.

William nodded, puffing on his pipe and lost in thought for a moment. 'Some sights is right,' he said eventually. 'Some I wouldn't want to see again. You know, there was one time . . .'

He broke off to look at his daughter. 'Should I tell him this story?' he asked her. 'The one about the village, you know, and the house?'

Avis's mom nodded and Avis saw her reach over and squeeze Dad's hand. It was funny because it was like how Mom squeezed *her* hand sometimes. It was the be-quiet-and-listen squeeze, not the I-love-you one.

'This was the spring of 1917,' William said, 'about two and a half years after that picture was taken. We'd been chasing Jerry back a few hundred yards – which in that war, by the way, was a lot of ground – and it'd meant night-fighting. Up and over before dawn. Pitch-black except for gunfire and flares. You'd be tripping over dead friends before you'd gone ten bloody feet. Anyway, this was a particularly nasty one. Nobody knew what the hell was going on – least of all the officers – and I just kept running forward. That's all they wanted us to do, you know, just run forward, dodging the machine-gunners' bullets, and if you lived long enough to reach somebody in a different uniform give him the benefit of your bayonet. Or a bullet, if you had the time and space. So I kept going, running blind like everyone else and, next thing I know, I've reached a trench. Barbed wire up in front of it of course but some poor swine had been cut down right on top of it and I just ran over his poor dead back to get through. Jumped down into the trench, swinging the old bayonet – as if it would've done me much good if the trench was full of Jerry – and looked round. And it *was* full of Jerry. But all of them dead. Blimey. Didn't know what to do. Better keep going, I supposed, and I started clambering out the other side of the trench and – just as I got my head over the rampart – the bullet hit me.'

He paused for a long satisfying pull on his pipe. Paused also, though Avis was too young to know this at the time, with the instinctive narrative cruelty of a storyteller who'd reached an appropriate point in his tale at which to let his listeners suffer a moment of suspense.

'You took a bullet?' said Dad (too young for Korea, too old for Vietnam). 'It hit you?'

'Hit the helmet, actually. Felt like somebody'd been hiding in the dark and smacked me right in the forehead with a bloody big sledgehammer. Knocked me right back down. Flat on my back in the bottom of the trench, out cold for at least an hour or so.

'Next thing I know, I open my eyes and I think I'm blind. I can tell it's daytime because I'm not looking at blackness, I'm looking at solid grey, but that's all I'm looking at. Can't see a thing. Not a thing. Fine state of affairs. What the bloody hell am I going to do now, I think. Then I feel the moisture on my face, you see, and I realize it's just fog. We used to get some terrible fogs those early spring mornings and this one was a blinder. I stagger up, still can't see more than half a yard in front of me, and realize that everything's very quiet. No guns. No grenades. No shouting. Battle's long over. So I haul myself out of the trench and take a look around. Fog's not quite as thick as where it had settled in the trench but it's still thick. Can't see a thing. Can't hear a thing. No bloody idea what to do or which way to go. Got to be careful, you see. In that sort of fog somebody who comes strolling in from out of the mist is as likely to get shot from a British trench or foxhole as he is from a German one. But I can't hang around either. Can't wait for the fog to clear because, for all I know, the area's still held by the Hun. So I just start walking.

'I must have wandered around for more than an hour before I realize that the fog's getting a little thinner. It's still there, wafting round in great cloudy chunks, but I'm beginning to be able to see through it. And so I see that there are buildings a couple of hundred yards in front of me and over to the left. Still no sound, no sign of activity. Nothing else to do so I head over toward these buildings. After a hundred yards or so I realize that I'm walking on an honest-to-God road instead of what used to be some poor farmer's fields and that what I'm heading for is a village – or what's left of it.

'Can't have been much to start with, mind you. Just a few stone-wall houses gathered around the road with some bigger structures that were probably . . . oh, I don't know . . . church, schoolhouse, things like that. But now, it's dead, all of it. And long dead. Must've been shelling, I suppose. There's no glass in any of the windows and precious few roofs. No chance of any people. This was old damage, not recent.

'But by now my stomach's doing its best to remind me that I haven't eaten for a long time and my feet are doing their fair share of complaining too. So I figure I'll go in one of these houses, see, and have a root around in what was left of a larder and look for food – might get lucky and find some stale bread or mouldy cheese – and then get my feet up on a couch, maybe even a bed, and wait around for the fog to clear. Then I might be able to work out which way's which and take myself off in a direction that'd bring me to our lads and not Jerry.

'So I look at the houses and I see that one of the nearest still has a bit of a roof on it, might be some stuff in there that's survived, you know, so I go in. No need to break in – no bloody door.

'Now, with there being no doors or windows, the fog is inside as well as out and, with there being walls and ceilings, it's not dissipating half as fast as outside so it's nearly as thick as when I woke up in that bloody trench. So I'm stumbling through the place, tripping over steps and uneven flagstones and what-have-you, trying to find whichever room might have been the kitchen once upon a time, using my hands as much as my eyes, and then all of a sudden I get this funny feeling that I'm not alone.

'It wasn't as if I'd heard anything else moving about in there – and I certainly hadn't seen anything – but I just got this eerie sense that there was somebody else in there with me. Of course, my mind starts racing then and I start to think about some Kraut lost like me, woke up in the fog like me, wandering around like me till he finds this place too. Maybe finds it first, maybe gets his head down just like I was going to, and then hears something – hears me coming in – and gets up nice and quiet and gets his rifle ready and sits there waiting to get a good look at whoever's going to come through his door.

'So I stand where I am – which is in a hallway a couple of feet shy of a door to another room – and flatten myself against the wall. Not much I can do about it, I reckon. If he's in the place and ready then he'll have the drop on me and there's no way I can take him by surprise. So what the hell – I shout to him. "Hey, Fritz!" I yell, top of my lungs. "Tommy! It's Tommy!" Echoes through the whole bloody house. Not a word back. I rack my brains for some German but I don't suppose *sauerkraut* or *auf Wiedersehen* are going to do me any good. Then I think, well we all do Latin at school. Jerry too, probably. The universal language, old Rev Wilkinson used to tell us when he wasn't busy rapping our knuckles for not knowing how to conjugate properly. "Pax!" I shout out. "Pax!"

'I let it ring out for a while but there's still no answer. So I start to think about the odds. If he's here – and of course I don't know that he even is – and he's doing what I wanted to do then he's probably upstairs in the bedroom. If I don't go up the stairs, he's not going to get a bead on me without coming down and, if he comes down, I'll hear him and turn the tables on the swine. So bugger it, I think, and edge my way along to the doorway through the fog – which is even thicker when I get into the room except that it seems to have settled heavily so that the bottom half of the room, up to about knee-height, is invisible but the top half is just misty and I can make out enough to see that this must have been the parlour when people still lived here; there's a sofa, a couple of armchairs, even a piano over by what used to be the window.

'Now, there's obviously not going to be any food in there so I don't even know why I walk over towards the piano, but I do. I edge past one of the armchairs – which has its back to me so that whoever used to sit in it could look out of the window – and go and stand by the old Joanna. God knows why. I couldn't play or anything. Maybe I just wanted to touch it to remind myself that there was a world somewhere where pianos were played, a world where there was music and a fire in the hearth and beer on the table. I don't know. Anyway, just as I'm lifting the lid to have a look at the keys, the hairs on the back of my neck stand up and I get, even stronger than before, that sense that I'm not on my own in there.

'I drop the lid – made a hell of a racket – and swung round. My heart nearly stopped, I swear; there's a man sitting in the armchair right behind me!

'I didn't even think – didn't even know what I was doing till my leg was halfway up – but I draw back and I kick the bugger right in the throat with all my strength. And his bloody head comes off! Flies right off his shoulders and shoots across the room, smacks into the far wall and drops to the floor.

'Good job I hadn't found anything to eat because I would have been sick. Not just at what happened, you see, but because the stench starts up then. Bloody awful it was, like a slaughterhouse nobody'd cleaned for a month. The poor bugger must have been sitting there dead for weeks, skin and flesh so ripe and rotten that a kick could take his head clean off his neck. I hadn't smelled him when I came in because he was intact, I suppose, but by God, now that I'd opened the poor swine up, the stink from his rotted innards nearly made me faint.

'I couldn't have eaten then anyway but the other thing was that it could well have been mustard gas that killed him. Any food I might find, in that house or in the whole village, would probably have poisoned me. I up and ran. Didn't give a thought to any imaginary Jerry, just legged it out of the room. Halfway down the hallway though, I stopped. I felt bad, you see. After all, he wasn't an enemy. He was probably just some poor old Frenchman caught up in it. For all I knew, his own son could have been out there somewhere in the trenches with us. So I half think I'll go back in there, find his head, and put it back with the rest of him. But the fog, you know. I'd have to get on my hands and knees and root round and . . . well, I've got no excuse . . . I just didn't fancy it, that's all. I let myself out of the place and follow the road out through the village and beyond. Couple of hours later, I find a bunch of Tommies being marched along by a corporal who seems to have some idea of where he's going and I fall in with them till we're back safely behind British lines.'

The Frenchman's head became a family joke, Avis remembered as she turned the corner onto the dark stretch of street that, within two blocks, would bring her to her door. Neither tasteful nor particularly funny, it had nevertheless, when she and Danny were growing up, been the standard question in her house whenever somebody was seen to be searching for something: What are you doing? Looking for a Frenchman's head?

She hadn't used or heard the phrase in years and she was damn sure she'd never mentioned it to Fern. So what the fuck was it doing in Fern's dream? Never mind that – what the fuck was Avis's *grandfather* doing in Fern's dream? Okay, so at least his presence explained the phrase. But what the hell explained *him*? She'd rooted round for twenty minutes last night trying to see if she had a photo of the old man in his younger days to show to Fern and get a confirmation but she hadn't been able to find one and Fern – the stress of what she'd unconsciously been through finally outweighing her excitement – had collapsed into her own bed five minutes into Avis's search anyway. Which Avis was kind of grateful about because, while she was happy to elicit information from Fern, she still didn't feel ready to explain in return what was going on. Because she didn't fucking *know* what was going on.

Postponing any follow-up questions from Fern had been the main reason she'd delayed coming home from work tonight and had instead joined Wendy for an open-face turkey sandwich at the Carnegie Deli. Which had been great but which was also the reason – or, more precisely, the fat-count of its gravy was the reason – that she'd taken the subway instead of a cab so that she could walk home at this end. Which also would have been great . . . except for the sudden presence of the grinning junkie beside her.

She didn't even know where he'd come from, didn't know from which benighted doorway or rat-infested alley he'd slipped out and found her. He might have been shadowing her for minutes or might just this second have broken into her life. She didn't know. All she knew was that he was here now – a half-step ahead of her, walking backwards, between her and the street – and that his wacked-out huge-pupilled eyes were fixed on her and that clutched in his weaving hand was something that glinted.

'I'm gonna cut you, you fucking bitch,' he said, his voice a stiletto giggle. 'I'm gonna cut you good.'

Avis screamed. Even as she did so, though, she threw her glance away from him further down the street. She was only twenty feet from her door. Without waiting to tell herself how stupid it was – how he was in front of her and turning and running in the opposite direction might have been the smarter move – she took off, flinging herself forward and angling herself in toward the dark wall of the building beside them.

It took him by surprise. It gained her three seconds and a few feet and saved her from the first angry swipe of his slashing arm. She caromed off the wall, pushing herself into a new start with her hands as he swung round and started his pursuit.

'Get back here, bitch!' he screamed, his voice full not only of anger but of an absurd indignation as if he couldn't believe that somebody had disobeyed some fucked-up street propriety that required victims to do as they're told.

Avis didn't look back. She didn't want to see him. She could hear his pounding feet gaining on her and that was quite enough. She screamed again. Surely John or Mike or Fern would hear her. Surely the door would open as or before she reached it – because she knew that she wouldn't have time to find her key and open the door herself before he'd be on her, slashing and slicing.

'Shut up!' his apoplectic voice screamed at her back. 'Shut the fuck up!'

Avis closed the distance between her and the door. It still wasn't open. She cried out in despairing disbelief and hammered on it with both fists before, propelled by some instinct, she threw herself to the far side of it at the last second before the junkie slammed into it himself.

She turned to face him, pressing herself back against the cold brick of the wall, her eyes wide in terror.

He straightened up too, viciously calm again now that the chase was over, and moved out onto the sidewalk directly in front of her. He giggled.

'Watched your legs while you ran,' he said. 'Good legs. You're going to open them up for me.'

Something snapped in Avis. Something that put her terror on hold and allowed her unlimited access to her disgust. 'Fuck you,' she said, her voice devoid of any emotion, 'you stupid ugly piece of shit.'

The junkie's eyes glittered at her as if he liked that. His hand started weaving again like a snake trying to mesmerize its prey.

'Dirty mouth,' he said, in a voice that was more excited than disapproving. 'Filthy. Gonna have to cut your tongue out now.'

There was a frozen second while he let her think about that and then he leapt for her. He should've made it – God knows Avis wasn't going anywhere – but he didn't. The front door opened behind him and a figure, blurred by motion, launched itself at him from the doorway, grabbed his raised arm, yanked it behind him and, with an audible cracking sound, broke it at the elbow.

While the junkie screamed, the figure behind him hooked a foot in front of his legs, pulled it backwards, and, with a simultaneous push in the small of his back, sent him tumbling down into a face-first smash on the sidewalk.

The figure stepped forward, placing a foot on the neck of the fallen thug to hold him in place, and Avis got her first clear look at her rescuer. It wasn't John. It wasn't Mike or Fern. As impeccably clad as two nights earlier, the silk of his top hat shining in the moonlight, Avis's ghost smiled at her.

He was dressed identically – the tuxedo, the topper, the white gloves, the curious blue buttonhole flower – but this time his outfit was completed by a midnight blue domino mask wrapped around his eyes. Avis remembered the little man in her dream who foretold the wearing of this mask and then remembered her manners.

'Thank you,' she said, her voice shrunken with shock. 'How did . . . how . . .' She had a thousand questions and no idea how to begin. The figure assumed the one question in which she wasn't even interested and gestured down at the moaning-with-pain junkie.

'It was nothing, my dear,' he said. 'A little trick I picked up in the Orient.'

His voice was attractive. Not only was its timbre rich and low but its accent and intonation were as elegantly archaic as his mode of dress. He looked at Avis quizzically as if waiting for her to resume the conversation and then, with a quick grimace of embarrassment at the social blunder of expecting a lady to speak to a stranger, spoke himself.

'Forgive me,' he said, 'in all this excitement I quite forgot that we had not yet been introduced.' He bowed slightly from the

93

waist. 'The Blue Valentine,' he said. 'At your service, ma'am.'

Through the two holes of his mask, his eyes twinkled at her with an assured charm that stopped just short of the arrogant. Avis looked at him – at his six-foot and well-proportioned frame, at his handsome square-jawed face, at the easy elegance of his manners and his clothes, and at the foot that effortlessly kept pinned to the ground the vile scum from whom he had rescued her – and realized that in anything approaching normal circumstances she could very easily be enormously attracted to him. The circumstances, however, were anything but normal and she wanted some damn answers.

'Avis Llewellen,' she said. 'Are you real?'

The Blue Valentine made an interested face. 'Ah,' he said, 'a lady who speaks instantly of the verities. How refreshing. As to your question . . .' He paused and looked down at the junkie. 'I'm sure this ruffian could attest to the undeniable reality of the breaking of his arm.'

He looked back at Avis and continued, 'I'm here. I breathe. I act. I feel I could pass any practical test that science could devise. But I will not mislead you. Your question, I know, is concerned with more than appearance, no matter how solid that appearance may be. No, my dear, I am not real. I am a ghost.'

'What the *fuck*?!' came a cry from the ground, cut off into a strangulated groan as the Blue Valentine increased the pressure of his foot on the junkie's neck.

'Silence, sir!' the Valentine snapped.

'But why?' Avis asked, trying to stick to the subject at hand and doing her best to ignore the sudden note of cruel pleasure she heard in the Valentine's voice.

The Valentine looked at her and shrugged. 'Perhaps Manhattan has need of me again,' he said.

'Again?' Avis asked. 'You've been here before?'

'Well, not as a ghost,' he replied, a laugh in his voice. 'This was my address,' he said, gesturing at Avis's front door, 'my headquarters, rather. My time was the thirties, ma'am, a decade the glory of which was spoiled only by the depredations of the underworld. I was one who helped do something about that. The police – at least their uncorrupted members – would do their best but

94

their hands were tied by the law. I did not represent the law. I represented justice. And my hands were free. And very busy.'

Avis's mind was reeling. What the hell was this guy talking about? 'Are you serious?' she asked, almost ready to believe that everything that had led up to this moment and this utterly bizarre conversation had been part of some elaborate prank.

The Valentine stared at her, not offended by her question but decidedly puzzled. 'Perfectly,' he replied. 'And now, for a reason known only to Heaven, my hands are free again.'

He took his foot from the junkie's neck, stooped, hauled him to his feet, twisting his one good arm behind him, and began to march him forward away from the front door.

Avis, still dazed and confused by everything that had happened, stood back passively to let the Valentine force his captive past her and toward the beckoning shadows of an alley some yards further on.

The junkie squirmed in his grip. 'What the fuck are you doing, man?' he cried. 'Stop it, you're hurting me!'

'Wait!' Avis called. 'What are you doing? Where are you taking him?'

The Valentine paused and looked back at her. 'To justice,' he replied simply.

The junkie twisted his head painfully round to fix his terrified and plaintive eyes on Avis. 'Make him stop!' he called to her. 'I didn't mean nothing. I was just fucking around!'

His voice segued into a cry of pain as the Valentine increased the pressure on his arm to silence him. Avis gasped in sympathy.

'No,' she said, 'let him go. Please. He's hurt enough. Don't do anything else.'

'Your forgiving nature does you credit, my dear,' the Valentine replied, 'and your concern is most becoming. But I suggest you meditate more on what he intended to do with *that*,' he gestured with his free hand at the cut-throat razor that was still lying on the ground where the junkie had dropped it, 'than on what I intend to do with *him*.'

'Why do you have to do *anything* with him?' Avis asked – but she noticed that her voice now was smaller and its tone less outraged. Her eyes had found the razor and her mind had pictured the uses for which it had been intended and her protest at the Valentine's vigilante ethos had become somewhat tempered.

'Alas, dear lady, it is my nature,' he said. 'God's pen is laid down and all our parts written.' He nodded at the man he held. 'And just as this leopard cannot change his spots, no more can I resist changing them for him. Permanently.'

With another cruel jerk of the captive arm, the Valentine urged the whimpering junkie further towards the deep black shadows of the alley. At the last moment before the darkness swallowed them, Avis's paralysis broke and she ran after them. She'd only gone three feet, however, before the Valentine turned to her with an admonishing hand which froze her in her tracks again.

For a moment he simply held her gaze and then very slowly, still not taking his eyes from hers, he shook his head from side to side.

Avis watched them disappear. She said nothing. She did nothing. She simply waited till she felt she could move again and then turned and walked quietly back to her front door. She'd gazed deep into the Valentine's eyes and known that argument or pursuit was certainly pointless and quite possibly dangerous. She had seen nothing there of mercy or kindness, seen only a deep cold fury that would see itself satisfied, a buried and bestial rage that, despite the elegance and superficial politeness of the man, would, at the last, brook no denial of its hunger, no interference with its feeding.

# 11

## *The Fields of Heaven*

He was watching his new flower form. A moment before it had
been a pebble.

It was a trick the Companions had showed him. All in the head.
A question of mental relaxation. A simultaneity of surrender and
control. He'd decided not to believe in the hardness of the pebble
any more and its edges had softened. It was a clump of soil – how
could it ever have been anything else? And once it was a clump
of soil then it was easy to believe that it was not a loose clump
lying on the surface of the grass but simply an exposed patch of
earth. And why shouldn't this patch of earth contain a seed? Why
shouldn't it contain something that was already rooted, something
eager to be born? And now it was a flower. And who couldn't
believe in a flower when it seemed so at home, so natural in such
fields as these?

He smiled, reached down, and plucked it. Fragile but solid in
his hand, its reality was beyond question. He raised it to his nose
and breathed in its rich perfume. Beautiful.

Of course, he wasn't as good at this yet as the Companions
were. He couldn't casually sweep up a handful of leaves of grass
and, by the time he brought it up to chest height, be holding a
glass of wine. Nor could he catch the sounds of people's words
in the air and compress them in his palm into intricate figurines
of translucent jade. But his lack of expertise was only to be
expected. He hadn't been here very long.

Actually, he wasn't sure that was true. It was very difficult to
judge time here. And tiresome, too. The Fields of Heaven were a
constant moment, an instant of for ever in which nothing changed
except by action of the exercised will. He remembered the night-
fall that his friends had given him when he'd asked: A huge

and placid lake had appeared beneath those distant hills and the massive glowing sun had vanished, to be replaced by a jet-black sky festooned with uncountable stars in new and nameless constellations, all reflected in the newborn lake so clearly that he had felt his grassy bower had become a magic carpet suspended between two views of a vast night sky, endless and glittering. It had lasted exactly as long as he had wanted it to and then his perfect late afternoon had returned.

He laid his flower back down on the grass, looked away, and thought of its large yellow petals as the wings of a butterfly. When he looked back it had already flown away. He spotted it a few yards off, flitting back and forth between two flowers as if remembering its recent kinship with them. He gave it the gift of believing it would have a very long life and then carefully dismissed it from his thoughts and settled back against the astonishing comfort of his tree and closed his eyes.

From a vantage point nearby, two of the Companions watched him ease himself into sleep.

'Flowers and insects,' said the one who was currently in the shape of a multi-faceted fifteen-foot diamond and whose complexion alternated irregularly between the calm of pale yellow, the passion of bright red, and the melancholy of a colour which has no earthly name. 'Such a poor imagination we have to work with.' He made himself a temporary head, solely in order that he could shake it disparagingly.

'But at least we have it with which to work,' said the other, who at present was choosing to be without shape but of whom fragments could occasionally be glimpsed, caught by the sun, as strands of its essence swam between the molecules of the air like microscopic sea-snakes navigating the infinitesimal caverns of an invisible ocean. 'And everything we need from him he has already imagined.'

'Then let me play with him,' said the first, transmutating into a fluorescent green and glass-fingered capuchin monkey with a second head dangling umbilically from its navel. 'Let me give him a glimpse or two of the spaces in which he actually sits. Because if I have to look at his pathetic vision of a piss-poor paradise a moment longer I'll need to grow a second oesophagus just to handle all the puke.'

The second, solidifying into an aquamarine finger of fire that blazed three feet above the ground and spat cherry stones, laughed dutifully but spoke warningly. 'No shocks,' he said, 'nothing to disturb the stasis. He's our conduit. Lose him and we lose it all.'

The green monkey began to vibrate, suddenly whirlwinding itself into a furious oscillation that squeezed and stretched its flesh into the shape of a Möbius strip along which ran a single eye, pulsing forward as if pushed by a rapid peristalsis. 'Then I shall be patient,' it said, 'until we ride the cloud.'

'Good,' said the fire, 'now let's visit him. I'm nervous when he sleeps. He might wake up elsewhere.'

He opened his eyes from a sleep that was as dreamless as all his sleep was here with a sense that someone was coming. Glancing over to his left he saw two of the Companions walking over toward him and, pulling himself upright, he gave them a wave of greeting. He looked at them carefully. He thought they were the two who had been with him earlier but he couldn't say for sure because it was always difficult to tell any of them apart.

It was curious, he thought, not for the first time, how a race (Were angels a race? He wasn't sure.) who could, at a whim, transform the reality around them into whatever they wished it to be were themselves so blandly similar to each other. Because they were all essentially the same person – each of them a sober-suited and short-haired man of medium build and unprepossessing features.

Now, he wasn't a stupid man. Hadn't been a stupid man when he was alive, wasn't a stupid man now. He didn't think for a second that that middle-American middle-management look was what they *really* looked like. He assumed it was an appearance adopted entirely for his benefit – part of an orientation process or something. He'd never been particularly religious but he was familiar with the phrase *blinded by glory*. Perhaps newly arrived humans were incapable at first of handling the sight of the Companions' true selves.

99

The two arrived by his tree and sat down cross-legged beside each other and in front of him, looking at him with the same open friendliness with which they always looked at him. He thought about it for a moment. He didn't want to rush anything but what the heck, it never hurt to ask.

'I know those aren't your real faces,' he said, grinning at them as an adult would grin at children caught in a harmless lie. He all but laughed with unmalicious delight as he saw the Companions look sharply at each other, an expression almost of panic crossing the face of one. The other looked back at him and replied, in a voice that was a mix of the curious and the cautious.

'What do you mean?'

'Come on, now,' he said, still gently chiding, 'I'm fairly settled in, don't you think? I've accepted the transition, surely? I don't think I'll be shocked or blinded. Heaven looks how I thought it would. I imagine you do too.'

'Ohhh,' said one of the Companions in a slow sigh, as if relieved that he hadn't been referring to something else. 'I understand.'

A glance passed between the Companions as if they were conferring telepathically and then they both looked back at him. One of them nodded solemnly.

'Very well,' the other said.

'Do I need to close my eyes?' he asked them.

'Oh, I don't think so,' came the reply.

With no more formalities, the change began. The Companions didn't move at all but the air in front of them shimmered and shifted and glowed briefly with a golden radiance. When it settled again, the Companions no longer had the appearance of mid-west businessmen.

Sitting cross-legged opposite him were two angels. He'd been right. He was neither shocked nor blinded. They were beautiful but unsurprising. He knew what angels looked like. Everybody did. And here they were before him. The real thing. Classic. Storybook. Robed, winged, and haloed.

He smiled at them. They smiled too, first at him and then at each other. And then one of them began to laugh. A giggle at first, escaping clenched lips that did their best to contain it, the laugh grew and continued to grow – despite a reproving glance

100

from the other angel – until it was a helpless breathless unceasing howl of utter hysterical amusement as at some grand and private joke.

# 12

Fern, Mike, and John had sat her down. They'd held her while she freaked. They'd brought blankets to wrap around her while she shivered. They'd made coffee. They'd poured alcohol. They'd made soothing noises. And now they were really pissing her off.

John had started it. Big fucking surprise. They'd listened through her gabbled and garbled account of the background to what had just happened outside the house, of the Valentine's first brief appearance, of the hauntings she'd suffered the previous day, of Fern's far-from-normal sleepwalking and her own far-from-normal dream, and they'd been very good. No overt disbelief. Very few questions. Just noises of concern. Then she'd made the mistake of describing the Blue Valentine's appearance.

'Sounds like Fred Astaire,' John had said.

'Do you like Fred Astaire?' Fern had asked, as if the merits of some dead dancer were obviously of more pressing interest than anything Avis was talking about.

'Guys don't like musicals,' Mike had announced in reply and now they were off and running and Avis was sitting back in stunned silence, listening, and ignored by all of them.

'Yeah, yeah. I know,' said Fern, 'guys like the Three Stooges.'

'Bullshit,' said John. 'Guy-characters in *sitcoms* like the Stooges. It's a shorthand for beer, pretzels, and nothing-queer-about-me. *I* like Laurel and Hardy.'

'But do you like *musicals*?' Fern asked.

'Guys don't like musicals,' Mike repeated.

Fern looked at him. 'That's a nothing-queer-about-me response, too,' she said.

102

'What's your point?' said Mike. 'You saying I'm latent? Protesting too much?'

'Chill out,' said John. 'I don't mind musicals. But I prefer Gene Kelly to Fred Astaire.'

Mike nodded. 'Right,' he said. 'Guys prefer Gene Kelly to Fred Astaire. Nothing queer about Gene. Except his name.'

John looked at him. Was he kidding? 'It's spelled differently,' he said.

'It is?'

'Yeah. But you're right. Astaire's too camp.'

'No, no, no,' Fern broke in, 'everybody always says that. But it's the other way round. *Kelly* is the camp one. All naked forearms and puppy-dog energy, bouncing round in tight T-shirts and sailor pants like some Tom of Finland fantasy. Astaire is a model of heterosexual sophistication.'

Avis couldn't take any more. 'You guys are incredible!' she shouted. 'What's the point of this fucking conversation? Didn't you hear what I *said*?'

'Yeah,' said Fern, 'you said he looks like Fred Astaire.'

'Actually,' said John, '*I* said he looks like . . .'

'He looks nothing like Fred Astaire!' Avis interrupted. 'He –'

'They just share a tailor, right?' said Mike.

Avis leapt to her feet, shrugging off the blanket that had been wrapped round her. 'Shut up!' she shouted. 'All of you! Don't you get it? Won't you hear what I'm saying? There's a *ghost* out there! A ghost who broke somebody's arm and who's taking him off somewhere!'

She broke at the end into incoherent sobs of frustrated rage. That seemed to be a more lucid argument than her words had been – at least for Fern, who stood and rushed to her, putting an arm round her shoulder.

'Honey, honey,' she said soothingly, 'it's all right. You're safe now. It's all right.'

From the corner of her eye Avis saw John and Mike exchange a glance, a tiny thing but one that contained a world of judgement. They believed she'd been attacked and chased, no doubt, but believed very little else. Maybe some guy had helped her out, maybe not. Everything else was the product of hysteria – and specifically female hysteria. She looked into Fern's eyes, searching for a different response, but she could read little past the concern and sympathy.

'I don't know if it *is* all right,' she said, in answer to Fern's well-intentioned assurances. 'I don't know if I *am* safe now. I don't know if any of us are.'

'But the guy who attacked you – he's gone, right?' said Fern, urging Avis with her eyes to acknowledge this as a first step to calming down.

'He's not who I'm worried about,' Avis replied, 'it's the guy who took him.'

'Took him where?'

Avis looked at Fern, yearning for something more than sympathy, yearning not to be humoured but to be understood and believed.

'To justice,' she said. 'Whatever the hell that means.'

Robert Flynn wasn't flying any more. Not even descending to reality's terminal gate but touched down and de-planed. He was real straight now. Stone-cold sober. Fuck knows, a crack high didn't last long at the best of times, even when bolstered by a hip-flask's worth of cheap vodka, and it was amazing how conducive to sobriety a broken arm, a lacerated head, and a heavy shot of dick-shrinking terror could be.

Robert was in some building's basement, a basement that was clearly a clothing manufacturer's sweat-shop by day. The place was packed chaotically and to bursting-point with piles of cloth, racks of shoddy designer knock-offs, and heavy industrial sewing machines. He'd seen that much just after the wacked-out son-of-a-bitch in the blue suit had used Robert's head as the tool with which to smash the low side window halfway up the alley and get them in here and just before the crazy bastard had smacked him on the back of the skull with something fucking heavy and knocked him out.

Now he couldn't see anything because there was some kind of cloth blindfold tied over his eyes. All he knew was that he was flat on his back on a hard cold surface and that some kind of binding was keeping him there. The binding wasn't just on his

104

body. Straps across his forehead and chin kept his head as incapable of free movement as his body. He assumed he was still in the basement – because he didn't feel like he'd been out that long and because there didn't seem much point to bringing him here and then having to drag his unconscious body somewhere else – but that didn't mean much because he wasn't sure exactly where the basement was. On the short trip from the street where he'd found the little blonde cunt that he should have been having fun with by now he hadn't been paying much attention because of the pain of his broken arm and his confused terror. But Robert didn't really care where he was. All he cared about was that he wasn't alone.

The freak in the fancy-dress costume – the guy who'd called himself the Blue Valentine – was moving around and beneath him, testing and tightening the makeshift bonds (Leather belts and duct-tape? That's what it felt like.) which secured Robert to whatever was the flat cool slab on which he was lying.

'What are you doing?' Robert asked. His voice was an impostor. That couldn't be him speaking. That voice was tremulous and little, was helpless and afraid. He didn't sound like that. He'd never sounded like that.

'Punishing the guilty,' the top-hatted psycho replied, his tone half flat, as if giving an answer that he had repeated so often in so many circumstances that it had become an invisible phrase to him, and half distracted, as he was much more concerned with the final tightening of one of the bindings than with explaining either his actions or his intentions.

'You're not the fucking police,' Robert said, 'you've no right to do this. You've no authorization.'

He wasn't shouting. He'd learned real quickly not to shout. He'd done it once moments after first regaining consciousness and the blue-suited fuck had broken one of the fingers on his good hand in response.

Robert felt the Blue Valentine give one last testing tug to the bonds and then heard him straighten up beside him. He felt the bastard's hands at his head and whimpered in fear but then realized that all he was doing was taking off the blindfold. Robert blinked against the dim light of a single work-lamp that shone on them both and then swivelled his eyes in his trapped-in-place head to find the Valentine. He was looking directly at Robert and, though there was a small smile on his lips, the eyes behind the mask were cold and unforgiving.

'You have proven yourself a villain, sir,' he said. 'And that is all the authorization I require.'

He moved away for a moment beyond the point to which Robert's sight could stretch and Robert, swinging his eyes back to his immediate surroundings, was able to see finally the circumstances to which he had been brought.

He was strapped in place on the bed of one of the large sewing machines. Directly above him, connected to the bed by a swivel arm and a set of runners down the length of one side, was the machine itself. It seemed to glare down at him like the cruel alien head of some giant insect with the shiny chrome needle-housing and the long sharp needle itself as the beak and the vile exploratory proboscis. Robert felt his stomach lurch in fear as he looked at it.

'The fashion world's technology seems to have progressed since last I walked the earth,' the Valentine said as he walked back up beside the machine and took up a position by what was, though beyond Robert's field of vision, presumably a set of controls. 'But I rather think I've got the hang of it.'

The Valentine's unseen fingers began playing with buttons and dials as if selecting or programming a series of settings and his voice, musing privately, seemed to confirm this. 'Height . . .' he said, 'length . . . duration – ooh, that's an interesting one, isn't it? . . . and style. Right, let's see what happens, shall we?'

Robert screamed as the Valentine hit a start button and the machine clattered deafeningly into life. The head slid rapidly down the set of runners while turning through various angles on its arm. Having locked into a straight-down stance, it slammed its way back up the runners to halt jarringly in a position directly above Robert's face and then, with a percussive hydraulic hiss, it dropped at great speed, stopping only when the glistening point of its terrifying needle was no more than half an inch from his flesh.

'No! No!! Please!!' Robert howled in anguish, his entire body vibrating with spastic tremors of fear.

'Don't worry,' said the Valentine, his voice full of an undisguised glee at the activities of the machine, 'this is only the demonstration run.'

As if on cue, the needle jerked into stunningly rapid activity, alternately drawing itself up and thrusting itself down from within the housing, stabbing the air above Robert's horrified face uncountable times per second.

The Valentine hit the stop button and the roar of the machine ceased along with its manic activity. The only things Robert could hear in the exaggerated silence that ensued was the freight-train thumping of his palpitating heart and the hand-saw rattle of his panicked breath.

The Valentine leaned over Robert's helpless form, leaning a casual forearm on the head of the machine, and looked down at him with an almost sympathetic expression on his face, like that of a doctor about to give you the really bad news.

'Everything you fear is going to happen,' he said, 'is going to happen. There is nothing you can imagine here that I have not imagined first.' His voice was as calm as that of a death-row chaplain and offered as little hope for anything this side of the grave.

While Robert began to weep, the Valentine reached down somewhere below the bed of the machine and came up bearing a large reel of heavy-duty thread which he attached to the housing and fed through the eye of the needle.

'Please, no,' Robert sobbed, 'I'm sorry. I'm sorry. I'll never do it again. I promise. I promise!'

The Valentine was back at the controls punching in a new set of parameters and he spoke with the half-attentive air of the busy technician, not even looking at Robert.

'I think you're making the mistake of assuming this has something to do with rehabilitation,' he said. 'Whereas, as far as I can tell, his function is entirely that of punishment.'

'Whose function?'

'What?'

'You said *his* function.'

Robert's eyes were on the Valentine as he backed away slightly from the side of the machine, removed his opera hat and, holding it in one hand, stared at it with a look that was not only interested but almost puzzled.

'This . . . this . . . person,' he said, gesturing at his own body with his free hand while continuing to stare at the hat. 'This Blue Valentine.'

'What's going on?' said Robert, now as confused as he was terrified. 'What are you talking about?'

'Oh, never you mind,' said the Valentine and hit the start button.

Robert's lungs gave it their best shot but the scream itself was a poor effort – a bubbling, spluttering aborted thing, drowned at birth by the blood that filled his mouth as the furious needle hammered forty puncture wounds into his lips, dragging the heavy thread insistently through each incision, pulling the lips tightly together, and sewing his mouth firmly shut before working its agonizing way across the whole area again and putting a neat filigreed hem around its work.

It's understandable that while this was going on Robert hardly noticed the Valentine pulling up a tailor's chair and sitting down. The hat was still in his hands and he was still looking at it curiously as he began to talk.

'Gateways used to be very common, you know,' he said, 'not that they were needed. Your world was as fluid as everyone else's once upon a time. You've only got yourselves to blame. I've heard your stories about serpents and fruit but they're all only metaphors for ossified wills and atrophied imagination. Before the Fall. There *was* no Fall. There was only a Forgetting. And twenty thousand years of regret.'

He paused and looked over at Robert, thrashing and writhing in his bonds and making inarticulate grunts and howls from behind the thread that sealed his bruised and bloody mouth. 'Is this making any sense to you?' he asked rhetorically, expecting no answer. 'No? What a particularly stupid race you are. Stubborn and vicious, too. Long habit of burning anyone who tried to tell you the truth, I understand. Even the alchemists, stumbling in the dark as they were, had to dress what they were doing in the language of commerce to be allowed to pursue their sense of the secret.'

108

He stood up and walked back over to stand beside the machine and look down at Robert's white-with-shock face and bulging plaintive eyes. He drew a white handkerchief from his tuxedo jacket's breast pocket and wiped away the film of blood from Robert's mouth. He stared intently at the machine's handiwork.

'That must hurt,' he said, in a tone not of sympathy but of academic interest. 'I don't imagine it's much comfort to you to know that you're at a pivotal point in the history of your entire benighted species. The Great Work is about to begin. The lead will become gold. The dross will remember its divinity. It's a time of reconciliation, my poor bleeding friend, a time of reunion between Man and all his sundered brethren.'

He shoved the bloodied handkerchief into a trouser pocket and replaced the top hat on his head.

'Well, I'd like to stay and chat,' he said, 'but I think I'd better get back in character. We can't afford to break the connection at this delicate stage. He needs another day or so before we can be sure the presence is established firmly.'

Robert saw a sudden absence wash over the Valentine's face, an absence that lasted only a second but during which Robert felt a fleeting hope that the bastard was dead because it looked for all the world like life was passing from him, that a soul was making its farewell. But he wasn't so lucky. The Valentine staggered slightly but that was all. The look of momentary vacancy was followed by a look of momentary confusion, as if the Valentine had forgotten where he was and what was happening, and then he got right back to business.

'Perhaps now you have some idea of how a victim feels,' he said, looking at Robert's sealed mouth. 'Mute and helpless. Hoping, perhaps, that someone will arrive to offer help. For them, that hope, however small, is real. For you, I'm afraid, that hope is useless. I have already arrived. And after me, there is nothing. I am the last word.'

He leaned over and, despite Robert's frenzied wrigglings, ripped open the bound man's T-shirt to expose his chest. Moving back to the control panel of the machine, he punched in another set of programmed instructions, looking back and forth from Robert to the machine's head to the panel, calculating by eye the distances

109

and positioning involved. Satisfied, he slipped his hand into an inside pocket of his jacket and produced a small white card which he held up in order that Robert could see it. It was a business card, though one without either phone number or address. All that was on it, delineated in bright blue ink, was a cross-hatched rendering of a flower, the stem of which curved elegantly over the words THE BLUE VALENTINE which were printed in a neat and unpretentious typeface in the lower right-hand corner.

'The police department will not have seen one of these for many years,' he said, 'but a diligent search through their records should remind them of a time when they came across them quite frequently, a time when my activities made their lives simpler. And you, sir, will be their first signal that that time has come again, that the Blue Valentine has returned.'

Snatching up a pin from a pin-cushion on a nearby work-table, he thrust it through the centre of the card and then nonchalantly jabbed it deep into the meat of Robert's chest, anchoring the card there as he stepped back and hit the machine's start button again.

Behind its muffling stitches, Robert's mouth grunted and squealed in pathetic and pointless protest. His body, too, writhed madly in a useless attempt to avoid the pain as the busy and uncaring needle stitched and hemmed the card to his flesh.

The Valentine waited till the machine stopped and the head retracted and then put his hand to his breast pocket. Apparently surprised at not finding his handkerchief there, he fished in his trousers and brought out the already blood-stained cloth.

Through the mist of his weeping eyes, Robert saw the puzzled look cross the schizophrenic son-of-a-bitch's face and realized that the Valentine had no memory of that other personality, the one that had prattled esoterically about the nature of the Universe while watching Robert suffer, the one which had used the hand-kerchief to wipe Robert's mouth for him. In other circumstances Robert might have given a shit, might even have wondered what it meant, but the circumstances were what they were and so he hardly registered it – other than to wish uselessly that, if the bastard suffered from multiple personality disorder as all the signs

110

suggested, some gentler self would emerge within the next few moments to free him from his torment.

The Valentine leaned over Robert's body, handkerchief in hand, and paused. He looked at the pattern that the blood-flecks made on the surface of the business card and gave a small smile. Like an aesthete surprised by an accidental artistic flourish and deciding that he liked it, he straightened up and put his handkerchief away without doing any wiping.

'Our time together is nearly at an end,' he said to Robert as he turned once more to the control panel, again estimating by eye exactly where he wanted the machine to go. 'There were two lessons you needed to learn. The first was that victims are mute.'

Pressing the last of the buttons, he stepped back and bowed formally, like a magician respectfully presenting his last trick to an audience. With perfect timing, he finished speaking just as the machine kicked back into life, just as the torturing head slid eagerly back up its runners and swivelled on itself to take up a position immediately above Robert's face.

'The second lesson, sir,' the Blue Valentine said, 'is that justice is blind.'

The head descended with robot obedience.

The needle chattered with insect fury.

Robert learned his lesson.

# 13

Avis was amazed. Sixty years ago, you could buy a knockout designer dress for the kind of money that nowadays, if you were lucky, might just stretch to burger, fries, and a Coke at a really shitty restaurant.

Typewriters were expensive though, and radios too – but halitosis, acne, and baldness could be cured, it seemed, for pennies. The baldness ads made her laugh. Judging by their frequent appearances in the newspapers and magazines, it looked like men were as gullibly ready to smear all kinds of God-knows-what shit on their hairless skulls in 1935 as they were now. What dorks. Shave it off and strut. Look at Sean Connery, for God's sake. She'd fuck him in a heartbeat and you don't get much balder than that.

She was sitting at a table in the New York Public Library. She'd been sitting there for nearly three hours now and she was finding it increasingly difficult to stop being distracted by the advertisements. She'd been strict with herself at first. Hard news only. Consequently, her head was full of Roosevelt New Deal rhetoric, Hindenburg explosions, and the search for Scarlett O'Hara, but her immersion in the newspaper archives of 1930–1939 had yet to yield even the tiniest reference to a gentleman adventurer operating under the name of the Blue Valentine.

She'd thought it was going to be easier. She didn't know she was going to be rooting through bound archives of long defunct papers and magazines herself. Not that it was the library's fault. It too – in the person of Joel Marsh, the librarian who'd been unlucky enough to get the Avis gig – had seemed to think, three and a half hours ago, that a quick skim through a computer file or two would yield reference numbers to shelves and books and

112

that within minutes she'd be browsing through contemporary reports and post-contemporary analyses of the Valentine's career. No such luck. There was nothing on the mainframe, no reference at all that Marsh could find for her. As far as the New York Public Library was concerned, the Blue Valentine might never have existed.

Joel – as he insisted she call him – had been tireless in his efforts to help her. Avis would have liked to believe that that was a testimony to the devotion that Manhattan civil servants felt toward their bosses, the public, but she rather had the feeling that it was testimony instead to the devotion that late thirty-something male librarians with no ring on their finger felt toward cute twenty-five-year-old blondes who knew how to make big helpless eyes and bite their lower lip in pensive and adorable frustration. She assumed that had she been a guy – or a woman with a nastier attitude and a less-short skirt – she herself would have been trolling back and forth to the shelves and dragging down the astonishingly heavy bound volumes and staggering back to the table with them. As it was, all she had to do was look up every half hour and there would be Joel, smiling his it's-no-trouble smile as he brought the next batch of daily history to her. Like the song said, she enjoyed being a girl.

She had no idea why exactly she felt so full of beans today after all that had happened last night but she figured it was to do with two things: she had woken up facing the fact that she was on her own in this, that her housemates were willing to offer nothing more than sympathy, and paradoxically, that very acknowledgement had been an empowering rather than a debilitating thing. She was taking action; she no longer felt like the passive victim of everything that was going on. Even calling in sick, lying through her teeth to the personnel department at work, had felt decisive and good and this investigative trip to the library, fruitless as it had been so far, was making her feel better too. She wasn't kidding herself that reading up on what a ghost may have done in his corporeal life was the equivalent of getting rid of his incorporeal self but it was a start. Knowledge was power and she was arming herself.

Or not. Page after editorial page on the growing crisis in Europe and, depending on the political stance of the editor (or, more likely, the proprietor), whether or not America should get involved was beginning to wear down her attention and her patience. It wasn't like she didn't know how it turned out – fall of Poland, fall of France, Battle of Britain, Pearl Harbor, Roosevelt, Churchill and Stalin, thousand-bomber raids, D-day, death of Hitler, The End. Domestic news was shrinking as she reached 1939 and she was beginning to despair of ever finding anything useful to her. And of course she was also getting paranoid that she'd missed a small column or two back in 1934 or 1935, that the records of the Valentine were slipping from her view as easily as he himself had done that first night.

She was halfway through a fifty-six-year-old Blondie and Dagwood strip in the comics section of a Sunday paper and wondering how come both of the Bumsteads looked identical to how they looked in the strips that still ran now when a voice interrupted her.

'A-ha!' it said. 'Now you're looking in the right places.'

Avis looked up to see Joel standing to one side and slightly behind her and looking over her shoulder at the comic strip. She smiled at him and pushed her chair back and round to face him, admiring silently the resolve that kept his eyes on her face instead of sneaking a quick look at her legs as they slid out from under the table.

'What?' she said.

'The funny pages,' he said.

She shook her head and gave him a questioning look. 'I'm not with you,' she said.

With a secretive smile, he handed her a piece of paper, an eight-by-eleven sheet still warm from a Xerox machine, that contained a reproduction of a single page from a magazine article.

'We don't have an original,' he said. 'I had to print it out from the microfiche files. Should charge you a quarter.' He laughed as he said the last bit to assure her he wouldn't actually be making her pay.

'What is it?' Avis asked.

'It's a very tedious polemic from some pundit of the time building an end-of-civilization-as-we-know-it spiel from a court case

114

that was going on. Two guys from Bay Ridge had kicked the living crap out of a guy who'd assaulted their sister.'

'Yeah?'

'Yeah. And screw him, I say. That's what brothers are for.'

'Mm. Not all of them,' Avis said, trying to imagine Danny doing anything so primal and brave on her behalf.

'Whatever,' said Joel. 'Read the last sentence. The last full sentence, I mean. The article ran on another page or two but we didn't need them.'

Avis looked down to the bottom of the page and found the sentence to which he was referring. The Valentine's name leapt out at her even before she read it and she felt a rush of pleasure along with genuine gratitude at Joel's tenacity. She figured she owed him at least a coffee date and she made a mental note that as soon as he got round to asking – and she *knew* he was going to ask – she would use the I'd-love-to smile instead of the I-guess-you've-earned-it one. Then she read the sentence and all other thoughts gave way to confusion.

*Such actions*, it read, *such attitudes, have no place in a society that calls itself civilized and are more appropriate to the Scarlet Wizard or the Blue Valentine or to any of those other fictional vigilantes from the pages of the penny-dreadfuls.*

She read it twice. She read it three times. The words didn't change. Other fictional vigilantes. Fictional. She looked back up at Joel, who was still grinning with the triumph of his discovery.

'Fictional?' she asked.

'I wish you'd been clearer,' Joel said. 'I wouldn't have wasted your time with the newspapers. We're in completely the wrong section. Here.' He handed her another piece of paper, this one much smaller and with hand-written information on it: a book title and a reference number.

Avis took it and stared at it stupidly, still numb with shock.

'It's on the fourth floor,' Joel said. 'C'mon, I'll walk you to the elevators.'

Avis stood up and made as if to follow him. Then she hesitated and gestured at the table, still creaking under the weight of all the newspaper files.

'Wait,' she said. 'What about all . . .'

115

Joel cut her off. 'I'll get them later,' he said, 'don't worry about it. Come on. You've spent all morning tracking this guy down. Don't you want to move in for the kill?'

Avis, regaining a little of her composure, managed to give him a reasonable imitation of her best smile as they left that section of the library. She even did him the small kindness of walking slightly in front of him so that he could check out her ass as they headed for the elevators but her mind was racing with the implications of this new information. Close in for the kill? Sure, she liked the sound of that. But she'd thought she was tracking a man who, while he might not be alive now, had once been as real as she. That he was a ghost was, God knows, weird enough but now she was suddenly in the land of the exponentially weird. Exactly who, or what, had she encountered last night?

Five minutes later, Avis had a big book in front of her that might give her part of the answer.

She was in a partitioned cubicle at the rear of a different section of the library. She wasn't even sure what the section was called, hadn't even checked the name over the door as she came in. She'd just followed Joel's directions semi-blindly and, using the reference number he'd given her, had pulled this heavy over-sized volume from its shelf and brought it with her to this semi-private cubicle with its single chair and small table.

She felt bad about Joel. He'd left her at the elevators downstairs. She'd remembered, before the doors closed over her, to thank him for all his help but he must have registered the change in her manner because she saw him hesitate at the point when he would have asked her out and the moment slipped away from him. Maybe, if she felt up to it, she'd stop by his desk on her way out and give him another shot.

She liked this section. It suited her current mood. It was much quieter, much less busy. And these cubicles were cool, too. The big tables downstairs you had to share with anybody else who wanted some research space. Here you got your own nook, complete with your own little art print on the wall behind your own little table. She looked up at the one that graced her cubicle. At first she thought she was familiar with the picture but realized

116

that it wasn't the one of which she was thinking. It wasn't 'The Garden of Earthly Delights' at all but a more modern rip-off, a kind of late-surrealist pastiche of Boschian madness, a landscape busily peopled with grotesques large and small. There was one neat trick among the thievery, though – along the bottom of the picture, deliberately small and compositionally insignificant in order to stop you noticing them at first, two or three distorted and misshapen creatures stared directly out at the viewer. The effect was to turn the picture into a window on a world which was as interested in looking at you as you were at it. Neat.

She took her eyes back down to the book and flipped it open to the title page. *An Encyclopedia of Popular Fiction*, it said, *Edited by Gary Hoppenstand*, and, down at the bottom of the page, *Bowling Green University Press 1982*. She grabbed sequential handfuls of the hundreds of pages and turned them en masse to get to the index. She ran her finger down the B's and there he was. She turned to the cited page and began to read the entry – which wasn't even under the Valentine's name but that of his creator.

> **READ, NORBERT** (1911 –) *b. Cedar Rapids, Iowa.* American short story writer, prolific in the pulps, most notably Aylward Jacobs's *Strange Thrills*, where, after a succession of non-series stories, he invented Valentine Dyson, better known under his nom-de-guerre of the Blue Valentine, a name he took from the blue flower he habitually wore in his buttonhole. (Read – a sloppy researcher and stubborn writer – consistently ignored the letter-column cavils from horticulturally-inclined readers who pointed out that there was no such flower as a Valentine, blue or otherwise.) First introduced in 'Best Served Cold' (ST Aug 1937), Dyson, a Shadow-type nemesis of evil, is infamous among pulp scholars for being the most vicious and amoral of all such cloaked or masked avengers, making Maxwell Grant's Shadow and even Grant Stockbridge's Spider seem models of restraint by comparison. Merciless and inventive in his punishing of evildoers, Dyson would think nothing of leaving kidnappers dangling from chains while the cellar in which they hung filled slowly with corrosive acid ('Three Nights of Bondage', ST May 1938), shoving a trapped murderer's head through a hole in a New York skyscraper's huge clock-face and waiting for the massive minute-hand to

117

slowly and bluntly decapitate him ('Blood-song of Broad-way', ST Nov 1939), or (in a device borrowed from Shake-speare) entertaining a gang-boss to a lavish banquet, most of which consisted of the baked, roasted, or flambéed bodies of his twin sons. Only when he found himself staring into the undissolved eyeball of one of them in an otherwise per-fect *crème brûlée* did Boss Hollis catch on – at which point the unflappable Dyson (despite being surrounded by other guests, all of whom were armed thugs) opened a hastily-shaken bottle of Dom Perignon and fired the cork explos-ively into the open-in-shock mouth of his enemy who choked to death on it while Dyson made his escape ('Where the Worm Has Slept', ST Feb 1943).

Despite popularity with the magazine's readership, the Blue Valentine's eleven appearances in *Strange Thrills* were never collected in book form. Indeed, Read's only appear-ance between hard covers was in the 1946 anthology *Bedside Creeps* (Harpers, ed. William Irish) which reprinted his 1938 non-series story 'Big Thunder'.

Read worked solidly for a decade from the mid-30s, with rarely a month going by without his by-line appearing in at least one magazine but, unlike other pulpsters, he graduated neither to the slicks nor to Hollywood. Instead, he simply ceased writing at the end of World War Two when his brother-in-law offered him an executive position in the oil industry. Never a great stylist (his prose at best serviceable, at worst leaden), he is still remembered fondly by old-time fans for the fecund nastiness of his imagination.

Avis finished reading the entry and sat looking for some time at the small black and white reproduction of a magazine cover that took up a couple of inches of one of the columns devoted to Norbert Read. It showed a thuggish gangster with his arm around the waist of a woman he was dragging away with him. Avis noticed that the woman (big surprise) had managed to lose most of her dress in the process and was showing a hell of a lot of stocking-and-garter-belted thigh and that one breast was only a nipple shy of popping out of the clinging silk that contained it. Avis might have had an opinion about that but she was too busy staring at the figure who, blazing .45 in hand, occupied the rest of the picture, plainly about to rescue the girl and punish the gangster. It was the Blue Valentine of course and, fictional character or not, he was completely identical to the man she had met last night.

At first she put the eerie feeling that had crept over her in the last few minutes down entirely to this pictorial evidence that, in some bizarre fashion, her ghost was absolutely who he claimed he was. But the feeling continued to grow, revealing itself eventually as a conviction that she was being watched. She closed the book and took a quick glance over her shoulder. There was nobody around, nobody at all. It had been like that when she arrived and she'd liked it. But she wasn't sure she liked it now. The quiet and calm of this section suddenly felt less pleasantly peaceful than it felt unpleasantly isolated. A little carefully, a little cautiously, she got to her feet. Her hands went to the book but she decided that walking down between the tall narrow shelves to return it to its rightful place wasn't the most attractive option in the world right now. Suddenly she sensed, rather than saw, a tiny blur of movement above and in front of her. Startled, she looked up. There was nothing there. She was staring only at the wall and the sub-Boschian print that hung there, the surreal landscape with its tiny figures . . . Wait. Something was wrong.

Avis couldn't swear to it but she thought, when she had noticed them earlier, that she had counted three of the curious figures who pressed against the limits of the picture and stared out at the viewer. Now there were only two. One of them had gone – and gone with it was her feeling of being observed. Avis had a new feeling now, a feeling that she liked even less, a feeling that somewhere, somehow, a scout was reporting to its superiors.

# 14

Fern tipped the empty glass over and placed it in the centre of the card table.

She looked at it there – surrounded by the twenty-eight small pieces of paper, a hand-written letter of the alphabet on twenty-six of them and the words YES and NO on the remaining two – and deemed it all pretty good for a makeshift version. She'd played it this way once before, back at college when what-the-hell-was-her-name down the hall of the dorm had burned her actual Ouija Board after she'd been freaked out by a late-night video viewing of *The Exorcist*.

Fern figured anyway that, if it was a question of communing with spirits, there had to be a better through-line when the letters were written by the person doing the communing than when they were just printed on some mass-produced piece of crap. If the graphologists were right and your handwriting showed your inner self then there was less chance this way of a crossed line; the spirits would know who was calling – the bit of your essence that you'd scrawled on the paper would be more of a beacon shining through whatever darkness they needed to cross before they could settle in for a nice chat.

She heard the main door to the apartment open.

'Avis? That you?' she shouted.

'No. Just us chickens,' came the reply. It was Mike's voice and, seconds later, its owner entered the room along with John.

Fern glanced at her wrist watch.

'It's four-thirty,' she said. 'What are you guys doing home?'

'I got off early for a doctor's appointment,' said John, 'but I'd fucked up the dates. So I called Mike, asked if he wanted to bail and share a ride. What the hell is that?'

120

He was staring at Fern's card table set-up with a pre-emptive contempt ready for whatever explanation she might offer.

'Party games?' said Mike. 'Did I miss someone's birthday?'

'Only if you count ghosts as people. Right?' said John, throwing his topcoat on a sofa and leaning in for a closer look at Fern's handiwork.

'Right,' said Fern. 'But I don't think yesterday was his re-birthday. Avis said she saw him a couple of nights ago. Remember?'

John gave her one of his looks, the one that courteously gave you time to call yourself an idiot before he did it for you, while Mike pulled up one of the folding card chairs and sat at the table. Fern ignored John and looked at Mike.

'So what do we do?' he asked her.

'You never done this before?' Fern said.

He shook his head.

'Well,' she said, 'we all rest an index finger on top of the glass –'

'And whoever thinks of the funniest line first pushes the glass to spell it out,' said John, interrupting.

'Yeah?' said Mike, a little disappointed, a little worried that he was going to be the big loser in this game.

'Only in the cynical prick version,' Fern said. 'We're going to play it the way normal people do.'

'Normal,' said John. 'Yeah, right.'

'Ah, take a pill, John,' Mike said. 'Let's play it.'

Fern smiled at Mike and continued her explanation. 'What we *don't* do is push it,' she said. 'We wait for the spirits to move the glass and then we ask them questions.'

'No shit? Does it work?'

'Sure it does,' she said, 'provided you have an open mind.'

'Or an empty head,' said John.

'Fuck off,' Fern snapped. 'You want to do this with us or not?'

John raised his hands in mock-surrender. 'All right, all right,' he said, 'I'm game. But let's get a little atmosphere going, don't you think?'

Fern shrugged non-committally but Mike was enthusiastic. 'Good idea,' he said, getting out of his chair and heading for the windows. 'John, get some candles.'

John looked at Fern as Mike began drawing the blinds. 'You got any?' he asked.

'Sure,' Fern said, 'there's a couple on my dresser if you want to get them.'

'I hope there's no embarrassing lingerie lying round in there,' John called over his shoulder as he headed toward the door to Fern's bedroom.

'You wish,' she shouted after him.

Mike closed the last blind. Before the room went completely dark, however, he hit the dimmer switch for the overhead light and brought it up a little.

'I'll kill it as soon as he lights the candles,' he said. 'So what are we going to ask?'

'I don't know. What's going on. What Avis is seeing. Stuff like that.'

'You believe her? You really think she saw something?'

'I don't know. But we're going to find out.'

John came back into the room, carrying two candles, one green and one black. Both of them were heavy and substantial, each six inches high and three inches in diameter.

'How much do you pay for these things?' John asked, incredulous.

'About five bucks each,' Fern replied, as John laid them down on two corners of the table.

'Jesus,' John said. 'Five bucks? They're *candles*, Fern. They *melt*.'

'So?' Fern said as John struck a match and Mike killed the lights. 'They're beautiful. Hand-made.'

Each candle was intricately carved – the green one with intertwining leaves and vines, the other with a finely detailed unicorn raised on its hind legs in a posture of play or aggression. John put the match to each of their wicks.

'And now they're going to be un-made,' he pointed out.

'There is a beauty in the ephemeral,' Fern declaimed in her best grad student voice, 'to which not all the towers of Ilium can compare.'

'Who said that?' Mike asked, taking up his place again at the table.

122

'I don't know,' Fern replied. 'Read it somewhere. John, you had a good idea. This is cool.'

She was talking about the atmosphere. The room was lit only by the candlelight now and the table was a fragile island of clarity in a pool of darkness. The flames swayed gently in breezes that crept in through the blinds and the shadows of Fern, Mike, and John danced exaggeratedly within the faint orange glow on the wall immediately behind the table.

'Yeah,' Mike said, 'cool. John – get some music on. Piano or something.'

'Your other servant got the day off?' John asked, not moving.

'It's the penance you pay for scepticism,' Fern said. 'Find that French guy.'

John moved over to the CD rack. 'What's his name?' he said.

'I forget,' Fern replied, 'but the cover's got umbrellas on it.'

'That's a lot of help,' John complained, bending down and leaning one CD after another out of their moorings.

Fern gestured to the candles and asked Mike if he liked them.

'Sure,' he said. 'Very nice.'

'Don't you think the unicorn is sexy?'

'What the hell drugs are you on?' John asked from over by the CDs. He snatched one out and showed it to Fern. 'This the one?'

Fern squinted across the darkness. 'Yeah,' she said. She and Mike watched as John struck another match to illuminate the controls on the CD player and slipped the disc into the tray. As he sat down to join them at the table, the simple and haunting notes of Erik Satie's first *Gymnopedie* filled the room.

'All right,' said Fern, 'fingers on the glass, please.'

She put her finger on first and John and Mike followed suit. She looked at Mike's finger and could see the blood swelling beneath the skin around his nail.

'No, Mike,' she said, 'no pressure. Just lean it lightly.' He relaxed his finger and she continued to talk, her voice very low and quiet.

123

'Now everybody just breathe easy. Try and clear your minds. Don't concentrate on anything. Let whatever happens happen.'

A few moments passed. Fern was pleasantly surprised that John was as quiet and still as Mike. Maybe there was hope for him yet. He was so uptight and wired that she'd always had him stashed in the heart-attack-before-forty file but maybe he was going to surprise everyone after all. She was so busy noticing this that it was only after Mike's whispered *Wow* that she realized the glass had begun to move.

It was a gentle motion, slow and circular, and the circumference it was describing was barely more than that of the glass itself but it was real and it was enough to further charge the atmosphere in the room.

'Nobody's pushing it? Really?' asked Mike in a hushed low tone.

'Nobody's pushing it,' said Fern. 'Right, John?'

'Right,' he whispered, surprised at the truth of it.

Fern waited a moment while the movements of the glass grew stronger and the sweep of its circling wider. The music, with its sparse and beautiful gesture of a melody, was the only sound in the room other than the tiny noise of the glass's rim against the vinyl of the card table top and the quiet and steady sound of all their breaths.

'Is there someone who wants to talk to us?' Fern asked eventually, directing her voice at the glass.

There was a sudden, but not violent, increase both in the speed of the glass's movement and in the space that that movement covered. Mike reacted with an audible intake of breath.

'Is it William?' Fern asked softly. 'Is it Avis's grandfather?'

'What?' said John sharply.

'Shhh,' Fern whispered, frightened that any break in the mood might send whatever spirits were gathering back to their particular beyond.

The glass began to make wide sweeping movements, no longer circular, shooting back and forth in curving arcs, each one wider and more urgent than the last as if whatever unseen force was guiding it was straining at some barrier and trying to reach Fern's handwritten letters.

124

'Okay,' said Fern, talking now to her housemates rather than the glass. 'Very slowly, very carefully, take your fingers away.' She lifted her own finger clear as she spoke.

Without comment, John and Mike obeyed.

Without pausing, the glass continued to sweep over the table.

'My God . . .' Mike said under his breath.

'I don't like this,' said John in a small and uncomfortable tone that Fern had never before heard issue from his mouth.

'It's all right,' she whispered soothingly, 'just stay still.'

The glass, at the apex of one of its swings, finally reached a letter. It paused there for a second and then swept back across the table.

'T,' Fern said aloud, watching excitedly as the glass found a second letter, 'H.'

Now that it had started, the glass's speed became astonishing. It fairly flew over the table, pausing only briefly at letter after letter. Fern's voice accompanied it.

'E . . . Y . . . R . . . E . . . L . . . I . . .'

'They . . . relish?' said John. 'They relinquish?'

'S . . .' said Fern, an edge in her voice to tell him to be quiet.

'They realize?' Mike suggested.

'Realize what?' said John. 'That they can't spell?'

'Quiet!' Fern hissed. 'T . . . E . . . N . . . I . . .'

'It's not *they*, it's *they're*!' Mike said, hushed but urgent.

'N . . . G . . .'

The glass jetted back into the centre of the table and began again simply to move in small circles, its message completed.

'*They're listening*,' said John. And he wasn't very happy about it.

'Who's listening?' said Mike. 'And who's telling us about it?'

Fern looked at him and shrugged. She didn't know the answer to either question and for the first time since the session began she felt a tiny twitch of anxiety in the pit of her stomach. Whatever the message referred to, it clearly struck some kind of warning note. She remembered Avis telling her about the other voices, the voices Fern hadn't heard but which had issued from her unconscious mouth. If they could have voices, they could have ears. And they could want their business kept strictly to themselves. Fern

125

suddenly began to wonder if this little game had been such a good idea after all.

Suddenly, the flame on the black candle flared wildly, jetting upwards an impossible six inches or so.

'Shit!' Mike shouted, startled, as, simultaneous with the flame's eruption, the glass began hurtling itself furiously around the table again, crashing into position by one letter after another. It oscillated back and forth between six of them, spelling out its new message again and again.

*getout getout getout getout getout*

'Oh fuck,' John squealed, throwing himself backward from the table and lurching awkwardly to his feet, his chair falling to the floor behind him.

'Can we make it stop?' Mike shouted at Fern.

Whether they could or not, something else did. The glass was suddenly lifted clear of the table and flung violently against the far wall, where it shattered in the darkness. At the same time, the sound coming from the speakers mutated, shifting jarringly from waltz-time piano chords to a deafening and bone-chilling shriek, something that was at once unknown but, on some cellular level, down deep in genetic memory, was hideously and deeply familiar, a massively magnified sound of animal fury like a snort or whinny from the flared nostrils of some giant beast forgotten by history. And behind it, growing in volume as if rapidly approaching the reality of the room from whatever forest of the fantastic in which it had started, was the galloping thunder of the creature's hooves.

Fern and Mike were already scrambling to their feet, ready to join John in his eagerness to flee the room, when the black candle shivered upwards and outwards in a tremor of becoming.

Fern screamed and John sobbed in terror as the impossible insisted on happening. And on happening fast. The candle swelled to ten times its original size in less than a second, its wax body oozing and rippling out into new dimensions and its flame blooming into a foot-high fire already frighteningly close to the ceiling.

The wax, as if acknowledging the new fury of the flame atop it, began to melt even as it continued to grow, falling away in streaming rivulets from some central shape that was emerging from its ruin and eager to be born. The transforming mass was already taller than a man as the animal sounds suddenly shifted in focus, no longer seeming to come from the stereo speakers but instead from right there on the table as the transmutation completed itself.

Mike whimpered in horror, falling to his knees in weakening shock. John, his run interrupted by a paralysingly literal fascination, was flattened against a wall, his hands and his back pressed against it for support. Fern thought he was trying to say something and then realized that the twitching movements she saw his mouth making were merely some spastic and unwilled reaction to what he was seeing. She looked back to the place on which his bulging terrified eyes were fixed.

The table, its legs long buckled beneath the weight of the thing that had come to them, was a crushed heap on the floor and had been kicked aside. Taking its place in the centre of the room was something else entirely.

Lit by the glow of its impossible mane of fire, reared on its hind legs and kicking its front legs furiously in the air, the great black unicorn was claiming its new territory, jerking its mighty head up and down as if practising angles of attack for the two-foot-long black ivory horn which jutted from its brow above and between the glittering rage of its ancient blood-red eyes.

# 15

'Take my advice. Nice girl like you? Shouldn't be living here.'

Well, you're just *full* of opinions, aren't you? Avis thought, staring pointedly and silently out of the side window of the taxi as the cabbie – short, stout, stupid woolly hat – went on to enumerate various true-crime stories that he (or the friend-of-a-friend-of-a-friend) had witnessed in this neighbourhood. Enough already, she said to herself as she glanced at her watch. Six o'clock. God, was that all? She felt like she'd been listening to this windbag for hours but apparently it was only twenty minutes from the time he'd picked her up outside the sandwich shop to which she'd gone after leaving the library. She didn't think he'd stopped talking since. She'd already suffered his views on politics, television, and the pointlessness of space exploration all the way down 7th Avenue – with all of which she'd disagreed, to all of which she'd said nothing other than an occasional *uh-huh* or *really* – and she certainly had no need of him telling her about the dangers of the area in which she was stupid enough to live while he was in the process of being stupid enough to drive her right through it. She wondered how he'd react if she told him – provided of course that she could get him to shut up for longer than two seconds – that she knew just what he meant and, by the way, did he know that along with the muggers, junkies, hookers, gangsters, and scum-without-portfolio that he was talking about there was a whole new breed of menace – psychopathic vigilantes in posh suits who stepped out of the long-trashed pages of sixty-year-old pulp fiction with the express purpose of giving nice girls like her a really fucking hard time.

This pleasant imaginary one-upmanship allowed her to blank most of what he was whittering on about until, with a whole new and far from welcome *Do I make my point?* tone, she heard him say, 'See what I mean?' as the taxi pulled to a stop outside her front door.

'What the hell . . . ?' Avis said as she scrambled to get out of the back of the cab. She stood on the sidewalk, not even noticing as she slammed the taxi door closed behind her, staring in disbelief and an embryonic sickness-of-heart at her wide-open front door and at the uniformed cop standing beside it with a walkie-talkie in his hand and an interested look on his face.

Only when the honking of the cab's horn drew her attention to the fact that she still had to pay the guy did she look around the street and register the two patrol cars pulled up further down the kerb. She didn't like this. She didn't like this at all. Without looking, she fumbled in her purse and shoved a bill through the cabbie's open window into his outstretched hand. She had no idea what the bill was – could've been a single, could've been a hundred – but it must have been acceptable, including tip, because he drove off without another word. Had she had the mental space to spare, she might have been glad at this evidence that at least some things could button his lip for him but she wasn't thinking about that. She wasn't thinking about anything other than her growing certainty that something terrible had happened.

She didn't move as the taxi pulled away. She didn't want to. She didn't want time to carry on. Perhaps if she didn't move, if she didn't walk up to the cop by the door, if she didn't hear what he had to say, if she didn't walk into the house, then none of it need be true. As long as she remained exactly where she was then none of it need have happened yet. Not really. Not as long as she didn't move.

But the choice wasn't hers. Time – in the person of the cop – insisted.

'Miss?' the cop said. 'Can I help you?'

Can I help you? *Can I help you?* She remembered Mike saying that just two nights ago in the kitchen. Mike. John. Fern. Oh God.

Pushed forward by concern, she headed straight for the door, not even answering the cop, not even looking at him. He grabbed her arm as she walked past him, stopping her from going in.

'Miss? Miss!' he said, demanding her attention.

She turned to look at him.

'What happened?' she asked simply.

'Do you live here?' he asked in return.

'Yes,' she said. 'What happened? Why are you here?'

'Hold on a moment,' he said, looking at her with . . . what? Caution? Sympathy? Suspicion? He brought the walkie-talkie up to his face and hit a button. A distorted voice barked out an unintelligible question at him.

'Young woman out here,' he said into his machine, 'another resident, apparently.' Another burst of scratchy electronic babble came back in reply. Avis couldn't make out a single word but the cop – a young man, Avis finally found time to notice, younger possibly than her – must have been used to it because he clicked the walkie-talkie off and nodded at her.

'All right, miss,' he said, 'go on in. Detective Gerani will meet you there.'

When she tried to remember things later, Avis found that she had no memory of moving through the house. As far as she could recall, she went straight from hearing Gerani's name on the street outside to falling, faint with shock, into his arms in what used to be her living room and was now the site of the atrocity.

'Easy, easy,' he said, catching her and holding her – more with an almost-annoyed pragmatism than with a comforting concern – and shouted across the room to another uniformed cop to bring her a chair and some water.

Moments later, sitting and sipping, Avis looked up at Gerani – a fifty-year-old plain-clothes in a suit that was certainly plain and was also getting to be too small – and repeated the question she'd asked the cop outside.

'What happened?' she said. Odd – she hadn't realized she was weeping till she heard the sobs in her voice.

'Kind of speaks for itself, doesn't it?' he replied, his voice neither kind nor cruel but simply flat and professional.

It did. The room was a charnel house – blood splashed on the walls and floor in huge elaborate washes as if some housepainter just out of Bedlam had been interrupted in his perverse take on redecoration and left his work unfinished. There were three zippered bodybags on the floor along with a destroyed card-table. A police photographer was taking pictures of a small waxy mass that sat in the middle of the carpet as if a candle had burnt out there.

'You live here?' Gerani asked after he'd watched Avis take in the sights. She looked at him and nodded.

'And your name would be . . . ?' he asked.

She had to swallow before she could make her mouth form words. 'Avis,' she said, 'Avis Llewellen.'

She noticed a look pass between Gerani and the uniformed cop who had brought her the water. It was carefully and professionally non-expressive but they clearly both reacted to the name as if for some reason it was familiar to them.

'Where've you been this afternoon?' Gerani asked, his voice perfect in its neutrality.

'The library,' Avis replied, her mind finally starting to move beyond the merciful numbness caused by the enormity of what she was seeing to a clear assumption about who was responsible for the fact that she was seeing it. 'Did you get him? Was he still here?'

'Was who here?' Gerani asked.

'The Blue Valentine,' she said.

'The what?'

'The killer.'

'Whoa. Wait a minute,' Gerani made a waving signal with his hand and the other cop pulled out a notebook and a pencil. 'What did you say his name was?'

'The Blue Valentine. That's what he called himself. He . . .'

Her voice broke off as a fresh and devastating wave of horrified realization swept through her. Fern, Mike, and John were *dead*. Dead. Lying there cold and lifeless in the middle of the fucking room. Zipped up and finished. They'd never move again, never laugh or smile, never say her name, never do anything. A terrible choking cry of despair welled up from deep inside her and she lapsed into hysterical weeping.

Gerani gave her about five seconds grace during which, through the tears that clouded her vision, she saw him signal to the photographer and get handed a batch of what looked like Polaroids. He flicked through them rapidly, selected one, and put the rest away in his pocket.

'This Blue Valentine,' he said to her, 'can you describe him?'

She looked up at him, sniffing her way back to coherence. 'I can show you a picture,' she said and reached into her purse, ignoring or hardly noticing another of those bland but meaningful looks that was exchanged between Gerani and his colleague.

She pulled out a folded-over Xeroxed sheet. She remembered making the copy just before she left the library ninety minutes ago, back in pre-history when she was still treating this almost as a game. She handed it to Gerani.

He looked, without expression, at the copy of a copy of the old magazine cover, at the masked Valentine swinging to the rescue of the gangster-clutched cutie, and then held it up, without comment, for the other cop to see it too.

'Yeah. Well, that's very interesting, Ms Llewellen,' he said. 'Now let me show *you* something.'

He held out to her the Polaroid that he had separated earlier from the pack and she took it from him, bringing it close to her eyes in an attempt to make sense of the image. She wished she hadn't. What had at first looked like a wet and crumpled pile of old clothes thrown on top of an oil-spill resolved into a picture of Fern, her body twisted and gored, her blood spread out around her in a butterfly-wing shock of colour. Her hand was outstretched and rested on the carpet beneath some more of her blood. But the blood hadn't spilled in that spot. Fern had chosen to put it there, transferring it with her dying finger and scrawling a word with it. The word was AVIS.

Gerani let her look at it for a few seconds.

Then he read her her rights.

The room was very grey.

The walls were covered in two-foot-square tiles of a curious kind that might have been more at home on the floor, covered as they were in a dark-grey synthetic wool. The carpeting itself – a single fitted piece rather than tiles – was a lighter grey and the very big rectangular table that took up most of the room was topped with a vinyl or Formica that was a shade somewhere between those of the walls and the floor.

Avis sat in one chair on one side of the table and the woman who was talking to her sat opposite her in another. Avis had realized halfway through their conversation – which was being pointedly recorded on the tape of a fast-spinning open-reel recorder that sat between them on the table – that the woman was probably a psychiatrist rather than a detective. The detective – maybe Gerani, maybe somebody else – sat, Avis assumed, on the other side of the big smoked-glass panel that all but filled one of the smaller walls of the rectangular room.

There was an ashtray on the table immediately in front of Avis and she was astonished at quite how close she'd come to filling it in the relatively short time she'd been there. The psychiatrist didn't smoke and Avis was grateful for her tolerance. No pointed looks, no advice that those things'd kill her. Avis figured that when they got people in this room they usually had more pressing things on their mind than the longterm health of their visitors or the dangers to themselves of second-hand smoke.

'Why didn't you call the police?' the woman asked her. Avis had just got through telling her about the previous night and the Valentine's rescue of her from the junkie.

'I don't know,' Avis replied. 'It just didn't occur to me.' She knew that sounded lame and shrugged apologetically. The woman showed no response, simply moving on to her next question.

'Were you angry with your roommates when they didn't believe you?'

'Yes,' Avis replied truthfully, 'but not . . .'

'It's all right,' the woman interrupted, 'nobody likes not being believed. Would you say that you felt unacknowledged, that your feelings were being invalidated?'

Avis bit her tongue. She was impatient with psycho-babble at the best of times and it was particularly infuriating to her now that this woman was mentally ticking off some pre-digested notions of what may have been the emotional triggers of some imagined homicidal behaviour on Avis's part when her friends were dead and the real killer was somewhere out there, loose, impossible,

133

and dangerous. God knows, she was aware how crazy her story must sound but she hated the way it was being ignored completely other than as another indicator of her own unbalanced state.

'Yes,' she said, 'but I couldn't blame them. I know it sounded unbelievable. I know it sounds unbelievable to *you*. But I . . .'

The woman cut her off again, homing in once more on what to her was the interesting angle.

'Did you feel the need to somehow prove to them that what you were saying was true?'

'Oh for God's sake,' said Avis, finally snapping. 'What do you think? That I'd slaughter three friends of mine to convince them I'd seen a ghost?'

'You think that such behaviour would be wrong?'

'This is ridiculous!' Oh, wait a minute. She knew what that one was about. 'Yes,' she said in a calm and, she hoped, annoyingly patronizing tone, 'such behaviour would be wrong. I am perfectly aware of the difference between good and evil, between right and wrong. So there goes *my* plea of insanity, right?'

The woman said nothing. All right. Fuck it. Avis was through being a good girl.

'Except there won't *be* a plea. Because there won't be a *case*. Okay?' She turned in her seat to speak directly at the smoked-glass panel and to whatever unseen listeners stood beyond it. 'If you'd quit listening to me fence with Sigmund Freud's groupie here and go out and check what I fucking *said*, you'd find my movements accounted for. Joel Marsh. Librarian. Wanted me bad. And the sandwich shop. Big guy. Glasses. Tell him I'm the snippy little bitch who sent back the eggplant parmigiana because it tasted like somebody'd already eaten it once. Trust me, he'll remember.'

She turned back to look at the woman opposite her.

'You can turn the tape off now,' she said. 'I've said all I'm going to say.'

The holding cell made the grey room look like a palace.

It was deep in the bowels of the precinct house, which Avis thought was damn appropriate because it was full of shit – human shit that was ready to be expelled from the body of society, flushed down the toilet of the legal process, and swept into the sewers of various penal institutions. Avis's immediate problem was that one particularly unpleasant turd – a coke-habit-thin forty-year-old in an eighteen-year-old's skirt with eyes that could have been painted on her closed lids for all the life they contained – had decided that for the moment her function in this world was to give Avis grief.

The cell probably held thirty women and twenty-eight of them had found something fascinating on the far side of the cramped-to-begin-with space they all shared once the dye-job whore had started in on the jail-time virgin. Avis calculated it was about five in the morning by now and she figured that this trouble would have come down on her much earlier in the four hours that she'd been cooling her heels amongst her new peers if the bitch that was causing it hadn't been noisily sleeping off her last high for most of them.

It had started with a request for a cigarette – which Avis had granted. She realized now that that had probably been her mistake. In this woman's world, maybe handing over a smoke when asked was not a civil courtesy but an indicator of weakness, a sign of surrender or submission. And if you gave in once, you'd probably give in again. After pocketing the matches Avis had handed her to light the bummed cigarette, the woman (who called herself Trixie – and Avis hadn't even laughed, though she'd wondered how many other Trixies were in the cell scattered among the three or four Jades and the several Crystals) had then requested the whole pack. Avis had refused and so Trixie had started in on the insults and, when Avis simply looked away and refused to make further eye-contact, had started in on the threats.

She was still going strong with those now, though her tone had moved from a loud and vague aggression that was probably as fake as her nails to a quiet descriptive litany that bordered on the perversely salacious and was probably as real as the black shadows beneath her eyes. Avis was sitting next to someone who was getting off on the fear she was causing her to feel and who would doubtless get off even more when the pain her excited mouth was promising moved from the descriptive to the real, from the potential to the practical.

It made Avis sick. She was in a police station for fuck's sake –

so she assumed that if she were to scream for help it might actually *arrive*. But she hated the cops so much at the moment that she really didn't want to do that. Besides, this streetwise skag could probably make a halfway decent start in the fucking-up-Avis department before New York's finest could even get the cage open. And what pissed her off most was that the last few days had, if nothing else, shown her far darker terrors than anything this nasty little bitch could conjure up but that this knowledge was useless to her at the moment because, while her experiences may have taught her that there are worse things of which to be frightened than some brain-dead cocaine whore, it hadn't necessarily taught her any skills to use on those occasions when the immediate cause of fear *was* said brain-dead cocaine whore.

'I'll peel your face clean off, you cocksucking bitch,' Trixie whispered with an all-but-erotic energy. 'Your uptown friends won't even piss on you.'

Avis turned to look at her. The vicious little monster sounded like she was getting to the point where words would no longer be enough anyway and Avis just didn't have the fucking patience any more.

'Why don't you finger yourself while you talk?' she said. 'You'll come much quicker.'

What amazed Avis even more than the steadiness and the bored-with-it-all sound of her own voice was the fact that Trixie remained exactly where she was. Avis had expected to be suddenly fighting for her life or at least her features but that didn't happen. Trixie didn't leap on her, nails flying and secret razorblade drawn from whatever hiding places people like her used. Trixie didn't throw a punch. Trixie didn't launch a kick. Trixie didn't do anything. Trixie didn't even speak. Trixie just sat there and continued to look at her.

Avis almost gave way to an expressed astonishment that would have broken the moment but then she read, in the sudden doubt in Trixie's eyes and the sullen silence of Trixie's mouth, what her own face must look like and was all at once aware of the clenched-teeth drawn-lips tightness of her mouth and the impenetrable coldness of her eyes. She realized too that her entire body was trembling – not, unbelievably, from fear, but from fury. It appeared that she had after all learned a skill from everything that had happened to her in the last few days – the skill of harbouring an anger so deep that, once roused, it couldn't quit and the further skill of conveying that fact with a glance, the ability to look deep into the eyes of your enemy and tell it wordlessly that, win or lose, you would hurt it as much as you possibly could and that somebody would have to kill you before you'd stop.

'Listen to me, you loathsome old whore,' she said, her voice a stiletto of intent and sincerity, 'if you're going to do something, then do it. Otherwise, fuck off.'

Trixie chose to fuck off. She stood and moved over to join another group of women and, although she kept snarling insults back over her shoulder, her movement away from Avis spoke louder than her words and Avis let it go. It was over, she realized, and realized further that it was over because she had chosen to make it so. She liked that. She liked too the fact that she was left completely alone for the two further hours it took before a female police officer came to let her out of the cell.

Back upstairs, she had a brief conversation with Gerani. He was unapologetic but polite in his acknowledgement that everything Avis had claimed she'd been doing the previous afternoon had eventually checked out. They'd called Joel Marsh late yesterday but he hadn't checked his messages till this morning – at which point he'd immediately called back to provide one half of her alibi. And the guy in the sandwich shop did indeed remember the customer who'd complained about his eggplant.

'So it looks like we've got a psycho running round loose,' he said after his summary – which was as close, Avis figured, as he was going to get to a you-were-right-and-we-were-wrong. But they were still wrong. She said nothing in immediate reply to him but her mind was racing. She could insist on her certainty that whatever was responsible for the deaths was stranger than a common or garden psychopath but she held her tongue. Just because they now believed her innocent of murder didn't mean they were ready to believe she wasn't out of her mind. She knew that however much she tried to convince them, however much she might actually *succeed* in convincing them of what she believed, police minds were incapable of acting on the kind of information she would give. It wasn't a question of their individual abilities to believe in the impossible – though she doubted frankly that a mind that chose a profession which dealt in numbing detail every day with the cold specifics of crime and punishment and used as its primary tools reason and hard evidence was necessarily primed for the kind of investigation of the esoteric that would be required – but more that they were part of a system and that that system simply couldn't function around such information. It would be nothing more than a wrench thrown in the machine. Fine. It didn't matter. Let them look for the thing in the blue suit under whatever terms they wanted. If they found him, good – either she *was* out of her mind and a jail cell would in fact hold the human he proved merely to be or they would see for themselves that they had captured something quite different from what they were expecting.

'I can give you a description,' she said eventually. 'He really does look like the guy from the book.'

'You already gave us a description,' Gerani said. 'We've got it on tape.'

'Yeah? I didn't remember.'

'Well, it's been a long day for you. A tough one, too.' For the first time, his tone softened and his eyes let through a certain sympathy. Avis didn't suddenly start assuming they'd be getting drunk and eating peanuts together any time soon but she was grateful for this small indication of fellow-feeling.

'Will I have to . . . will you need me to . . . ?'

She didn't want to say it. He helped her out.

'Identify the bodies? Yeah, maybe. We're not sure about relatives yet.'

He saw how much this bothered her. 'It won't be too bad,' he said, as kindly as he could. 'Their faces weren't marked. That's all you'd need to see.'

'What did he do to them?' she asked, her voice as small as her desire to know.

'Stabbed,' he said. 'Or skewered, more like.' Seeing her flinch at that, he slipped into a clinical tone that was more merciful. 'Some big, heavy pointed object. Not a knife, something round –

138

like a horn or a tusk or something. We didn't find the weapon. Was there anything like that in the house that he could have used?'

Avis shook her head, pale with the horror of what had been visited upon her friends.

'All right, listen,' he said, 'that's enough for today.' He held out a card from a small pile on his desk. 'That's my number. Why don't you check into a hotel and give us a call so that we know where to find you if we've got any more questions. Okay?'

Avis took the card and nodded.

'That's it?' she said.

'That's it.'

He was already sorting through some other case files on his desk before Avis had reached the door. That really *was* it for him, she thought, as she let herself out into the crowded and busy reception room. Just one more case among many. To be dealt with in turn and by rote. To be remembered only in office hours, to be thought of less in terms of tragedy than of timecards. It was different for her. Very different. For her, that was far from it. It would be with her every waking – and probably every dreaming – moment from now until it was resolved.

As she made her way out of the precinct house into the grey Manhattan morning she realized that, if it was to be resolved at all, the resolution would be of her making. She was not only personally involved, she was personally responsible. And she didn't mean that what had happened was her fault – though God knows a substantial part of her felt that it *was*. She meant that she was taking responsibility. This case was as much hers as it was the police's. Let them chase *their* Blue Valentine – a psychopath running round in clothes he'd borrowed from an obsession – through their everyday world of fingerprints and house-to-house inquiry. She was going to take charge of the real investigation, the one that would take place in a world of imagined horrors made flesh, of ancient dreams set walking.

She flagged a cab and directed the driver uptown. She made herself think of Fern, of Mike and John. And she apologized to their spirits for having no tears for them. She was dry-eyed and level-headed and glad of it. One day she would cry for them again but as of now her grief was on hold. Her weeping would wait until whatever had crept into this world was sent back out of it and whatever door through which it had crept was closed for ever.

# PART TWO

## In the Ruins of
## the Kingdom

# 16

'But we'd keep the climax, of course?' the man behind the desk said.

He said it with the friendliness and casualness that was *de rigueur* for all orders in this town, but Larry Webster recognized it nonetheless for the order it was. He stared over the producer's shoulder and out of the big plate glass window to the view of the Hollywood hills beyond the other side of Sunset. He'd never heard of this guy and neither had his agent nor any of his friends but if he could find the rent for this fourth-floor suite in the DGA building then he had access to money. And if he had access to money then his orders were worth listening to. Larry took his eyes away from the falling hills and the insured-against-falling houses perched precipitously down their sides and fixed them back firmly on those of the other guy. He smiled sincerely. Time to agree enthusiastically. Time to peddle that we're-two-people-sharing-one-vision shit, along with its useful undercurrent of and-I'm-lucky-to-be-working-with-such-a-genius.

'Absolutely,' he said. 'Who in their right mind would change that? It's so . . . so . . .' he paused, knowing in fact precisely what he was going to say, but mugging the effect of a man making the effort to search for the elusive absolutely correct phrase, '. . . so *visual.*'

The producer beamed. Larry smirked internally. It always worked. Most producers knew jack-shit about anything but the one thing they'd usually managed to pick up was that, though story and dialogue were important, film was about *pictures*. They also learned, or were told soon enough and often enough by people who were supposed to know, that writers never got that. Were, in fact, incapable of understanding it. After all, their trade

143

was words. And God forbid the possibility that someone was capable of understanding two aspects of something.

'That's right,' the producer nodded enthusiastically.

Larry could almost hear the engine running. *Thank God I found a smart one*, the guy was thinking. Smart. Jesus Christ.

'You know,' the producer continued, 'it's very good to hear you say that. A lot of writers . . .'

Larry raised a politely interrupting hand. Time to bad-mouth the rest of the tribe.

'Hey, tell me about it. Film's about images. Worth a thousand words, right?'

'Right.'

Boy, they were getting on well.

Larry'd actually felt comfortable even from the start of his pitch. The guy'd listened attentively, smiling and nodding and making no interruptions. Larry'd done the usual stroking about the guy's perspicacity in finding the story and then carefully pointed out that it was essentially a one-act piece the way it worked now. That had gone over fine. No resistance. So he'd fed him some log-line single-sentence simplicities about ways in which a three-act structure could be overlaid without damaging the story's integrity and all he'd got back was a series of interjected fines and greats. Larry was beginning to think he was in the dream situation he'd heard about from other screenwriters but which he'd never really believed could happen. It was like the guy didn't really have any opinions about how the thing should be done. He just wanted it done and was prepared to pay for it. He was almost impatient with Larry's telling as if ready for him to shut up so that he could write out a cheque and wait for Larry's screenplay to be delivered. Maybe he – or maybe somebody for whom he was fronting – needed a legitimate way of getting rid of some money fast. Frankly, Larry didn't care. In the twenty-four hours since his agent had put him up for this meeting he'd found out that her carelessness in an earlier deal's small print (he was, after all, only a B-client for the agency so why should attention be paid to the minutiae of his contracts?) had cost him a guaranteed first-draft shot at a TV spin-off of a movie he'd written a couple of years back and therefore also cost him potential years of lucrative TV residuals. After some mutual screaming on the phone he'd fired her and felt good for three hours till a look at his bank statement and his overdue bills and several unreturned phone calls from other agents (his last on-screen credit had been two years ago so who remembered the courting they'd done of him back in the fifteen minutes that he'd been hot?) had filled him with an unusually large dose of the usual freelancer's panic. He wanted this job. And it was really beginning to look like he might be about to get it. He dragged the conversation back to the topic of the climax.

'You know, though, there's a couple of things we need to consider about the ending,' he said.

'And what would those be?' the producer asked.

'It's great,' Larry reassured him, 'visual. Strong. Some state-of-the-art CGI effects, it'll look *amazing*. But it's kind of self-contained. And it's kind of bleak.'

The producer just looked at him. Shit. Had he lost ground?

'I *love* bleak,' he hastily back-pedalled. 'But it's really the self-contained thing. If we're going bleak, let's go *globally* bleak, you know what I mean? Open up the end of the picture so that there's a sense that what we've just seen happen is only the beginning. Target the audience. Global threat. You know, like *Body Snatchers* – *You're next! You're next!* kind of thing. See what I'm saying?'

The producer beamed. Phew. Good save.

'You're exactly right,' the producer said, enthusiasm back in his voice and stronger than ever. 'Exactly right. Global threat. An open-ended picture. Good. Very good.'

'Great,' Larry said in a talking-frankly-with-another-seasoned-professional tone. 'You know, I only mentioned the bleakness because – you know how it is – you and I might be right there with it but I always worry about those studio guys.'

'There'll be no studio guys. I'm making this picture.'

Larry suddenly felt a little nervous. This was either very good or very bad. 'What do you mean?' he asked.

'I mean I'm making this picture. Or, more accurately, I'm paying for it. I hire you. I hire crew. I hire a director. The picture gets made. Much simpler that way, don't you think?'

Okay. He was either crazy or very *very* rich. Oh, how Larry prayed it was the latter. That passing and casual *I hire you* had not been lost on him.

'Yes, I do,' he replied. 'But – forgive me, I have to ask so I know what angle to take on the script – what kind of budget are we talking about?'

The producer shrugged. 'Whatever it takes,' he said. 'Don't worry about that. Write it the best way you can. I'll look after everything else.'

He opened a drawer in his desk and suddenly there was a wad of bills in his hand. A wad of thousand-dollar bills.

'I understand from your representative that eighty thousand dollars is your quote for a first draft?'

Larry was in shock. 'Uh-huh,' was the best he could manage.

Eighty grand was his quote, that was true. But you never got it like this. You never got it all at once and you never got it in cash. There were negotiations, there were agents and lawyers, there were signature payments, commencement payments, completion payments, all of which served both to eat away at the sum involved and to amortize what was left over the several months projects could take and turn what always sounded like impressive money to non-industry friends into something approaching merely an average salary. But not this time. This time a guy was waving a bundle of cash in Larry's face and seemed ready to let him walk out of here with it.

'I'll be frank with you,' the producer said. 'I'm in a hurry to get this thing done. A single draft is all I'm after. If I give you the money now, can you get me the script in a week?'

A week was impossible. Out of the question. He'd have to generate fifteen pages a day. Who could do that?

The producer put the wad of notes down on Larry's side of the desk.

A week wasn't bad. It was an adaptation, after all, not an original. Eight hours' sleep and a single meal break and it was only a page an hour. Who couldn't do that?

'Sure I can,' he said and scooped up the wad as if that was the way he always did business.

As Larry placed the money in his pocket, the producer smiled, stood up, and held out his hand. The meeting was apparently over, their business apparently done. Larry got to his feet and took the proffered hand in a firm shake.

'Thanks for the faith,' he said, 'thanks for the opportunity.'

'No. Thank you,' the producer said, 'and congratulations. You've done more than take a job today. You've joined a winning team.'

Larry was well-versed in masking his contempt for the self-congratulatory pep talk crap in which most people who made pictures habitually indulged but only the solid weight of the bundled eighty grand in his jeans pocket kept his face straight when the producer, continuing to speak, crossed the line from par-for-the-industry hyperbole to self-deluding absurdity.

'We're not just making a picture,' the guy said, his eyes shining with the lunatic fervour of a televangelist, 'we're making history.'

Irma had brought flowers.

*Somebody* had to make the old man's room look nice, she thought, and God knows those doctors and the empty-headed young husband-hunters who played nurse during the day weren't going to do it.

She fluffed them out nicely in the vase on his bedside table. Beautiful. An explosion of colours: purples, yellows, reds, and whites all set off against the bright greens of their stalks and leaves, the bouquet brought the whole room to life. It wasn't just a question of decoration, either. She'd learned enough through her years of service to know that not all medicine comes in pills or syringes. Patients were people. And people needed more than drugs or scalpels to help them get better. They needed – their souls needed – things to make them feel it was worth getting better. They needed flowers. And friends.

'There you are,' she said to him, 'don't they look nice? Smell nice, too. I bet those perfumes are reaching you, aren't they? Makes a nice change from disinfectant, I'll bet.'

The old man didn't reply. Didn't even twitch an eyelid nerve in response. Poor old thing. Terrible to be frozen like that. Not dead, not alive, but somewhere in between. But Irma believed he'd be coming back even if the doctors didn't. And when he came back it would be flowers and kindness that brought him, not their charts and machines. Flowers and kindness and good news. Like the unexpected and head-spinning development of a week ago.

'That was an exciting day, wasn't it?' she asked him as she moved back across the room to her chair. 'Bet you needed the week just to calm down, am I right?'

148

She looked at him mock-accusingly once she'd settled herself. 'Fancy you keeping secrets from me,' she said. 'Who'd have known you were famous? You're too modest for your own good, that's your problem.'

Shaking her head at him, she dipped into her holdall and brought out the book she was reading. 'Now you just rest for a while,' she said, 'and we'll talk later.'

She hadn't got more than three pages in when there was a gentle knock at the closed door of their private room.

Irma looked up, surprised and not necessarily pleased. She glanced at her watch. It was only eight-thirty at night. It couldn't be that idiot security guard yet. It was usually at least midnight before he checked in. But who else could it be? It was half-an-hour since her shift started and any last little interruptions by the day-timers always happened within the first ten minutes of her getting here. Folding the corner of her page to mark her place, she put the book down and walked over to the door as a second knock, louder than the first, came from the other side of it. Hmm, Irma thought, Pushy too. She reached the door and opened it halfway, standing firmly in the gap she made so that whoever this was didn't get the idea they could just breeze into the room without her say-so.

She found herself looking at a small blonde person. Pretty, she supposed, if you liked that sort of thing.

'Yes?' she asked.

The blonde looked up at her and Irma could see her fighting the urge to peer round Irma's shoulders and check out the room.

'I hope I'm in the right place,' the visitor said. 'I'm here to see Norbert Read.'

Avis looked at the dried-out old battle-axe in the nurse's uniform blocking the door to the room and waited for an answer.

'Are you family?' the nurse said eventually, and Avis heard more in her voice than the suspicious caution of an appointed guardian. There was an underlay of astonishment there, and something more. Was it *disappointment*? What the hell was *that* about?

149

'No. No, I'm not,' Avis said. 'I just wanted to . . . it's really important that I see him. Could I come in?'

A new light went on in the nurse's eyes.

'Oh,' she said, as if filled with sudden understanding. 'Are you a *fan*?'

Jesus, lady, what planet are you from? Avis thought. A fan? Like there was anybody still alive who'd ever heard of the old geezer apart from Avis and Florence Nightingale here. But Avis wasn't dumb and she sure had no problem with lying. She'd seen and heard the change for the better in the nurse's manner as this absurd possibility had hit her so what the hell – if fandom was the car that would get her where she wanted to be then she was hitching a ride right now.

'Yes, I am,' she said, smiling at the older woman (who, you know, was probably not much more than forty when you looked closely and when her face relaxed) in what she hoped was a suitably humble and beseeching manner. 'I heard Mr Read was here and I just had to come by and tell him how much his work has meant to me.'

The nurse smiled. It took years off her. 'Well, that's very kind,' she said. 'I'm Irma Vanborough, Mr Read's personal nurse.'

Avis heard the pride in Irma's voice at this last bit and realized that in some (probably unconscious) fantasy she was more than his nurse, she was the great man's trusty executive assistant, part of whose job entailed screening potential visitors. Okay, Avis. Kiss that ass.

'Oh,' she said, impressed, 'it's so nice to meet you, Irma.' She put out her hand and turned up the heat on her smile. 'I'm Avis Llewellen.'

Her hand was taken by Irma and shaken firmly and her smile was returned. But the door wasn't opened any wider and Irma still wasn't budging.

'How's Mr Read doing?' Avis asked, knowing that pushiness was the wrong button for this broad. 'I was hoping I could ask him some questions about my favourite stories.'

Irma's face dropped into a mask of concern.

'Oh,' she said sadly, 'didn't they tell you at the desk?'

'Tell me what?' Avis asked, suddenly anxious.

150

Irma gave her another sympathetic look and then stood aside. 'All right, dear, come in.'

Dear. That was progress. Avis threw her some gratitude and then walked around her into the room and into disappointment. It was immediately clear that, even if he had any light to shed on the current activities of his long-ago creation, Read – still, silent, barely breathing, wired up to a plethora of machines – was in no position to strike a match.

'Oh no,' Avis said. 'Coma?'

Irma nodded sadly as she crossed the room to her patient. She paused to fluff up some flowers in a vase beside the bed and then stood there stroking his brow. That was a little weird. There was plainly no harm in the woman but Avis wasn't entirely sure she should be wandering around unattended.

'More than two weeks now,' Irma said.

Avis felt flattened and defeated. It had taken her nearly a week to track Read down. Joel Marsh from the library had been invaluable, giving her a crash course in the various means of using various records to locate somebody who was no longer listed in the phone book, but now all that research seemed wasted. The thrill of realization she had felt on remembering that, while there had been a year of birth, there had been no year of death in the encyclopaedia entry on Read had kept her excited and hopeful through the last few days – though she'd been of course far from sure that an eighty-four-year-old retiree would have anything useful to offer her – but now, even that slim hope was crushed. Read was, almost literally, a dead end.

She stared over at him and his neurotically attentive guardian and had no idea what to say. She had an irrational urge to shake his fragile octogenarian shoulders and scream her questions – unformed and imprecise as they might be – at him in some ridiculous belief that the importance of her needs and the urgency of their expression would do what fourteen days of expensive medical attention had failed to do and wake the poor old bastard up.

'What happened?' she asked Irma instead.

'A car crash,' Irma replied and then looked down at her silent charge. 'You never regained consciousness, did you? Poor old thing.'

'Do the doctors think there's any hope?' Avis said.

Irma made a contemptuous face. 'Doctors,' she said dismissively. 'There's always hope,' she added, clearly speaking not for the collective opinion of the medical profession but for herself, 'I've treated coma patients before. They need to know they're missed, that's all.'

Avis watched as Irma stroked the old man's brow again.

'Look,' she said to him in almost a private whisper, 'you've got another visitor. Her name's Avis. You'd like her, you old rascal. She's a pretty young thing. And she's come to tell you how much she likes your work. Isn't that nice?'

Avis blanked the pimping aspect of what Irma had to say. 'Does his family come by often?' she asked.

'He has no family,' Irma said sadly. 'No family, no friends. Nobody in the world. You know, the lawyer who pays his bills hasn't even been to see him. Not once.'

Avis was confused. 'But you called me *another* visitor,' she said. 'I don't understand.'

Irma's face lit up with pride and excitement. 'That's what's so wonderful,' she said. 'You know,' her voice dropped into a sharing-a-confidence tone, 'until a week ago, I didn't even know that Mr Read was a famous writer.'

Famous? Avis let it slide. Irma was on a roll.

'And then we got a visitor,' she continued, 'a very important man. From Hollywood. A producer. And he'd just bought the rights to one of Mr Read's stories! He's going to turn it into a movie!'

'He came here? Was Mr Read *talking*?'

'No, no. He came by just to see that Mr Read was being well taken care of. He seemed very concerned that he be looked after. He even offered money. That wasn't necessary, of course. But isn't that nice? Isn't it exciting?'

Avis supposed that it was. But it was also too damn much of a coincidence and she was getting a very strange feeling about it.

'What was his name?' she asked.

'You know, dear, that's the strange thing,' Irma replied, 'he must have told me but I can't recall it.'

I bet he didn't, thought Avis, I bet he just charmed his way in here, sized you up in a second, pressed all the right buttons, and got you so hot and bothered you didn't even think to ask.

'What did he look like?' she said, knowing that that would seem like a weird question but hoping that Irma's enthusiasm would keep her from noticing. It did. She went straight into it.

'He was *very* handsome,' she said.

Oh God. That was enough. Avis all but tuned out after those first words. As soon as Irma said them, Avis knew exactly what had happened and precisely who had been standing in this room just a few days ahead of her.

Irma's mouth and memory were working overtime but Avis's eyes were fixed on the bed and on the frail figure of Norbert Read. Did he know? she wondered. Did he get some sense somewhere of what had been in the room with him? And did it feel familiar?

Odd phrases from Irma's approving and apparently never-ending litany broke through into her consciousness – *square-jawed, striking, should be on the other side of the cameras if you ask me* – but Avis was hardly listening. She was already wondering just what this new twist meant in the strange story in which she was caught up. She was wondering what this meant for Norbert Read. She was wondering what this meant for her. She was wondering what the hell Valentine Dyson was doing in Hollywood.

153

# 18

It was the end of the evening.

From the terrace in the garden of Steve Gruber's house atop the hills on Mulholland Drive, the slow purple explosion of the California sunset had given way to night and, below him, the immense vista of the San Fernando Valley was laid out before Gruber's eyes, its lights brighter, more numerous, and more densely packed than the stars that interrupted the black and cloudless sky above.

Fuck the stars, Gruber thought. The lights below were his heaven, a heaven whose rewards were more easily imagined and more readily realized than any vague promise of distant glory suggested by the lights above.

It hadn't always been that way. He remembered how, in college, after long drunken drives to the hills, it would be the stars, not the cities, that drew his eyes and filled his being with a plangent sense of metaphysical desire. But he'd learned. They had something he wanted, sure. But he couldn't name it and you couldn't buy something you couldn't name. There were no deals you could make, no contracts you could sign. Steve Gruber had grown up and the stars had grown cold and insignificant, their heat the concern of faraway alien worlds and their meaning the concern of priests, philosophers, and other losers.

He drained the last drops from his last glass of seventy-five-bucks-a-bottle Bordeaux and turned back from the edge of his terrace to walk back into his seven-dollars-a-square-inch house. The twenty-five-dollars-a-minute hooker had already left and Steve was already showered and ready for bed. Like the town in which he thrived, Steve was an early-to-bed and early-to-rise guy. He was up at five-thirty every morning and, Highway 101

154

traffic permitting, at his desk by eight to get any paperwork out of the way before the phone started ringing at nine. He'd have the phone in his ear until six-thirty. On a slow day he'd log maybe one hundred calls. He preferred the less-slow days because then he was too busy to be tempted to fill the space between real calls with any one of the thousand jerk-off calls that would normally be fielded by his assistant. Like the dick who'd called four times today about 'an investment opportunity' and whose fifth call Steve had allowed through to amuse himself by putting the no-track-record stiff in his place.

'Well, you've got some fucking balls. I'll give you that,' Steve had said when he'd finally understood that no, he hadn't heard wrong the first time, the jumped-up little fuck was basically asking Steve to give him – *give* him – a million dollars flat for an associate producer credit and ten per cent of eventual profit. No negative pick-up, no overseas rights. A credit and ten per cent of what would probably be fuck all. Well, balls he might have. A hope in hell, he didn't. Steve had told him, with a great deal of pleasure, that he could kiss his white ass. Two times.

'I'll call again tomorrow,' the guy had said, annoyingly unflustered by Steve's contempt. 'By then I think you may have had cause to reconsider your position.'

Steve had gone ballistic. 'Listen, you little prick,' he'd said, 'is that any kind of a threat? Because, if it is, I'll have you shot. You hear me? I'll have you fucking shot. I can do it. I know who to call.'

The blood had been pounding in his head so hard that he hadn't even heard the phone go dead halfway through his outburst. Steve's unresolved fury had been almost physically painful. He'd had to go out into the main office and fire an intern just to exorcise his rage and tonight's hooker had gone home with a big tip but with welts on her ass that would keep her out of work for maybe three days.

And it wasn't over. Steve was going to find out about this guy and crush him like a bug. It wasn't just personal. The business worked in certain ways and this guy seemed not to give two fucks. The lack of respect was appalling.

He tugged the huge sliding glass door along its track and shut

155

it behind him, clicking its lock into place and hitting the ARMED button on the home security console before turning in to his living room. His system was state-of-the-art. And it needed to be. Lot of freaks out there. Lot of have-nots wanting what he had. Lot of losers wanting his winnings. But he'd paid for the best and he knew that, within thirty seconds of a door or window even being *breathed* on after he'd retired for the night, there'd be a car on its way with armed men inside and sympathetic judges waiting the other side of a dead intruder.

So, given all this, it was particularly galling when Steve heard, coming from his kitchen, the unmistakable sound of one of his three hundred dollar designer dining chairs being slid back across his thousand dollar terracotta floor as if somebody was adjusting their position at his table.

The very unbelievability of somebody being able to get in should have allowed Steve to luxuriate in anger before fear took any kind of hold but it was surprising how quickly his puffed-up outrage gave way to that shrinking of the self that accompanies terror. There was somebody in his house who had not been invited and it was beyond question that therefore they meant him harm. Steve's toughness was of the kind that relied on litigation or second-hand muscle to back it up and he was suddenly in a situation where neither was immediately available. He felt frightened and small as he froze in place, holding his breath and waiting for another sound to give him any kind of clue as to what he might be facing.

For four long heartbeats there was nothing and then, finally, a different noise came from the kitchen, a sound that was odd enough to free Steve temporarily from his paralysis and send him – cautiously, quietly, and slowly – toward the open plan archway entrance at the far end of the living room. It was a sound he remembered from childhood and recognized from the homes of business associates crazy enough to keep pets: it was the sound of a dog lapping thirstily at a bowl of water. What the fuck was going on? Had one of his idiot part-time Mexican domestics or the stupid little whore he'd used an hour ago left a window open somewhere – a window through which a coyote or a stray dog had clambered into his house?

156

He was in no hurry to have some flea-bitten-at-best and rabid-at-worst creature take any defensive nips at him but his fear was smaller and more controllable than it had been and he walked through the elegantly arched hole in the dividing wall ready to show the animal who was boss. It was only in the second before his eyes gave him the impossible answer that he thought to ask himself the question – if what he was hearing was a dog of some kind quenching its thirst, then who exactly had filled its bowl?

It had filled it itself. That much was immediately obvious. The bowl was on the table, not the floor, but the creature's snout was no longer in it. It had straightened up as soon as Steve entered the room and now leapt to its feet, the chair flying away behind it, and turned to face him.

Steve's legs went absurdly weak. He staggered and all but fell. He was staring at a six-foot-tall figure in an evening suit. From the tip of the highly polished black shoes to the crisp edge of the starched white collar of the dress-shirt, it was a powerfully built man. From the thick dark-brown fur of the throat to the black-flesh tips of the erect ears, it was a massive German Shepherd.

Steve recognized it at once. It was – or had been – a dummy, a dressed and made-up model from the FX shop of one of his first movies, made back before he'd left that low-budget horror shit long behind him and moved on to the kind of classy picture with which he deserved to be associated. He'd claimed it from the boys at Image Animation to use as window-dressing for a Halloween party five years ago and since then it had been languishing in one of his closets.

But it wasn't languishing now. Now it was heading straight for him, its lips curled back from its dripping and pointed fangs in a furious snarl of territorial anger and its arms raised wide, human fingers spread, ready to grip and hold its prey beneath that terrible canine mouth. Its growl was deafening, unending, and terrifying.

Steve screamed. His brain knew what to do – turn and run and never stop running – but his body was slow and pathetic and he'd hardly moved an inch before the thing had seized him by the shoulders, lifted him effortlessly off his feet, and thrown him back to slam painfully against his kitchen wall. The breath was blasted

157

out of his body and he sank to the floor, slipping gracelessly forward to lie helpless on his back, gasping for air as the creature strode towards him again and stood over him. Steve began to cry, huge blubbering sobs belching from his throat and snot and tears running from his nose and eyes.

The creature's growl subsided. It was dog enough to recognize surrender in a weaker member of the pack. Steve, heart pounding like it would rip itself free of its arteries, saw, through tear-filmed eyes, the creature cock its head to the side and look inquisitively down at him.

Then it opened its fly and pissed all over him.

*Simultaneity.*

*While it was watching the human squirm beneath the scalding torrents of piss through the eyes of the lifeless thing it was inhabiting, the Companion was also looking at one of its fellows – still, like it, in angel-drag – in the Fields of Heaven.*

*'There's a phone on the wall above him,' it said. 'I think he'll be ready to talk business.'*

*The other Companion saw its colleague's satisfied grin – faces had their uses – and, it too being in simultaneity, also saw its own borrowed hands moving to a phone in an office two or three miles from the Gruber house.*

The creature, with the confidence of one who knows no threat is coming from a particular quarter, turned its back on Steve and walked back to the table.

Suddenly, the phone rang, startling and deafening in what had been, save for Steve's diminishing sobs and the sound of the creature's shoes, a silence.

Steve's head jerked up at the sound, his eyes going plaintively to the phone, not daring to get up and answer it. He looked over to the creature, who was now seated back at the table, and, astonished, saw it shrug at him in a gesture of careless permission. Rising shakily to his feet, Steve scrambled gratefully to the phone and grabbed it from the wall.

'Hello?' he said, his voice tremulously pregnant with the desire to scream out what had happened to him and beg for help, and the fear of what the creature would do to him if he did.

'Mr Gruber,' said a voice Steve recognized from earlier in the day, 'watch your creature closely.'

What? He hadn't said anything. How did this –

'Look. Right now,' the voice said.

Beyond questioning, stunned and defeated, Steve looked over at his table. The creature's huge monstrous head swung towards him, its mouth parted in a canine parody of a human smile. For a second, Steve felt a fresh stab of fear but it turned quickly into a mix of confusion and relief as, before his eyes, life left the creature.

It was instantaneous and complete. Sitting clumsily and floppily at his table was an FX shop dummy so plainly inanimate, so utterly different from what it had been a moment ago, that Steve knew he'd never again be able to use the word *lifelike* when describing one of these technician's marvels. He knew the difference now. He'd been in the presence of life and now he wasn't. The difference was so marked, the contrast so complete, that if it weren't for the dampness of his clothes and the inescapable stink of the creature's urine, Steve would find it impossible to believe that what had happened had happened. The voice on the other end of the phone resumed.

'I'm sure you're a little shaken, Mr Gruber. I quite understand. There's no need to talk. I left details on your office voice-mail of how to get the money to me. I'll look forward to receiving it tomorrow. Good night to you.'

The phone went dead.

At the other end of the line, the man whom Avis would have recognized as Valentine Dyson looked at the phone he'd just hung up and smiled. It was good that Gruber had crumpled so easily. After all, the creature would have faded back into lifelessness in a few more moments anyway. Unlike the body he was occupying, access could not be maintained for more than minutes and specific control was difficult. Still, it had done its job.

He picked up a clipboard from the desk and put a check next to the neatly typed name of Steve Gruber. Gruber's name was the last on a list of twelve. All of the names had checks by them.

Avis had asked herself what the hell Dyson was doing in Hollywood. He was doing what any self-respecting producer does: he was raising money.

# 19

It was all right when she had stuff to do. Otherwise, the apartment bothered her.

It had been thoroughly cleaned, of course, and she'd stayed in a mid-priced Best Western for the first week after the killings but Avis wasn't rich and the sick pay (Gerani had got a police psychiatrist to vouch for her traumatized condition to personnel and she'd scored a month off at two-thirds salary) wouldn't cover the mortgage, let alone the expense of an additional place, so she'd had to move back in. Even so, there was no way she'd have spent a single night there if it wasn't that she knew now that Valentine Dyson had business elsewhere and was unlikely to be haunting the Bowery any time in the immediate future.

It was his business elsewhere, of course, that was giving her stuff to do so, in a perverse way, she supposed she should be grateful to him. This very afternoon, for instance, she might have been sitting here picturing her friends moving around the space they'd once shared with her if she wasn't busy getting annoyed at still being on hold.

'Hello?' she said again into the muzak-filled void of the phone. She knew no one could hear her but . . . well, but nothing, really. She knew no one could hear her so trying to remind them of her presence was pointless, nothing more than a Pavlovian response to holding a phone to her head. If you were on the phone, you spoke into it at intervals, no matter how pointless it was. Maybe part of her thought that if she kept piping up then the switchboard person at the other end of the line would somehow sense her voice even if she couldn't hear it. And maybe she was right – God knows she'd been right about odder things in the last two weeks – because suddenly the sickening music box version of the love theme from *The Towering Inferno* or whatever piece of inane crap it was disappeared and the line came back to life.

'Susman, Caleph and Tyne,' said a voice marginally less robotic than the music it had replaced, 'good afternoon.'

Avis groaned internally. This had happened twice already: the woman had put her on hold and then come back to her as if it was a brand new call.

'Yes,' she said, 'I'm still waiting for –'

'Can you hold please?' the voice interrupted her and before Avis could scream any objection the godawful music was back.

This was ridiculous. How did anybody ever speak to any of these guys? Was there a *code* or something? Did they issue a PIN number to their A-list clients which you were meant to spit out the second the phone was picked up?

She'd first called the day before yesterday and at least then she'd had what passed for a conversation – she'd asked for Roger Caleph and been told that he was out of the office all day. She'd even been asked for her number and she'd left it. But there'd been no returned call all day yesterday and now she was stuck playing this one-sided game of tag with the office operator. She'd got Caleph's name and number from Irma, Norbert Read's nurse, and if the silly old bag had had half a memory Avis wouldn't perhaps have needed to be strung along like this. All she wanted to know was the name of the story for which Dyson had bought the film rights but Irma – after first reverting to her initial snot-tiness and playing who-the-fuck-wants-to-know for a couple of minutes – had eventually admitted that she couldn't remember. If she hadn't bitched earlier in Avis's visit about Read's lawyer never visiting him, Avis might have been as stalled as she'd first felt on seeing Read in his comatose state. But Caleph's name and, more importantly, the name of his firm had for some reason – probably resentment – stuck in what passed for Irma's memory and after a couple more minutes of ring-kissing Avis had pried the information from her. She wondered if – ooh, hold on. Signs of life.

'Susman, Caleph, and Tyne. Thanks for holding.'

'Roger Caleph, please. I've been holding five minutes now.'

'Oh, I'm sorry.' Yeah. She sounded it. 'Here you go.'

A click of transference and then another voice.

'Roger Caleph's office.'

'Mister Caleph, please.'

'Who's calling?'

'Avis Llewellen.'

'Will he know what this is concerning?'

'Tell him it's about Norbert Read.'

'Hold a moment.'

At least there was no music this time. Avis decided she'd count to twenty-one and that would be it. He made it by thirteen and, in an unconscious courtesy, wasted no more of Avis's time on introductions.

'So how's my favourite client?' he said. The voice was brisk and friendly but the accent would have sounded more suitable describing how easily legs can break if payments aren't made.

'Still in a coma,' Avis replied, deciding that, despite Caleph's apparent lack of solemnity, a witty answer was not exactly appropriate.

'Yeah. It's a terrible thing. What can I do for you?'

Avis Llewellen, girl detective, had her cover story ready. 'I'm a freelance journalist,' she said, 'and one of my markets is *Writer's Digest*.'

'Uh-huh.'

Wow. The usual non-committal lawyerishness but no accusation of lying. Cool.

'I have a friend who works at the hospital and I heard about Mr Read's film sale.'

'Uh-huh.'

'I figured there was a nice piece there about . . . you know, good things coming to those who wait or whatever. I mean, it's a long time since he was an active writer so this must have been quite a surprise.'

'I'll say. I never represented Norbert as a writer. Hell, I wasn't born when he quit. It's the first deal I had to do for him with regards to his stories. So, if you're looking for background and stuff, I don't think I can be much help to you.'

'Oh, no. No, that's fine. I've got all my research material,' Avis

163

said, her fingers patting the Xeroxed sheets of the article from Hoppenstand's encyclopaedia that she'd gone back to the library to get. 'It's a really simple question. My friend didn't know what story it was that this producer bought, so I was hoping you could tell me.'

Caleph laughed. 'Oh, sure,' he said, 'it was called "Big Thunder".'

That rang a bell. Avis scanned the Xeroxes quickly.

'Oh,' she said, finding the reference, 'now has that story been reprinted since it was in *Bedside Creeps* in 1946?'

'Wow. You *do* do your research. I –' he broke off for half a second and, when he resumed, his voice was markedly different – aggressive, suspicious and fast. 'Is this a copyright check? All rights reverted to Norbert when the magazines folded. I got paperwork to prove it. And, by the way, misrepresentation on the phone is a criminal offence.'

Avis leapt in the first moment he took a breath.

'No, no,' she assured him, 'I couldn't care less about that. It's not my business. I'm just fascinated why anybody would buy such an old and – forgive me – obscure story.'

Caleph calmed down. 'Okay. I'm sorry,' he said. 'And no, you're quite right, the story's never been reprinted. None of them have. Like I said, first deal I'd done that didn't involve stock transfers or the price of crude.'

'So how did the producer know about the story? Where did he read it?'

'Christ, I don't know,' Caleph said, 'they read all the time, don't they? Or have people read for them.'

'But this one's been out of print for decades.'

She could almost see him raise his arms in a shrug.

'You got me,' he said, 'and I'm sure your readers will be fascinated by it all. But all I know is that Norbert's made no money from writing for half a century – his career's as dormant as the old guy himself's been for the last three weeks – and then I get a phone call. So – you tell me. Do I look a gift horse in the mouth or do I do the deal for him? I do the deal, right?'

'Right.'

'Right. Now, listen sweetheart, I wish you the best of luck and

164

I'm glad I could help but my phone's lighting up like a landing strip so, if you'll excuse me . . .'

'Sure, sure,' said Avis. 'And thanks very much.'

'No problem. Bye.'

The phone went dead and Avis dropped it back in the cradle. She picked up the Xeroxed article and looked at it again in an unfocused manner as she thought about the phone call. She was excited. Caleph had done more than give her the name of the story. He'd confirmed the relative inaccessibility of that or any of Norbert Read's work and, therefore had, in effect, given her a second confirming description of the man who'd bought it – because, she was convinced, it had been bought without being read. It had been bought by somebody who had no need to read it. Somebody who already knew the story because it had been written by his own creator.

Avis Llewellen, girl detective, was doing all right. Subterfuge, investigation, deduction. She had them all down pat. Of course, she still had no clear idea of what exactly it was that she was investigating but, hey, give her a chance. She was new at this. And what counted was that she had her next clue. *Big Thunder.* She didn't know why it was important but it was clear that it was. And, like all good detectives, she had a contact. She was sure Joel Marsh would be thrilled to hear her voice again.

# 20

It cost her eighty-five dollars. Avis had never paid that much for a book in her life. Didn't know you *could* pay that much for a book. Her trip to the Mystery and Imagination Bookstore in the Village, though, had taught her that you could actually pay a lot more. Within a locked glass cabinet near the front of the store she'd seen a copy of *The Thin Man* as she was about to write out her cheque (like she'd brought that kind of money in cash. Who knew?) and because she'd always liked the movie and because this edition of the book looked cute – all old-fashioned lettering and silly studied posing by Dashiell Hammett (it had to be the author himself, she'd assumed – if you were hiring a model for a cover shot you'd presumably hire somebody better looking) – she'd asked how much it cost, figuring she'd throw it in with the copy of *Bedside Creeps*. She'd almost turned white when the nervous-mannered-but-friendly woman behind the counter had quoted a four-figure sum at her, assuring her that it was a genuine first edition, not a later printing disguised in an earlier dust jacket. Avis had passed on that one and counted herself lucky that some vagary of rarity or collectibility had not added a zero or two to the price of the book she *was* buying.

She was sitting back home now, holding her purchase in her hands. The book smelled funny, smelled *old*. The pages were yellowed and curiously brittle and Avis felt nervous turning them. On the title page she saw a notice which said that the book had been produced in keeping with wartime restrictions on paper. What the hell kind of sense did that make? She could understand, if there was a paper shortage, people using *less* paper by printing the words smaller but what was the point of using *crap* paper and printing the words normal size? This stuff felt not only as if it might come away page by page from the spine if she flipped through too vigorously but as if the individual pages could crumble between her thumb and fingers if she gripped them too tightly. She was also more than mildly convinced that her itchy eyes and her constantly-at-the-point-of-sneezing-but-not-actually-doing-it nose were a consequence of whatever hibernating germs and dust mites she had liberated by opening this thing. Eighty-five dollars. Jesus Christ.

She scanned down the contents page to find the Norbert Read story, checking out the titles and the other authors' names as she did so in case there was anything or anybody she might actually have *heard* of. There wasn't. But there was 'Big Thunder', on page 162 – which was kind of a relief because, she realized, she'd failed to check in the store that the book she was buying actually contained the story in which she was interested. Avis Llewellen, smart shopper. Ralph Nader would be very proud.

She curled her legs up underneath her, settled back comfortably in the corner of the sofa, turned – carefully – to page 162 and started to read 'Big Thunder' by Norbert Read.


A WELCOME cooling breeze blew over Mickey Calhoun as he settled comfortably against the small rock supporting his shoulders and patted his satisfied stomach, legs stretched out in front of him. The picnic was going well, he thought. That business with the crazy Indian had seemed to pass from everybody's mind and the whole town had spent a happy midsummer afternoon. Steaks and ale and homemade pastries. Lemonade for the children. Waltzes and polkas played for dancing by Sherman McCoy and his high school brass band. And pretty girls made warm and glowing by the sun. Yes, things were good for the small Kansas community of Big Thunder that August day in 1912.

Mickey, a big broad Irishman of some thirty years with a mane of thick red hair, looked down from his vantage point on the high green plain to the nest of wooden buildings that was the town. Deserted by its inhabitants for this town picnic, it seemed peaceful and untroubled as if it too were enjoying a moment of relaxation, a respite from the everyday matters of business and work and school.

Main Street looked like a child's model to him, a small neat set of painted wooden structures lined up on either side of the wide sandy thoroughfare. Mayor Jenkins was planning to bring in men to lay tarmac over the ground come the fall and soon, Mickey supposed, automobiles would arrive to glide up and down the blacktop where once horses trotted. His thoughts turned to the future of the town and what other changes history might bring and then, swinging the other way, replayed for him the immediate past and he remembered the town meeting of a week ago when the plans for the picnic had been discussed and suddenly interrupted by the raised voice of Billy Twofeathers . . .

'It must not happen!'

The shout from the back of the room startled everyone and heads turned to look at the standing figure of Billy Twofeathers, the Indian who helped out in the stables of Matthew Potter's saloon. Murmurs of disapproval were silenced by the banging of Mayor Jenkins's gavel on the lectern behind which he was standing on the platform at the front of the town hall.

'Now, Billy,' the Mayor said, 'what are you doing in here?'

The Indian had let himself in through the doors of the Town Hall and had obviously been listening as the Town discussed the arrangements for the forthcoming Saturday picnic. Now he shouted back to the Mayor across the length of the room.

'There must be no dancing on the hill!' he cried. 'And no eating of meat!'

Angry mutterings were renewed among the fifty or so seated people and more than one menacing look was directed at the Redskin. Tommy Randel caught Mickey Calhoun's eye and a silent agreement passed between them. If necessary, Mickey and the big ex-soldier would handle this – a swift well-placed kick to the horse-riding part of the Indian's anatomy would soon restore the meeting to order!

Mayor Jenkins again banged his gavel and the townsfolk's faces turned expectantly to him.

'Well now, Billy,' he said, smiling, 'it wouldn't be much of a picnic, would it?'

Some appreciative laughter from the assembled multitude broke the angry mood in the room but the Mayor's answer failed to placate the excited Indian.

'The hill is sacred!' he cried. 'The spirits of our ancestors must not be disturbed!'

More murmuring followed this declaration, this time of the confused variety rather than the angry. And then old Doc Woodbridge rose to his feet, waving his hand for the Mayor's attention.

'Speak up, Doc,' said the Mayor.

'Seems as how I recollect some old stories from when this here town was just a collection of tents and expectations,' mused the kindly-faced old medical practitioner, 'and I reckon what Billy here is talking about is that a lot of his forefathers might be buried up on that there hill. Fact, I recall that the very name of our town came from one of his people's stories. Ain't that right, Billy?'

The Redskin nodded enthusiastically.

'Big Thunder!' he shouted. 'This is the place of Big Thunder!'

'So the h— what?' called a voice from the crowd, to a few low chuckles from the men and one or two shocked and disapproving glances from the women. Once again, the Mayor had to bang his gavel to calm everyone down and get them all looking in his direction. Having got everyone's attention, he paused and looked hard at Billy with that stern magisterial eye that had had many a Friday night drunk or Saturday night brawler quaking in their boots. For, as well as being the elected Mayor of Big Thunder, Rudyard H. Jenkins was also its appointed Judge.

'I wouldn't expect you to understand this, Billy,' he said, his voice calm but firm and brooking no nonsense, 'but we got here what we call a democracy.'

His gaze widened to take in all of the people as he continued. 'What say we put it to a vote?'

Well, that was about it. Once the Judge proposed a simple motion and the room was filled with deafening, *Ayes!*, the defeated Redskin turned and left without a single further word. He could probably still hear the ringing cheers of the crowd from several hundred yards down the street.

Mickey came back to the present, smiling both at the memory and at the pleasantness of the day and the sweet drowsiness that was

169

starting to creep over him as the late-afternoon sun continued to warm his well-fed body. The two or three pitchers of beer he'd swallowed were certainly contributing to his sense of sleepy well-being too!

He looked around him. Seemed like everybody else was feeling the same way he did. Two or three old-timers were already full asleep, blissfully ignorant of their loud snores that were reverberating in the air. Several kids were curled up near their mothers, fighting sleep, their young excited eyes looking round for one more event, one more piece of fun before snoozing.

In fact, everybody was off their feet. Some, like Mickey, had found themselves small smooth rocks to act as pillows. Others were simply stretched out on picnic cloths that they were using as blankets. One or two were in the shade of trees, their heads propped up against the trunks. Mickey felt a great sense of wellbeing which he somehow knew was not just his alone. The entire population of the town was settling into a late afternoon siesta. The sun was warm. The breeze was cool. The air was sweet. And a calm and peaceful silence was settling over the green hill above Big Thunder.

Mickey shuffled his body, crossed his big powerful arms behind his head, took a deep relaxing breath which he let out slowly, and closed his eyes. Maybe forty winks wasn't a bad idea. A welcome velvety blackness swam up to meet him and he let himself fall into it. Within two minutes he was sound asleep.

'Ouch!'

Mickey sprang into sudden wakefulness at the sharp piercing pain in his upper leg.

'What the . . . ?' he growled, pulling himself instantly up into a half-sitting position, his legs still stretched out in front of him. The suddenness of his movement caused a bee to take flight from his leg – a bee that had stung him in his sleep.

Mickey swung his arm angrily at the buzzing insect to swat it but it was already flying away from him. Mickey rubbed at his leg, which was now throbbing painfully from where the winged creature had deposited its venom.

'D— !' he muttered beneath his breath and then glanced quickly around shamefacedly in case any of the women or children had heard his profanity.

It was unlikely that they had. With astonishment, Mickey saw that everyone was completely asleep. Not a single figure was standing or even sitting. Everybody was laid out, dead asleep. Old, young, and middle-aged, male and female – all were sleeping! More than a hundred people up there on that hill and not a single one awake!

Mickey felt a cold unease settle into the pit of his stomach. He wasn't sure why. After all, the sun was still shining, the air was still sweet. There was very little of threat or danger in the scene before him. The only sound was the ripple of the small late afternoon breeze through the grass. Nothing harmful in that, he thought – and then stopped himself. His anxiety worsening, Mickey realized that that tiny rustling was indeed the only sound he could hear. The only sound. There was no buzz of insects, no chatter of crickets, and there were no birds singing. The entire hill was devoid of the sounds of life!

Scrabbling into a more upright position, Mickey scanned the vista before him more thoroughly. It was when he saw the two horses tethered in the distance to a tree that he began to feel certain that something was deeply wrong. The leads from their reins stretched tight to the low branch around which they had been wrapped, the horses too were lying asleep and motionless – not even an unconscious flick of the tails to shoo away troublesome flies. Which meant there were no flies. Or at least no troublesome ones. No conscious ones.

A sudden thought hit him. A sudden *hope*, he might even have called it were it not that to name it as such would have implied an acknowledgement that he was in a situation where hope was necessary. The bee! He had been woken from his sleep by a bee! A bee which buzzed, flew, and stung was undeniably a bee that was awake. He glanced around . . . and his heart sank. Not five yards from him, he saw a small dark-brown object lying on the grass. He didn't even need to go closer to it to know that there was his hope, brought low and silent.

Mickey started to think. The bee had obviously been awake mere seconds before. It must have flown up onto the hill and then been caught and affected by whatever it was that was causing this unnatural sleepiness. Indeed, he realized, that was probably why the insect had stung him in the first place. It had landed on his leg and been afflicted by the strange drowsiness that was affecting all other life forms on the hill and, in its confusion at what was happening, responded with a defensive instinct by utilizing its sting. Far from the annoying pest Mickey had thought of it as being, the insect had in fact been a friend to him. Were it not for the sharp pain of its venomous barb, he too would still have been a victim of this bizarre unconsciousness.

He paused in reflection. And so what? a small voice inside his head was saying. What is there to be afraid of in sleepiness? What is there of fear in peaceful, relaxing slumber? What of dread in the dreams of a summer afternoon? Mickey conceded the point. Perhaps he was being foolish. After all, to an independent observer, who would look the happier – the single man made anxious by the sleep of insects or the hundred-and-more people peacefully snoozing away in well-earned rest on a Saturday afternoon? What was the matter with him? Who could deny the attraction of such a sleep? Who would not like to lie back and let the pressures of life slip away and be comforted by a pleasant drowsiness? He was silly to be alarmed. He had been startled by a sting and was suffering from the anxiety that all sudden wakings invoke, that was all. But the sting wasn't hurting now. It wasn't even throbbing. His leg felt good. His whole body felt good, felt deliciously relaxed. His mind, too, was calmer now, all doubts and fears receding. His eyelids were growing heavy. Perhaps he too would sleep now. Perhaps he would again lean back and take advantage of this wonderful and peaceful afternoon. His mouth opened slowly in a satisfying and relaxing yawn and he rolled his head languorously round on his shoulders. Yes – to settle now, to relax and drowse, what could be better? To sleep, perchance to –

'No!'

The roar tore out of his mouth, ringing loudly in the otherwise eerie silence of the hill as, with a Herculean effort of mind, Mickey ripped himself free of the spell that had almost had him again. From the reserves of his will, Mickey raised his arm, an arm all but gripped in lethargy, and, swinging it from as far back as he could, slapped himself across the cheek with all the strength he could muster!

172

Once again, his mind was clear. And once again – and even more than before – he was afraid. He slapped himself again. And again.

'Stay awake, Calhoun!' he shouted to himself. 'For God's sake, stay awake!'

He leaped to his feet. Or at least, that was the intention. Halfway through straightening up, a wave of overwhelming dizziness hit him and caused him to stagger and all but put him back on the ground. With a grunt and a muttered curse, Mickey threw one arm in front to hit the grass with his hand and support himself and pushed himself back up again. Standing upright, he breathed deeply to try and clear the wave of nausea that followed in the wake of the dizzy spell.

'What in the name of the Lord is happening?' Mickey called out, looking round in distress at his sleeping fellow townsfolk. The nearest recumbent figure to him was that of Susan Johanson, the pretty nineteen-year-old daughter of Swedish Pete the Blacksmith. Mickey turned his face to her.

'Miss Johanson!' he cried urgently. 'Susan! Wake up!'

Answer came there none. Susan continued to lay there, her only movement being a small delicate fluttering of her beautiful eyelashes as if somewhere far away she was dreaming happy dreams. Mickey started to walk toward her, every dragging step of his legs an effort akin to wading through waist-high mud. He looked at her, lying there so peacefully innocent – little knowing that she and the rest of the town were in the grip of some dangerous and evil spell!

A sudden thought came to Mickey, and with it a chilling certainty as to the root cause of whatever was happening, as his mind was filled with a memory of the night before . . .

He had come out of the saloon after enjoying an evening in the company of his friends and, as he made his way along Main Street, had glanced up to the hill which was to be the site of the next afternoon's picnic. It had been a cloudy night, no stars visible through the banks of dark grey above, but, just as Mickey had glanced over to the hill, a cloud had slid away from the moon and the silver lunar light had broken through. There had been a figure silhouetted on top of the hill and Mickey had stopped in his tracks, surprised. The figure had had its arms outstretched to either side as if in some kind of invocation. Mickey had had only a second to see it before another

173

bank of cloud obscured the moon again and the figure disappeared from view – but that second had been long enough for the ruddy Irishman to be convinced as to its identity!

'Billy Twofeathers!' he had growled then – and growled it again now as he continued to try to press his way to Susan Johanson, fighting both the physical oppressiveness of whatever it was that pulled and tugged at his legs and the lethargy that every second threatened to overwhelm his mind and lure him back into the deadly drowsiness that was gripping the rest of the people of Big Thunder.

Billy Twofeathers. At the time, Mickey had just shrugged and continued on his way home. Now, he remembered how a few people had spoken at the picnic as to the whereabouts of the Redskin. It seemed nobody had seen him all day. Mickey, cursing the Indian under his breath, was not surprised nobody had seen him. The treacherous dog must have lit out of town after putting his diabolical plan into action!

The breeze picked up a little and Mickey's eye was drawn to the booted feet of Susan Johanson as the wind played with the frilled hem of her skirt and lifted it an inch or so before letting it fall back, more carelessly arranged than before. Mickey found himself looking at the beautiful paleness of Susan's calf. She was a very pretty girl and, though Mickey felt a bit guilty about looking at what perhaps only her future husband should ever see, he couldn't help but stare. She was a *very* pretty girl. And she looked so peaceful, so calm and relaxed. Mickey was sure she wouldn't mind him looking. He meant no harm. Indeed, harm or guilt or anger seemed such foolish notions, seemed as nothing when set against the peace that had come to the people. Mickey was sure, in fact, that the only impolite thing a person could do on such an afternoon was to refuse to join in the communal ease and wellbeing that everyone was feeling. Susan would like him a lot more, he felt, if he lay down somewhere near her and joined her and the others in their sleep. He could almost hear her sweet little voice asking him to join them. How could he refuse her? It would break her heart if he –

No. No! Mickey pulled his eyes away from Susan's leg. The terrible sleepiness had almost had him again. He couldn't afford to let his guard down for an instant! He reached one hand over to his other arm and, gathering some flesh between his thumb and his forefinger,

174

pinched himself painfully with as much pressure as he could bear. He kept squeezing until his eyes were watering and he felt the creeping lethargy withdraw again, slipping away from his mind and leaving it clear – at least for the moment.

A sudden barking broke startlingly into the eerie lifeless silence which had surrounded Mickey since first the bee sting had woken him. He swung his body round, his eyes scanning wildly to locate the source of the sound. There! At the bottom of the hill, a few hundred yards from the town, he saw a young dog galloping through the grass, barking joyfully as it leaped and bounded, chasing something Mickey couldn't see from this distance – a butterfly, perhaps, or simply a windswept leaf. Mickey's heart leapt with pleasure at this simple sight. The canine creature's delight and energy, its simple instinctive joy-in-life, was like a tonic to the troubled Irishman. He was about to whistle for the dog but stopped himself. Why bring it up here where it too would simply fall victim to the dread sleeping sickness that had claimed all life atop the hill? He watched the dog disappear over a small rise, its barks dying away in the distance as it pursued its quarry.

Mickey thought quickly. To try to wake the townsfolk on his own was dangerous for all of them. At any moment, he too could succumb to the insidious drowsiness of whatever black magic was at work up here. And it wasn't as if a simple shout or shake would wake them anyway. It had taken a bee sting to rouse him. He needed something at least as noticeable. Something loud and sharp-sounding. He cursed himself for not bringing a gun up with him to the picnic. But somebody must have brought one!

His eyes scanned the people nearest him, his hand all the time finding other unbruised areas of his arm to pinch in order to ensure his wakefulness. There! Not forty yards from him, he saw the glint of sunlight against polished metal as the solar rays bounced off the revolver displayed in the holster of Dale Andrews, a ranch hand out at the Middleton place who'd come into town for the picnic because he was sweet on Widow Meachum's youngest girl. A rapid blast of six bullets into the air would surely rouse at least some people and provide Mickey with some help in dragging others away down the hill and out of the reach of the pernicious influence of the supernatural sleepiness.

175

Mickey started forward. Once again, he felt the dragging sensation against his legs as if he were wading through a vat of treacle. Each step forward, each half yard gained, was a massive effort of both muscle and will. The Irishman hesitated. Forty yards. Nothing to a man of his size and strength on any normal occasion – but now? He weighed an alternative as his head turned to look down again at the deserted town. The distance to it was much greater, of course, than the distance to Dale Andrews' gun but it wasn't simply a question of distance. A five-minute run at the most would get him to town, where he could soon locate a shotgun or two. Allow ten minutes for the uphill journey back and even so he'd be back here before twenty minutes had passed. Once more, he looked over to where Dale slumbered in the shade of a tree. So much nearer . . . even with the terrible effort of pushing his way through the unseen and unnatural force that retarded his progress, he would surely reach Dale sooner than twenty minutes. But then he remembered how twice already he had almost fallen back into the sleep that held the others in its unnatural grip and his mind was made up. He couldn't afford the risk of surrender to the drowsiness that heading for Dale entailed. The town was the better choice.

He turned around and began walking in the other direction. If he'd thought this was going to be instantly easier, he was swiftly disappointed. Even after he'd started on the downward slope of the hill that led toward town, he was still having to force his every step through the unseen retardant.

'Come on, Calhoun!' he snapped at himself. 'You're a big tough guy. What's a little afternoon walk to you?'

He realized that the very sound of his own voice was actually a help to him in keeping at bay the ever-present, ever-threatening lethargy. So, as well as continuing to pinch himself, he began to sing aloud in a resounding baritone that made up in volume what it sorely lacked in tonality!

He was halfway through the second verse of 'The Girl in the Shadowed Doorway', a sentimental ballad about lost innocence that he'd first heard in a vaudeville theatre in New York on his only trip to that city some seven years earlier, when, with a sudden shock as if someone had pushed him in the small of the back, he found himself running headlong down the hill. He was free! He'd broken

176

through the barrier of the evil force's sphere of influence! With a whoop of delight, Mickey slowed himself and turned back to look up the hill. Not only was he physically more at ease but there was no hint, not even a lingering trace, of the lethargy that had been a constant threat mere seconds before. Cautiously, he stepped back up the hill a yard or so. Yes. There it was. He could feel it both in his head and in his body – his limbs felt heavy and slow and his mind was dulling at the edges. As quickly as he could, he backed down again and was once more in full possession of his faculties and in full control of his body. He was about to turn once more to face the town and continue on his downward quest when something stopped him. It was something just at the corner of his vision and he turned his eyes more fully to it.

Up on the hill, a small object was rising. Mickey narrowed his eyes, the better to achieve a clarity of vision. It was a bird! A bird rising up from the death-like sleep on the grassy summit! Mickey's entire system flooded with an overwhelming sense of relief. Perhaps the nightmare was over!

But wait. A slow surprise showed on Mickey's face as he realized that the bird's wings were still folded around its body and the speed of its ascent was astonishingly slow – perhaps as little as a foot every five or six seconds. Flight in such a posture and at such a slow speed was aerodynamically impossible! Mickey's initial surprise gave way to other emotions as his heart sank and he was once again plunged into the depths of despair. And this time it was worse than before – for not only was the bird not flying (which was enough to depress his momentary sense of relief) but, still unconscious of anything that was happening to it, it was being raised by some unseen supernatural means. Whatever evil forces were at play here were now levitating the innocent creature, drawing it up from the ground toward the sky! What in the name of heaven was happening?

Mickey realized that for the last few minutes the sound of the breeze atop the hill had been growing in volume and that the breeze itself had been growing in intensity. The very breeze that had so prettily fluttered Susan Johanson's dress up from her calf was now a strong and powerful wind, whipping and howling across the grassy summit, playing around and over the sleeping people. Playing around and over and beneath . . .

With a cry of despair and denial, 'No! No, it can't happen! It mustn't happen!' Mickey realized what was about to occur and, despite the risk to himself, threw himself back up the hill. Within seconds, he was once again surrounded by the unseen retardant and struggling upward as a man would struggle through quicksand. His progress was even slower because now he was making his way uphill, not down. But he pressed on despite this, and despite the pernicious sluggishness of mind that even now was seeping back into his brain, sapping his will and urging his surrender.

His eyes wide in horror, Mickey watched helplessly – still many yards from the summit above him – as the process that had begun with the bird (one of the lightest creatures caught in the sleep trap) now continued. Ahead of him, impossible as it seemed, the sleepers were rising!

As slowly – but as diabolically surely – as the bird before them, the townsfolk were being raised into the air. All of them still on their backs, all of them still asleep and unknowing, they were levitating upwards! Like involuntary participants in an unwilled exodus to a promised land where all the promises were dark, the people were rising in their scores. Some were already higher than others – children, women, lightly-built men – but all of them, every last one, were now off the ground and were slipping inexorably upward. Nearly two hundred people in the air being taken God knows where by God knows what!

The very slowness of their ascent simply added to the horror for Mickey because although most of the floating sleepers were not yet even six feet from the ground, he was still many yards from them and, he realized with a profound horror, there was no chance at all that he could achieve the summit before each of them was beyond his grasp. It was hopeless!

Mickey hesitated, stopping for a moment his struggle against the invisible quicksand and in that very moment he realized that the threat to the rest of the town's inhabitants was a threat to him also because, as he paused and stood still, he felt a lightness creep beneath the soles of his boots and his body swayed gently and lifted slightly. The wind was playing around him, whipping into his face and eyes, and he understood that it meant to take him too, to make him a member of the hellish exodus!

178

With a cry that was half anger and half terror, Mickey spun round to face the town and then threw himself to the ground face down. His powerful hands clawed into the grass and the soil beneath and he began to crawl forward and downward, his eyes fixed on the town below. He couldn't be more than ten yards inside the evil force's sphere of control, he told himself as he inched forward through the unyielding and invisible quicksand, but it was the longest ten yards Mickey Calhoun had ever had to cover in his life. He felt the nightmarish supernatural wind playing over his body and trying to get beneath him as he crawled onward and desperately he flattened his body as best he could, pressing himself into a tight embrace of the precious grass below him as his mighty hands seized, gripped, and pulled, seized, gripped, and pulled, never letting go with one hand until the other had firm anchor again. He now had three enemies to contend with: the mental fog that was constantly trying to overwhelm him and seduce him into surrender, the air that was turning his limbs to lead as he struggled to make his way through it, and the terrible ungodly wind that was hovering over and around him like a bird of prey looking for an opening. Mickey's gritted teeth were bared in a grim snarl of animal determination as, summoning all his reserves of strength, both physical and mental, he fought on, gaining inch by precious inch. To make matters worse, every hard-won step of progress was accompanied and haunted by the terrible mental anguish of his knowledge that he could do nothing to help his fellow man, that he had failed, that somewhere behind him the poor innocent townsfolk of Big Thunder were disappearing up toward the sky and to what he could only assume would be some awful fate!

The air grew shadowed and dark around him as if something was blocking the sun. He couldn't afford to turn his head and look for fear the wind would have him. Once his grip on the earth was broken, Mickey knew, he was lost. There were no trees or structures nearby, nothing which he could grab as a secondary anchor if he was lifted. But what did this darkness mean? What was happening behind him? Keeping his eyes fixed downward on the town, Mickey struggled on, his muscles aching with the effort of his progress. Surely he must be close now to the edge of the invisible barrier? A thrill of terror ran through him as he considered the possibility that

179

the sphere was spreading, that the point at which he had broken through earlier was no longer the limit of the horror. He refused to believe it. He couldn't allow himself to believe it for then all was lost. He had to keep believing that any moment now he would be clear, that any moment now he would be free. Groaning with the strain, he redoubled his efforts.

'Come on, Calhoun!' he muttered to himself. 'Come on!'

The darkness was deeper now. He could hardly see the greenness of the grass below and before him. It was as if the world had been drained of colour. It wasn't the darkness of night, he realized, but that terrible oppressive darkness that presages a storm. It was as he was thinking this that he suddenly realized he was free. He'd done it! His arms were suddenly moving freely and he was scrabbling down the hill at a much faster pace, his limbs untroubled by leadenness, his mind unfogged and clear.

'Thank God!' he shouted. 'Thank God!' as he raised himself to his feet again. He swung round to look up once more at the summit and his selfish joy at his own salvation gave way to a terrible despair as he saw what was happening to his fellow townsfolk.

The darkness he had experienced was due to a massive roiling grey cloud that had gathered as if from nowhere on what had been mere moments before a cloudless blue sky. The cloud obscured the sun and dominated the vista of the sky. Mickey had never seen its like. Indescribably huge, its solid grey mass seemed almost alive in its constant bubbling movements as if it was a chemical compound at boiling point.

As well as the cloud, the sky was full of people. The sleeping inhabitants of Big Thunder were now impossibly high in the sky, so high that they seemed, from Mickey's viewpoint, to be very small – almost like tiny play figures torn from a child's grasp and flung upwards. Before Mickey's appalled gaze, they began one by one to disappear into the vast cloud, vanishing into its bubbling and rolling greyness. It was beyond belief but it was happening and Mickey watched, frozen in helpless horror, as hundreds of people were drawn into the impenetrable darkness of the cloud like an unending stream of victims being fed into the insatiably hungry maw of some indescribably huge beast.

Mickey rushed forward almost unconsciously, shaking his fist at

180

the heavens in powerless rage. Remembering only at the last moment that he himself was in danger, he froze and prepared to leap backwards only to realize with a shock that the air around him still felt normal and that his mind still felt clear. Tentatively, he moved further forward, extending his arm out ahead of him to test for the leadenness of limb that was an indicator of the presence of the dangerous field of influence. Nothing! A little more boldly, he began to trot up the hill. Still nothing. He rushed forward until he was once again on the summit. He was moving freely, his mind was completely his own, and the wind that whistled around him was merely that – a wind, not some insidious and unnatural trap of diabolic transportation. Having done its job, having captured the entire population of Big Thunder save Mickey Calhoun, the mysterious energy had vanished as magically as it had come. The hill was safe again. But small comfort that was now to Calhoun as he stood alone atop it, gazing upward at the terrible huge cloud above.

What to do now? Mickey had never felt so powerless. Give him an honest enemy to fight and he would be as brave as the next man and more resourceful than most, but this was beyond his ken. People must be told, he knew that much, and yet something in him rebelled at the notion of simply walking away while his entire town was lost up there in that monstrosity.

Suddenly, the sky darkened even more. Mickey looked up. The movements of the cloud were growing even more furious and its colour was darkening toward blackness.

*Crack!* Mickey started in shock as a jagged streak of forked lightning lit the sky. *Crack!* Another. And another! The lightning was not hitting the ground. Instead, it was jagging and dancing all around and over the cloud as if simultaneously erupting from within and piercing from without. The lightning increased in frequency and intensity while at the same time the cloud seemed to swell and pulse ever more furiously as if they were racing each other to some terrible climactic event. And all the time, the darkness was growing deeper and more oppressive.

The cloud began to change hue, purple and pink patches appearing over its surface as if it were bruising wherever the lightning hit. An ominous low rumble began to build in the air, deeply disturbing and, despite the lowness of its pitch, painfully loud. Mickey clapped his hands over his ears, pressing them tight in a vain effort to keep the sound out. It built and built and, just at the point where Mickey thought his senses could take no more, it broke in an equally deafening massive clap of thunder, which reverberated in the startling silence afterward for several seconds. And then came another. And another.

Mickey stared upwards, most conscious thought forgotten, lost in the terror and awe produced by what he was seeing and hearing. Suddenly, making all that had come before seem like a mild summer storm in comparison, the sky seemed to explode as a hundred lightning bolts erupted simultaneously and the roar of the thunder was like nothing ever heard before on earth . . .

Then all sound stopped. The lightning ceased. There was, for a brief second or two, nothing but the ominous presence of the massive cloud – which, as Mickey's eyes recovered from the blinding effect of the massed lightning and saw it clearly again, was now no longer grey but a terrifying and portentous deep red. And then the silence ceased as the cloud broke. And the rain came.

It came all at once. There was no initial drizzle. It was as if the cloud had simply split apart like tortured and inflamed skin over a pustulant wound that had been stretched beyond endurance and finally burst. From a completely dry day it moved to a drenching driving blinding powerful rain that instantly covered the hill and everything else within the radius below the huge cloud.

Mickey was soaked to the skin at once. The rain fell and it kept on falling, its intensity and violence such that it felt as if the rain would never cease.

But it was neither the intensity of the rain nor the threat of its unendingness that drew the despairing cry from the depths of Mickey's soul, a cry that transformed itself within less than a minute to the terrifying and hopeless laughing cackle of the incurably insane. No. It was its taste. Its smell. Its colour. For the rain that fell on Big Thunder that day was a rain of blood! It was blood that poured from the wounded skies, blood that flooded over the grassy summit of the hill, blood that pounded into Mickey Calhoun's upturned face, stinging his eyes, invading his nostrils, flooding his mouth. And, in his last second of sanity, Mickey knew and understood the nature and the provenance of these crimson streams that were

182

soaking his skin and staining his clothes, transforming him into a bedraggled liquid-logged scarecrow figure of horror and madness. It was, in a manner of speaking, only what he had wished for. As these scarlet rivers and nothing more, the townsfolk of Big Thunder were returning to the earth that had been their home.

Some weeks later, the plains town of Fiddler's Ferry, some one hundred miles west of Big Thunder, gained a new inhabitant. Nobody ever learned the real name of the drifter who wandered into town one afternoon half-starved and completely insane, though the townsfolk soon christened him Paddy, on account of his Irish features and colouring.

'Must've been a strong man once,' people would say pityingly whenever they chanced to catch sight of the poor madman's six-foot frame. The preacher, in a spirit of Christian kindness, took him under his wing, allowing him to sleep in the church barn in return for the few menial tasks the retarded man was capable of performing.

Paddy, if spoken to directly, would look away quickly like a nervous animal and he never spoke himself. Indeed, the only sounds people ever heard from him were the terrible heartrending howls of complete terror that would emanate from the barn where he would hide burrowed in hay bales whenever a storm hit town.

For the most part, though, Paddy could get by as much as people like him ever could and, though mothers would often cross the street with their children when they were about to cross his path, most of the town realized he was harmless. His most disconcerting trait, in fact, was a nervous habit he had of suddenly, prompted by nothing, looking to the sky with an expression of soul-deep dread, as if in fear of some unspeakable doom that might suddenly and unexpectedly come from the clouds to claim him!

THE END

Avis finished the story and closed the book.

She had mixed feelings. It was a good story, she supposed, but she'd felt distinctly uncomfortable with all that name calling of the Native American and that had kind of poisoned the rest for her. Billy Twofeathers. Redskin. You just couldn't say that stuff.

It was offensive. And, frankly, she thought the people of the town in all their white-folk smugness had gotten what they deserved. She wondered if Norbert Read had ever stopped to think that maybe the townspeople were the villains of his story.

But okay. Enough of that. Her opinion of the story wasn't really the point. Valentine Dyson's opinion, on the other hand, could be very important. This story – and not, interestingly, a Blue Valentine adventure – was the one he'd picked, the one out of which he intended to make a movie. And what, by the way, was *that* about? Who was *he* to make a movie? Weren't there rules about that? Didn't you have to go to school or something? Of course, it was difficult to think of rules applying to someone who had somehow transformed himself from ink to actuality, from thought to flesh –

Avis went cold. Her stomach was suddenly both tight and hollow. She was very frightened and she didn't know why exactly. All she knew was that she'd been riding two trains of thought – the Valentine-made-flesh, the choice of this story – and there'd just been a collision. Somewhere in the wreckage was an answer, an answer which frightened her, but the wreck was still burning and she was blinded by the smoke. She had to read its signals, had to decipher the fire of this unholy alchemy –

And suddenly she knew. Why had Dyson picked this story? *To work on it the same spell of transmutation by which he himself had been conjured.*

Was that logical? No. Was that rational? No. Was that possible? Yes. If the Blue Valentine himself could be somehow brought to a life beyond the imagined, then why couldn't anything that that helpless old man had once dreamed up have the same magic worked on it? She remembered the terrible voices that had issued from Fern's mouth. *Using his favourite is good*, they'd said. Her mind was racing now, making connections that logic laughed at but instinct knew to be right. *His favourite*. The he was Read, the favourite Dyson. There were powers she could neither name nor imagine behind what was happening, powers that could somehow bring the imagined to life. The voices had referred to a Chinese dragon. *Not his*, they'd said, *the focus couldn't hold*. For a moment, her focus couldn't hold either. For a moment, reason got in the

184

way. For a moment, she found herself almost laughing at what she was considering: creatures from another dimension . . . demons from beyond time and space . . . monsters from the heavens . . . God knows what from God knows where using the artefacts of mankind's imagination to invade reality and, for some reason, having a special relationship with the products of Read's mind. It wasn't just Dyson. They'd referred to . . . what was it? *The Corridor Walkers*. They were his, the voices had said. Just like the Blue Valentine. Just like Big Thunder. Oh my God. Could it happen? Could the massive blood-cloud from Read's silly little story be made to sail beyond its fictional sky and out into the real one? It seemed absurd. Seemed unbelievable. But so did phantom vigilantes – and Avis had three dead friends to weigh against disbelief in that department. She was operating in a world in which the impossible was already wandering around buying up film rights and torturing junkies so she had to put aside any decisions based on twenty-five years of life in which the real was the real and the paranormal was something hosted by Robert Stack in bite-size TV chunks and trust instead her experiences of the last week or so. Dyson was intending to float the hungry and terrible cloud of 'Big Thunder' over the heads of humanity and she absolutely believed he could do it.

But why a movie? Dyson had popped into existence without the need of a celluloid intermediary, so what was the point of making a film? Why waste time and energy (and presumably a shitload of money) on doing that?

She hadn't even finished forming the thought before the answer flooded her with fear – a fear that was sudden, stomach-churning, and all-encompassing, a fear like that which would follow the finding, by idle fingers, of a lump in the breast.

Multiplicity.

She had a vision of a thousand screens across America, each one showing a movie called *Big Thunder* and each one giving impossible birth from the coloured light that played across it to the monstrous reality of which that coloured light was merely a reflection. She saw the skies above Manhattan suddenly full of a bubbling red death, the air above America filled from horizon to horizon with Norbert Read's impossible clouds, voracious and inescapable. She saw people in their thousands drawn screaming into the sky. She saw the blood-storm that would follow when those clouds burst and she thanked God for the limits of her imagination when she found herself incapable of picturing America after the rain.

# 21

In the Fields of Heaven, a safe distance from the tree beneath which their human guest sat, several of the Companions were gathered.

Four of them, even though they were out of his sight, remained – amused by the codified banality of his vision of themselves – in the form of angels, their gold and silver wings folded elegantly about their pure white robes and their halos glittering above the Italianate curls of their hair. A fifth was present as a series of small dark Lucite rings, the interweaving orbits of which spun in gyroscopic fury around an unseen centre, and the sixth existed at the moment only as a harmony, a pair of vibrations in space that sang a two-tone chord that might have been recognized, had there been human ears to hear it, as the opening of the final wordless verse of The Marcels' version of Rodgers and Hart's 'Blue Moon'.

'The stone is in the fire,' one of the angels said, 'and the twelve gates are open.'

Two of the other angels flowed together as the first spoke, their impostor flesh merging and transmuting into a thin pool the consistency of water and the colour of mercury that hung upright, suspended a few feet above the ground. Bubbles broke rapidly from the pool's centre, bursting successively into words.

'They will be called back into the illumination of the righteous,' the pool said, 'and all will be freed from the sheaths of substance.'

A third voice emerged from somewhere to the left of the spinning Lucite rings. 'And our guest is all right?' it said. 'Not bored yet? No awkward questions?'

'He seemed happy some moments ago,' said another of the angels, 'he was making squirrels out of fallen twigs and dust.'

The harmonious duotone became a discordant triad as a slow contemptuous groan escaped the invisible Companion. The other two notes disappeared but the groan continued as its owner solidified into a sandstone obelisk threaded throughout its eighteen-foot height by pale and sightless worms.

'Oohhh,' it said, 'the Work better happen fast. I don't know how much longer I can resist turning his eyes inside out.'

The angel who'd reported the creation of the squirrels tried to placate the obelisk. 'He's not as innocent as he was,' it said, 'he changed one of the squirrels into a pack of Marlboro when he thought I wasn't looking.'

'So he puts appetite before sentiment,' the obelisk replied. 'Big deal. Each is as dull as the other. If he'd smoked the squirrel we might be getting somewhere.'

The mercury pool shimmered into the solidity of a star-shaped mirror and spoke sternly. 'We *are* getting somewhere,' it said, 'and disturbing our guest will not widen the path but close it. Your impatience is not appreciated.'

'But boredom may soon be an issue,' the angel who'd seen the Marlboro miracle said. 'And we can't afford to have his mind wandering. Perhaps he needs new distractions. A new kind of companion or two.'

'Very well,' the mirror replied, 'but remember the times in which he was a young man. Flesh yourself appropriately.'

Nodding distractedly as the flesh of its face began to run in streams like opposing rivulets rushing from a central fissure, the angel walked away, its body stretching and splitting as it went.

He was leaning his head back against his tree, ready for another dreamless doze, when, just as his eyes were closing, he became aware of movement off to his side. He opened his eyes again and saw two figures walking toward him.

Startled and most pleasantly surprised, he scrambled to his feet. It was two angels who were approaching but, though they were winged and clad in the same heavenly raiment as the others with whom he had spent time here, they were decidedly different.

'Oh, there you are,' said one of them, 'we've been wanting to come and say hello for the longest time.'

188

'We've heard such a lot about you,' the other added.

He swallowed hard. He could almost feel a blush rising to his cheeks, as if he was once again the awkward and shy young man from the sticks that he had been so many years before. He felt a strange mix of pleasure and guilt in looking at them. Pleasure because they were sure nice to look at and guilt because he was less than confident that the mildly libidinous rush he was feeling was entirely an appropriate response to a pair of angels – even when one had the rusty-blonde hair and the saucy eyes of the young Ginger Rogers and the other looked like the celestial proto-type from which God had, in his infinite kindness to mankind, once fashioned Myrna Loy.

'Well, it's . . . it's certainly a pleasure,' he said, 'a pleasure to . . . to meet you both. Gosh.'

The angelic girls giggled delightfully at the flattery of his embar-rassment and both of them moved closer, reaching out simul-taneously from either side of him to rest their hands on his arms. He'd never really noticed, in his times with the male angels, just how sheer were the white robes that they wore and just how much those robes could cling revealingly and tantalizingly to the figures concealed beneath them. He swallowed again.

'There's no need to stand,' the brunette said, her voice just the decorous side of an intimate whisper. 'Why don't we all three settle down here and . . . oh, I don't know . . . get comfortable?'

He couldn't answer at first. His head was swimming from the delicate caressing pressure of their small warm hands and the sweet fragrant smell of them – part innocent and part wicked, half babypowder, half champagne.

'Doesn't that sound like a good idea?' the blonde asked, her eyes plaintive and appealing, like her poor little heart might break if he didn't grant them this tiny favour.

Norbert Read nodded. Hell, yes. It sounded like a swell idea.

# 22

Avis checked the time difference and then dialled the number from the copy of *The Hollywood Reporter* that she'd found in a newsstand in SoHo.

'Production,' said a voice, not unfriendly but determined to let you know that it was busy.

Production. That was all. No company name. No nothing. What did that mean?

'Oh,' said Avis, 'I'm not sure I have the right number.'

'What number were you calling?'

Avis gave the number she'd dialled.

'Yes,' said the voice, 'production. Can I help you?'

'Is this the office for *Big Thunder*?'

'Yes,' said the voice, a note of undisguised impatience creeping in to its less-than-polite-to-begin-with tone. 'Is there somebody you want to talk to?'

'Valentine Dyson?'

'Who?'

'Thought so. Problem is I'm not sure which name he's using.'

'I'm sorry?'

'He's the producer, I suppose. Hold on . . .' Avis grabbed at the *Reporter*, already folded over to the page which listed current productions, and ran her finger down the column of tiny typeface. Before she could even find the list of names again, the voice interrupted her.

'Can I help you?'

Now the voice was pointedly rude. Fuck you, thought Avis, but held it in. Ah, here it was. 'David Vial?'

'He's on set.'

'Can I talk to him?'

'This is the production office.'

The hell with this. 'Yeah? So?'

'What?'

'"This is the production office",' good imitation, just the right mix of snotty and stupid, 'is that supposed to mean something to me?'

'It's supposed to mean we're busy.'

Ooh. Very arch.

'Yeah? Well, it doesn't. It means you're a stupid fucking prick with far too much attitude for somebody who answers phones for a living. I . . .'

*Click.*

Avis held the phone a moment longer and then dropped it in its cradle. She smiled. She supposed she'd been silly but she didn't feel silly. She felt good. And she hoped that, at the other end of the disconnected line, the guy to whom she'd been speaking felt bad. She hoped he felt really bad. She hoped that, in some small way, she'd helped to completely ruin the little bastard's whole fucking day.

She wasn't even sure if calling had been a good idea anyway. Suppose she'd got him on the phone, what could she possibly have said? *Hi, this is Avis Llewellen. We met in New York before your career change. Listen, I know what you're planning to do and I'd like you not to. Okay?* Yeah. Might've worked. In a month with K in its name.

She knew there was no point calling the police. Her friends' killer had left no fingerprints and she couldn't see the basis of her assumptions – *he bought a Norbert Read story and the nurse said he was really good-looking* – prompting an enthusiastic phone call from Gerani to the LAPD. And she certainly couldn't share with Gerani her fears about the nature of the movie that was being made without going right back to the top of his known crazies list. In other words, the thing there was a possibility of Gerani being interested in nailing him on was probably alibied and the thing that Avis actually wanted him to be stopped from doing was beyond the possibility of Gerani choosing to act on it – other than recommending that Avis keep on taking the pills. Or, to be even more succinct, Avis was fucked.

191

At least, she was fucked if she remained sitting here in New York. She had no idea what precisely she could do were she to be in Los Angeles instead (Picket the shoot? Tell the press? Ask Dyson to stop? Blow his fucking brains out?) but she was beginning to feel that that was where she had to be. Three of her credit cards were maxed out (big surprise) but she thought she could squeeze the price of a round-trip flight out of a fourth. Round-trip flight. Shit. New York to LA. What was it – five hours? Six? Even at this completely theoretical stage she felt the familiar beginnings of her familiar dread. Flying. Sitting seven thousand miles above the earth in Death's cupped palm and gritting your teeth against the opening of His fingers.

She was going to *do* that? Voluntarily? She was going to put herself back up there on a mission that was not only unfocused but was barely understood? The sick thing was, her questions were less than hypothetical. She was doing it. She knew she was doing it. She had to.

But, Jesus, the world better be *damn* grateful once she'd saved its fucking ass.

# 23

'Cut!' Larry called. 'All right!'

The set exploded into spontaneous applause as the fifty extras were lowered on their filament wires safely back to the floor. Larry didn't know for sure if fifty people was a record for wire work but he was certain it was pretty damn close. His wire wranglers – straight out of film school like eighty per cent of the crew – had regarded the challenge as something of a graduate thesis and Larry was more than ready to sign their diplomas. The shot had looked impressive enough live and, through the video feed, it was nothing short of fucking beautiful. The massive cyclorama with the painted sky read completely real and the dangling extras – as the sleeping inhabitants of Big Thunder – had all relaxed perfectly into the pull of the wires as they lifted them toward the death-cloud (which would be electronically added to the image later by the computer wizards). Larry was ecstatic.

'Cool as fuck,' he said to his First Assistant Director, 'let's move on.'

'One for safety, Larry?' the Director of Photography asked.

Larry glanced at his watch and then instinctively looked over to where David Vial was standing. Vial caught his eye and picked up on the unasked question.

'It looked fine to me,' he said, 'but you're the director.'

God, that was right. Larry still couldn't get over it. It wasn't even three weeks since Vial's casual *Would you like to do it yourself?* had turned him into a hyphenate. Larry Webster, writer-director. Right up there with Orson and Woody and precious few others.

The DP and the First were looking at him, waiting for a decision.

'Nah. We got it,' he said. 'Print it. Let's get ready for the reverse on Jonathan.'

The instruction, passed on by the First's megaphone, sent the crew into a flurry of activity as lights, cameras, and backdrops were repositioned on another part of the huge soundstage. Larry knew he had at least ten minutes before they were ready for him so he lit a cigarette – in the kind of casual defiance of the many posted NO SMOKING signs that befitted a writer-director – and walked over to where Vial was standing.

Larry had to hand it to this guy. Nobody knew who he was or where the fuck he'd come from but Vial was amazing. Nobody'd worked this fast since Corman. The pace he'd set up in their first meeting when he'd asked Larry to do the script in a week had remained constant throughout pre-production and showed no sign of slackening yet. Three editors were assembling the movie as Larry shot it (he'd already agreed to give up even any pretence at a director's cut), the first five reels were locked already, and a negative cutter was making it permanent. Some little Mozart three weeks out of USC was scoring it right now, mixing studios were on hold for two days after wrap, and even the fucking *theatres* were booked. Somehow he had the money and somehow he had the powers of persuasion. Exactly how he'd done it Larry had no idea but, however he'd done it, this movie – which had neither a studio nor a high-profile distributor behind it and which still had a day to shoot, for God's sake – was opening on 700 screens in ten days' time.

As Larry reached him, Vial was still staring at the cyclorama. There was an intense look in his eye as if he was somehow still seeing the extras floating up there, or as if he was seeing the shot as it would finally look with the computer-generated images added and the hungry monster cloud hovering above it all. Screening the entire sequence in the theatre of his imagination, even, and watching the cloud turn blood-red and burst into its terrible rain. For a moment Larry felt a tiny and passing chill of discomfort. There was something not quite pleasant about Vial's gaze, a hint of some hidden and secret excitement about the shot that was his alone and that struck Larry as far from healthy, as if all that money and effort was being used to realize some completely personal obsession and that the rest of it didn't matter at all.

194

*Don't go crazy on me*, Larry thought, *not now*. Eleven days from now, Vial could paint himself green and jump off the Hollywood sign into a carefully positioned threshing machine for all Larry cared – hell, he'd even shoot it for him if that's what he wanted – but until then, until Larry's movie was in the theatres and agents started kissing his ass again, he wanted Vial's obsessiveness to remain focused and practical.

'Looked good, huh?' Larry said, and was relieved when his voice seemed to pull Vial back into the everyday from whatever secret world his mind had been inhabiting.

'First-rate,' he replied. 'Congratulations.'

'Hey,' Larry said, remembering something that had been bothering him since his first coffee this morning, 'I checked out the press kit your office got ready. Great. Great, but . . . I don't know . . . you hyped this last effect a little much, didn't you?'

'You think?'

'Well – "an experience no audience has ever had before". I don't know. I mean, I'm sure the CGI will look spectacular but that makes it sound like we've got some special technique in there. Sensurround. 3-D. You know what I mean?'

Vial looked at him, the threat of a small smile somewhere behind his mouth. For a moment, Larry felt as if he was about to be let in on a secret but then Vial simply shrugged.

'It's publicity, Larry,' he said. 'We need to pull them in, don't we?'

'Right, right,' Larry agreed, 'but couldn't it backfire? I mean, it might pull 'em in for the first weekend but word-of-mouth could kill us if they're disappointed.'

Vial let out a laugh, a strange single thing as much like a bark as a chuckle, and held Larry's eye.

'Oh, they're not going to be disappointed,' he said.

# 24

Joel Marsh was already at a booth in the Waverly Coffee House when Avis squeezed her way through the lunchtime crowd – students, actors, writers, wannabes, and a couple of old folkies who looked like they'd been there since 1962 waiting for Bob Dylan's next set and steadfastly refusing to believe the rumours that he'd gone electric and fucked off to Europe with a rock'n'roll band – and sat down opposite him with an apologetic smile.

'God, sorry,' she said, 'subway.' He lived in the city. She had no need to elaborate. Of course, he'd come from further away than she had and made it on time but, hey, she was the girl.

'No problem,' he said, smiling. She'd have read that as casually magnanimous if he'd been a little more skilled at hiding the erotic delight that shone in his eyes at the sight of her. Bless him. His attraction was so obvious, and his ignorance of its obviousness so complete, that it was positively endearing. She returned the smile and grabbed at a menu.

'Did you order?' she said.

'Just a coffee,' he replied. 'Figured I'd wait for you.'

'Wow. You're a real gentleman.'

'And one who bears gifts,' he said mysteriously and pulled up a briefcase from beside his feet under the table.

Uh oh.

'Really? What?' She kept her voice casual but she hoped to Christ he wasn't going to pull out anything expensive or romantic. It was a lunch date. A first lunch date. She hoped he had a sense of proportion. She'd only called him, in fact, because of some weird private superstition of hers: whenever she was going to fly, she needed to let somebody *know* she was flying – needed some-

196

body to be ready to call the 1-800 number that the newscasts would post for people to check the casualty list. The last thing she wanted was an inappropriate overture as the relationship it sought was unlikely.

She needn't have worried. What he drew from his briefcase was many degrees lower on the turn-a-young-girl's-head scale than the jewellery or flowers she'd feared. Cased in a clear plastic sleeve, it was some ancient and yellowing magazine. With the instinctive care of a bibliophile, he eased it from its sleeve and passed it over the table to her.

'I know you found the book you were after,' he said, as Avis held its brittle fragility in her hands and stared at the cover, 'but I was in Comic Universe yesterday and I thought I'd check out the pulps for you. They're not specialists. Not much of a stock. But I struck lucky.'

Avis was holding an issue of *Strange Thrills*. Dated February 1937, the painted cover showed three white-faced men in sunglasses and black coats pursuing a fourth down a dimly lit city street. The painted face of the pursued, foregrounded and terror-stricken, and half-turned back to stare at those behind him, sold more of the menace the three figures were presumably intended to convey than did the rather bland renderings of the three themselves.

In the lower right corner a yellow box floated above the image and contained the words THE CORRIDOR WALKERS BY NORBERT READ. A little groan escaped Avis and she laid the magazine down. Joel looked at her face and freaked.

'God, you nearly turned white,' he said. 'What's the matter? Are you okay? Here, drink some water.' He pushed his own untouched glass of water across the table top to her and grabbed at his coffee, taking a healthy swallow in an unconscious echo of the act of an example-setting parent.

Avis picked up the glass and took a sip. Joel was right. She felt awful. The magazine was a confirmation of the wild logical leaps she'd made after reading 'Big Thunder' and remembering the bizarre dialogue that had poured from Fern's mouth. She had a hideous conviction that somewhere in the city in the last few weeks these creatures had 'performed their function' or whatever

197

euphemistic phrase it was for killing somebody that one of Fern's voices had used.

'Did you read the story?' she asked him hollowly as she put the water back down.

'Skimmed it,' he said, his concerned eyes flicking over her face as if worried she was still about to faint. 'Writing's not real good but I guess the story's okay. Kind of Bureaucrats from Hell or something. People in an office building keep seeing these three guys in black prowling the corridors with sunglasses and clipboards. Nobody knows who they are or what they're doing. People start not showing up for work, then start showing up dead, that kind of thing. Central character investigates, gets too close to the truth, and they follow him onto the streets and kill him. They got reptile tongues. That bit was kind of cool.' He took a breath. 'Are you okay?'

Avis sighed. 'Not really,' she said.

'Jesus,' said Joel, 'did I bring the wrong gift.'

'No. No, you didn't. It just took me by surprise, is all. But it's good, I guess. It's more evidence that what's going on is really going on.'

Joel gave her a careful look. 'Okay,' he said slowly, 'and what is going on?'

'Shit, Joel,' she said apologetically, 'I didn't ask you here to dump this stuff on you. I . . . I don't know . . .'

'Hey, we gotta talk about something. Right? And it's not like I get out much – so we're not going to discuss new movies.'

Avis groaned. 'Oh, we might,' she said.

Joel might have asked her what that meant but a waitress interrupted them and asked if they were ready to order. Joel's eyes checked if Avis needed a minute but her eyes said it was okay so he ordered a pastrami sandwich and Avis got a grilled cheese. By mutual instinct, they avoided getting back to Avis's story until the food hit the table.

'You really want to hear this stuff?' Avis asked, half of her sandwich halfway to her mouth.

'Sure,' he said, busy laying his sandwich open and carefully placing rings of raw onion on top of the meat. Avis took this as a reassuring sign that he harboured few illusions about kissing

198

her any time soon. She waited till he looked up at her and then narrowed her eyes in mock inquisitiveness.

'How's your tolerance for really fucking weird?' she asked.

Joel shrugged. 'Try me,' he said.

Forty-five minutes later Avis stopped talking.

Joel laid down his fifth refill of coffee and looked at her. 'Well,' he said, 'despite there being a month or so left, I think it's safe to say you're the front runner for my most-interesting-lunch-date-of-the-year award.'

That got a little laugh from Avis. She liked him. It was a very smooth way out of her story for both of them and she appreciated it. He'd been a great listener, too. The only interruptions had been very specific questions when she hadn't been clear in her telling. There'd been no attempts to rationalize, no attempts to persuade her that perhaps something hadn't really happened or that her reading of it was wrong. He hadn't tried to cut her short, he hadn't laughed, and nor had he suddenly remembered an important appointment somewhere outside the asylum. In fact, though she was smart enough to know it would be seen as no compliment if she told him so, he'd listened like a girl – he hadn't assumed from the get-go that she was an idiot and he hadn't assumed two minutes in that she was out of her fucking mind. He might think it, but he'd let her talk and she was grateful – more grateful than she knew she'd be. Just getting it all out there in sequence made her feel better. She told him that and thanked him for his patience.

'Patience, my ass,' he said. 'It's fascinating.' He caught himself there. 'Don't get me wrong,' he said hastily, 'it's terrible about your friends. Just terrible. But the rest of it, what's happening, it's ... I don't know ... all the clichés – astonishing, amazing, whatever. Jesus Christ. *Jesus* Christ. Have you thought about *why* this is happening? Have you wondered what the reason is?'

That took Avis by surprise. Not only his readiness to discuss it (and the staggering implication that he might therefore *believe* her) but the question itself. A reason. A motive. She thought for a second and then gave him the honest answer.

'No. No, I guess I haven't. I suppose I just assumed it was ... I don't know ... *malice.*'

Joel nodded. 'Right,' he said, 'of course. Bad things have happened. Something even worse is threatening to happen. What the hell else *could* you think? You have to read evil as the motivation – but, God, it's all a bit fucking elaborate to be summed up as just . . . I don't know . . . meanness, isn't it?'

'Evil can't be elaborate?'

'Its forms certainly can – but the complexity of a thing's form can often blind us to the simplicity of a thing's essence.'

Avis – who'd done most of the talking and so who, unlike Joel, still had half a sandwich left – took the semi-coagulated grilled cheese away from the mouth that had been just about to close on it.

'Whoa,' she said, 'rein it in, professor. I've got my reputation to think of. People might think I'm having lunch with a philosopher.'

Joel laughed. 'You are,' he said.

'Get out of town,' Avis said. 'Really?'

'Sure. Doctorate and everything. Did two years' teaching. Couldn't get on the tenure stream. Lost the gig.' He paused for another sip of coffee. 'Do you have any idea how *useless* a philosophy degree is once you're out of the academic womb? Went back to a City College to learn how to librarian. And that, kids, is how you get to be thirty-seven years old and still in an entry-level job.'

Avis sipped at her coffee. She hadn't kept up with Joel's refills and it was cold. She waved at the waitress for a warm-up and looked back at Joel.

'God,' she said, 'I'm sorry.'

'Don't be,' he said. 'You know what the cool thing is? I really like my job. Surprises the hell out of me, but I do. Besides, my entire generation had the most protracted adolescence in history so I'm probably not that unusual. Of course, most of them had disco and cocaine and I had Schopenhauer and symbolic logic but . . . I don't know . . . now they're trapped in Nick At Nite nostalgia and I feel my life is just beginning so I guess I got the better deal.'

He laughed again, and then buried his face in some serious coffee-swigging as if a little embarrassed by his self-revelation. Avis took the opportunity to look at him more closely. She'd liked what he said. His story made him more real to her and she found

200

she could, bizarrely, *see* him better now. Could get past the older-guy-equals-invisible equation and actually see his face and read and enjoy its Eastern European origins.

She saw that face unchanged down the centuries, saw that broad nose and thick beard in the time-lost glow of some ancient campfire, in the vanished streets of some long-levelled village. She wished she had her blood-history on her face as clearly as he did. Wished she could be a Celtic priestess to his Bulgar prince . . .

Jesus. She stopped herself right there. Where the hell was she going with *that*? Joel Marsh was not her type. Emphatically not her type. Maybe once she hit thirty she'd be looking for someone like him but she figured she still had five years left of her girls-just-wanna-have-fun decade. She was still checking out buns, not braincells. Still looking for Brad Pitt, not Bertrand fucking Russell.

She was relieved as the waitress arrived – despite the you-guys-are-taking-a-long-time-on-a-small-cheque look on her face – and broke the mood by refilling Avis's cup.

'That's good, Joel,' she said, 'good that you feel that way. But, if you don't mind exercising your former profession, tell me what you think. Philosophically. Tell me what you think this is if it isn't just an exercise in evil.'

'You know,' he said, 'I'm not sure it matters what I think. Analysis isn't always a useful companion to action. If a guy's swinging a punch at you, the time to consider the significance of his deed and wonder who's got the moral high ground is *after* you've side-stepped and slugged him on the chin.'

Avis grinned. 'So I should just get off the plane, grab a taxi, and pop him in the head?' she said.

Joel suddenly looked puzzled and bothered. 'Wait, wait,' he said, 'what plane? What are you talking about?'

She hadn't told him that bit yet, hadn't told him of her decision to fly to LA and confront Dyson. Which was weird, given that that was the *only* bit – the flying, at least – that she'd intended to tell him.

'I'm flying there,' she said. 'I have to.'

'When?'

'Tomorrow.'

'*Tomorrow!* Jesus.'

'The clock's ticking, Joel. Took me five days to get a damn ticket. Could've gone straight away, of course. First Class. Three thousand dollars. In my dreams. Tomorrow's the first flight I could get for less than half a grand.'

'But what are you going to *do*?' he said, his concern for her touchingly clear on his face and in his voice.

Avis pursed her lips and raised her eyebrows. It was a damn good question. 'Philosophically?' she said. 'Punch him in the face. Actually? I've no idea.'

# 25

In the twenty-two and a half hours between Joel seeing Avis into a cab outside the Waverly and Joel rushing into his top floor apartment, breathless from the five flights of stairs in his no-elevator building on West 11th, he – and all of New York – had enjoyed a brief respite from the greyness of its winter. It was still cold as a Republican's heart, of course, but the sky was that deep and brittle blue that he'd always loved and the sun, despite its bankruptcy of heat, was bright and forgiving.

Fumbling at his pants pocket to put it away, he nearly dropped his key in his haste to get across his living room to the phone. God, he was a fuck-up. Not only had he not taken the coffee house napkin containing the treasure of Avis's phone number to work with him but he'd forgotten to check the time of her flight. She might already be in the air or at least in a cab on her way to the airport. He glanced at his watch again. It was still a couple of minutes after noon.

He picked up the phone and started dialling, laying the book he had brought from work beside the phone and flicking it open to the pages he'd marked while holding the phone awkwardly between his chin and his shoulder.

He finally took a breath as the connection went through and he heard the first ring. Holding the book open with one hand, he took hold of the phone with his other and calmed down. Okay. It was ringing. The matter was no longer in his hands. She was either in or not.

After the hectic pace of his dash home, the ten seconds or so that the phone rang seemed very long and relaxed. Joel looked round his room, blessed temporarily by the sunlight that came in the windows, and wondered if – on the off-chance he ever got her back here – Avis would like his place or not. It was tidy at least, though his dusting schedule was not all it should be. Lots of bookcases. Lots of books. The walls were bad, their turn-of-the-century plastering a tribute more to haste than to smoothness, but they were hidden by the bookcases and by pictures. The pictures were good. She'd like them, he thought. They showed the range of interests of a well-rounded man, he hoped. The framed *Casablanca* one-sheet (original, bought with a ridiculously huge part of one of his student loans but bought, thank God, before the market for such things exploded) would show her he was hip and in touch with the culture of his own country (Christ. Did it do that any more? Did somebody Avis's age even know who Bogart was? Maybe he should trade it in for a Pearl Jam poster or something.) and the series of prints by Tiepolo of commedia dell'arte clowns (Not original. Are you kidding?) would show her he was sophisticated and had an appreciation of the older cultures from which his country had sprung. Maybe she'd like his place. Maybe she'd like him.

After five rings, her answering machine clicked on. Joel groaned. Had he missed her? Maybe she was screening.

'Avis? Hi,' he said, 'it's Joel. You there? No? Damn. Maybe you haven't left yet. Just at a store or something. Listen. I was thinking about . . . you know . . . about *it*. I got reminded of something. Checked it out at work. This is from an essay by John William Adams. He was an English poet. Early Edwardian. Not a bad poet but his prose was a bit over-precious. Anyway. I can't help feeling this section is . . . I don't know . . . related to the issue at hand, let's say. Hope your machine doesn't have a cut-off timer. Here goes:

> Their boats were fragile. Moored in the docks of Europe, anchored in Liverpool, Southampton, or Rotterdam, they may have looked strong to emigrant eyes, may have seemed huge and firm and built of promises and new beginnings – but imagine them; tiny constructions of wood and canvas braving an ocean whose size was unimaginable and whose latent fury was terrifying.
>
> But they never sailed empty.

204

There was a hunger for exploration and escape that was stronger in the disenfranchised children of Europe than the fear of the ocean or the mysteries of the New World.

The emigrants were fleeing. Pogroms and potato famines, of course, but was that all? As much as they were sailing to a dream of self-determination, they were sailing *from* something else – something older, darker, and rarely discussed; the mythic woods marked on no maps save those of the imagination. The flight to America was a flight to reason, to forests free of magic histories, to air free of secret shapes between the atoms, to a day free of voices that whispered in forgotten languages, to a night free of impossible hands that found their frightened dreaming shoulders.

But some plagues cannot be burned away. Some vermin cannot be escaped by water. The people on those ships did not sail alone. Like the black rat or poison spider hidden deep inside forgotten cargo, something else sailed with them, stowaways in the best hiding place of all – the human heart. Burrowed deep inside the soul like the eggs of parasites laid beneath the skin of our subconscious, ready to hatch anew beneath Manhattan skies.

'Okay. Another thing. One of my grad students did a paper once on how the figures of American popular culture are the equivalent of old folklore archetypes. Old myths in new clothes. That would be like Adams's parasites hatching anew, I guess. Look, I don't know how much use any of this is but I'm trying to help you understand it all. Knowledge is power, etcetera. And there's something there, I think. Myths – or things we've turned into myths – trying to break back into this world, using our own representations of them as their points of access. Now it's still not the *why* I was after but . . . I don't know . . . I'm rambling . . . Shit, this has got to be the longest answering machine message in history. Look, call me. Soon as you hear this. Soon as you can. Fly safe. I'll talk to you. Bye.'

Joel put the phone down. He felt ridiculously disappointed that he hadn't heard Avis's voice, hadn't been able to talk to her before she left. He'd managed to continue pretending all the way through his rush home that the imperative which drove him was the conveying of this information to her but, now that the information was conveyed, he could no longer pretend that the urgency in his heart was anything other than what it was – a simple longing for Avis herself.

Good God, Joel, he told himself, you're thirty-seven years old – what's with this high-school crush on a girl who's probably not even interested, a girl you hardly know? He had no answer, of course. The heart is not amenable to reason and has little interest in debate. He liked her. He really liked her. And that was that.

Except that it wasn't. Because she was in a strange and terrible situation and was flying right now directly to the heart of it and so the usual nervous feeling that accompanies an infatuation was mixed in in this case with an anxiety for Avis's wellbeing that was going to keep him more than mildly fucked-up until she was safely back in New York.

He looked at his watch again. Despite the detour home he could probably make the class before the last two or three of the students dragged their reluctant selves in. Once a week, he had a gig as a tutor at an extension class in which most of the students were general public enthusiasts but with a few credit-gathering and far from enthusiastic undergraduates thrown in just to help make the experience a little more unpleasant for all concerned. The library elders were cool about it – mainly because Joel in turn was cool about covering the few late-evening shifts that government cutbacks still allowed.

Patting his pockets to check on keys, billfold, and glasses – a stupid Pavlovian habit he'd picked up from his dad – he turned and headed for his door.

He was already back in rush-mode so he didn't look around his living room before he left. Which was a shame because, had he cared to cast a backward glance, he might have noticed that something strange had happened. The sunlight was still bathing his walls and the pictures they held in unseasonal brightness and the pictures themselves were still hanging exactly as they had hung when he'd looked at them while waiting for Avis's phone to pick up but, within the pictures, something had changed.

The six Tiepolo prints – beautifully rendered engravings of eighteenth-century stage scenes – were now simply that. Stage scenes. The figures who had occupied those stages – contorted, masked, and motley-clad representations of the characters of the lost art of pantomime – were no longer present. It was as if a call had gone up from some unseen theatre manager that a better venue had been found. Joel's walls held only empty stages. The players who had trod those boards had moved on, called to another performance, summoned to a different drama.

Joel made good time on his run to the subway station and the subway train he caught made good time on its run up the city. So much so that Joel, looking at his watch as the train pulled into the station at which he'd thought he'd have to transfer, realized that he'd only in fact be ten minutes late were he to take his usual (and preferred) route after all. He debated it for a few seconds as the doors stood open. Screw it. He'd teach a better class if he got there happy. He let the doors close, rode one more station, and got out at 72nd.

Within three minutes of starting his walk across Central Park, he knew he'd made the right choice. Might be the last bright day before Christmas and, besides, he was still a little freaked by the whole Avis thing and the walk would help calm him down, help him make more smoothly his transformation from harried love-struck librarian to wise and wisdom-imparting philosopher.

The park got quieter and less populated each week as winter started to bite – and the area his route took him across was never one of the busier stretches anyway – but nevertheless he was a little surprised by how few people he was passing today, especially given the unexpected sunlight. It was strange, actually, how convincingly the sunlight made it seem as if somehow the year had simply folded itself over the harshest weeks of winter and sent him out into a brisk day in early spring. And the park was collaborating in that illusion. Was it ever really this green at this time of year? Were that many of the trees and plants perennials or evergreens? Strange that he'd never registered that before. In fact, as he turned through a clearing that he used practically every week, he was astonished at how *much* of a clearing it felt like today, surrounded as it was on all sides by burgeoning hedges and bushes, by trees that seemed not only richer in their foliage than he would have thought natural at this time of year but which were much more densely packed than he'd ever noticed.

In fact, he began to feel a little uncomfortable. The clearing felt suddenly less like an open way through a city park, a way traversed by scores of people every day, and more like a secret and special place contained within dense woods, a place into which few people ventured, and then not wisely. A spot of unknown but suggestively specific purpose bounded on all sides by the thick (and still thickening? No. Impossible, surely?) trees and bushes. Joel, suddenly and unpleasantly aware of how deeply he was surrounded by the woods, noticed something else, too. It no longer felt like the one o'clock he knew it to be. The sunlight had begun to take on a strange quality that he had observed before, but only in late afternoon. The sun was far from down but somehow its disappearance was becoming anticipated by the day. It was as if the light was pregnant with darkness, the afternoon latent with twilight. The blueness of the sky had given way to something else, to a still bright but icy whiteness. The entire atmosphere had changed and Joel felt like the place into which he had come was a place where he had no desire to be but – bizarrely and unsettlingly – a place which very much wanted him to be there.

Joel quickened his pace. He was an educated man. He was able to make certain associations and he wanted to be many yards out of the clearing before his mind dwelt on them. He wanted to be somewhere where he could feel foolish rather than afraid when he thought of sacred groves, of appointed places, of sites of offerings. But the brain is faster than the feet and no matter how much Joel kept such thoughts from his conscious mind, his cells were already screaming their recognition somewhere in his subconscious.

Joel looked around. Where the hell *was* everybody? Not only could he no longer see another living soul, he couldn't even *hear* them. It was ridiculous. He was probably within fifty yards in any direction of more than a hundred people and he felt completely and utterly alone.

Unfortunately, things didn't stay that way.

Suddenly, there was a whoosh of sound and a flurry of blind-ingly imprecise movement startlingly close to him. He threw himself instinctively to one side, gasping involuntarily, as the movement resolved itself into a flying man.

No, not flying. Tumbling.

Joel watched, astonished, as the acrobat completed his cartwheel dive and landed upright a few feet in front of him, grinning madly at Joel as if awaiting applause.

It didn't come from Joel but applause there certainly was, along with laughter and whistles of encouragement. Joel looked beyond the acrobat to find the source and blinked disbelievingly. There were things there that had not been there before. There were things there that simply should not have been.

Stretched and hung between two trees at one edge of the clearing was a large and heavy sheet of canvas. About ten feet tall and twenty feet long, it was painted with a street scene, a stylized and simple representation of the urban streets of eighteenth-century Italy. That was unlikely enough, but at least it was merely painted. What was in front of it was, impossibly, flesh and blood.

For a moment, Joel was mercifully free of fear. He was so completely certain of what was going to happen to him that he moved beyond terror to a simple poignant regret. He would never see Avis again. His wishes there, his unfocused hopes, indeed all his hopes and wishes for his life, were not to be realized.

Ahead of him, standing before their canvas backdrop, were the clowns. There were three other acrobats to join the fellow who'd cartwheeled past Joel and then there were the major players: Harlequin, Pierrot, Pulcinello, Columbine, and, in front of them and plainly the man in charge, the figure known in the commedia tradition as Il Dottore, the Surgeon. Joel recognized them all. It wasn't difficult. He'd looked at them every day for years in the prints on his walls. Joel had always prided himself on keeping his sense of wonder as he got older and a little part of him was almost pleased to see them. My God, he thought, Avis was right. He remembered her theory that anything of the fantastic, not just the products of Norbert Read's imagination, could be brought to life, remembered too that those things which weren't Read's could not last long, that the focus couldn't hold. He tried to find comfort there as he stared at the company of grotesques ahead of him but

209

he had a horrible feeling that the focus was going to hold just long enough.

The Surgeon, an almost comically bizarre little man with tiny glittering eyes and an absurdly full beard, took several steps toward Joel while his compatriots stayed where they were, each of them smiling a strange half-smile that promised both a secret and unpleasant knowledge and a close proximity to the borders of sanity.

The Surgeon looked at Joel, cocked his head, and grinned.

'As the day is long, sir,' he said, 'an excellent surprise.'

He paused to bow elaborately to Joel and then continued with his introduction. 'You have stumbled, sir, upon Europe's finest comedians.'

Joel's sense of wonder had fled, shrieking, along with any other complexities of response. Now what he felt was very precise and very unpleasant. Fear and nothing but. His heart was beating dismayingly fast and distressingly hard in his chest and a cold sweat covered his entire body. He was trembling all over and he tried his best to keep that tremor out of his voice as he replied.

'I'm sorry,' he said, 'sorry to have disturbed you. I had no idea you were here.'

The Surgeon made an exaggerated and sudden play of looking around himself. 'Yet here it appears we most definitely are, sir,' he said, and narrowed his eyes at Joel. 'And should we be elsewhere?'

Joel, loathing the appeasing tone he heard whimpering in his own voice, shook his head and raised his hands placatingly.

'No, no,' he said, 'of course not. You can be wherever you want. But *I* should be somewhere else. I'm running a little late.'

He made as if to move past the Surgeon but the latter raised his hand in a staying motion.

'An appointment?' he asked.

Joel nodded.

'We too have an appointment, sir,' the Surgeon said, waving his hand expansively to indicate the rest of his troupe, 'but regrettably have eaten our map.' He belched, as if to illustrate his point, and continued, 'Where does your business take you today?'

Joel looked helplessly past the Surgeon to the silent unwavering smiles of the other clowns. 'I . . . I have a class to teach,' he said.

'In what discipline, sir, if I may enquire?'

'Philosophy.'

The Surgeon's face creased into an exaggerated mime of a man most impressed with the company in which he has found himself.

'Philosophy!' he said. 'A fine trade indeed, and one never to be confused with the training of frogs, which is – and I speak from experience – a much overrated profession.'

Joel smiled weakly in response and again started to move, stepping to his left in order to walk past the Surgeon – who stepped to his right in order to stop him.

'We have played for crowned heads, sir,' he said, his tone mildly insulted. 'Would you leave without letting us play for you?' He raised his hand in a gesture of command and shouted over his shoulder, 'Players, prepare!'

Behind him, Pierrot and Pulcinello bent down to a hessian sack and began to draw out musical instruments – a trumpet, a cornet, and a bass drum.

'Thanks. Really, thank you,' said Joel, knowing his desire to leave was pointless but expressing it anyway, 'but I have to go. You'll have to excuse me.'

'And leave you unsatisfied, sir?' the Surgeon replied. 'An unsatisfied audience is the saddest thing in the world, save a one-legged fish in a barrel of pork.'

Pierrot and Pulcinello raised the horns to their lips and blew while Harlequin, with enthusiastic vigour and a healthy contempt for any established rules of rhythm, pounded the bass drum. The clearing was suddenly filled with their deafening and vile music, dissonant and grating and suggestive in its piercing discordancy that whatever entertainment to which this formed the overture would be far from amusing.

Raising his voice to be heard above the din, Joel pressed his point with the Surgeon. 'Really,' he said, 'there's no need.'

'But I insist,' said the Surgeon, and this time his voice was as sharp and as cold as the two huge and gleaming butcher's knives which he suddenly produced from the deep pockets of his coat and held upright in each hand to either side of him.

211

Before Joel could react with anything more than a gasp of fear, two of the acrobats launched themselves forward in a series of somersaults which ended, with impressive precision, with an acrobat standing on either side of Joel and each holding one of Joel's arms in a strong and restraining grip.

'A brief diversion in your busy day, sir,' the Surgeon said. 'An entertainment entitled *Your Last Sight on Earth*, and guaranteed to please. Silence!'

This last was to his fellow clowns, who dropped their instruments immediately and moved into their assigned places before the painted backdrop. The Surgeon's cry of silence, though, seemed more than a simple instruction to stop the music. Like the cry of a priest who served a god forgotten or forbidden, it was an invocation to the medium in which their pantomime art was practised. Joel, like the single dissenter in a crowd of the faithful, shattered the silence with a scream of protest.

'No! Let me go! Somebody help me!'

He would have said more but the small red ball that one of the acrobats fished from his pants and shoved firmly in Joel's mouth silenced him. At a nod from the Surgeon, who followed behind ready for his own part in the wordless comedy, the acrobats hustled Joel over to the backdrop where the play was already in progress.

Harlequin and Columbine were in the middle of a pantomime argument – Harlequin, with angry looks and pointing fingers, was accusing Columbine of something which she, with fervent eyes and imploring hands, was denying.

Pierrot, shamefaced and afraid, was flattened against the backdrop, trying to look invisible. Pulcinello wasn't letting him, tugging at Harlequin's sleeve and pointing at Pierrot. Harlequin nodded and Pulcinello, hunchbacked and capering, rushed over to the cowering moon-faced clown, flipped up Pierrot's long tunic, and shoved his head up and under it for a close examination of Pierrot's groin.

Columbine buried her head in her hands, her body wracked with huge silent sobs, as Harlequin awaited the hunchback's judgement. It wasn't long coming. Pulcinello emerged, holding his nose, and shook his head at Harlequin with an expression

212

that suggested he had little cause for jealousy in that department.

The acrobats moved Joel, struggling in their grip, into the action, bringing him onstage between the arguing lovers. Columbine threw her hands up to her cheeks, her mouth open in a noiseless gasp of shocked recognition. Harlequin, pointing an accusing finger at Joel, used his eyebrows to ask Columbine about him. Columbine, blushing prettily, could no longer deny. She stared at Joel, her hands fluttering over her heart and an exaggerated look of infatuation on her face. Yes, this was indeed her secret lover.

Joel did his best to shriek his denial, his reluctance to play the part in which these creatures had cast him, but the gagging ball muffled his protests and all his increased struggling did was to make the acrobats grasp him even more painfully.

Harlequin, face darkened with betrayal and rage, ordered Pierrot, Columbine, and Pulcinello away. The Surgeon, now wearing a judge's wig plucked from the hessian sack, crossed paths with them as he entered the action and walked up to Harlequin to offer legal assistance. Harlequin pointed accusingly at Joel again and beat his breast. The Surgeon, sympathetic, proffered his knives. Harlequin looked at them, considered, and shook his head. The Surgeon dropped them to the grass and dug back in his pockets for another solution. He brought out a duelling pistol. Again, Harlequin declined. The Surgeon tried one more time and produced a lobster in one hand and a lump of cheese in the other. Harlequin gave him a look. This was no time for humour. Or supper.

Suddenly, the Surgeon tapped his temple and jabbed his finger up in the air, miming the birth of a wonderful idea. He pointed to the backdrop. Harlequin nodded excitedly. That was more like it! He gestured to the acrobats holding Joel and they backed him off, circling round so that they were directly in line with the centre of the backdrop and several yards away from it.

The Surgeon rushed to one end of the canvas and Harlequin to the other.

The acrobats lifted Joel bodily off the ground, laying him forward in their strong and unshakeable grip like a fleshy missile about to be launched.

213

Harlequin and the Surgeon each grasped a side of the backdrop.

The acrobats swung Joel between them – once, twice, three times – each swing building up momentum . . .

Nodding each to the other, Harlequin and the Surgeon yanked at the canvas cloth and it fell away from between the trees.

Joel's eyes bulged in appalled disbelief. His body jerked in uncontrollable spastic twitches as his terror, watered by what he suddenly saw, flowered into a new fullness.

The removal of the backdrop had revealed not, as he might have hoped had he had mind to spare to hope, the open expanse of the rest of an unbewitched Central Park but something else entirely. Ahead of him, hovering impossibly in space and shimmering like a heat-haze mirage, was a massive whirlpool-like maw that stretched back into a dark and dizzying infinity of some space other than our own. Circular, ribbed, and pulsing, it was like an impossible tunnel hollowed through the nightmare organic rock between dimensions. And from way back in its darkness came the sharp sound of whirring blades.

With a final swing, the acrobats launched Joel directly into it.

The play was done.

Undaunted by the absence of applause, professional to the last, the remaining players formed a line and bowed to the empty auditorium, holding in their hearts for comfort the unheard approval of their unseen patrons.

# 26

The little girl in the aisle seat two rows down from Avis and on the other side of the plane had slept right through take-off, right through the banks and turns that took the DC-10 to its cruising altitude of 35,000 feet somewhere above Pennsylvania, right through the service of peanuts and soft drinks, and was only now being awoken by her mother in preparation for dinner.

Avis had obsessed on the kid. She couldn't fucking believe it. Couldn't believe (and envied and resented) the child's complete obliviousness to the insanity in which she and all the other passengers were willingly taking part. Was she too young to know that they were all risking their lives? That they were all sitting in a fragile pressurized tin can packed with thousands of gallons of potentially explosive fuel? And sitting in it *miles* above the earth? And what the hell was her mother thinking, exposing her daughter to such danger?

Avis herself couldn't have slept if she'd been offered a million dollars per snore. Unlike the selfish little brat across the aisle, *she'd* spent the first forty-five minutes of the flight (not to mention the two hours preceding it) in a stomach-clenched state of hyper-awareness, gripped by an anxiety that was at best a constant bubbling discomfort and which occasionally broke surface as a body-sweeping cold sweat whenever the plane did anything at all that broke the illusion that it was an earthbound and stationary object.

The guy in the window seat next to Avis didn't seem interested in conversation, thank God, so she hadn't had to freeze him out in order to keep her attention focused obsessively on every little sound the aircraft made. Not that she thought she could *do* anything if she heard the sound of the wing coming apart or the fuselage igniting. It was just part of her flying superstitions. She had to pay attention. She was responsible. If her guard slipped, if she relaxed for a moment, something would happen and it would be her fault. Like the ads used to say, it was the only way to fly.

The little girl – what? Seven, eight years old? – was fully awake now. She sat up in her seat and, very self-possessed, wriggled her head around as if an invisible chiropractor was adjusting her neck. It was a curiously adult gesture and it held Avis's gaze. Which meant that when the little girl suddenly swung her head round over her shoulder to stare instantly and unerringly at Avis, Avis in turn was still staring at her.

Their eyes were locked for a second before Avis could conjure the automatic smile appropriate for such occasions – *Oops, we're strangers and we're looking at each other, lucky neither one of us is a psychopath, huh?* – but, weirdly and unsettlingly, the little girl neither returned the smile nor looked away. Avis felt her own smile falter as the child regarded her coolly for several seconds with a flat, unblinking, but curiously intent expression, her eyes wide and fixed as if she was staring at someone or something which she recognized but with which she wasn't yet sure how to deal.

It was odd enough to have been creepy even if they'd been on the ground and in Avis's heightened state it was downright disturbing and she was considerably relieved when the kid finally looked away and turned to her mother, pulling at the sleeve of the woman's dress for attention and then leaning her little body upwards to whisper in her ear.

During her daughter's whispering, the mother glanced back several times at Avis and hissed a few whispers of her own at her little girl. Avis wondered what the hell was going on. Had she done anything? Had she somehow inadvertently frightened the kid? God knows, she was always far from sure what her face looked like when she was flying. Maybe the friendly little smile she thought she'd sent out had actually been a grimace of anxious terror that read to a child's eyes as some vague stranger's threat.

After a few more exchanges in their whispered argument,

216

accompanied by increasingly determined pulls on the maternal sleeve, the mother threw one more glance back at Avis and then reached down and unclipped her daughter's seatbelt.

The girl stood up, left her seat, and walked the small distance up the aisle to where Avis, increasingly freaked by it all, was sitting.

Avis turned her uncomfortable eyes to the guy beside her, eager now for some conversation, keen to establish her credentials as a normal human being for her fellow passengers before the child, probably loudly, accused her of God-knows-what. But his face was buried in a book, the bastard, and Avis turned back with impeccable timing to see the girl stop by her seat and stare at her again. Okay, Avis. Make your face normal. Make your voice normal. Get this over with.

'Can I help you, sweetheart?' she said, making damn sure the people in the rows in front and behind her heard what a kind and reasonable adult she was.

'I was dreaming,' the girl said.

'Were you, honey?' Avis replied. 'I saw you sleeping. Was it a nice dream?'

The little girl shrugged an it-was-okay-I-guess shrug. 'Are you Avis?' she said.

Oh. Fuck.

Avis nodded dumbly.

'The soldier said to tell you you're going the wrong way,' the little girl said.

The remaining four and a half hours of the flight were probably the most turbulence-free that Avis had ever enjoyed in the air. But she didn't notice.

Sheryl – as the little girl had belatedly introduced herself – had had nothing further to say regarding her dream and, after asking Avis if she too was on vacation and did she think the in-flight movie was going to be any good, had returned to her mother and not looked at Avis again for the rest of the flight.

Avis hadn't really needed any more information, anyway. The simple message that had been forwarded to her had been a model of brevity and precision. Avis knew who the soldier was – her

217

long-dead grandfather popping up yet again in the dreams of people who were strangers to him – and his opinion of her journey was patently, and depressingly, clear. It was a warning that she was heading into danger. She'd known that, of course, but this was an unpleasant confirmation from beyond the grave. Avis didn't know why the opinion of the dead should carry more weight than that of the living but she felt that it indubitably did. She wondered, as she'd wondered when Fern had seen him, why her grandfather wasn't appearing directly in her own dreams but she thought she knew the answer. Avis didn't dream well. She wasn't very good at it. Maybe she didn't sleep deeply enough. Maybe, when asleep, she surrendered less of her consciousness than she ought to, remaining tethered to reality's causeway instead of braving the deeper waters that surrounded the dream country. Her grandfather found it easier to reach sailors who were braver than she. Sheryl was a child – her young soul less far from direct access to the collective unconscious than were the ossifying minds of dreaming adults – and Fern, with her New Age obsessions and constant eagerness for the paranormal, must have been someone whose dream-life was always in a state of readiness for contact with the beyond. But, even if he had to use intermediaries, William's messages were getting through and Avis felt even more unsure about the wisdom of confronting Dyson than she'd felt when she got on the plane.

She tried to accentuate the positive – at least Sheryl hadn't passed on a message that said the plane was going to drop out of the sky. On every other flight she'd ever taken, Avis would have given her eye teeth for any kind of assurance – supernatural or not – that the plane was going to end its trip with a slow taxiing into the terminal zone rather than in a massive fireball thousands of feet above it, but this time that thought was scant comfort. This time all she felt was a realization that terror, too, had its hierarchies and that her fear of flying was as nothing to her fear for herself and her world if she failed to stop Valentine Dyson from conjuring Read's big thunder.

She couldn't believe the light when she emerged from baggage claim (not that she had any baggage to claim – she'd flown with

218

a single carry-on holdall – but the only way out to the taxi ranks was through the massed hundreds of suitcase-searchers) and saw her first California afternoon. It was winter, for God's sake, but you'd never know it from the deep blue of the Los Angeles sky and the air that – once you filtered out the overwhelming fumes of diesel and gasoline – actually *smelled* warm, smelled like the air in a sauna that had been turned off for an hour or so but which carried the memory of heat in its molecules. But she didn't feel over-dressed in her heavy December-in-New-York coat because it was late afternoon and, despite the light, the day was growing cool. LA was a desert, she remembered being told sometime somewhere by someone, warm in the day, cold at night.

She walked over to the posted TAXI sign, got a cab without any wait at all, and told the driver she was looking for a cheap hotel in Hollywood. The driver swung round in his seat to look at her as he pulled out into traffic – Avis reflecting, through the annoyed honking of the car horns of the other drivers he inconvenienced, that at least the road habits of cabbies were the same on either coast – and gave her an appraising glance. It was only an hour later, after she'd seen the parade of hookers on Sunset and seen the sleazy motels that presumably functioned as their bases of operations, that Avis realized he'd been deciding whether or not to take her somewhere where the night manager might be looking for the rent in trade not cash. She supposed she should be flattered that he drove her instead to a Days Inn that catered to the less well-heeled tourist and was only a few blocks walk from the address of the rental studios where Dyson was making his movie.

It was before they arrived at the Days Inn though, and during the drive across town after exiting the freeway, that Avis received a shock only marginally less disturbing than Sheryl's dream message. The cab had been stuck at a red light and Avis, glancing around her through the cab's filthy windows, had seen a large billboard on top of a three-storey building. It was a striking piece of minimalism – a jet-black background with a single shard of silver lightning forking across its centre. No advertising copy, no words of any kind. Avis wondered what it was for. A new perfume? A heavyweight bout? There were no clues at all to the nature of the product it was supposed to be hyping. What kind of promotion was that? What the hell did they want you to do? Guess?

As the cab crawled its way to the corner of the next block things became clearer. A second billboard was there to follow up the first. This one had the same solid black for its backdrop but where the lightning had been there was now – in letters small and unpretentious and of the same silver hue as the lightning – only the single phrase, *It's Coming*. Avis began to understand. It was one of those serial advertising strategies, a method of hooking drivers into playing the advertiser's little game so that the attention they paid to the final puzzle-solving billboard was stronger than it might have been for a single splash announcement. Avis resented such blatant manipulation as much as the next consumer. But it always fucking worked. Annoyed with herself for doing it, she nevertheless found herself peering forward, ready to check out the next billboard.

When it came a block later, it was as plain as the first two: the black background and a simple phrase. But this time the phrase was *Big Thunder* and there was a six-digit date underneath it. Month. Day. Year. And the date was the day after tomorrow.

The cab took the right at the corner where the third billboard stood and Avis twisted in her seat to keep it in view for as long as possible, waiting for the optical illusion to be over, waiting for her mind to stop playing tricks on her, waiting for the real words to swim into focus and replace those that her anxiety had painted there. Because it couldn't be true. How could it be? How could Dyson have made this happen so quickly?

'You all right?' the cabbie suddenly said. 'You going to be sick? Don't throw up in my cab.'

Avis wondered what the hell he was talking about and then heard the low moan that was escaping her mouth and which had presumably been escaping it for the last minute.

'No,' she said, 'no, I'm fine.'

'Because if you throw up,' he continued, as if she hadn't answered at all, 'I won't clean it up. You'll clean it up. Understand? And I'll charge you double.'

'I said I'm all right!' she snapped. 'Just drive. And hurry up. I'm not here sightseeing.'

The cabbie stepped a little harder on the gas and didn't try to argue but he made a disgusted noise in his mouth and shook his head as if weary of idiots. Avis glared into his rearview. Fucking prick. She was really looking forward to stiffing him on the tip.

If Avis had had anything like a plan, it had involved somehow stopping the film before production was completed. Not that she'd figured out a method of doing that. Joining the union and calling a strike? Norma-Rae Avis. Shooting a star? Black Widow Avis. Persuading the marketing department that the story sucked? Siskel and Ebert Avis. But, whatever it might have been that she might have done, it was apparently too late for it now. If the billboards said Dyson's film was to be released in two days, then she had to assume that it was true. And if it was true then she had no time to waste on worrying about how it had come to be true. She had no time to waste, period.

She called the production office number as soon as she'd checked in to her two-notches-above-disgusting room and, unlike the time she'd called from New York, she was calm and precise.

'David Vial, please,' she said.

'May I ask who's calling?'

'Tell him it's Avis Llewellen. His friend from New York.'

The voice asked her to hold on. It was already after seven. She hoped he was still there. She hoped he'd take the call.

'Hello?' said another voice – a voice which, though she'd heard it only once before, she recognized instantly.

'Valentine Dyson,' she said.

'Not any more,' he replied very calmly. 'Can I help you?'

'Do you remember me?' she asked, suddenly and painfully aware of how without strategy she was, how unprepared and how powerless. She did her best to keep all that out of her voice.

'Oh, yes, I think so,' he said, 'didn't we meet outside Dyson's former headquarters?'

His voice, placid as a breezeless afternoon, hovered somewhere in the no-man's-land between politeness and boredom. But that

221

was good. It pissed Avis off enough to pull her right past nervous-ness and into a needling aggression.

'That's right,' she said. 'My place. The place where you mur-dered three of my friends.'

'Actually, I didn't,' he said, 'though I can understand why you'd make that assumption.'

His dismissive calm was more convincing than any angry denial would have been but Avis refused to be drawn into an argument about the specifics of how her friends died. Their deaths, much as she hated to admit it, were no longer the issue.

'I know what you're going to do when the movie opens,' she said. 'I read the story.'

'I see,' he said, and paused briefly before continuing. 'How exactly do you expect me to respond to that information?'

'You know what? I don't give a shit how you respond. I'm more interested in how the police and the press will respond.'

He gave a little laugh. 'I've not been in this industry very long, my dear,' he said, 'but I think I can say that, were you to make your theories public, you'd probably achieve little more than helping to double my opening-night gross. For which I'd thank you – except that, as you seem to know, I'm not in it for the money.'

'So what are you in it for? The fame?'

'No. Not the fame,' he said. 'The glory.'

There was something in the way he said it, something about the way his voice almost backed away from the word that made Avis uncomfortable and reminded her – like she needed reminding – of the bizarre nature of that with which she was dealing.

'This is a local call,' she announced.

'Really? How local?'

There was a mild surprise but no menace in his voice but still Avis bit her lip before taking the plunge.

'Less than half a mile,' she said.

'Then why don't we meet?' he said. 'I could even screen the picture for you if you'd like.'

What did he think she was? Stupid?

'I wouldn't like,' she said.

222

'I assure you, nothing would . . . happen.'

'No. Wouldn't want to spoil the premiere, would you?'

'Premieres,' he corrected. 'Simultaneous. Midnight in New York. Nine in Los Angeles. An hour either way for the other time zones.'

Avis groaned internally. Everything he was saying was an admission that she was right, was a confirmation of her fears.

'Let's meet somewhere neutral,' she said. 'Somewhere with lots of people.'

'You're in no danger from me, Avis, but as you wish; there's a pub-restaurant a couple of miles down Sunset. British-style. The Cat and Fiddle. The patio's always crowded. Lots of people. Shall we say an hour from now?'

Was she going to do this? Well, what the hell *else* was she going to do?

'All right,' she said, 'an hour. Will you be wearing your blue valentine?'

She'd meant it as an ironic jab but he laughed. Charmingly. Like they were making a *date*, for Christ's sake.

'I think the suit's at the cleaners,' he said. 'Don't know what I did with the flower.'

'It doesn't exist, you know. There's no such flower.'

'You mean there didn't used to be any such flower. Just like there didn't used to be any such *me*. Yet here I am. And I'll see you in an hour.'

He killed the connection and Avis put her phone down. He was right. She had to get over insisting on a reality that was past its sell-by date. The rules had changed. The flower existed. He existed. And, in two days time, the reality behind his film would exist as well.

He was right about something else, too. She was in no danger from him, at least not tonight. And the reason she was in no danger *from* him was because she posed no danger *to* him. She was no threat at all. His film was ready and she couldn't stop it from being shown. She was just an amusing diversion for him in the run-up to the glory he was awaiting, someone to whom she could talk more freely than to most people, someone to whom he could brag and pontificate.

223

Okay. She'd meet him. He'd talk. She'd listen. She'd ask questions. And, when he'd given her some understanding of why all this was happening, she'd look into his eyes one last time and then she'd kill him.

# 27

The Cat and Fiddle's patio was as crowded as Dyson had promised. Avis looked at the hordes of Young Hollywood smoking and schmoozing under the open sky and tried to imagine that many people choosing to sit outside in New York at this time of year but of course it was ridiculous. It just wouldn't happen. They'd either freeze to death or be so wrapped-up in winter clothing that boozing or socializing would be no fun. Here, though, jackets on the guys and extra sweatshirts on the girls were the only concession to winter, apart from the several – and, to Avis's blood at least, unnecessary – gas heaters that stood scattered guard around the grey stone courtyard. The courtyard itself, studded with glass-topped tables and wrought-iron chairs, was beautified by an over-abundance of plants and trees and brought to life by the cacophonous merging of a hundred different conversations.

There were as many people standing in chattering groups between the tables as there were sitting at them – a stylish crowd, predominantly good-looking, one or two faces Avis even thought she recognized from small parts in movies or sitcoms – and she had trouble locating Dyson at first. Then a particularly tall girl (tiny waist, skinny legs, huge breasts – how was *that* combination possible?) moved to the side of the group of which she was a part and, through the newly made gap in the crowd, Avis saw him.

He was at a table alone and he was already looking at her. There was a smile of welcome on his face and, gentleman that he was, he rose to his feet as she made the short trip over to the table and pulled back a chair for her.

'It's nice to see you again,' he said.

Avis wished she could say the same. In fact, she wished she

could say anything – because, as she sat and as she watched him seat himself again, she was suddenly overwhelmed with the insanity of it all. She looked at his impossibly handsome face – of course it was impossible, it had never existed, it was a wish-fulfilment face dreamed up decades ago by a much-less-handsome pulp fictioneer – and was speechless.

'May I order you a drink?' he asked just before the silence was about to become embarrassing. Avis shook her head, then reconsidered. She swallowed and found her voice.

'Screwdriver,' she said.

He smiled, half-turned, and, before his hand was even raised, a pretty girl in black was at his side, order pad in hand. He passed on Avis's request and was very graceful in ignoring the over-flirtatious manner of the waitress. Avis realized she was looking at a cliché. She waited till the girl had moved across the courtyard into the bar before asking him for confirmation. 'She's an actress, right?'

Dyson – or Vial or whatever the hell he wanted to call himself – nodded.

'And she knows you're a producer?'

'Well, she doesn't know that specifically,' he said. 'She's making certain assumptions based on age, manner, clothes, and locale.'

Avis was about to ask a follow-up question and then caught herself. Jesus Christ, she wasn't here for a conversation about the sad ways in which Hollywood worked.

'How vital are you to what's going to happen?' she asked instead.

'That's an interesting question,' he said, and he actually sounded like he meant it. 'The occupation of this flesh was of course of paramount importance to get our project up and running but I don't suppose it need have been me that occupied it.' He paused and looked at her quizzically as if weighing up her ability to follow what he was about to say. 'You see, the problem is that the concept of *me* is a little difficult for us, anyway. Separate selves are . . . oh, I don't know . . . occasionally convenient, some-times pleasurable, but always temporary. What's interesting is that I've been here for some time now and, despite myself, I can feel your reality . . . *congealing* around me, feel its ludicrous

226

pretensions to permanence binding me as effectively as it binds all of you, can feel myself hardening into this brittle inconsequence that you call being human. It's very strange. Perhaps in time I might even grow, as you all do, to love my prison, might fear my release from it, might, as you all do, call it death.'

He paused again and gave her a strange half smile. 'I mean, I don't know,' he said. 'Give me a few more days and I might actually be nervous sitting here watching your hand fiddle with your purse, waiting for its opportunity to draw out whatever killing tool it is that you've brought along with you.'

Avis went cold. Her hand, in pointless denial, leapt away from her purse and then snatched back at it as if afraid he might take it instead.

Dyson didn't move at all. Still infuriatingly calm, he asked, 'What is it?'

Avis opened the purse and half drew out the large and cruelly sharp butcher's knife that she'd bought not half an hour ago from a hardware store. She felt stupid and useless and his grin didn't help.

'My, that's a big one,' he said. 'Should I be flattered, I wonder?'

Avis found his equanimity neither impressive nor amusing. He wiped the smirk from his face.

'Let me explain something,' he said. 'As your first question implied, I'm now somewhat irrelevant to the process I've initiated. *Big Thunder* – do you think it sounds too much like a Western? I got a few comments about that – will open nationwide in two days whether I'm here or not. So killing me would be only an act of personal revenge. But you can go ahead if you like. I assume I can bleed. I've been observing this body's functions whenever I could spare the time. I even had sex a few days ago. It was nice. But dangerous – I nearly slipped the skin during orgasm. So if you killed me, I'd actually be interested to see what would happen. I should warn you, though, that this flesh is still imprinted with the Blue Valentine's behaviours. Swing that knife at it and it might snap your arm, wring your pretty neck, and run me out of here before anybody else even noticed we were fighting.'

Avis just stared at him. Using the knife was out of the question – not just because of his warning (delivered with the same

227

impersonal calm as everything else he said) but because it felt completely pointless. Everything felt completely pointless. It was over. She'd lost. This smiling monster sitting opposite her was going to have his way with the world and there was nothing she could do about it. She felt hollow and empty, like a terminal patient who'd moved past protest and was simply waiting for the end. The only thing she had left was curiosity.

'What in God's name are you?' she said.

'The orphans of ecstasy, Ms Llewellen,' he replied, 'the angels of exile. We are the brother you've forgotten, the child you've buried, the self that you've denied. For thousands of years we've watched you from the other side of the mirror. Now we're smashing the glass.'

'Why?'

'There's nothing else we can do. You've forced us to it.'

'Right. Like we're the bad guys.'

Dyson looked at her and nodded. 'Yes. As a matter of fact you are.'

Avis's face filled with angry denial but Dyson raised a silencing hand before she could speak.

'Look, there's something you should understand,' he said. 'Your world wasn't always the way it is. Once it was fluid and graceful and matter and man were as liquid as water. And we were not strangers – all the worlds bled into each other. But, millennia ago, you closed the doors. Reason flourished, belief withered, and magic withdrew from the world. And every day that you continue to insist that the world is solid forces us further into hiding.

'Don't misunderstand me. If you shivering apes want to stay fearful, fleshed, and fragile, it's no ephemeral skin off my impermanent nose. I frankly couldn't care less. But the whole of creation is linked, every dimension interconnected. You're a blocked artery in the heart of the Divine and I'm here to perform the bypass. I'm not the Devil's butcher, Ms Llewellen, I'm God's surgeon.'

'Tell that to the thousands of people you're going to kill on opening night,' Avis said.

'There will be casualties,' he acknowledged, 'but we're not

228

ultimately here to harm you. We're here to heal. We're here to answer the cries of help you've been sending out since the Forgetting.'

'Cries of help? What the fuck are you talking about?'

'Some of you dream, Avis. And some of you – artists – dream in pictures or words or music. That's the faint echo of the faculty you once had. You put a premium on imagination – look where we're sitting, think what this town was built on – but you don't realize it's the bastard stepson of a greater parent, an atrophied remnant of the magic you once wielded. Sad shattered thing that it is, it's still your only means of remembering and our only means of access.'

'Screwdriver and a Scotch rocks,' the waitress said, placing the drinks down on the table. Avis sat back, jolted by the sudden intrusion of reality into the unreal conversation they'd been having. Dyson, though, made the transition effortlessly, pulling cash from a billfold and tipping the girl generously. His borrowed eyes watched her walk away and then, with equal ease, he turned back to Avis and resumed.

'Your collective unconscious wants this, Avis,' he said, 'I promise. You threw away something precious and the memory of mutablity, the ghost of transmutation, has bedevilled you ever since. What was the Alchemists' dream but a recovery of such powers? They sought to rediscover the protean gene and to translate themselves back into angels. Now their experiment is to be completed. Your world is the lead that is to enter the furnace of the sages and remember that it is gold. What will happen in two days time is not the destruction of the world but its transformation.'

'Pretty talk,' said Avis, 'and just how exactly is mass murder going to accomplish all this?'

'Your world has a terrible gift for marginalizing the incredible. People believe in UFOs, for example. People believe in ghosts. But those beliefs, and the stories that support them, somehow never inform the culture. They're minor ripples in a pool that insists on its own stagnancy. They're filed away and ignored.'

*That other stuff*, thought Avis, remembering her own filing away of such matters and silently conceding his point. She saw his

229

leasehold eyes glitter with excitement in his imagined flesh and knew her concession was no secret to him.

'But *Big Thunder* will be too large-scale to ignore,' he said, sipping at his Scotch. 'The deaths are irrelevant. What counts is the massive psychic assault the nature of those deaths constitute. When the clouds cover America, when the bodies float and the blood-rain falls, surely then the blinkers will fall off. The Great Work will remember itself. Renew itself. Paradise will be regained.'

Avis grabbed her screwdriver, tipped it back, and drank it down like it was a soda or plain water. She clunked the empty glass back on the table and stared at him.

'Thanks for the drink,' she said and, pulling her purse toward her, made to leave. She had nothing else to say. She had no doubt he believed everything that he'd just said. She had no doubt that his magic was going to work, that the clouds would escape the screen and that ninety minutes after his film started playing the world she knew would be changed for ever. She had no idea whether that change would be the profound metaphysical alteration he was talking about or simply a terrible post-apocalyptic nightmare. She didn't know and she didn't care. All she knew was that she was human and that, right or wrong, she wanted the world to stay as it was. She'd always assumed that she was as ready for the miraculous as the next girl but she'd never dreamed that when it came it would come demanding blood. Dyson promised a New Humanity but it was a promise that was poisoned for her by an image of those new humans rising to their feet bathed in the blood of their parents, knee-deep in the viscera of those who had come before. Fuck him. It was a lousy deal. It was like sitting down to bargain with God and then catching sight of his red glinting horns. She stood up. Dyson made no attempt to stop her or to persuade her to stay.

'Stay indoors on Friday,' he said, as calmly as if warning of a slight summer shower and concerned she'd catch a chill. 'The book of terrors is brief. The book of wonders lasts for ever.'

She walked away without a word and without a backward glance.

# 28

The motel didn't have cable.

Which meant that after two-thirty in the morning Avis's insomnia had had nothing but paid programming to entertain it. Which meant that when she'd finally slipped into sleep at about four a.m. she'd already been subjected to more than ninety endlessly recycled minutes of a brain-destroying infomercial in which some lunatic and ugly Brit with an insufferable voice demonstrated, with an enthusiasm that should surely have been reserved for at least the second coming of Christ, the virtues of a set of (admittedly reasonably priced) cooking utensils. Her last conscious thought had been to wonder whether, if she called the 1-800 number and promised to buy his entire stock, she could prevail upon him in the names of decency and peace to just shut the fuck up.

The TV had still been playing four and a half hours later when Housekeeping knocked on the door and shouted through it. Avis had groggily told them to come back later, fumbled for the remote, killed the early morning news, and fallen back asleep.

She woke again at a little after midday thanks to the noisy departure of a couple in the room next door. Because the closed blinds were good and heavy the room, save for one inch-thick band of bright California sunlight on the far wall, was still dark and Avis couldn't believe the time on the radio-alarm beside her bed. She also couldn't believe how groggy she still felt, how her body was urging her mind back into sleep and how her mind wasn't putting up much of a fight about it. She'd had enough friends suffer from depression (and tell her endlessly about the symptoms) to know what this meant. She'd given up. She was in retreat, her body and mind shutting down to avoid facing the appalling facts of her defeat and what it meant for her world. But realizing it didn't change it.

As her eyes closed again and her arms pulled the bedding tight and cocoon-like around her, a thought came to her. It was a free thought, not something she consciously generated, just one item in the parade of semi-conscious images and phrases that flitted across the screen of her passive mind as it fell rapidly back toward sleep. Her grandfather. He was out there somewhere in some region of the dream country. Maybe she could visit. Maybe this time she could find whatever unmarked route had previously eluded her. She didn't seize on the thought, knowing instinctively in her hypnogogic state that conscious focus would kill its possibilities. Instead she let it go, allowing it to give way to everything else that was crowding into her surrendered mind – nonsense phrases, irrational images, impossible sounds. Some began to last longer than others.

She was running down a street in New Jersey, trying to keep sight of an ice-cream van.

She was at a boxing match, refusing to look at the blood-soaked ring and the knives that grew out of the forearms of the combatants.

In a rock pool an octopus was dancing.

She was looking at a doll's house. The house got bigger or she got smaller. She looked up at a window. A blue-dressed little girl with long blonde hair looked out at her. The little girl's eyes were silvered glass. Avis could see her reflection in them. She got smaller again until one looking-glass eye was all she could see and she walked toward her own reflection but it got very dark and the reflection disappeared and it wasn't a looking-glass at all but instead was an entrance to a cave and so she went through it and came out the other side and she was on top of a hill and she walked down it and turned to her left and found she was looking up at a huge waterfall that pounded down onto dark rocks below and she stood looking at the waterfall for a long time and it made her feel helpless and sad and then a phone started ringing and she was very annoyed and she tried to ignore it but it kept ringing and she realized that she had to open her eyes.

The phone was next to the radio-alarm. Avis was furious at it.

232

She hadn't found her grandfather but who knows what might have happened if this fucking ringing hadn't pulled her out of the place she'd been. It was useless now. She wasn't groggy at all. She might as well answer it. Only as her hand lifted the receiver from its cradle did it occur to her, with a chilling jab of anxiety, that as far as she was aware nobody knew where she was. As her automatic hand lifted the phone to her ear she was suddenly convinced that Dyson had thought better of his contemptuous mercy of last night and had tracked her down to initiate the end of the business between them.

'Hello?' she said.

'Every waterfall was once a stream. Every stream has a source,' said the voice on the other end of the line.

Avis had no time to react because she was suddenly and horribly aware of the ominous low rumble outside her window. She dropped the phone and tried to scramble out of bed, her panicking legs trapped and tangled in the sheets as the rumble built to a deafening rushing roar and the massive waterfall smashed through the windowed wall, shattering brick and mortar as effortlessly as glass with its sweeping and unstoppable force. It filled the room in less than a second, lifting Avis's bed effortlessly and flinging it toward the door. She wanted to scream but her mouth was already full of water. She couldn't breathe. She couldn't see. But she could hear herself screaming. How was that possible?

She opened her eyes and jolted upright in a true waking, her scream cut off as she came back into her body. For a terrifying second or two her eyes scanned the motel room like those of a wild animal cut off from the herd and surrounded by predators. Gradually, her heart rate slowed to normal and she took a deep breath. All right. This was real now. The only sounds outside her window were those of a city going about its day. She clambered out of bed and rushed to the blinds, drawing them open hurriedly. Good. The forecourt of the motel. Cars. People. A closed-for-the-season pool. Sunlight. Reality.

More slowly, more calmly, she walked back to the bed, sat down on its side, and looked at the phone. It hadn't rung at all in real life. But its analogue in the dream country had brought her a message. The voice that had spoken to her before the waterfall

233

smashed into the room was one she knew. Even if not in person, her grandfather had finally managed to reach her.

After a shower, after dressing, after looking at the various brochures laid on her bedside table advertising the tourist pleasures of southern California and not being surprised that she found it difficult to summon up any enthusiasm for visiting them, she accessed her home machine from the phone. She only heard three beeps so was astonished at how long it took to rewind. Somebody'd been fucking long-winded.

The first message was from her bank, advising her she was ten days late with a house payment. The second was a tele-marketing cold-call. The third was Joel.

She curled up on the bed as he went on and on, strangely comforted by the sound of his voice. She wished she'd got to know him sooner. Maybe then she wouldn't be alone out here. Maybe then she wouldn't be alone when the world was reinvented. Maybe then she would have had a human hand to hold as humanity dissolved.

Joel's voice may have been a source of comfort but the substance of his message was different. It fed her anxiety – made her feel, with its historical perspective, that there was a kind of predestination to what Dyson was doing, that his victory was inevitable and that, as he himself had implied, humankind had always known that this day would come.

As soon as the message finished, she called Joel's home number. She got his machine, told it she was an idiot and should've tried the library first, hung up and dialled again. After a quick game of roulette with the automated switchboard she eventually reached somebody in Joel's department and asked for him. It was during the minuscule pause before the voice replied that Avis began to get an unpleasant sense that something was wrong.

'Who is this?' the voice asked with a strange carefulness.

'A friend,' she said, trying not to worry yet.

'When did you last see Joel?'

Oh Christ.

'I don't know. Two, three days ago?' Which was it? She was

234

losing track. Plane flights. Time differences. Too much sleep. Too many dreams.

'Mmm. Well, the problem is nobody's seen Joel for more than twenty-four hours now. We're all getting a little anxious.'

Avis took the phone out of her face and hung up without replying, cutting off the puzzled *Hello? Are you still there?* from the other end.

Joel was gone. People closer to him mightn't know it yet but Avis did. While she'd been curled up on the bed listening to his voice, Joel had already been lost. His long call to her, as surely as the dream phone call from her grandfather, had been a message from the dead. Dyson, or the forces Dyson represented, had killed him. She leant down, rested her forearms on her knees, cupped her face in her hands, and wept.

Why did he have to be killed? Dyson had made it sound like murder wasn't the purpose of what was happening. Lying sack of shit. His film was finished, his scheme in place. What harm could Joel do? So what if he was approaching some kind of understanding of what was going on? She herself had been given the whole story and yet was obviously being spared.

Drying her eyes, she sat up. Grief had given way to an insistent curiosity. Maybe things weren't as cut-and-dried as she thought, as Dyson obviously wanted her to think. She hadn't been killed and Joel had. Why? What was the difference between them? Avis was vain enough to entertain the possibility that Dyson liked her (you know, *liked* her) but not vain enough to assume that he would seriously risk scuppering a plan he'd waited on for centuries for her sake. She thought back to the other deaths, to Fern and John and Michael. Unlike Joel, they hadn't even known what was going on. Wait a minute. That wasn't strictly true . . .

Avis's mind was racing now. She suddenly felt she was heading somewhere, felt as if various things she knew were about to come together and give her a new insight. She remembered the scattered letters and the shattered glass in the bloody chaos of their living room. Fern too, like Joel, had perhaps been about to access some of the truth. And she and the others were killed for it. And if Avis had been at home with them that day she was damn sure she wouldn't have been excused from the slaughter.

So, if she'd been with Joel instead of out here, would she too have discovered the limits of Dyson's strange mercy?

But the fact remained that she knew more now than all of them and yet was being allowed to live. She'd thought that that was because her knowledge was now useless. The killing of Joel gave the lie to that so it had to be something else. Had to be . . . had to be where she *was*. It wasn't just access to the truth that put you in danger, it was being in a position to act on that truth. Which meant that there was still something that could be done if you were in the proximity of . . . of what? Of the source of their power? But their power wasn't centred anywhere, according to Dyson, other than the human imagination itself or the products thereof.

Wait a minute, wait a minute . . .

What had her grandfather just told her? *Every waterfall was once a stream. Every stream has a source.* She'd rushed out here ready to attack the waterfall – Dyson's film – and of course had been overwhelmed. It was too big, too inevitable, too powerful. Jesus Christ, was she slow. Jesus Christ, was she stupid. She'd been told on the plane she was going the wrong way and had read that as a simple warning about her own safety. No. She was fucking up. She was going the wrong way. Duh. She'd needed to turn around and head for the source . . .

She took a breath and whispered a name.

'Norbert Read . . .' she said.

No wonder Dyson could afford to be nothing more than amused by her. No wonder he could afford to let her live. She'd consciously removed herself from the place where she might be anything more than powerless, where her knowledge might do her some good. Out here, she was no threat. New York was a different matter.

God, it all made sense now. If works of imagination were the points of entry for her opponents then why hadn't this scheme been initiated decades or centuries earlier? She remembered again the voices in Fern's mouth and how her grandfather had let her eavesdrop on them. Chinese Dragons. Corridor Walkers. And Read's favourite, the Blue Valentine. Fuck, Dyson had said practically the same thing – *the occupation of this flesh was of paramount importance*. This flesh. The Valentine's flesh. Something that would give them what all previous points of access couldn't. The ability to work through time. To stick around. To get a damn movie made. To send out *Big Thunder*'s clouds on so large a scale that it would suffice, perhaps, to – what had Dyson said? – let the blinkers fall off.

Read was the key, and an even more vital one than she'd realized. Access through the products of human imagination they might always have had but access wherein the focus wouldn't hold, temporary access, was useless for any major scheme. Read was a special case. An astonishing and, for all she knew, unprecedented gift to them. It was his coma. His fucking coma. That limbo state he was in, neither living nor dead, gave them some kind of permanent access not merely through an imaginer's work but through an imaginer's brain. So what if Read had been by critical consensus a third-rate imaginer and even less of a craftsman? He was *theirs*. He could let them through like never before, he could let Dyson – or the thing that was occupying Dyson's flesh – through a gate which would stay open into a focus that would hold.

New York. Norbert Read. The source.

When Housekeeping came into room 212 an hour or so after its last guest had checked out, they – in the person of Juanita Ramirez – found a rather strange situation. Not the strangest Juanita had ever seen in her three years of chambermaiding and certainly not the most unpleasant or disgusting, but odd nonetheless. The TV set had been unplugged, all the pictures in the bedroom had been turned to the wall, and the mirror in the bathroom had been completely covered by a large bathtowel Scotch-taped to the wall.

# 29

The guy in the cowboy hat was doing his best not to take out his frustration on the middle-aged woman behind the counter. He knew it wasn't her fault. It was just that every time she *told* him it wasn't her fault, it pissed him off some more.

'Yes, I know, Mr Trusler,' she said. 'But it's not my fault.'

Carl sighed. 'Okay,' he said, 'then whose fault is it?'

'It's nobody's fault, sir,' she said, in almost as good an imitation of patience as he'd managed himself, 'it's the weather.'

'No. You see, you're not listening. I *know* it's the weather's fault that the planes aren't taking off. I *know* it's the weather's fault that we're stuck here at three in the morning irritating the hell out of each other. But it's not the weather's fault that I can't get accurate updates, is it? See, if I knew it'd be two hours, I'd stay. If I knew it'd be eight hours, I'd get a room. You with me?'

The woman made a sympathetic face. 'I don't know what to tell you,' she said. 'I'm doing the best I can.'

Carl nodded, did his best to smile, and moved away from the desk to the banks of seats in the gate's waiting area. He sat down heavily and looked at the girl sitting opposite him.

'Nothing new,' he said.

The girl nodded in acknowledgement but then quickly looked away, avoiding further eye-contact. Carl wasn't insulted. He was a doctor. He was trained to recognize the signs of anxiety and, man, she had a plethora. Still and silent, body posture stiff, face muscles tense, movements quick when necessary and non-existent when not. Poor little thing must be scared of flying, he figured. This waiting must be terrible for her. It put his own feelings into perspective. All *he* had to deal with was boredom and frustration. For her every additional minute of delay must make the terror worse.

Every additional minute of delay *was* making the terror worse but, for the first time in Avis's life, it wasn't the thought of getting on the plane that was bothering her. She wasn't even thinking about the flight itself. She had no doubt at all that when she got on the plane she'd get off it safely at the other end. It was the possibility of *not* flying that was making her worry. That, and what was to happen once she reached New York.

She'd been sitting here for hours now. The airport staff had been round long before midnight trying to organize hotels for those stranded but Avis had been one of the volunteers to simply sit it out. She didn't want a room. She didn't want to be alone. She didn't want to be spotted through whatever windows into this world might be open in a hotel room. She didn't figure they were actively looking for her yet – Dyson was probably confident she'd swallowed his half-truths and was burrowing down in the shitty part of Hollywood waiting for the apocalypse to pass – but she wasn't taking any chances. That's why she'd unplugged the TV and covered the mirror back at the motel along with turning the pictures to the wall. She remembered being spied on by the painting in the library and she wanted to be unobserved. She preferred to stay here in the airport lounge. Among people. Among the clean clinical lines of modern middlebrow architecture.

She was already refining her theories about how they got to you. Realism was probably not a problem. Arid photograph-like representations of aspects of this reality were presumably not gateways. She couldn't see Dyson's fellow creatures stepping out into the world from the pages of a Jane Austen novel or from the bushes in a neo-classical landscape. It had to be only the flowerings of the grotesque imagination that gave them access. Richard Dadd, Salvador Dali, Steve Montiglio. Ovid, Shakespeare, Poe. It didn't even have to be high art. Hell, she was in more danger from a kid's comic book than she was from a Gainsborough portrait. Now, while she'd stayed in enough hotels to know that you wouldn't expect Surrealism or Symbolism on your bedroom wall she'd also seen enough tasteless decoration to know that, intentional or not, the grotesque could often be found hanging there. Some misproportioned horse in ridiculous colours or a hideously rendered big-eyed Parisian orphan might be enough for all she knew.

She looked up quickly as an automated voice crackled its way through the invisible speakers overhead. Something distorted was boarding somewhere but it wasn't her flight so she tuned out. Jesus, it was three o'clock. Actioning her ticket had cost her an extra hundred dollars for the short notice but it had got her a seat on a plane scheduled to leave at eight last night but that was now seven hours ago. The incoming flight had finally shown up around eleven-thirty and the plane was now sitting empty just the other side of the plate-glass windows of Gate 47A. She'd gone up to the counter an hour or two ago only to be told, as she'd been told three times previously, that there was a storm in New York and no planes were landing. You think that's a storm, Avis had almost said to the woman behind the counter. Wait'll you see what's coming.

Six hours later, after some troubled and useless sleep stretched out across four of the gate's seats, Avis – past caring whether she looked as bad as she felt – had taken herself over to the Donut franchise two or three gates away and breakfasted on two glazed buttermilks and a huge cup of coffee. The airport was filling up again by then and Avis had noticed several newly arrived passengers look at her in horror over their orange juice. Were they all going to look as rough as her when they'd suffered the delays that their car radios had warned them about, they must have been wondering. Probably not, Avis had wanted to reply. A profound knowledge that the world is about to end helps give that subtle hint of devastation around the eyes that tiredness alone can't deliver.

Another four hours had passed, broken only by complimentary breakfast trays handed out by airline staff (Avis had donated hers to the hungry ten-year-old of a couple a few seats away from her), before the dayshift staff at the counter had at last announced the plane would be boarding within the hour and now, nineteen unbelievable hours after she'd arrived at LAX, Avis was finally in a seat on board the plane listening to the captain advise the ground crew to depart and the flight attendants to prepare for takeoff.

Avis had no idea where her fear of flying had gone but gone it certainly had. As the 767 thundered down the runway she found herself urging it on, urging it up, as eager for the miracle of flight as any lifetime enthusiast. Come on, she whispered to the great machine in whose belly she sat. Get me there. Get me home. Get me somewhere I can do some good by doing something terrible.

Flying time was five hours and change and it put her on the ground at JFK at what would have been 7:30 in the evening in Los Angeles and was 10:30 at night in Queens.

The weather had some welcome for her. When she'd left California, she'd left bright sunlight and a temperature of eighty degrees. Here, when she walked out to the taxi rank, the night was dark and freezing and the sky was pissing on her.

She'd done her best to freshen up in the restrooms at the airport and on board the plane and she'd grabbed some sleep during the flight but she was still surprised that the cab driver didn't ask to see proof of ability to pay before he let her in his cab. She wondered if she'd ever looked worse. She wondered if it mattered, wondered if such things would ever matter again.

The cab pulled out, the meter clicked on. Avis gave the address, settled back in her seat, and stared at her watch. It was nearly eleven. In about an hour's time, all over the country, houselights would dim, curtains would part, and people eating popcorn and drinking soda would read the opening credits of the end of the world.

# 30

Norbert Read was finding it difficult to concentrate.

He'd wanted to bring into being some songbirds and a jug of
ale but the game of making required a certain degree of . . . well,
*focus* wasn't the right word because doing it relied as much on a
kind of surrender as it did on an exercise of will, but clarity of
thought, for sure. And clarity was something that he had been
finding elusive ever since the Myrna and Ginger angels had blush-
ingly and sweetly introduced him to a whole new level of celestial
pleasures, pleasures that he was far from sure would be listed in
the things-to-look-forward-to-in-Heaven books of any priests or
preachers he'd known back in his days on earth.

He gave up his attempts to manipulate the matter around him
and gazed again, with as much satisfaction as when he had first
seen them, at the Fields of Heaven – at the gentle slopes and the
perfect light, at the exquisite palette of greens and golds and blues.
The sight of it all would never grow tiresome, he thought. Or, at
least, *he* would never tire of it. He'd realized long ago, of course,
that his particular heaven, this pastoral expanse of a perfect summer's late-afternoon, was not necessarily one that would appeal
to everyone. Presumably therefore there were as many heavens
as there were people and he marvelled at the stunning mix of
efficiency and benevolence that characterized an Eternity that
could provide a personalized paradise for every soul which had
passed into its keeping. It begged the question, of course, of
whether equally-customized Hells were scattered as commonly
amongst this plenitude of infinities, but he didn't like to think
about that.

There was a sudden movement on the periphery of Norbert's
vision and he swung round, startled, to see a figure scurry down

the side of the slope that led to Norbert's favourite resting place.

The figure hunkered down into a half-crouch, his back flat against the grass of the hill as if trying to avoid the eyeline of anybody else that might be around. Norbert said nothing, stunned into silence by the sight of him. He was a man of about Norbert's age – or the age Norbert appeared to be in this ageless place – and he was in the battledress of a soldier from the Great War.

'Hello, old chap,' the soldier said, reaching into a pocket of his khaki trousers and pulling out a tin, 'care for a smoke?'

William Llewellen had stormed the Fields of Heaven from the limbo fringes at which it obtruded into the territories of the Dream Country. He'd waited close to the borders until night came as it always came in those places – drawn over the morphean geographies as the vast shadow of the great white bird that flew endlessly overhead – and then, under the brief cover of a darkness that dissolved once he'd made the transition into this anomalous protectorate, he'd slipped into their fields and crawled his careful way, belly as flat to the ground as if Jerry's machine guns were seeking him out, to the hollow where they kept their ignorant prisoner.

He made a couple of roll-ups, balancing his baccy tin on his knees, and handed one to Read who put it in his mouth and then snatched, almost unconsciously, at a stray molecule of air, transforming it into a tiny flickering flame with which he lit his own cigarette and then leaned across to William to light his too.

'Thanks,' William said, drawing the nicotine deep into his lungs. 'I see they've been teaching you tricks.'

Read shook the flame free of his fingers and nodded. He'd still not said a word, staring at William like a man would stare who, lost in a jungle for years, finds himself, upon emerging, tongue-tied in the presence of his own kind. William matched his silence, waiting for him to be ready to talk, as they each took several drags of their cigarettes and looked at each other.

'Where did you come from?' Read eventually said.

'From the outside,' William replied.

'There's an outside?'

'Oh yes, old man. There's an outside. There's many outsides.'

'And we can come and go?'

William took another drag. 'Not if they can help it,' he said.

Read narrowed his eyebrows. 'What do you mean?'

'Look,' William said, 'I have to make this fast. I'm a goner the second they spot me. Christ, how to begin? First things first, I suppose. Despite all evidence to the contrary, you are not dead.'

'Of course I'm dead!' Read said, sounding quite offended by the suggestion that he wasn't.

William shook his head. 'No. If you were dead, you wouldn't be here. If you were dead, none of this would be happening.'

'None of what? And where would I be?'

'You'd be where I am. You'd . . .'

'You're here.'

'Oh Christ. Look, let me get through this. Maybe it'll come clear. I'm in the Colourfield. That's where we all are. I'm only here to talk to you.'

'The Colourfield is outside?'

'You're not making this easy, old chap. The Colourfield is . . . somewhere else. Outside is the Dream Country. It's a place we have in common with the living but we inhabit it less than they do. I've been . . . how do I put it? . . . stationed there for a while. Because of my granddaughter. Because of what's going on.'

Read let a moment pass as he drew the last possible hit of nicotine from his cigarette, threw it away, and gestured at William's tobacco tin.

'Do you think you could spare me another of those?' he said.

Norbert listened, appalled and enthralled, through the duration of his second hand-rolled cigarette, while the soldier's sing-song voice told him many things. Told him that his Fields of Heaven didn't really exist. Told him that they were an unmapped area of what the soldier called the Dream Country that had been occupied by the Companions and customized wholly for him. Told him of the Companions' purpose and his unknowing role in it. Told him that the world he'd known for eighty-four years and had thought he'd left for ever some weeks ago was about to suffer an awesome change and that the vessel of that change was his own almost

244

forgotten story. He was patient and silent through all of it and then asked the obvious question.

'And why,' he said, 'is what they want such a bad thing?'

The soldier, for an unguarded moment, looked at him like he was barking mad. But Norbert was neither mad nor joking. It sounded like they were about to give to the world the gift that they had given to him – the manipulation of reality to a state most pleasing to the wielder of the willed imagination – and it was a gift he both enjoyed and treasured.

The soldier pulled himself together. 'Maybe it isn't a bad thing,' he granted, 'I don't pretend to be qualified to know. All I know is that the world we both knew is in danger. And I've been a soldier for unclear causes before. The Germans mightn't have been bad people – not in *my* war at least – but I wanted my children to grow up in a country I knew speaking a language I recognize. You see what I mean?'

Norbert nodded. He could understand that. But it seemed curious to him that someone this side of the great divide was reluctant to see light shed on the other. It was as if a butterfly chose to express its concern for a caterpillar by insisting on it remaining tethered to the ground, as if wings were a curse and crawling a blessing.

The soldier used Norbert's musing silence to make another point. 'Maybe they're wrong, anyway,' he said, 'maybe *they're* the failed experiment, not us. Maybe we're trapped in the flesh for reasons none of us can understand yet.'

He looked at Norbert with a silent appeal like a man who can't believe his argument is failing but who fears that it might be. Norbert, as he kept thinking, waggled his fingers in the air beside him. A cigarette identical to the two which the soldier had given him appeared between his index and middle fingers. By the time he raised it to his lips it was already alight. He looked at the soldier's face, hardly aware of what he had done, but saw an expression there that must have been close to the expression on the face of Kruschev when he gazed down from a plane onto the thousand swimming pools of California and knew that Communism was a lost cause. He felt bad. He liked the soldier. He liked his eyes. There was no dishonesty there, no unkindness. He was

245

about to ask what on earth, even if he was to agree with the soldier, he could possibly do about the situation anyway when matters were taken out of their hands.

For a second he thought it was his Myrna Loy angel who had appeared at the top of the hill above them but it must have been a trick of the light because the creature he actually saw there bore no relation to anything he had ever seen before, in this life or the last.

It was about nine feet tall and almost as wide. There was no face – nor anything resembling one – on which he could read emotion but from the frantic thrashing of the scores of long thin leather-like strands that radiated out from the central mass – pink and gelatinous and itself pulsing and quivering furiously – he deduced that the thing was unspeakably angry.

It rushed down the hill towards them, spinning over on itself at a stunning rate, the leathery thongs acting as temporary limbs as each of them connected with the ground, and, without pausing, headed straight for the soldier who was scrambling to his feet as fast as any man could but who appeared, in contrast to the whirling thing, to be moving in ridiculously slow motion. Within a second, the thing had enveloped him and, with a motion too fast for Norbert's eyes to follow, the strap-like limbs – wrapping, grabbing, pushing, pulling – had fed him into the effortlessly absorbing jellied heart at its centre. The soldier hadn't even had time to scream. Instantly, the creature was still. The amoeboid mass shrivelled to nothing and the whipping leathers became taut and stiff as if whatever had been contained in the thing's centre was being jetted out into them like blood to engorging organs. Then, like monstrous quills from a nightmare porcupine, they exploded outwards in as many directions as they pointed.

Norbert, crying out in alarm, threw himself flat on the ground but there was no need; despite the bullet-like speed of their trajectories, each spine blinked out of existence almost instantaneously. The only thing left to mark the creature's presence was a tiny black dot that hovered a few feet above the ground where the thing's centre had once been. Smaller than a housefly, it looked less like a solid object than it did a hole in space, a point of absolute negation.

246

For a second, Norbert was put in mind of a black hole in miniature and he was ready to feel himself and all the reality around
him drawn dissolvingly into its emptiness. But that state too
passed and, again quicker than he could actually see, the point
began to bleed forth matter – at first a tiny flood of white proto-
plasmic ooze and then suddenly, in a flurry of organic transmutation, the expanding mass shivered into its final shape and the
Myrna Loy angel was standing a few feet in front of him.

Her face, melted back fully into the beautiful features with
which he had recently grown so intimately familiar, assumed a
mask of delicate concern. A nausea passed through him and he
tried not to let it show.

'Norbert, are you all right?' she asked.

He nodded, not yet trusting himself with words.

'We were so worried for you,' she said, 'we try to keep our
borders safe but occasionally one slips through.'

'One what?' Norbert asked.

'Isn't it obvious?' she said and then, lowering her voice to a
whisper and looking round herself as if someone might hear. 'A
devil.'

The contrast between her perfect imitation of a plucky but
nervous girl and the whirling threshing hungry thing that had
occupied her place in this world and apparently shared as primal
matter that which functioned as her flesh was very marked and,
to Norbert's eye, ridiculous. He didn't see how she (it?) expected
him to believe in her schtick any more once he'd seen an example
of that of which it (she?) was capable. But – partly because he
*had* seen that of which she was capable – he kept his own counsel
and elected to keep the conversation on the level at which she
was pitching it. He really didn't want to make her angry.

'Devils?' he said. 'That's who lives in the Dream Country?'

She gave him a look such as her earthly model might have
given on screen to William Powell if she were to notice lipstick
on his collar or liquor on his breath, a look that was a mix of
suspicion and amusement. 'What's he been telling you?'

Norbert didn't answer her. He had his own questions. He
wanted to know what had happened to the soldier. Devil? He
didn't think so. He'd neither threatened nor harmed Norbert, and

247

his company, despite their philosophic disagreement, had been pleasant.

'Where is he now? Gone? *Really* gone? Or just gone from here?'

'Well, let's just say his visa has expired.'

She was trying to be cute but it wasn't working.

'So he's back in the Colourfield?'

He watched her as he said this. Again with that look. Stronger this time. Condescending and annoyed. Like he shouldn't know either that word or the concept behind it. Who did she think she was? Or perhaps the question should be, who did *he* think she was – because she obviously wasn't what his libido had allowed him to believe she was in all their previous encounters.

But her expression also told him that he was right and he was glad about that. What she'd destroyed had obviously been only the dream-flesh with which the soldier had clothed himself to come to the Dream Country. She'd obliterated his form, not his essence. That remained elsewhere, remained safe and untouchable in the Colourfield, in the state beyond this one, the state that was the real home, according to the soldier, of the genuinely dead.

Norbert felt a sudden stab of unparticularized desire, an unfocused longing to be there instead of in this place, this illusionary paradise which she and the other Companions had fashioned for his limbo self from his limited and human expectations. He had no idea what the Colourfield was but he yearned for it as a flower yearns for the sun or the tides for the moon. For a second he knew something that he had never consciously known through all his long years on Earth: the thrill of Heaven should be the thrill of the unknown and not of the familiar. He glanced away from the angel to look for a moment at the undeniable beauty of the fields that they had pulled from his imagination. Despite their beauty, he felt shallow and predictable and felt his paradise tawdry and mundane.

Suddenly, and for less than a second, everything before his eyes shuddered. His fields were still there but it was as if, as well as seeing them, he was seeing *through* them to a different place, a place that occupied, in an impossible simultaneity, the same

248

quadrant of space and time as they did, a place of bare rocks and terrible skies.

Norbert would have gasped except that he was still on guard against inviting any unwanted attentions from the angel and, as the fields shimmered back into dominance and the other place retreated, he turned to look at her again. She had her head cocked a little to the side and was regarding him coolly and appraisingly. He was less than sure that she hadn't seen the interpenetration along with him. He did his best to smile and waited to see what she would say or do. A beat passed and she decided to keep things on the surface.

'Listen, Norbert,' she said, 'I want you to put this out of your mind. It was an unfortunate incident and it won't happen again. I'm going to go and talk to my friends. You stay here and be good.' Her voice dropped to a lower register and a more intimate tone, a promise-filled whisper the implicit lasciviousness of which stayed just this side of propriety, 'And – *if* you're good – I'll come back. Soon. And I'll bring our little blonde friend with me. It'll be nice, Norbert. It'll be very nice. We can all do some new things together. Things we haven't let you do before. Things you'd like.'

Her eyes glittered at him through half-lowered lids. He did his best to mug a response that he hoped would fool her, that he hoped would appear as mindlessly lecherous as she needed to see to keep her happy and to keep him safe, as mindlessly lecherous as, he now realized, all the other looks she and her partner had pulled out of him in the past had been. He felt defiled and pathetic, felt like a monkey placating its masters, like a lab animal grinning at its torturers.

It must have worked. Lowering her eyes demurely, as if a little shocked at the abandon he was able to rouse in her, she left him. Placing her arms to either side of her, palms out like a novitiate eager to reveal her stigmata, she rose smoothly and elegantly into the air above him, her great golden wings beating against the sky. He watched those wings as they bore her away across the fields and remembered the caressing feel of their feathers on his back as they'd folded intimately around him in their secret moments together. For a brief erotic second he wished he was back in thrall to their illusion but the memory of what had rushed down the hillside to engulf the soldier came to him and cleared his mind with a wash of horror leaving him sober and unsettled. He sank into a crouch beside his tree and did his best not to think.

As soon as she was out of Read's eye-line, she folded herself into a shaft of light and was instantly present at a group of its fellows.

A carbon spiral five inches wide and forty-five feet high and studded with opalescent and pupil-free eyes addressed her and the others.

'Is it safe?' it said.

'I scattered the dream wraith,' the shaft of light replied. 'But he'd done some damage, I think.'

'How much damage?'

'Conceptual only. He –'

A large piece of curved tree bark used its termites to chew itself a ragged mouth and interrupted.

'Conceptual damage is the only dangerous kind!' it snarled.

'It's contained,' the shaft of light snapped back, 'he's placated. He's waiting for his playmates.'

There was a silence as a group consideration took place. The carbon spiral, collapsing on itself and blossoming outward again into something that might have been a wolf in a world that saw in five dimensions and heard in colours, expressed it for all of them. 'Keep him happy here, of course. But his other self should be guarded for this last crucial hour. Arrangements must be made.'

Instantly, the shaft of light split itself in two and one beam slipped from their collective sight, sliding between the atoms of the imagined sky to seek out a viable gateway in the relevant region of the sundered world.

250

# 31

The Cadenza Drive-In had been dead for three years.

That it had lived, outmoded by multiplexes, even that long, was amazing, John Martin reflected as he pulled the '63 de Ville – borrowed from his father's friend Norm on the promise of free help in Norm's hardware store next Saturday afternoon – into position among the other cars and reached out for the post-mounted speaker and pulled it in through the side window. And if *that* was amazing, then its resurrection for this four-day week-end was nothing short of a miracle. He loved the place and was happy to be back – even if he couldn't get a date. He wasn't going to miss something this special. Cadenza was a small town, halfway between Los Angeles and Santa Barbara and midway between the ocean and the desert. Why it had been picked as the place at which this movie's producer was going to introduce it in person he had no idea. But it was cool. John Martin loved the movies.

From the windows in the shabby office above the concession stand, David Vial looked out over the hundreds of cars that were filling the parking lot auditorium before the giant screen. He'd thrown a couple of thousand at Red Meachum, the owner of this place, to fix it up before the reopening but he had a strong sus-picion that most of the money had stayed safely in Red's chequing account. But that wasn't going to matter for very much longer. And at least the two major tears in the screen had been stitched up.

Red's wife, Julie, came over to him and handed him a glass of champagne. He turned back to look at the assembly of town dignitaries in the office and raised his glass to them. Red took the opportunity to turn it into a toast.

'To David Vial,' he said, 'a man who's bringing back a quality this industry sorely needs: showmanship.'

Vial smiled to himself as people echoed his name and emptied their glasses. Meachum was not only an idiot but a hypocrite. His loyalty to the industry he was pretending to be a part of was non-existent. The only reason the Drive-In was still standing was because Meachum was waiting for the right offer from a K-Mart or a strip-mall developer before wasting any of his own money in razing the place to the ground. Still, Vial liked being called a showman. He felt it suited his character. Just as the inherited behaviours of Valentine Dyson had governed his actions for his first few days on earth so too did the assumed personality of a Hollywood producer colour his being now. He wondered if it was a quality of human flesh that caused this cleaving to its outward appearance. Dress a man in a bloody apron for a few days and he'll soon be thinking like a butcher. What slaves they were to form. And how surprised they would all be very soon when form forgot itself.

He glanced at his watch and took another look at the all-but-full space below. He'd go down and talk to them in a minute and tell them how happy he was that his film was playing their backwater. And he'd be telling the truth. He'd had a production assistant scout around for a drive-in at which he could attend the movie because he wanted to be in a big space when the special effect happened. He wanted to be out of doors and beneath open skies when the Great Opening began.

With unconscious but unpleasant timing, the cabbie pulled up at the kerb just as Avis's watch clicked over to midnight. She paid him and ran. She was on borrowed time now. For all she knew, they'd changed the sequence of events in adapting the story to the screen. For all she knew, instead of being the climactic image, the death-cloud could open the fucking picture and its progeny be loose five minutes from now.

Atop its hill, sheathed in midnight rain, the hospital looked imposing and dreadful in its isolation, the only illuminated structure for half a mile. Avis thanked Christ, though, that at least it was a modern building. Clean, streamlined, and mercifully dull, no gargoyles prowled its roofs, no stone lions manned its doors. Even if they knew she was here, there was no obvious access-point for them. She was grateful Read hadn't been housed in an older hospital somewhere in the city. What she had to do was hard enough without some mock-classical Hippocrates stepping out of a bas-relief and chasing her, white and implacable, swinging a Grecian scalpel in its cold stone hand.

The hospital was very quiet. Catering as it did to long-term and well-heeled patients, it didn't have an ER and official visiting hours were long over. So there was no traffic and, on the outside at least, no people. Avis, conscious of the security cameras mounted on posts and swivelling to watch her, slowed herself down and walked across the plaza to the wide glass doors of the main entrance. She listened to the sound of her cab disappearing in the distance behind her as she waited for the doors to slide open. Once they did, she stepped through, more aware than ever as she stood alone in the lobby drawing the eyes of the security guard at the desk of how bedraggled she must look. The lashing rain that had soaked her over the few yards from the kerb to the entrance hadn't helped matters any, she was sure. Okay, she thought, go with what you've got. Be pathetic and distraught. A woman who looks like this for a reason.

She rushed over to the desk and laid her forearms on it, leaning urgently toward the so-far stone-faced guard.

'I've got to see Irma,' she said.

'Who?' the guard replied.

Good. She'd met Irma only that one time but the nurse had not struck her as the kind of woman to invite friendship or intimacy from her fellow-workers. Looked like she was right, thank God.

'Irma Vanborough,' she said, pitching her voice just the sympathetic side of hysterical, 'she's the night nurse for Norbert Read.'

That name the guard seemed to know. He ran his eye down a list as if to check a room number and made to pick up a house-phone. Before he could either dial or ask her who she was to Irma, Avis put out an imploring hand.

'Please,' she said, 'don't call. If you tell her it's me, she'll . . . she'll know. I want to . . . to tell her in person.'

She'd played it right. Without actually saying so, she had the guard assuming some familial tragedy. Probably a death, if he was reading right her nicely judged distress. The real urgency driving her to Read's room doubtless helped her performance. He put the phone back down and looked at her. He was swayed but not yet sold.

'I don't know,' he said. 'Rules are you should be escorted but there's only me and I can't leave my station.'

Avis didn't say anything. She gave him the big eyes. She swallowed hard and breathed heavy. Did her best to force a tear. Come on, she thought, I'm a girl, I'm distraught. Be a big guy about it.

'You know where the room is?' he said, still unsure but crumbling.

'Uh-huh,' she said, nodding, eyes pathetically grateful.

'Go ahead,' he said, 'have the nurse call me from the room, okay?'

'Thank you,' she said. 'Thank you so much.'

She turned, crossed the lobby, and headed down the first corridor, mentally rehearsing the route from her previous visit. Two lefts and a right. Fourth door down.

She didn't give the guard another thought. He'd be in trouble tomorrow but she had no sympathy to waste. He'd be alive. And the trouble he'd be in would be nothing compared to hers. He wasn't the guilty party. Wasn't even an accomplice. All he'd done was screw up on his job. He'd only failed in his duty. He'd only let the murderer in.

Irma put her book down and looked over at Mr Read. He was sleeping peacefully. She'd thought, an hour or so earlier, that he'd seemed troubled. His eyelids had twitched a little and there'd been a tiny tremble in his right hand. The doctors would say it was just muscle reactions, she knew, but she didn't like it. She didn't like to think that, wherever he was, he was being bothered by bad dreams. She'd stroked his brow and patted his hand and the crisis had seemed to pass. Now his monitors were steady, his body as still as ever, and his breathing the shallow and ragged thing that passed for normal in his diminished life. Poor old thing.

She'd make herself a coffee in a few minutes and maybe, if she found a passage in her book that she particularly liked, she'd read aloud to him. She knew he liked that.

The sound in the corridor that suddenly intruded into her thoughts was a tiny and careful thing but she registered it anyway. Maybe if she'd still been lost in her book she wouldn't have noticed but now she seized on it. It was the sound of footfalls approaching the door, she realized, but whoever was coming was doing their level best not to be heard at all. Irma rose to her feet, matching the cautious visitor in silence. Who the hell did they think they were, creeping up on her and Mr Read this time of night? Carefully and quietly, she crossed the room to the door, her ears straining to keep track of the noises outside. She could hardly hear them at all now but she sensed them, tuning in to their rhythm so that even when she missed one or two she could keep track of where they were. Silently, she slipped her hand around the door-handle, waiting for the nuisance outside to arrive directly the other side of the door. Somebody was about to get a piece of her mind, all right. Here they come. One. Two. Now. Irma flung open the door.

She didn't have time to scream. The creature revealed impossibly in the open doorway raised itself instantly on its powerful back legs and launched itself at Irma, its front paws smashing into her chest and knocking her to the ground. She had less than a second to see its huge black body, cat-shaped and sinuous, or register the impossible wings that sprouted from its massive shoulders before it rushed up her body, cracking ribs with its weight, and, opening wide its terrible jaws, ripped her face from her skull with one bite.

The Companion, at ease in its newly borrowed shape, stepped off the corpse, pushed it further back into the room with a front paw, and flicked the door closed behind itself with a swing of its mighty tail. It purred in satisfaction at the sight of the old man and the flickering machines that told of his hold on life.

Already, the mind-set of the beast whose imagined flesh it occupied was clouding its thoughts, simplifying everything down to an animal concern. But it didn't matter. Full consciousness could be surrendered for now. Once the leased metal that served as this thing's flesh re-solidified and forced the Companion back to its own territory, then its mind would regain its sense of itself. For now, one thing only was important, only one function vital. Guard the room. And kill anything that tried to enter.

Anthony Jaeger wiped the ashtray clean. These doctors killed him. You go to them with *anything* – a head cold, a cough, a pain in the neck – and the first thing they ask you is whether you smoke. And tell them you do and you get a lecture long before you get a prescription. But every night he cleaned this conference room and every night there was an ashtray or two that needed wiping. Talk about *Don't do as I do, do as I say*. Talk about motes and splinters. Talk about *Physician, heal thyself*. Jeez.

He walked over to what he called the History Wall at the far end of the big conference table, shot some Windex in the glass-protected face of Harry Edwards III, the railroad-baron-turned-philanthropist whose money had allowed the construction of the first hospital built on this site in the 1890s, and started wiping the portrait. Harry sat on one side of the wall and was matched on the other by an equally elaborately framed painting of Luther Carrington, the place's first chief surgeon. Between them, mounted on the wall – and, with all due respect to Harry and Luther, dominating it entirely – was the salvaged front door of the original building. A massive twelve-foot-high cast-iron thing from a more decorative age, it was each night the target of both resentment and admiration from Anthony. The resentment was because it was a bitch to polish and the admiration was because it was fabulous.

Tonight, though, as he moved from Harry to the door, Anthony felt something new: a shocked surprise. What the hell was going on? The central and imposing carving that gave the door its character was missing. There were no rivet holes to show where it might have been prised from the door for restoration – indeed, Anthony'd always assumed the door was all of a piece anyway, the whole thing one single casting – but instead a simple smooth surface uninterrupted in its black solidity. It was weird. It looked for all the world as if the seven-foot winged black panther that had sat there as a silent sentinel for more than a century had finally grown bored of its task and had simply peeled itself away and gone exploring. Or hunting.

'Did you get to meet her?'

Vial turned to Meachum, annoyed at the distraction that pulled him from the view through the office windows of the big drive-in screen.

'What?' he asked.

'The babe,' Meachum replied, keeping his voice low in case Julie heard. 'Her.' He gestured at the screen where the movie had just cut back to a close-up of the actress playing Susan Johanson, a part Larry Webster had expanded considerably from Read's original in order to give Mickey Calhoun some love-interest for the first two-thirds of the picture.

'Oh.' What a stupid question. 'Yes. Of course.'

'Man, she's hot,' Meachum said. 'Let me ask you – what would a guy have to do to fuck something like that?'

'Oh, I don't know,' Vial said, glancing at Meachum appraisingly, 'lose a hundred pounds and grow a brain?'

Surprisingly, Meachum didn't look offended – merely thoughtful, as if considering the possibility of doing those things. Vial was tempted to tell him that, come tomorrow, it might be easier than he thought but he decided against it. He'd have to watch his champagne consumption. It could loosen the tongue too much. He turned back to the window and continued to watch the movie.

Avis tried to hold her pace steady as she turned in to the final corridor, the one that contained Read's room. It wasn't only her feet that were racing. Her mind was on overdrive, too. Should she have called Irma away? Found a pay-phone, got through to the room, and told her . . . told her what? Ed McMahon's in the lobby with a camera crew and you've just won ten million dollars? What the hell else would pry her away from the old man's side? No. It had to be this way. She'd have to fight her if necessary – maybe slug her quick as soon as the door was opened – and then yank those wires clear of his fragile body and hold Irma off till he croaked. How long could it be? How long could the poor old bastard hold on without his life-support? Minutes? Seconds?

She reached the door and took a second to catch her breath and get her nerve. A second was *all* she could take though because, while breath and nerve could do with being caught, something else couldn't: her sense of right and wrong. That she'd buried as far below her consciousness as she could get it and she didn't want it burrowing out now to cripple her ability to act. She'd have time enough for moral reflection in the twenty years some disbelieving jury was going to give her.

Okay. Just do it.

She reached her hand out to the handle, her eyes moving down to assure her aim . . . and froze.

There was a tiny trickle of blood coming out from beneath the door.

Avis took an involuntary step backward and stared at the door, all of her senses suddenly alive to the possibilities behind it. Strain her ears as she might, she could hear nothing. But, as strongly as if she could see it, she felt a complete awareness of something inside the room, something just beyond the thin wood that separated her from it, something that was waiting with predatory patience and taking a silent stance ready to pounce on her the second she opened the door.

She was terrified. She wanted to walk quietly away down the corridor and leave whatever waited there far behind. But she didn't have the choice. The clock was ticking. She'd surrendered choice as soon as she'd left Los Angeles.

But that didn't mean she had to be an idiot. Pressing the handle down firmly and bracing herself to move, she shoved the door inwards while simultaneously throwing herself to the side.

The thing was fast. Hideously fast. But it hadn't expected Avis to move aside and the fury of its first leap sent it right across the width of the corridor to crash into the opposite wall, which bought Avis time to start running before it could turn and take her.

Had the Companion had a firmer hold on the metal-fleshed creature it was occupying, it would doubtless have elected to simply retreat and keep all further comers far from Read's bedside but its animal instinct was predominant. An enemy had come, had not died, and was fleeing. Pursuit was the only option its

258

borrowed instincts allowed and, giving voice to its rage in an eerie feline cry, half roar and half screech, it spun on its back legs and launched itself down the corridor after her before Avis had covered more than three yards.

Avis had had a half-second's glimpse of Irma lying dead on the floor, her head a bloody mask of raw tissue and that vile evidence of what the creature's talons were capable of lent her the speed of desperation as she flew down the corridor, only peripherally aware of how the monster's roar had woken the sleeping hospital, of how doors were flying open along the route of her flight and revealing men and women, nurses and patients, eyes wide in shock, mouths open in disbelief at what they were seeing, standing frozen in their doorways. Avis could hear somebody screaming. She wasn't sure that it wasn't her.

Her blood pounded deafeningly in her head, almost as loud as the sound of the creature's massive paws as they carried it thunderously along the floor behind her, gaining ground effort-lessly. It would be over in a second if she didn't do something. A gurney was parked outside one of the doors. Grasping its metal rail as she reached it, she flung it, wheels spinning, out behind her widthways across the corridor. The creature's impossible wings beat suddenly as if it would lift itself above the obstacle but it was too close. It hardly mattered. Its jet-black body slammed into it without even breaking stride and the momentum of the huge and powerful creature knocked the gurney to the side.

Avis, looking back over her shoulder to see the uselessness of her action, suddenly felt her feet betray her and she all but stumbled to the floor. Staggering and spinning, she flattened her-self against a heavily locked door, convinced that it was over.

Its prey suddenly stationary, the monster shifted angle, leant back on its hind legs, and sprang forward with breathtaking speed. Avis threw herself bodily to the side and hit the floor helplessly as the creature passed over her – its back leg, claws extended cruelly, lashing down and missing the flesh of her arm by inches – and smashed through the door into the room beyond.

Avis, scrambling to her feet, caught a quick glimpse of the emergency equipment stored in the room and then she straight-ened up and continued her panic-fuelled run. Somebody'd hit an

259

alarm and the air was full of its klaxon howl, mixing cacoph-
onously with the screams of the paralysed bystanders to create
an aural chaos.

Behind her, she could hear the roar of the beast and the sound
of its taloned limbs smashing out in frustrated fury at the machines
among which it had found itself. Big deal. That would occupy it
all of three seconds before it was on her ass again. If she had any
thought at all past running for her fucking life, it was the vague
notion, too shrivelled and pathetic a thing to be called a hope,
that maybe, if she could reach the end of the corridor, she could
somehow double back on herself through the corridor system and
get to Read while the thing was still behind her, could undo him
before the monster undid her.

She was maybe twenty yards from the corridor's end when a
figure turned into it, running from the opposite direction. It was
the security guard. At that moment she knew that all he could
see, looking past her, was open doors, a wrecked gurney, and
several horror-struck witnesses, so she was hardly surprised when
he stopped running, drew his gun, and levelled it at her as she
closed the distance between them to no more than nine or ten
feet.

'Freeze!' he shouted.

Before Avis could either obey him or not, before she could
shout anything back to him, she saw his face change, saw it
struggling between disbelief and terror, and knew that the thing
was out the door and heading for her again.

'Jesus Christ!' he screamed. 'Get down!'

Avis threw herself forward, spinning onto her back as the loud
reports of his gun echoed painfully overhead. She screamed at
the sight of the creature, mid-leap towards her, front legs
extended, mouth open wide in a roar ready to convert itself into
a killing bite.

The guard's bullets slammed unceasingly, one after the other,
into the thing's body, the shock of the impacts bringing it to the
ground before it could reach Avis. But – penetrating only slightly
the metallic cast of the creature's flesh – that was all the bullets
did and, within seconds, it was up and running again. But now
it had a new target. Useless though the guard's attack may have

been, it was still an attack and the creature, infuriated by it, swept right past the cowering Avis and leapt at the man who'd dared it.

The guard, staggering back in shock and fear, kept firing, his bullets as ineffective as before, as the monster buried the claws of each of its front paws deep in his face. The guard screamed in agony but his torment had only started. The creature's mighty wings began to beat and, dragging the guard with it, it rose into the air.

Still on her back, Avis watched in helpless horror as the monster, nine feet from the floor, its flight hampered by its burden and the confined space, bounced on and off the upper parts of the walls and the ceiling, smashing furiously from one to the next like a confused and gigantic insect seeking an exit to the light. The guard, muffled cries of pain escaping his skewered mouth, emptied his useless gun blindly at the belly of the beast, his dangling legs kicking and twitching below him as he was held inexorably in place by the hooked talons buried deep in the meat and bone of his face.

The creature's back legs reared up tight to its lower body and then thrust forward. The unsheathed claws took purchase in the softness of the flesh of the guard's stomach and, in one devastating second, as the legs pushed themselves powerfully down and back, the guard was disembowelled completely, his viscera pouring down like a Fortean rain of steaming flesh to the corridor floor below, accompanied by a chorus of screams from those watching horrified in the doorways.

Avis scrambled to her feet and rushed desperately back down the corridor toward Read's room. Casting a backward glance over her shoulder, she saw the creature drop the still-twitching body of the guard and launch itself in a perfectly angled diagonal dive at her, its front paws extended, claws scratching at the air in vicious rehearsal for the movements they yearned to make in her body. She was still several yards from Read's door and there was one direction only in which she could avoid the monster's lunge. She took it, throwing herself sideways into the equipment room the creature had smashed into moments earlier.

Not letting the sounds of the creature's landing just outside the

261

room panic her into a paralysing terror, she hefted the door – still in one piece, having given way at the hinges and the lock – back into place and, grasping at a heavy cabinet just inside the room, used all her strength to tip it over and shove it up against the door. She glanced around the room for something, anything, that could help her, unconscious of the tears of terrified anger that poured from her eyes and the moaning gasps of exhausted distress that escaped her mouth.

The creature, its wings retracting and folding back against its body, spun round in the corridor to face the newly blocked doorway, pausing only to growl a keep-your-distance warning at the one or two foolhardy souls who were venturing from their doorways out into the corridor.

The chase had gone on long enough. Its prey was just beyond this door. The game was over. Taking two or three steps backward, the creature tightened itself into a crouch and then, muscles rippling along the length of its body, leapt forward, jetting towards the door, all four feet off the ground. The door, and whatever was blocking it, gave way instantly and the beast continued in its forward dive as if there had been no impediment at all.

It had a second to see its quarry – standing waiting at the last, as if it knew there was no point to further flight, no use in further hiding, holding out ahead of it two small flat metallic objects connected by a trailing wire to a machine somewhere behind it – and then it made contact.

A terrible searing shock slammed through its body and an animal howl of excruciating pain was ripped from its mouth. Before it knew what had happened, it was on its back, writhing in agony, smelling its own melting iron flesh and trying uselessly to catch its breath.

Avis dropped the contact-pads of the whatever-the-fuck-you-called-it, the heart-starter, the shock-machine, the *thing*, thanking God for the popularity of medical dramas on TV which had allowed her to know what it *was* even if she didn't know what the hell to *call* it, and clambered over the cabinet and the door out of the room. She had no idea if she'd killed the bastard or not but – no matter how much she longed to watch it die, no matter how much she hoped that the consciousness driving it was in some way the same consciousness that drove Dyson and that he too was suffering – she wasn't sticking around to find out.

Out in the corridor again, she ran to Read's door. Dimly, she was aware of a man moving towards her from one of the other doorways.

'Fuck off!' she screamed at him, not caring whether his motive was to help her or to stop her. Incredibly, he obeyed her, shuffling back to his doorway, cowed and living proof of how people, in emergencies, will listen to anything that sounds like authority.

She slammed Read's door shut behind her and leant back against it, taking a precious second to get her breath and clear her head.

Irma lay dead on the floor, her ruined face painful to look at. When the world made sense again, Avis would find time for sympathy for the nurse. But not now. Now her business was with the other inhabitant of the room.

Read lay as he had lain for the last month, still and almost silent, the hum of the machines that kept him breathing louder than his breath itself.

Avis walked to the foot of the bed and looked at his helpless form, at his sleeping face. This was it. The source of all that had happened. The unknowing doorway through which the night-mares had come and the monsters had crept. The doorway which she could close with a few sweeps of her strong young hand, tearing from his frail elderly body the wires that gave him his fragile hold on life.

His face was peaceful and calm. Everything that had happened in the room and the corridor, everything that had happened in the city, everything that was about to happen in the world, had made and would make no impact on him. He'd slept through it all, ignorant and innocent.

It was a nice face, Avis thought, the face of a man incapable of committing consciously a tenth of the sins that had been com-mitted through the medium of his long-retired imagination. In a bizarre way, she realized, he was her partner in this terrible adventure. The only other human so intimately connected with all that had happened. She was sorry they'd never had, nor ever would have, a chance to talk.

She remained staring at him for some time, not moving, as still as he.

It wasn't so much that she decided not to do it, it was more a realization that she wasn't going to. Her entire body relaxed and she took several deep breaths. She felt strangely calm. She knew somehow that it wasn't a moral issue. Not really. It was a kind of Zen choice. She was not going to take action. Whatever would happen, would happen. And she would be no more responsible for it than Read himself.

The door exploded inwards, shattering into fragments at the force of the creature's leap. Without turning to see it, operating entirely on instinct, Avis flung herself to the side, falling low and awkwardly on her right arm.

As the monster's momentum sent it crashing into the bed, Avis could see that it was already very near death. Whatever brief hold the consciousness from Dyson's territory had had on it was slipping and that consciousness itself withdrawing, perhaps hastened in its retreat by the damage Avis had done to its borrowed body with the electric shock. The metal that formed the creature's flesh was remembering itself and the beast's movements were stiff and painful.

The force of the impact sent the bed careering across the floor, IVs, syringes, and catheters ripped free of Read's withered flesh. The monitors began to howl a warning that their patient was in trouble as the creature turned, its killing instinct an imperative even in the face of its own imminent death, and ran at Avis, its increasingly inorganic limbs creaking in protest.

She threw her left arm up before her face as the mouth of the beast came at her and screamed as its huge metallic teeth sank into her flesh. They'd made an agonizing inch's progress when they stopped. Avis, whose eyes had been closed in a final terrified surrender, opened them again and found herself staring into the glittering eyes of the monster. An unending malice shone from them, along with a frustrated rage as it became finally aware of the end of its awareness. The rest of the body was inanimate metal now, cold and immobile, as far from life as it had always been, and, as Avis watched, unblinking and as still as the beast itself, the life went from the eyes too, leaving behind two carved orbs of smooth and solid black.

There was a blessed second of silence and stillness and then suddenly the room erupted. From somewhere unseen and unreachable, Avis sensed, at the limits of her hearing, a terrible and unceasing roar of stymied fury. Tremors of intent rippled around the room, the walls and fixtures buckling nightmarishly, as if something was running at unbelievable speed from point to point on the other side of the room's reality desperate to find a way in. The lights flickered, the walls pulsed, the glass vase that held Irma's flowers swelled and shattered, but there was nothing here for it to use. Avis held her breath, awed by the sense of something huge and dangerous skirting the parameters of the world and kept at bay only by the smallness and dullness of the world's creations.

It passed finally and Avis breathed again. Still trapped painfully in place by the metal mouth of the cast creature, she turned awkwardly to look at Read. She gasped. The bed, knocked by the creature, was at the far end of the room. And Read was sitting up in it.

Even over the high-pitched squeal of the alarmed monitors, his breath was painful to hear. At once ratchety and shallow, she could hear it rattle in his ancient chest, each inhalation an incredible and agonizing effort. His entire body was trembling helplessly and drool was trickling inelegantly from the corner of his gasping mouth. But his eyes shone with complete clarity and focused unerringly on hers.

For a second, they held each other's gaze, saying nothing. Read took as deep a breath as he could manage, the agony it caused him horribly clear on his face.

'You have your grandfather's eyes,' he said, his voice a fragile wheeze but its tone one of peaceful understanding, comradely affection, and calm acceptance.

Avis could only choke a sob in response, her eyes brimming with more than the pain of the monster's teeth. Before she could say or do anything else, Read fell back onto the sheets, his life leaving him in a long thin gasp. He was dead before his head hit the pillow.

Avis began to weep uncontrollably, hardly aware of the people who were moving into the room behind her or their cries of incredulity and whispers of disbelief.

David Vial felt him die.

It was nothing more than a disturbance in the etheric rhythms that were as natural to his perception as sight or sound, but he knew instantly what it meant. Read had gone. The conduit was closed. He accessed the simultaneity for a moment but the rage and confusion there were painful. He caught a quick glimpse of the pastoral paradise they'd built for their guest dissolving away to an emptiness that nobody was even bothering to fill yet and then blinked himself back to the sundered world and Red Meachum's office.

Beyond the plate glass of the picture window *Big Thunder* was still playing but the secret life with which it had pulsed mere seconds before was gone. The moment had passed and the movie was just a movie. He stared at it and winced.

'Didn't quite work, huh?'

He turned, surprised, and saw that Julie had come to stand beside him. What was she saying? What did she know?

She gestured at the screen. 'The matte shot,' she said. 'Looked a little hokey.' She smiled sympathetically Vial felt a curiously personal anger. The film had been only a means to an end for him but now he felt suddenly defensive of its shortcomings. He wanted to say something unpleasant to her but, remembering who she was married to, he decided life had punished her enough.

'You win some, you lose some,' he said, shrugging.

By the time another hour had passed and the movie faded to black and started its end credits crawl, he was beginning to feel his tenure on the flesh weakening. The rules of access had returned to normal and it was probably only the length of time he'd already spent in this body that was keeping his consciousness in as much control of it as it was. Things would get cloudy very soon. He imagined there'd be a brief interim period when the Dyson per-

266

sonality would resurface to claim again its imagined body and shortly thereafter the flesh would dissolve away like every other leasehold.

He'd told the audience before the picture started that he'd be happy to answer questions at the end. It had been an empty promise, of course, but now he decided to keep it. After all, the audience had been disappointed. The movie'd played well enough, he supposed, but they'd heard the advance publicity and had doubtless been expecting something special at the climax. Larry Webster had been right after all. Promising something you can't deliver could kill the movie's second weekend. He didn't want that to happen.

Nodding at Red's questioning are-you-ready look, he followed the Drive-In's owner down the stairs from the office and across the lot to the small stage area in front of the screen.

Red tapped the microphone of the rented PA system and then introduced him for the second time to the crowd. Vial waited till Meachum had walked offstage and then strode to the centre through the chorus of honking car horns that greeted him. He realized that he didn't know if that signalled derision or was a drive-in audience's special method of applause. He didn't much care. He waited till it had died down and then adjusted the microphone's height and angle. It was an automatic gesture. He had no intention of wasting this moment with words.

He looked out over the California night to the sea of faces and car hoods below him and read their expectancy. He felt strangely warm towards them, like a father disappointed in his children but loving them nonetheless. Because here, in miniature, was the world's longing. Ignorant of what they wanted, still they wanted it.

So the film had been merely a film after all – its climax merely light and shadow, its secret glory still trapped within its celluloid? So what? He was here. They were here. It came down to this at last. A figure on a stage and a mass of people waiting to see what would happen next. It had always been like that. Whether Ritual or Vaudeville, they'd hear the rumours of the marvellous and come to it in an act of collective hope that this time they would not be let down. They flock to churches or caverns and await the

267

manifestation, await the tears on the cold white cheek of the marble Virgin or the rich red blood on the wood-and-plaster palms of the graven God. They gather, merchandising-clad, to hear the thunder speak in the guise of young men with guitars. Even here, before a battered screen slashed and torn by years of neglect, they come to see the wonders unfold. Everywhere and always, driven by the same impulse, they huddle in hope of the vessel of the revelation. And the impulse was simple. Free us from the everyday, it said, show us something bigger. Let us forget who and what we are pretending to be and remind us, however briefly, however imperfectly, of what we are. Give us a show. If the grand becomes the gaudy, we'll forgive it. If the magnificent descends to the mundane, we'll take it. A hint, a smell, a sense of it is all we need. Our disbelief is ready to be suspended and our secret selves ready to be revived.

All right. Vial let the silence build a moment or two longer and then kicked the microphone stand aside. He raised his arms for attention and then opened his mouth to a primal roar from the other side of the universe.

For long seconds, his deafening, ear-bloodying howl rang over the arena and when it stopped the silence was different from before. It was shocked and profound. Now his audience was ready – stilled and quieted and every eye trained irresistibly on him. He'd made them truly a crowd, their individual personalities dissolved into a mass openness to whatever was going to happen.

He spread his arms wider as if in invocation. He'd decided he wasn't going to stick around for the dissolution of his borrowed self. He was leaving early. He was going home. But he was going to show them exactly what that meant.

For a moment he shone. For a moment it looked as if he had simply turned to gold, his skin become luminous and its pores bursting to let him bleed light. It promised to be slow and glorious . . .

And then he exploded.

It was soundless, which only made it stranger. Without a whisper, without a scream, his entire body simultaneously crumpled and expanded, falling in on itself and blasting outward into its separate atoms with each atom having the fiery brilliance of a tiny star and celebrating their release by erupting into the space above the platform as their older brothers had once and for ever erupted into the spaces of the galaxies.

Out in the audience, no one screamed. Nobody sounded their car horn. Nobody did anything at all. Every adolescent heart was stilled, every teenage mouth reduced to silence. This was not a movie or a theme-park ride. What was happening was happening. There was no technique to applaud or revile, no illusion to which to surrender or to see through. It was as if they had been taken to the primary moment, to the second of singularity before time began. They were watching the birth of the universe in front of the tired Cadenza screen and there was no orchestral score to tell them how to feel.

Vial was no longer Vial but his brief and borrowed consciousness still hovered for a second somewhere both within and beyond the fecund cloud of light and energy that was his true self. He was ecstatic in his dissolution, filled with knowledge and possessed by clarity. He wanted to shout to the assembled humans, to let them know that they too would have this moment. That, at the time of their passing, they too would not only know everything but would be everything. But he had no voice and, besides, he had a decision to make. It had been his intention to take the world – or at least ten square miles of it – with him in this cameo apocalypse, to blast Cadenza into eternity and leave nothing but craters and questions behind but, just as he was about to do it, just as he was about to direct his scattered self to sweep across the plain like a terrible fire from Heaven that had come to cleanse this place of God's mistakes, he thought better of it.

A disaster with no survivors would allow a rational explanation. All he'd accomplish would be a confirmation of his defeat. Better to leave a story, to leave a miracle and a multitude who had beheld it. Leave them to see, leave them to talk, leave them to spark the imaginations of their hearers with another tale of undreamed possibilities. Let his action become mythic and the moment become enshrined.

Before the stunned gaze of a thousand eyes, the star-burst swept in on itself to become a twenty-foot tall pillar of golden flame around a raging whirlwind of cosmic dust. It spun and burned furiously for a second and then suddenly jetted upwards like a rocket-ship made of celestial fire, blasting itself up into the heart of the infinite with the speed of a guided missile.

From far below came the honking of a thousand car horns. This time the scattered consciousness that had been David Vial was in no doubt as to the meaning of the sound.

They were applauding.

The drive-in lot was a chaos of activity, people scrambling out of their cars, screaming at their neighbours to confirm their own visions, and tilting their heads to the star-filled sky above, straining for a final sight of the thing they had seen.

As every face looked to heaven, one last collective gasp was pulled from their mouths. From nowhere, an impossibly gigantic figure swelled into sight above them. Five miles high and transparent, his feet planted somewhere beyond the curve of the horizon and probably crushing Nevada, his suit the same midnight blue as the sky from which he seemed to be formed, a masked man in a top hat towered over the hills and valleys of California.

Touching his vast gossamer hand to the gargantuan brim of his impossible hat, Valentine Dyson took his final bow.

# EPILOGUE

## *A Flower for the Fallen*

Death, too, has a garden – which we tend
For love of those once living and the end
Of those who live. And, though our flowers spoil
In this world, they bloom still in foreign soil
Where, fed and watered by eternal streams,
We glimpse them once. And only in our dreams.

*Requiescat*, JOHN WILLIAM ADAMS

Avis left the black cab over by the main church building. She told
the driver – who was young and stupid but who seemed nice and
who'd done his best to flirt with her in his almost incomprehensible Liverpudlian accent – that she'd only be a few minutes.

It was a grey day in the north of England but she'd been told
that for March this was hardly unusual and she tried not to let
it depress her as she made her way through the weaving paths
of the churchyard among the headstones of the dead and the
flowers left by the living. She found the place fairly easily.

Her editor at Ballantine – the woman with whom she'd put
together Read's posthumous Blue Valentine collection that was
to be issued in the fall with a really cool Steranko cover – had
told her she was crazy to take a trip to Britain and spend only
two days there but her business here was very specific and she
had a life to get on with.

She'd handled the seven-hour transatlantic flight with complete equanimity – her fear of flying living only in her memory,
a thing she knew to have been true but incomprehensible to her

271

now – and was actually looking forward to the flight back. She didn't care how much people laughed at her, she *liked* airline food.

William's grave was simple. Avis stared at the carved inadequacies of its names and dates – WILLIAM LLEWELLEN 1895–1976 – and pondered on how little we put on headstones, on how their simplicities can deny the complex stories of the people who lie beneath them. William's stone, for example, didn't say SERVED IN FRANCE 1914–1918, or mention his 1930 marriage to Katherine, or name his six children. Her own mother, Barbara, was his third child, born in 1940. Nobody'd know that from William's gravestone, nor that she herself was born in 1970 and her brother Danny two years earlier. And yet, without the mouldering bones beneath this earth, none of those people would have existed and none of what they had done or had done to them would have happened. But she realized she was being wrong-headed. It wasn't the monuments of marble that mattered, but the monuments of flesh. Headstones aren't the repository of the stories of the dead. Those stories live on but they live on in the heads and hearts of the people that the dead leave behind.

Except that Avis knew now that it was more than that. She knew that somehow stories and the people that lived them survive in the Dream Country too. She knew that William Llewellen had come out of whatever eternity his spirit may have found to reclothe himself in dream-flesh and do his best to help his grandchild. She knew that death's division was illusionary and that stories never end.

She knelt down to lay the flowers she had brought on the grass at the base of the stone. Her heart skipped a sudden beat and for a moment she was chilled with a small but perfectly focused fear. Unnoticed by her earlier, a single blue flower was already lying there, a flower of a species that she knew not to exist in the world and which she had last seen in a tuxedo buttonhole three thousand miles away.

But her fear passed as she realized she was reading the flower's provenance incorrectly. It came not from Dyson but from his creator. Norbert Read was no longer in the clutches of his Companions and this impossible tribute had been laid here not by a defeated enemy but by an eleventh-hour ally. She thought of the swaying poppy fields of Flanders and the innumerable white crosses that would, according to her mother, every year during the television coverage of Remembrance Day bring unashamed tears to the eyes of the ageing and alive William Llewellen for his ageless and fallen comrades. She placed her flowers beside the blue valentine and rose to her feet, moist-eyed.

The cab picked her up where the graveyard's walkways met the church's main drive and cruised with respectful slowness out toward the main gate.

'Back to the hotel, love?' the driver asked, his voice quiet and as delicate as his accent allowed.

Avis nodded. 'Yes,' she said, 'thank you.'

She glanced over her shoulder for one last look back at the churchyard. William's grave was just visible among the many others. Avis tried to find Read's alien flower but from this distance it was impossible to pick out. Her own bouquet too was lost amidst the sea of flowers that washed over the entire cemetery, becoming an invisible part of a greater whole. The blue valentine's strangeness was something that was only apparent at close quarters and dissolved as Avis's distance from it increased. From here, as the cab nosed out of the drive and into the suburban traffic of her grandfather's city, there was nothing unusual about it at all. Impossible and unreal as it was, from whatever imagined garden in which it could have grown, it lay there now simply and honestly as merely one more flower for the fallen, one offering amongst many, its own strange story subsumed into the larger tale, the endless story of how we bury our dead and celebrate our grief.